CAPTAIN QUAD

NOVELS BY SEAN COSTELLO

Eden's Eyes (1989)

The Cartoonist (1990)

Captain Quad (1991)

Finders Keepers (2002)

Sandman (2003)

Here After (2008)

CAPTAIN QUAD

BY

SEAN COSTELLO

Library and Archives Canada Cataloguing in Publication

Costello, Sean
    Captain Quad / Sean Costello.

ISBN 978-1-896350-46-2

    I. Title.

PS8555.O73C36 2011   C813'.54   C2011-905493-0

Book design: Laurence Steven
Cover design: amy Bradley
Photo of author: Alfred Boyd

Published by Scrivener Press
465 Loach's Road,
Sudbury, Ontario, Canada, P3E 2R2
info@yourscrivenerpress.com
www.scrivenerpress.com

We acknowledge the financial support of the Canada Council for the Arts, the Ontario Arts Council, and the Government of Canada through the Canada Book Fund for our publishing activities.

 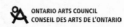

For my son, Steve...in the hope that someday he'll actually
READ one of his old man's books!
I love you, bud. I am so glad to be your dad.

ACKNOWLEDGEMENTS

A special thank you to Laurence Steven of Scrivener Press. As a publisher his sense of style is second to none; as an editor he is both fair and insightful ... and he's a terrific guy. I am both proud and honoured to be a part of the family.

Publisher's Preface
TO THE TRADE EDITION

Publishing a trade print edition of Sean Costello's *Captain Quad* is an act of faith...

...faith that the many readers of Sean's last book, *Here After* (Scrivener Press, 2008), are wanting more Costello fiction;

...faith that Sean's fans from the 1990s will remember how enthralled they were (meaning captivated, or captured, or enslaved) by his relentless storytelling;

...faith that those fans will want another look at Peter Gardner's claustrophobic madness, and his will-driven break into murderous flight;

...faith that new fans will want to know where the intensity of *Here After* came from;

...faith that all fans will enjoy some time travel into the world of the 1980s that Sean evokes with such precision;

...faith that readers both regional and national will appreciate Sean's evocation of Sudbury and environs: its rocks, trees, lakes, mines, slag, ice fishing, and exploding porcupines;

…faith that readers will be intrigued by how quickly the superficial social, cultural, regional, and tech differences fall away, leaving a riveting narrative;

…faith that long time fans will pass the word to the next generation that Costello is a writer they don't want to miss;

…faith that those fans will want to get a preview of what's coming next (fall 2012) from Sean Costello (see the intro chapter of *Let It Ride*, appended to the end of the book);

…and, most importantly, faith that important authors need to be kept in print.

ONE

—

THE LAST SONATA

1

June, 1983

THERE WAS A MOMENT in the dark of the wing, a startling moment that was part optical illusion and part raw nerves—but for the space of an eyeblink, it appeared to Kelly Wheeler as if Peter Gardner was headless. His body stood erect beside her, caught in an oblong of stage light, and there was nothing above the neat line of his collar but air, black air. It was absurd. She knew it was only a trick of the light... but for that eerie, spun-out first second she was convinced that someone had lopped off his head.

Then he shifted a half step toward her and that same oblong of light found his face, and he was grinning at her nervously, fingering the tight loop of his collar, looking like the groom at a shotgun wedding.

Chuckling at her bizarre misperception—one that had carried with it an alarming force—Kelly drew him back into the dark and hugged him. He was rigid with apprehension and she tried to reassure him.

"Don't panic," she told him. "You're going to play just like you always do—flawlessly." She kissed him lightly on the chin, her hand on the back of his neck feeling his tension.

Peter's eyes, the colour of sandstone, settled over the top of Kelly's head on the baby grand that stood waiting for him at centre stage.

"Yeah," he said. "Flawlessly. If only I could find my fingers." He poked his hands into the light with the fingers bent at the middle knuckles, creating the illusion that the distal segments had been neatly amputated.

Kelly, who was almost as nervous as Peter, jabbed him playfully in the ribs. Though eager to show him off, she felt guilty about putting him through all of this. He'd never played in public before—his music, he'd told her, was for himself and the people he loved—and it had taken all of her wiles to persuade him to appear at this final assembly. But he was good, maybe even great, and she wanted people to know it. She was proud of him.

Taking Peter's hand, Kelly returned her attention to the stage, where the principal, Mr. Laughren, stood reciting his annual address. It was June 28, the last day of school.

"As your principal," Laughren was saying, his round face the colour of brick, "I consider it my personal duty to prepare each and every Laurentian High graduate for the fickle and often treacherous road ahead…"

Peter said, "Gimme a break. Same old bullshit only deeper."

Kelly kissed him again, letting her hand slip to the sculpted small of his back. "Will you relax?"

"Relax," Peter said. "Right." He shifted the curtain a few inches, enough to allow Kelly a glimpse of all those impatient faces out there. "Look at those animals. The minute Laughren steps down they're going to eat me alive. They'll wolf down the tender bits, then take turns gnawing on my skull." He noticed his mother and kid brother seated near the front, eyes expectant and bright, then let the curtain fall closed.

Kelly giggled, only now beginning to appreciate how petrified he actually was. "This has really got you going, hasn't it?"

"Look," Peter said in his most reasonable tone. "Why don't we just skip this whole deal? Hop on the bike and zip down to the DQ for a Dilly bar? I mean, no one's going to care—"

"*I'm* going to care," Kelly said, cutting him off with her words and the wounded look in her eyes. "And your mother's going to care. And Sam."

"But—"

Both fell mute as Laughren's amplified voice swung toward them. "It gives me pleasure to introduce to you now a graduating student whom most of you know from his prowess on the football field."

"Oh, shit."

"Knock 'em dead," Kelly said, squeezing his hand. Then she was gone, down the steps and out through the stage-left exit.

"What most of you don't know about Peter Gardner," Laughren said, "is that academically he ranks among the finest students to have passed through Laurentian's hallowed halls."

In the decidedly unhallowed womb of the wing, Peter felt his face flush with blood.

"On top of all that, a certain Kelly Wheeler informs me that his musical talent approaches the level of genius."

Laughren glanced toward the wing and Peter shrank into the shadows again.

"Somehow Mr. Gardner has managed to escape us until now— but now we've *got* him. So before we at this final assembly bid him luck and adieu, let us welcome him, and lend him our keenest attention as he performs one of my personal favorites, Beethoven's 'Moonlight Sonata.'"

A scattering of unenthusiastic applause tinkled through the hall's big belly, and that made Peter even more nervous. It was hot, it was late and it was the last day of school. Summer waited outside like an acres-big carnival where all the rides are free. And in the face of all that, he was supposed to capture and hold the *keenest* attention of some twelve hundred hyped-up teenagers?

No small feat.

Grinning like a used-car salesman, Laughren waved him onstage. Reluctantly, Peter stepped into view, almost overcome by the urge to look down and see if his fly was done up...or if his pants were on at all.

The lights went down. A dramatically muted spot picked him up and followed him toward the piano. A fresh flourish of applause, punctuated by high hoots and happy hollers, swept against him from the orchestra seats, where the entire football team slouched in grinning disarray. Risking a sideward glance, Peter spotted his three best buddies, Rhett Kiley, Mike Gore and Jerry Jeter, frenziedly clapping their hands. Kiley's dark eyes were bloodshot, and Jerry's long, horsey face gleamed with a telltale beery flush.

"'Stairway to Heaven,'" Rhett bellowed, shrinking in his seat as Laughren's predatory gaze settled directly upon him.

Peter's knees turned to Silly Putty. Maddeningly, the piano seemed to glide away from him as he approached it. His tie—he almost *never* wore a tie—felt like a gradually tightening noose around his neck.

Somehow he reached the stool. He sat. His fingers brushed the keys and he felt better, more confident. He waited for silence, his soft brown eyes fixed on the alternating pattern of keys.

From her seat near the front Kelly looked on, her excitement contaminated now by a new emotion. Tiptoeing down from the wing a half-minute earlier, she'd met eyes with Peter's mother and had been struck by an open glare of resentment; brief but shockingly potent, it had rocked her like a savage backhand. And it occurred to her then that she'd seen that look before—glancing idly around while Peter played for her and finding those slate-coloured eyes fixed on her back from the adjacent kitchen, lingering an instant too long before shifting away; turning on the moonlit porch in time to see the living room curtain snap shut behind them while she and Peter sat chatting on the steps. And yet, when she spoke to Kelly, Mrs. Gardner was always gracious and kind. Before today, Kelly had always managed to explain that look away, putting it down to her imagination or to some innocent quirk in a decidedly quirky lady. But on this occasion there had been no mistaking its authenticity—Kelly had felt something go slack inside her in its force. She'd dropped her gaze immediately, feeling sweaty, guilty and afraid...but angry, too. She knew what that look meant, and its very senselessness infuriated her. Jealousy was for other girls, not for mothers. The woman just wouldn't give her a chance.

Kelly cast these thoughts aside, deciding to deal with them later. She refused to let a single nasty glance spoil her enjoyment of Peter's first public recital. Besides, by this time tomorrow they'd be free of their accustomed restraints, parental and academic alike. By this time tomorrow they'd be rolling west on Highway 17, embarking on the adventure of their lives, a cross country motorcycle trip to celebrate their graduation from high school.

Kelly settled back in her seat. Onstage, Peter sat hunched over the keys, eyes closed, a small muscle in his jaw working rhythmically. Waiting for silence.

Come on, everyone, Kelly thought, her excitement returning. *Shut up and let him play.*

As if privy to her thoughts, Laughren strafed the assembly with his most menacing glare. A reluctant, blemished hush wound its way through the aisles.

And Peter began to play.

And suddenly, as if compelled by some unseen force, the hush grew solemn and profound, becoming so total that within minutes the cavernous hall seemed empty of any living soul. No seat creaked, no page was riffled, no whispered phrase was uttered.

For a while there was only the music, untarnished and sweet, as at the best of times seeming to flow *through* him, as if apart from his own volition. It evoked within him a state akin to magic, and he allowed it to fetch him away.

In the audience Kelly felt her heart swell with pride. She'd chosen her seat carefully, so she could see Peter's face, and when his mouth widened into that funny, lopsided grin he got when he played, she knew she'd done the right thing. In the years to come this day would stand as a cherished memory for them both.

When it was done, when the last audible vibration perished on the air, Peter wondered for a moment if everyone hadn't just up and left, so perfect was the silence. Then a single pair of hands rang out (*My mother*, Peter thought ruefully, *I bet that was my mother*), and were immediately joined by another, and another, until soon the crisp, clean roar of applause filled the hall.

The lights came up then, giving Peter that naked feeling again, and he stood, bowing modestly. For as far back as he could see, the eyes of his audience looked misty and dazed. Even the jocks he called his friends wore expressions of mingled wonder, admiration and surprise.

He scanned the crowd for his girl. Where was she, anyway?

Now they were giving him a standing ovation. With the house lights up, Peter could see his mother out there, dabbing her eyes with a hankie. And his kid brother, Sam, hoisting the family reel-to-reel aloft like a trophy, an admiring grin splitting his zit-ravaged face. Spilling into the aisles, his teammates waved their arms like overgrown two-year-olds.

But where was Kelly?

"Pssst."

Peter heard the sound but was unable to trace it. Now Laughren was back at the lectern, clapping along with the rest of them.

"Pssst. Peter."

Then he saw her, standing in the shadows of the wing. He gave another quick bow then stepped offstage to join her. She hugged him mightily. Even in the scant light of the wing he could see the silvery tracks of her tears.

"Oh, Peter, that was wonderful."

Smiling like a sultan, Peter agreed with her.

Kelly composed herself. "Wanna get lucky?" she said, bumping her hips against his.

"Here?" Peter said, hamming it. "Now?"

"Cute. My place, dummy. My folks won't be back 'til ten."

Peter ran a hand through his thick sandy hair, which the sun had already begun to lighten. "What about Nell Tait's party? Didn't you say you'd die before you'd miss Nell Tait's cottage party?"

"It'll keep." She cupped his crotch in her hand. "What do you say?"

"Five minutes," Peter said. "Just let me say 'bye to my mom."

* * *

Sometimes Peter had a tendency to rush things a bit.

But today, in the curtained cool of Kelly's bedroom, he began almost painfully slowly, building her by degrees to a pitch before he entered her that scared her a little. Even once he was inside her and she was moving rhythmically beneath him, he remained in complete control. And soon, there was a heat building deep in Kelly's works, a tiny, dime-size glow that was the warm orange colour of a new spring sun and spreading concentrically outward. Something happened to her mind as the sensation rippled out from her belly and found her legs, a sort of unintentional yet irresistible disconnection, nothing like it had ever happened to her before, not *ever*, and before she realized it was finally, actually *happening*, she was caught in the tightening, gushing, heightening glory of it, murmuring rapturously to Peter and clutching him closer, trying to absorb him into herself.

The feeling lingered for a time, ebbing and flowing, and they lay awash in it, more in love than either could even begin to comprehend.

Then, dreamily, they drowsed.

* * *

A half hour later Peter jerked awake with a scream boiling up from his guts. He managed to contain it, dissipating its force in a hot rush of air, but the terror remained lodged like a fishhook in his throat.

He'd been dreaming about flying; nothing unusual for Peter. Hardly a day had gone by since his eighth birthday—when his father, in one of the few loving gestures he'd shown the boy, brought home an Aurora model of a Lockheed F-104 and the two of them stayed up until midnight assembling it—that he hadn't dreamed about piloting his own aircraft, carving the edge of the atmosphere, man and machine joined in perfect harmony.

But in this dark dream, things had gone abruptly, irreversibly awry. He'd been alone, high up, where the stars wink even in daylight and to the earthbound observer an aircraft seems little more than a pinpoint of light trailing vapour. His oxygen supply had failed, and in the delirium that quickly followed he lost control. Then man and machine were plummeting, dragged toward the globe like a thumbtack in the resistless pull of an electromagnet. Alarms flashed, dials spun helter-skelter, the whole instrument panel seemed to sneer like a savage face, the face of a machine come to malign and murderous life, shedding its charade of smooth obedience and replacing it with a furious, suicidal mutiny. *Die with me, fool,* it seemed to whisper in the vacuum of the cockpit. *Taste the flames of hell.* And when he opened his eyes he thought he was still in the cockpit, and the scream was hammering at the backs of his teeth.

Breathless, Peter pushed up onto his elbows. That spiraling sensation of free-fall was still on him, and it took several swooning seconds to still the spin of the room. Gradually his breathing settled, the images dispersing like wind-torn smoke.

Kelly lay with her back to him, her respirations shallow with sleep. As gently as he was able, Peter tucked an arm around her waist. Nuzzling closer, he kissed the back of her neck, high up on the nape. Kelly moaned, stirring slightly, then awoke.

"Hi, doll," she said. Her hand found Peter's beneath the covers and pressed it to her tummy.

Peter felt the beginnings of another erection and drew back his hips. Though they'd been going out together for nine months (and sleeping together for three of those), Peter hadn't fully overcome his shyness with her yet. But Kelly pressed her backside against him, closing the gap. Not sharing Peter's shyness, his penis grew almost painfully stiff.

"What's that in your pocket?" Kelly said.

"Banana," Peter said, his shyness forgotten. He kissed her again on the nape of her neck, high up, in the downy hair that grew there. "Wanna play bury the banana?"

Kelly Wheeler, whose mouth was wide and whose large brown eyes seemed always to betray a flicker of sadness, turned to face him. "That's what I like about you, Gardner. Always the romantic."

"We're keeping Nell Tait waiting."

The plan was to motor out to his uncle Jim's charter field on Highway 144, pick up the pontooned Twin Otter Peter had trained in, and fly to Nell's cottage on Halfway Lake. Peter had earned his solo license the summer before, and both he and Kelly were looking forward to the grand entrance they'd make at the party. His uncle, who'd trained him, trusted Peter implicitly. To accommodate his favorite nephew, he'd kept the Twin Otter free for this one special day.

"What time is it?" Kelly said.

Peter glanced at the bedside digital. "Almost four."

Kelly's fingers found the taut muscles of his shoulders and idly began to knead them. "You're still pretty tense," she said, and Peter detected a trace of injury in her voice.

"It's never been so good," he said.

"No. It's been good, but never *that* good."

"Did it happen?"

She smiled. "Uh-huh."

Suddenly pensive, Peter lay back on the pillow, resting his head in the hammock of his hands. Kelly lay with her head on his chest, one hand stroking his abdomen. His erection had subsided.

"What's on your mind?" she said. But she knew. Many of the same things reeled in her mind, too.

"I was just thinking that it's over. High school. Being a kid." This was only partially true. In the front of his mind was the dream, bright and jagged as a saw blade. He'd dreamed about flying before, many times. It was only natural. Aviation was his future; he lived for it. But this was the first time things had taken such a catastrophic turn, and there was no way he was going to tell Kelly about it. Her own nightmare was that he would someday perish in a crash. Thinking back on it now, he supposed his dream tied in with some of the other feelings he was having. The fears, the uncertainty about what Laughren had so aptly termed 'the fickle and often treacherous road ahead.' It was no longer a metaphor. "It's really over."

"Aren't you glad?"

"Until this morning I was overjoyed, ready to do back flips. But now that it's here…" He sighed. "I mean, after today, we're probably never going to see half of those people again."

Kelly chuckled. "I can think of more than a few I'm not gonna miss."

"Me, too…but you know what I mean." She did. "And it's not only that. Tomorrow we're off on our trip, and when we get back there'll only be a few days left before we move down to Kingston. I mean, here we are planning to live together, and we haven't even told our parents about it yet. Then there's military college. What if I spend three years down there and they tell me I'm not cut out for the air force?"

Peter's admission of uncertainty surprised and unsettled Kelly. Before today he'd never expressed even the slightest doubt regarding their future, particularly where flying was concerned—he was going to become a fighter pilot come hell or high water. But his sudden confidings pleased her, too. It meant he trusted her, and she felt that much closer to him for it.

She tried to hearten him. "You've already been through candidate screening and they've practically guaranteed you a spot."

It was true. He'd been to the Aircrew Selection Centre in Toronto the month before for a series of rigorous tests, and had done well. And he already had a private pilot's license.

"I know, I know." He seemed close to tears. "It's just…"

Then it dawned. "Is it your mom?"

Peter paused a moment before answering, surprised at how brittle his emotions had become on this of all days…and astonished at how, after just under a year together, Kelly seemed so unfailingly able to place her finger directly on the sore spot. He said, "When she kissed me in the auditorium there was booze on her breath."

Kelly made a small, disappointed sound in her throat.

"You know, I honestly thought she'd be okay. After my dad died—" Peter missed a beat, realizing with a jolt that it had been five years since his father's death from a heart attack "—it looked as if she was going to lose it completely. Jack Daniel's was her only friend in those days." He blew air through his teeth in a humorless chuckle. "I still don't know why she took it so hard. The old man was a total prick to her." He paused, remembering. "But then she seemed to come around. I can't say for sure, but I think I had a lot to do with it. The piano, the marks, football…all of that."

He turned to face Kelly. Tears had formed glimmering pools in his eyes. "Just lately, she's gone back to the boozing again. Nothing serious, just the occasional weekend fling…but I'm afraid once I'm gone, she'll slip back over the edge."

"She's still got Sammy," Kelly said, biting her tongue against an urge to verbalize her true feelings for Peter's mother; it could only worsen an already delicate situation. "He's only fourteen, but…"

"I've never said this to anyone, Kel. It kills me to even think it. But my mother doesn't love Sam. Not the way she does me. Sam was an accident. After me, she never meant to have another." He sighed. "I don't think Sam can help her."

"Try not to think about it," Kelly said, chilled—but not entirely surprised—by this admission. "You'll do what you can. But you've got a life of your own now." She kissed him. "And you've got me."

Seized by a sudden, fierce arousal, Peter shifted his body over Kelly's. Sharing his need, Kelly turned and lifted the raven locks from her neck, baring the nape.

Peter kissed her there, knowing how it brought her alive.

* * *

It was five o'clock and the end-of-June sun still hung high. For the past six days temperatures had skyrocketed into the high eighties and early nineties, and the forecasts offered no hints of a break. Uncle Jim's airfield—a six-bay hangar and a frost-heaved landing strip—was a forty-minute drive from the city, northwest of Sudbury on Highway 144. Peter and Kelly had been on the road for about twenty minutes now, and had just passed the turnoff to Dowling. The last of the city's mining-ravaged outskirts lay far behind them, and now rich pine forest stretched out for miles on either side.

Peter swerved out to pass a lumbering transport loaded with Blue Label, if you could believe the logo on the trailer.

Cuffing sweat from her brow, Kelly shouted over the roar of the bike. "Hey, let's hijack that truck."

Peter nodded, his silver Bell helmet setting off sunflares with the movement. "That'd make us a hit at the party," he said. "Beer, anyone?"

Onaping came next, then Cartier, twelve miles later. Beyond that, 144 was little more than a weather-bleached strip of concrete, running like a zipper between two thighs of bush.

Bush, bush, and more bush.

Lulled by the heat and the stuttering monotony of the centre line, Peter slipped into a logy semi-trance. He was aware of the vibration of the bike, the pressure of Kelly's hands on his hips, but these perceptions only added to the soporific effect. Gradually, his mind switched to autopilot.

His thoughts wound back absently to the events and sentiments of the now dwindling day, turning them over like Rubic's cubes, arranging them into different patterns. The porcupine toiling its way out of the ditch didn't even catch his eye. He might have picked it up with his peripheral vision, but the image didn't crystallize until it was already too late.

Then he did see its waddling bulk, and with a cold lump of terror in his throat he tried to swerve around it—

But in the last possible instant the doomed beast chose the direction of Peter's swerve as its own. With a swiftness anomalous to its species, it leaped into the whirring spokes of the Honda's front wheel.

The creature exploded, knots of raw tissue and fire-tipped quills spraying into Peter's face.

The front wheel locked at sixty miles an hour.

For the space of a heartbeat, unreality triumphed. Nothing happened. They simply hung there, neither in control nor completely out of it. Then reality resumed its treacherous reign and the bike flipped saddle-over-headlight, catapulting Kelly into space. Still clutching the handgrips, Peter watched her go, and for another tilted spasm unreality overswept him. That was *Kelly* out there and she was totally airborne, her flailing limbs giving the impression of someone swimming through the thick summer air.

Impossible.

There followed an infinite moment of downy free-fall...

Then the bike went over hard. Peter's first, terrified intake of breath stunk of gasoline, sun-baked pavement and scalding oil. His helmet struck the asphalt with a pistol crack and split like an egg, stunning him. Coloured pinpoints of light pulsed on his retinas, blooming like oil drops on water, and a dreadful flat horn bleat a single concussive note in his skull.

Peter thought: *I'm about to die.*

Then came the pain.

Four hundred pounds of pitiless machine pinned him to the pavement, grinding his body like a bug beneath a boot heel. Obeying the laws of friction and force, the bike swept him along before its load of momentum. He tried to roll away but couldn't, the weight of the bike clutching his leg like shark teeth. He could feel the blacktop rasping through his jeans, flaying off skin, planing down to bone. In a reflex, he thrust his hands out in front of him, but the asphalt chewed into them, too. He twisted at the waist, trying to distribute the scalding pain. Beneath his face, inches away, the flat gray back of the highway blurred incessantly past, and for a hideous moment Peter wondered if the still roaring Honda would mill and grind him until there was nothing left but a long bloody streak and a coagulated cluster of bone.

Now the concussive bleat in his head changed in quality. It deepened, seemed to exteriorize, becoming a deep-throated bellow overspread by a high keening shriek that whirled around inside his helmet.

But he was going to be all right. He knew that now. The bike was slowing, and although the world swam and the stars were out and the pain was titanic, he was still conscious. He would walk away from this one, scraped and bloodied, maybe a busted kneecap on the left—

Kelly.

The thought galvanized him.

What about Kelly?

He was lying on his belly, still facing north, when the bike came to an abrupt, begrudging halt. He craned his neck around and spotted her, several yards back on the roadside. She was hobbling toward him, one arm flailing over her head, the other dangling at her side, a fractured butt of bone jutting obscenely through the skin. There was blood and she was yelling something, but she was up and she was moving and she was going to be okay, too.

Relief surged through him. He waved, doing his best through the pain to grin...but Kelly was still yelling, really howling, he realized. What was she saying? He couldn't hear her over that infernal noise inside his helmet.

Pushing up on raw palms, Peter angled his gaze another twenty degrees and saw what Kelly was yelling about, beheld the source of that solid, bellowing roar.

The beer truck, rumbling like doom out of the heat shimmer, veering hard to the left in an ill-spent effort to avoid the over-turned bike. It bore down on him like the closing halves of a gargantuan jack-knife, locked wheels spewing white smoke...

And there was nothing he could do but watch.

The truck was thunder, the truck was the serpent-hiss of air brakes, the truck was the earsplitting howl of the air horn.

The truck was everything.

Punted like a pop can, the bike entered the air in a lazy spiral.

And Peter went under, past sunlight on polished chrome, past hot breath and foul smells into dark guts and a lifetime of hideous night-

mares. The right rear wheels of the cab rolled over his legs at the knees—
he could actually *see* them going over his knees—then he was tumbling,
over and over, faster and faster, a bit of cloth in a wicked wind.

The world became a bloodied pastiche of layered sensation: alternating glimpses of road and underbelly, road and underbelly; hot
whiffs of mechanical body fluids; the terrible, beastly moan of metal
straining against metal; raw pain screaming from every nerve fiber in
hellish concert with the air horn.

A *snap!*

(*That came*)

A deep, sickening, greenstick *snap.*

(*from inside me*)

Bright Light.

Dead? Am I dead?

no

It had passed over him. The truck had passed over him and now
he lay flat on his back on the highway. The Bright Light was not God's
celestial corridor but the sun, hot as slag on his face. He had jour-
neyed through a dark eternity that had lasted only seconds—and he
was still alive. Incredibly, he was still alive.

Legs busted bad… can't move…

The sun was so terribly hot on his face, he could feel the skin burning, he could feel that and he could hear the truck. The horn had fallen
silent, but now came the earsplitting artillery blasts of steel snapping
trees, and the jangling, shattering clangor of hundreds upon hundreds
of exploding beer bottles.

He could feel the sun on his face—

But that was all.

Where is the pain? Why is there no pain?

In his tottering mind Peter screamed out a prayer, begging for
pain, pleading for brutal, mind-eating, nerve-blasting pain—

Something hovering over him now, blocking the sun, pooling cool shadow on his face.

"Kelly?" A feeble whisper.

"Oh, Peter, yes, it's me. You're alive, thank God you're *alive.*"

Kelly. Above him, leaning over him, her voice hectic and high. Blood dripped from her shattered arm and freckled his forehead... wet, warm, tacky. He could feel that and he wanted to tell her he could feel that and nothing else...

But the truth of what that meant, the unspeakable horror of what that crisp interior *snap!* had been, turned the words to ash in his throat.

The world was swimming...

Swimming away.

There was a voice out there now, beyond Kelly's, and Peter prayed it was God's voice, if there was a God. He prayed it was God's voice calling him Home.

But it was only the trucker, stumbling toward them from his toppled rig. "Hey. Hey. You kids all right?"

Swimming...

Floating? Am I floating?

Kelly's voice. Kelly's touch. Kelly's hair tenting his face.

Then nothing.

Nothing at all.

2

THE HAGGARD FACE IN the west window startled her. *That's me,* Leona Gardner realized as her reflection resolved into ghostly focus; and in that moment she knew what she'd look like when she got old. Not a pretty sight.

Turning away, Leona took another stiff belt of Jack Daniel's, wincing at its bite and the hot tingle it sent capering through her body. Already comfortably plastered, she toasted the vacant chair opposite.

"Smooth sippin' Tennessee whiskey," she said, slurring the words. She snickered and lit another Tareyton.

Wreathed in smoke, she punched the rewind button on the reel-to-reel. Then, not wanting to, she glanced again at her reflection in the glass. Now it seemed to be speaking to her.

Look at you, it reproached her, its drawn lips unmoving. *A fine figure of a mother. You're a mess. A weak, disgusting mess. The boy's got to fly the coop sometime.*

"Fuck you," Leona said. And in a furious reflex, the hand holding the lit Tareyton shot out and clutched the yellow sheers, jerking them hard in an effort to obscure that mocking reflection. But the force she used was too great and the curtain rod let go, swinging down and batting a house-plant to the floor. Now there was a pungent burnt smell, and Leona realized her cigarette had ignited the sheers. Cursing again, she crushed the tiny blue flame between her fingers. Now there was a nickel-size hole, charred black at the edges.

Leona felt the scald of bitter tears.

Now Sam appeared in the doorway, his eyes behind his thick glasses puzzled and afraid, one finger worrying an angry-looking zit on his chin.

Leona glared at him. "What are you looking at?"

"Nothing," Sam said, dropping his gaze. "I just—"

"Then go about your business."

Head hung, Sam slouched back to his room.

On the kitchen table the reel-to-reel continued to spin. It had completed the rewind cycle, and now the loose end of the tape flapped annoyingly. Ignoring the fallen curtains, Leona clumsily rethreaded the tape, then hit the play button again.

Peter's music swelled from the whirring machine, filling her heart, quelling her pointless rage. She swilled and listened, her gaze straying through the living room archway to the piano by the big bay window. A white Yamaha. A baby grand. Peter had earned the money for it all by himself, starting with a paper route when he was only eleven.

Leona smiled. Whenever she thought of her boy, life's troubles seemed to just glide away. They were still there, of course—she wasn't *that* drunk. But for the time being they lost some of their nagging urgency.

The phone rang, jarring Leona out of her stupor. Raising her voice, she said, "Sam? Get that, will you?"

No answer.

"*Sam.*"

Nothing.

She turned down the volume on the recorder and wobbled to her feet. Weaving, she crossed to the wall phone by the doorway and lifted the receiver, almost fumbling it.

"Hello?"

A gruff male voice said, "Is this the Gardner residence?"

"Yes." A tiny dagger of fear slipped between Leona's ribs. "To whom am I speaking?"

"Mrs. Gardner. Who is this?"

"It's Sergeant Mitchell of the Sudbury Regional Police, Mrs. Gardner."

Dread reared up and kicked Leona Gardner in the stomach. *Peter.* Her Peter was up in that damned airplane...

"Is it Peter?" she said, abruptly sober. "Is it my boy?"

Sam appeared again in the doorway, his face expectant and pale.

"I'm afraid so, Mrs. Gardner. There's been an accident."

Leona's legs failed her and she sat down hard, her teeth clacking together as her fanny struck the floor. Sam took an uncertain step toward her.

"Is he...?"

"His condition is listed as critical. He's in surgery right now, at University Hospital. I regret having to give you this news."

The receiver plopped into Leona's lap, her hands thudding limply to the floor. Jumping its attachments, her small engagement diamond skidded across the linoleum and vanished among the dust kitties under the stove. Leona sat with her back to the wall and gazed without seeing at her feet, her pallid face stricken with shock.

Sam took the receiver and put it to his ear.

"Mrs. Gardner?"

"This is Sam, Peter's brother. Please, what's happened?"

"Your brother's been involved in an accident," the officer said, his voice formal and low. "He's badly hurt, Sam. He's in surgery now."

Sam said, "Oh," his thoughts whirling crazily. "What should I do?"

"You and your mom should get over to the hospital, son."

"Okay," Sam said. He simply could not envision his brother hurt. "Where…?"

"University Hospital," Mitchell said. "Is your mother all right?"

Sam looked down at his mother, still gaping doll-eyed at her feet. "I don't think so."

"Is there someone you can get to help? Is your father home?"

"I'll get a neighbour."

Mitchell apologized again.

"Good-bye," Sam said, and broke the connection.

Five minutes later Jimmy Maslak, the Gardners' nearest neighbour, was helping Peter's mother into the front seat of his van. Sam sat in back. They drove in silence to the hospital, six blocks away on Paris Street.

3

KELLY'S PARENTS WERE ALREADY there, seated in the small angular enclosure that served as a waiting room for the OR and ICU. Otherwise featureless, the room contained a dozen orange vinyl chairs, a compact colour TV and a single threadbare couch. In a far corner an ancient native woman sat alone, rocking in her seat and murmuring low, throaty prayers, working a worn set of beads through fingers that were crabbed with arthritis.

Sam, who had met the Wheelers only once, greeted them somberly after seating his mother by the door. No, they told him, there had been no news; they had arrived only minutes ahead of Sam and his mother.

While they waited, Sam did his best to calm his mother, though it was all he could do to keep from going to pieces himself. Not in his bleakest nightmares had he imagined that any harm might come to his brother. In Sam's admiring, fourteen-year-old mind, all of this was unthinkable.

He looked gravely at his mother, dreading what might happen should Peter not survive.

Sometime later, a thin, carrot-haired man in a lab coat two sizes too big for him strode into the room. Every face tilted up and beheld him, but he moved to the corner where the native woman sat praying, and drew up a chair. Compassionately he took her withered hand. Fragments of his speech reached Sam's ears.

"...very sorry...all we could, but..."

The old woman began to weep, her tears seeming to Sam almost foreign, coursing over those parched, weather-worn cheeks. She continued to rock a while longer. Then, with the doctor's help, she rose to her feet and shuffled out of the room, leaning heavily on her cane.

For her, at least, it was over.

* * *

News for the Wheelers came about an hour later, and it was good: Kelly had suffered a few minor friction burns, none of them disfiguring, and a compound fracture of her left forearm. Her fracture, the surgeon told them, would heal nicely, and he anticipated no loss of function.

Without a backward glance, the Wheelers accompanied the doctor to the recovery room.

Following this, Leona withdrew into silence, her face set like hardened wax. Even through the shock and her lingering drunkenness she understood that their turn was next, and the prospect paralyzed her.

Oh, Peter, her mind kept repeating. *Oh, Peter, oh, Peter...*

His own mind a blank, Sam gazed out the window overlooking Ramsey Lake, at the westering sun and its streaked, blazing glory.

* * *

At five the next morning, nine hours following the Gardners' arrival at the hospital, a tall, tired-looking man in OR greens shuffled into the waiting room. He glanced around briefly, then moved stiffly toward them.

"Mrs. Gardner?"

Leona's face tightened, as if preparing for a physical blow.

"Yes," Sam said, taking a deep breath. "And my name's Sam. I'm Peter's brother."

The doctor—DR. LUND, his name tag said—scanned the room once more. Then he drew up a chair and sat facing them, the harsh light of the overheads casting his eyes into deep, unreadable shadow. Sam remembered the native woman and braced himself.

"Is he dead?" Leona blurted, the shrillness of her voice startling both the surgeon and Sam. "Please don't tell me he's dead."

"He's not dead—"

"Oh, thank you," Leona said, clutching the doctor's coat sleeve. "Thank you, thank you, thank—"

"But he is seriously injured."

Leona released the man's arm and shrank back in her chair. In that instant of silence the hard-wax consistency of her face seemed to soften and run.

"Both of his legs were badly broken," the surgeon said. "His right shoulder blade, clavicle, and forearm were also fractured, but not as seriously as his legs. Six ribs—"

"Will he…" Sam swallowed hard. "Will he walk again?"

For the space of an instant the doctor appeared cornered to Sam, as if wanting only to flee this knife blade of truth. For many years afterward, in the fretful sweats of his slumber, Sam would wish that he had kept his mouth shut. It was as if, by asking, he had created the terrible answer.

"Peter… sustained another fracture," Lund said, the breath sighing out of him. "In his neck. A very serious fracture. His spinal cord was injured. Torn, actually. I'm afraid the damage will be permanent."

"What does that mean?" Leona said. "What does that *mean*?"

"I'm terribly sorry, Mrs. Gardner," Lund said. "But your son is paralyzed. From the neck down."

4

DOWN THE HALL FROM the waiting room stood a single orange door. A sign identified the area beyond it as the intensive care unit. As Sam approached that door, it swung hermetically inward, startling him. His mother, shambling along next to him, didn't notice. Following Dr. Lund's tragic news, she'd wandered off in search of a bathroom. Now she reeked of hard liquor.

In the corridor beyond the door, a barrage of alien stimuli assaulted Sam's senses: the pungent odours of disinfectant and disease; the jumbled beeps of unseen monitors; the cycle and hiss of life-support systems; and as the nurse led them deeper inside, the frightful sight of the cubicles. In which of them, Sam wondered, barely coherent, had they installed his brother? None of them, he suddenly felt certain. It was a clear cut case of mistaken identity. Peter was over the city right now, flying Uncle Jim's Twin Otter. God, how he managed it Sam didn't know. Sam had gone up with him once and had almost tossed his cookies. Peter had really razzed him over that—

The nurse had stopped walking. Unheeding, Sam bumped into her. She glanced at him, regretful, before stepping into an eight-by-ten cubicle and drawing the curtain aside.

Several seconds passed before Sam was able to focus his eyes, before the room agreed to stand still. It was impossible to take it all in at once, and for a giddy instant Sam believed there really had been a case of mistaken identity. It wasn't Peter in that bed. No way. He didn't know who the poor bugger was, with his legs in casts and tubes snaking out all over him and his eyes swollen shut and his head swathed like a Sikh's and a machine inflating his lungs—but it wasn't his brother.

Then his mother was falling to her knees at the bedside, wailing like a holocaust victim, clutching the unmoving hand of the body on the bed.

Peter's hand.

Sam dropped to his knees, too. Then forward, onto his elbows, swooning in a near faint.

* * *

Time ceased to have meaning in that windowless cell, the only sign of its passing the repetitive hiss of the ventilator. Twelve cycles a minute—Sam had absently counted it out.

And twelve times each minute his mind refused to credit what his senses told him was true.

That's Peter in that bed. That's really your brother.

But how could it be? Peter was like the sun, always there, above harm, a vigorous force bringing life and warmth wherever he turned his face. Sam could be blackly depressed—and these moods came often enough in the stormy crucible of his adolescence—and Peter needed only to grin at him or pull one of his Jack Nicholson impersonations and Sam immediately felt like a prince, unable even to recall the bulking concerns that had plagued him only moments before. Though no match for Peter academically, Sam never felt as if he lived in his brother's shadow, but rather in his light. Peter always had time for his goofy kid brother...

Sam looked up and saw his mother glowering at him, her gray eyes baleful and measuring. Stricken, he turned away. The first seeds of guilt sprouted then.

It should've been you—that's what she's thinking. See how she looks at you? You've got no right to be walking, no right to be breathing, no right...

Sam made a decision then. A choice. Killing himself would be pointless, although in that room and in that moment he felt no fear of death. But if he died, he couldn't help Peter. And for the first time in their lives together, Peter needed him instead of the other way around, the way it had always been.

His brother needed him.

Sam decided to become a doctor. He would devote his life to spinal cord research, and he would find a cure.

Sam's back straightened a little with this resolve. Some of the pain leaked out of his heart.

Yeah. A cure.

* * *

Several hundred breaths later, a nurse rolled Kelly Wheeler into the ICU in a wheelchair. Her arm, encased in plaster, lay cradled in a sling across her chest. There was a small friction burn on her chin and another on her cheek. To Sam, it looked as if her entire body was humming, so bright and alert were her eyes. She too failed to recognize the body on the bed, and for an instant that same fugitive hope tugged at the corners of her mouth.

Then the truth struck home, stark and immutable, and Kelly's face collapsed in anguish. Her head rolled back and a tortured moan built inside her; it twisted up through her chest and out through her mouth and Sam wanted to hold her. His little boy's crush on his big brother's girl congealed inside him in shades of green and shamefaced red—but he wanted her in his arms. He took a halting step toward her, then a brisk one back as his mother clutched Kelly in a tortured embrace.

"Oh, dear God," Leona cried. "Give back my boy. Give back my perfect, beautiful boy."

Head hung, Sam slunk out of the room.

* * *

Later that long, shattered day, Kelly had a nurse wheel her back to her room, a semiprivate on the second floor. She climbed into bed, curled up in a ball and cried. It hurt to cry, but she couldn't help it. Huge sobs convulsed her, hot tears soaking her pillow. Every inch of her hurt. She was fractured and bruised, abraded in places she hadn't known existed, bound up in so many yards of gauze she looked like the Mummy's Bride.

But all she could think of was Peter. So strong, so vital. As near perfect as nature allowed. Her lover. Her man. Smashed like a priceless Ming vase.

When his mother clutched her, Kelly had come close to pushing her away. The stink of liquor had come off her in waves, and Kelly had felt rage twisting savagely inside her. *Look at you*, she'd wanted to cry. *And look at your boy. Do you realize how much he's suffered over you? The worry you've caused him? And now just* look *at him.*

But compassion had won out, and Kelly returned Leona's grieving embrace. She'd noticed Sam starting toward her and wished she could have held him instead. But Sam had stalked silently away. Hours later, when Kelly left the unit for her room, Sam had still not returned. She feared the shock might destroy him. Like their mother, Sam had lived for his older brother.

Like Kelly herself.

Sometime during the brown haze of that afternoon, her parents came in and tried to console her. Not meaning to, Kelly drew herself shut and wished them away. Finally they left, babbling nervous good cheer and unwanted promises as they shuffled out of the room. They didn't understand.

In ICU Kelly had tried to drag some information out of Peter's mother, but the woman only blubbered nonsensically. With Sam gone, she'd turned next to the attending nurse. "How is he?" she'd asked. "What are his injuries?" But in the fashion of all health professionals the nurse had been deliberately vague. Refusing to be put off, Kelly had stirred up a fuss until finally the nurse paged Dr. Lund, who came by to explain things to Kelly. He, at least, had been honest. Brutally so.

Quadriplegic.

A cold, anthropological sound. Hearing it, Kelly recalled the grisly illusion she'd experienced in the stage-left wing the day before, that freak trick of the light in which Peter had appeared headless. She recalled, too, the force of that illusion, how it had seemed almost premonitory.

But he hadn't become a body without a head, which might have been more merciful; he'd become a head without a body. Permanent nerve damage, the doctor said. If he recovered from his coma, which was still uncertain, he'd be thoroughly dependent. He'd never walk again, never move his arms again, never do anything but blink his eyes, breathe, and just...lie there.

Permanent.

But what about Kingston?

What about flying?

What about us?

Permanent.

Kelly wept. She wept and wished for death.

* * *

The first of their school friends began wandering in later that afternoon. Though they came of their own free will, they appeared trapped to Kelly, nervously shifting, unable to meet her gaze. And it occurred to her then that she didn't really know them...and they didn't know her. They'd come only to ogle. And once they'd seen what they'd come to see, they were sorry. In a few of their faces Kelly witnessed a disquieting awareness being born. *Christ*, that look said, *we really can be hurt. Even killed.* For these vibrant kids Kelly was an exhibit, unwelcome proof of their own vulnerability. Even Kelly's closest girlfriend, Marti Stone, was in and out like a church mouse.

Of them all, though, Peter's football cronies were the worst. Huge flexing hulks, so unlike Peter in both intellect and physique, yet Peter mixed with them easily, earning their trust and respect. They skulked into Kelly's room, gawked at their feet, stammered out clumsy condolences and then ran, literally *ran*, the instant they were outside the door. Only Rhett Kiley overstayed his welcome. He hung around after the others left, grinning stupidly, making Kelly feel uneasy with his quick, canny eyes.

"Bummer," he said from the foot of the bed.

Kelly looked out the window, the covers drawn up to her chin.

"He was a good shit—"

"He's not dead, Rhett," Kelly said, sitting up. "He's hurt, but he's not..." Tears glazed her eyes.

"Hey," Rhett said, "I'm sorry. That's not what I meant." He sat on the edge of the bed and placed a hand on Kelly's thigh. Kelly tensed beneath the covers, but Rhett did not withdraw his hand. He released a long, woeful sigh—but his gaze touched the tanned dome of Kelly's shoulder like a dead fish.

In a single motion Kelly covered her shoulder and snugged her knees up to her chest, displacing Kiley's hand. Unperturbed, he let it rest on her foot. She could feel it tighten around her ankle.

"What I meant was, if you need a friend, Kelly—"

"Oh, that's sweet." Tears boiled out of Kelly's eyes, bringing Kiley smartly to his feet. "I bet Peter'll be real pleased to hear that his *friends* are looking out for his best interests."

Kiley's eyes darkened menacingly. "Aw, forget it," he said. Then he turned and stormed out of the room.

"You better hope I do," Kelly said to the empty room. "You bastard."

There were no other visitors that day, and Kelly was glad. She didn't want their company, didn't want their gawky condolences.

She only wanted Peter.

* * *

After leaving ICU Sam had gone for a long walk, back along Paris Street toward home, then west on York to Regent. Once downtown, he completed a rambling loop through the business district and found himself back on Paris Street.

Now he stood on the Paris Street bridge, overlooking the train station and the bedlam of the railyard below. The air was muggy, stubbornly static. In the west, the last light of day sent up enormous fans of peach and violet, crimson and shimmering gold. The pigments, though breathtaking, were mostly artificial, the result of sunlight filtered through tons of industrial effluent, sulfur dioxide and untold other pollutants spewed daily into the atmosphere by the numerous Nickel Ridge smokestacks. Peter had worked in the mines over the past three summers, earning money for college and to help make ends meet at home. Once Sam was old enough, he'd probably wind up there, too. It was tough, backbreaking work, but the money was good. And he'd be needing that money soon enough. It must cost a bundle to get a medical degree. He'd have to save-save-save. If he really tried he could probably find a night job, too, in a restaurant, maybe, or one of those all-night gas bars. Earn a few extra bucks during the school year. And there were government grants to be had if you were eligible. Sam remembered seeing Peter hunched over the application forms this past spring, wanting to obtain the maximum but ashamed to admit on paper that his family lived near the poverty line. He'd told Sam then that they might lose the house if their mother couldn't hold down a job. The employment agency she'd been attached to for the past five years hadn't called her in months, and Sam knew why.

She'd become...unreliable.

No, there was no way he could expect any support from her. She was always complaining that they didn't have a pot to piss in. Sam knew she got a monthly allowance from the provincial Family Benefits Program— "Welfare by any other name," he recalled Peter saying with obvious shame—another from Canada Pension, which their father had paid into for years, and a third small chunk from the life insurance policy the old man had taken out when he signed on at the mines.

But if the government weren't picking up the tab for Peter's medical expenses, Sam knew, they'd be out in the street tomorrow.

Oh, Jesus, Peter. I'm so sorry.

Overhead, flying low, a two-seater Cessna swooped past in preparation for landing on Ramsey Lake, the big in-city lake upon whose east bank the hospital stood. Sam craned his neck to watch it buzz by. That strange nebula-glow in the west flashed off a pontoon and struck Sam's eyes, bringing tears...

Sam's primal shout was lost in the roar of the Cessna's engine. Once tapped, the grief came in an unstoppable flood. A few folk tooling by in their cars glanced briefly his way, but no one paid him much heed. He stood there raging at the sky, clutching the guardrail, until his head ached miserably and his legs no longer betrayed him. Then he trudged back to the hospital.

Where the waiting began.

* * *

For Kelly and Sam that first week snailed interminably. Kelly was discharged on the second day following the accident, a circumstance that proved more an inconvenience than anything else. It meant she had to go home to sleep rather than just down the hall to her gloomy semiprivate. More than once during that week she beat the inconvenience by grabbing a few fretful winks on the too-short couch in the waiting room.

Sam, too, kept restless vigil, slouched in a chair by the wall or standing at the foot of Peter's bed, watching for some sign of life, some small hint of responsiveness. His brother's quadriplegia had by sympathy induced a kind of emotional paralysis in Sam, an inner numbness from which he seemed unable to free himself. The truth was impossible to grasp, so Sam's mind simply shoved it away, like snow before a rumbling plow blade. He kept brushing closer to that cold curl of truth, but could never quite bring himself to touch it. He spoke to no one, made eye contact with no one, trusted no one. Peter had been his only friend, the one he'd turned to when the going got tough.

But now the tough weren't going anywhere. Not ever again.

Leona turned to Jack for solace: Jack Daniel's. And, curiously enough, to God. A lapsed Catholic who'd last glimpsed the inside of a church on the occasion of Sam's first communion, Leona took up worship with a zealot's fervor. Before going to the hospital each morning, a ritual she practiced with at least equal zeal, she plodded up to Saint Joseph's Church on Boland Avenue. A high-spired Gothic cathedral with a mullioned rose window and twin louvered towers, Saint Joseph's boasted the largest parish in the city. And each morning at seven its cool shadow consumed her. At the marble font in the central portal she blessed herself, and at the big wrought-iron candelabrum beneath the north tower balcony she lit a candle in Peter's name. Then, hunched in a pew near the back, she prayed, remembered fragments of legitimate prayer slung feverishly together with nonsense verse of her own creation—or, more precisely, Jack Daniel's.

Jack in one hand, an unopened missal in the other.

Nights, too, Jack was her only comfort. A few times in the dark of the living room Sam tried clumsily to console her and thus be consoled himself, but Leona just shrugged him off. Installed on the couch in front of the silent TV, she guzzled and wept and listened to Peter's music on the reel-to-reel. Beethoven's "Moonlight Sonata." She raised her chin proudly each time the audience broke into exuberant applause. Then she rewound the tape and started over.

One late night Sam felt a long-dormant rage reaching a fusion point in his chest. He lay there in the stuffy dark of his bedroom and swore that if she rewound that tape just one more time he was going to go out there and toss the whole thing through the front fucking window. This emotion, dark and utterly foreign, clotted sickly inside him—but it continued to build. And the third time she rewound the tape after that dark pledge was taken Sam did get up and go out there. But instead of grabbing the recorder, which in his heart he knew housed the last repository of his brother's talent, Sam seized the bottle instead, shame and disgust funding his rage. "Give me that thing," he roared, his face an impossible beet red. *"Stop this."* He snared its glass neck—but Leona's grip tightened, bringing into play lightning reflexes Sam had never imagined her possessing, not in this inebriated state, and now they were engaged in a grotesque tug-of-war, Sam grunting on the verge of tears, Leona snarling like a hell-hound. In a freak canceling of opposed forces, the bottle broke free, its amber contents sloshing stormily. It flipped once, spun through an uneven arc and shattered on the edge of the piano lid.

Animated by a fury that towered over Sam's, Leona lurched to her feet and struck him a whistling backhand, the jagged claws of her stoneless engagement ring raking Sam's acne-spotted face, bringing blood. Sam reeled back, clutching his cheek, tears of bewilderment stabbing his eyes. Leona brushed past him and wove her way to the piano, her chin jutting out before her like some weird damage detector.

Prisms of glass and tracking puddles of booze littered the instrument's lid. Volatile liquid dripped to the rug from the Yamaha's polished heel. Leona snatched a doily from a side table, knocking a lamp to the floor, and began gingerly sopping up the mess with it. A gouge embedded with glass marred the lid near its edge, and when Leona spotted it she swung on Sam like a crazy woman, her eyes as red as Sam's face had been only moments before.

"Are you out of your mind? This is Peter's *piano*." She resumed her frantic mopping, one finger darting repeatedly to the gouge in the wood, as if to scrub that away, too. "Why don't you just get the hell out of here? Eh, Sammy? Why the hell don't you?"

Sam did.

And found himself back at the hospital.

5

THEY WERE ON THE bike, cruising north on Highway 144. The air was sweltering, the sky an eerie metallic blue...and any minute now that fucking porcupine was going to waddle up onto the road.

But this time he'd be ready.

The spot where the beast would appear was easy enough to identify. The blacktop beyond it was all gouged and slickly wet looking, and in the bush to the right it appeared as if a tornado had chewed out a ravening path.

But Peter knew better. It was no tornado but a big, beer-filled tractor trailer. It was behind them right now, waiting to flatten him—but this time he'd swerve the *other* way and old porky would just sashay on by, startled but still intact, and he and Kelly would boogie on up to Nell Tait's cottage party, he could feel Kelly's hands on his hips, and afterward they'd cruise back home and catch a few winks, and in the morning they'd be on the road again, free for the summer, off to see the country, make love, plans for the future...

Yep, this time he'd be ready.

The porcupine waddled out of the ditch, so slowly that Peter had to chuckle inside. This was going to be a cakewalk. Maybe he should just pull over and wait until the witless creature had crossed the road and the truck had blown harmlessly by.

Slowly...

On the soft shoulder now, its stupid eyes meeting his. Hesitating, about to cut back...

Peter's fingers tightened on the handgrips, preparing to coax the bike into a gentle curve around the doomed beast.

Lots of time...

But in the last possible instant during which control was still his, an invisible hand seized the handlebars, Fate's hand, freezing the wheel, damning his efforts to guide it.

The porcupine exploded—

And in hideous fast forward the scene played itself out again, until the hiss of air brakes became the mechanical chuff of a ventilator.

Peter jerked awake from his coma. He'd been coming up slowly for the past thirty hours, but had shown no outward sign. Now a spasm skipped through him like a stone on still water. His whole body flinched—but the sensation reached only his neck. His eyes fluttered open, his vision fuzzy from the ointment the nurses had placed in them to prevent the drying of his corneas. His head felt as heavy as a wrecking ball, dead weight, and there was something jammed into his mouth, a plastic-tasting tube of some kind, tied in place with a cord around his neck. The cord chafed the corners of his mouth like a riding bit. He couldn't breathe through his nose, and his body...

Where was his body?

(snap)

Peter moaned as the memory flashed back, but no sound came out of him. It was blocked by the tube in his throat. He closed his eyes against the bite of tears and sent a fierce command to his fingers.

Move.

Nothing happened.

Move, damn you.

But his fingers remained motionless. He couldn't even be sure they were there. He tried his toes next. His feet, arms, legs…

Nothing.

Peter's mouth widened in a silent scream around the tube that now kept him alive. Then he lapsed willingly back toward coma. And beyond.

And in the years to come, he would have time aplenty to rue the shrill cry that dragged him back again.

* * *

"*He moved.*"

Leona Gardner popped to her feet like a spring-loaded toy. She'd been sitting in her usual spot, in a chair by the bedside, stroking Peter's hand, when his eyes fluttered open and his mouth yawned wide. Her purse, which had been cradled in her lap, tumbled to the floor, spewing its contents under the bed. Her Bible fell with it.

"He moved," she shrilled again. "Did you see it?"

Now Sam was up too, and Kelly, and the nurses were filing into the room. All of them stood in silent tableau.

* * *

There was a brisk sense of acceleration away from that voice, of dizzying free-fall. The exhilaration was tremendous, and it was only in facing the depths of his descent that Peter understood what was happening. He was tumbling into death's dark warren.

Fear slowed his fall. Terror stopped it completely.

And Peter opened his eyes.

There was a cheek pressed against his, hot and wet, and a boozy waft of breath…

Mom.

"Peter, baby, I'm so glad you're back. I was so afraid, I've been praying. I knew you'd be back, I did."

He tried lifting an arm to embrace her.

Nothing.

He lifted his head instead, coughing as the rigid tube prodded something deep in his windpipe. Leona drew back a bit, and Peter saw Sam standing on tiptoe behind her. Kelly was there, too, her bruised face beaming with relief.

Peter tried to speak, but the tube left him mute.

"He's tryna say something, Sammy," Leona slurred, missing the terror in Peter's eyes. "C'mere. Try to read his lips."

Both Sam and Kelly drew nearer. Still smiling, Kelly placed a hand on Peter's forearm—and abruptly withdrew it, a chill skating through her. His skin was cold and dry, abnormally smooth. It was like touching the arm of a dead man.

They watched Peter's mouth. His chapped lips formed unintelligible syllables, the tube getting in the way. He angled his head to one side, wedging the tube in the corner of his mouth, and tried again.

"Can," Sam said aloud, thrilled as a kid at Christmastime. "Can't?" He repeated the word to Kelly, who agreed, then looked back at his brother. "Can't...moo..."

Can't move.

Sam's heart fell. So did Kelly's.

How were they ever going to tell him?

"That's just for now, Peter," Leona said, and Sam felt kicked by the thoughtless cruelty of her lie. He grabbed her arm, but Leona charged ahead. "Couple of months tops, honey, then you'll be good as new." She beamed, stroking her son's matted hair. "Honestly."

Peter's eyes welled with relief...then doubt seemed to harden their shine. He looked at Sam, then at Kelly, hoping for confirmation. But neither of them could meet his gaze.

He retured his gaze to his mother.

"Good as new, sweetheart," she told him. "Just wait and see. I'm praying for you, honey. Praying every day."

* * *

In the middle of the week that followed, a balding, potbellied physician by the name of Harrison Lowe strolled into Peter's room and told him he was going to be extubated that morning. A few days prior Peter had learned the meaning of the term and had been looking forward to it ever since. It meant the tube in his throat would be coming out and he'd finally be able to speak. He'd been breathing without the benefit of the ventilator for two days now and felt more than up to the task of carrying on without the tube. Above all else, progress was paramount in his mind. Stated bluntly, he wanted the fuck out of here.

A couple of months, his mother had told him. True, she'd been drunk at the time, probably had been since the accident, but surely she'd have gotten it right, even drunk as she was? Something as important as that...

Kelly and Sam, both of whom had been practically living at Peter's bedside, had studiously avoided the topic—not that Peter had been very much able to stimulate conversation—and there had been something in Sam's eyes when their mother told Peter the good news—a slap-faced sort of surprise. Shock, maybe? Whatever it was, it had badgered him ever since. And it had joined an inner voice, a dark, doomsayer's voice that plagued him in the trench of the night.

Wake up, son, that deceitful voice told him. *You're a gimp, a veg, a head. You're paralyzed from the neck down.*

And you're going to stay that way forever...

But that was a lie. His own mother had told him so. All he had to do now was sit tight and persevere, just as he'd always done, and before long *(couple of months tops)* he'd be out of here. Kingston could wait if it had to. He was a prime candidate, like Kelly said. They'd hold his spot for him, surely they would...

As Dr. Lowe and the nurse prepared to remove his tube, Peter realized what that look on his brother's face had been. It had been shock all right, but happy shock, wordless shock. Both Sam and Kelly had feared his injuries were permanent, and Leona had kept the good news from them until Peter was awake enough to share in it, too. That was why they'd seemed so stunned.

Peter's neck muscles tightened. The nurse had slipped on a pair of disposable gloves and now she was leaning over him, reaching for his tube with a suction catheter coiled like a snake in one hand. Reflexively, Peter twisted his head away... but her deft fingers slipped the catheter into the tube and began worming it down his neck. She'd done this before, many times, and although Peter knew she was doing it for his own good—"We've got to keep all that mucus from building up down there"—he wanted to slap it out of her hands. It made him hack like hell when it touched—

A cough scraped its way up Peter's throat like the blade of a rasp, causing a throb in his eyes and a croupy wheeze around the tube in his trachea. Tears bleared his eyes as tenacious yellow mucus streaked up the length of the catheter, mercifully obscuring his view of the nurse's face and the revulsion that contorted it. She withdrew the catheter slowly, dipped it into a basin of water—and snaked it into him again.

When Peter's coughing subsided, the doctor stepped forward. His blue eyes gleamed around pinpoint pupils.

"Good," he said. "That's what we like to see. Okay, now..." He grasped the end of the tube between forefinger and thumb. "Deep breath—"

And before Peter could blink, the tube was dragged up and out, snagging on his teeth before vanishing from his sight line. He heard it thunk unceremoniously into a bedside wastebasket.

"There," Dr. Lowe said, apparently pleased with himself. "How does that feel? Better, hmm?"

Peter tried to say yes, to thank him, but all that came out was a dry croak of air. He nodded instead.

"The hoarseness will go away," Dr. Lowe said. "Give it a day or two. For now you can whisper—"

And for a bitter moment that dark voice heckled again: *Wow, man, just think of it. You can whisper. Top athlete, musical prodigy, Ontario scholar, soon-to-be jet pilot, and all you can do is whisper.*

"—and before you know it you'll be talking a blue streak."

Then the guy—and that was exactly how Peter viewed him in this woeful moment of mute communication, as an ordinary guy caught in a shitty situation—seemed to read the unspoken question that reeled behind Peter's eyes...

And he was gone, a jovial "See you tomorrow" all that was left to ring in Peter's ears.

* * *

The spasms began in earnest during his third week in ICU. He'd suffered a few of them already, mild ones, quivery little starts that stole through his body or shimmied his legs. Spinal shock, they told him it was—although his mother kept insisting these movements were a sign of his imminent recovery—the body's predictable reaction to spinal cord injury. From the shelves of his shoulders to the soles of his feet his muscles were totally flaccid—no tone, no reflexes. But when the spasms came, their force was Herculean, at times seeming vigorous enough to snap his spine all over again. On top of all this, he got frequent spontaneous erections (whose presence he couldn't feel, and this embarrassed him repeatedly), his blood pressure took regular nosedives, leaving him faint whenever they sat him up, and his heart knocked along at an all-time low of thirty-eight beats a minute.

His bladder was distended almost constantly, necessitating the full-time placement of a catheter, and sometimes, it became downright difficult to breathe.

One early morning, with Sam's and Kelly's help—his mother, thank God, had been absent—two nurses and an intern hoisted him out of bed and propped him up in a chair. Much ceremony surrounded this process—apparently it represented a big step forward. To Peter, however, being hauled about bodily was one of the most humiliating experiences he'd ever endured, right up there with having a student nurse pad into his room to give him a sponge bath and find his pecker standing stupidly at attention, a yellow bladder catheter waggling obscenely from its tip. The feeling of helplessness, of utter dependency, was huge, and in its shadow Peter could barely contain his despair. Only his mother's promise kept the outbursts at bay.

(couple of months tops)

He was going to get better.

Shortly after they plunked him in the chair, a spasm like a mortar blast almost slammed him onto the floor. His arms jerked up and his legs jackknifed violently, sending the food Kelly had been spooning into him all over the chair, the floor, and Kelly herself. A second spasm took him an instant later, and this time Peter gave voice to his pain. The tears came as they lifted him back into bed, scalding, humiliating tears, and in a tantrum totally out of character for Peter Gardner he ordered everyone out of his room—Sam, Kelly, the lot of them.

When they had gone, he wept in the miserable silence.

6

FOR KELLY WHEELER THAT first summer passed like a debilitating disease, moment by painful moment, sometimes threatening to kill but most times just laying her flat. In spite of her parents' protests, she canceled her position at Queen's University in Kingston, where she'd been among the first accepted into the honours phys ed program. And although she would later reapply and be reaccepted, on that drizzly morning in August when she called the registrar's office to relinquish her slot, the future she had grimly decided upon had a different face entirely.

The night before, sitting on the grass in Bell Park on Ramsey Lake, she'd discussed her plans with Marti Stone, who'd been her closest friend since the third grade. Though disappointed—both girls had dreamed of becoming teachers for as long as either could remember—Marti had encouraged her to go with her heart. And if that meant putting off her education for a while, even indefinitely, then so be it. If she didn't at least try to work things out with Peter, she might regret it for the rest of her life.

Marti left the park ahead of Kelly that night, and Kelly spent a long time just lying on the grass, gazing at the moon. There were tears, and a heartache so intense it had a physical quality, but it felt good to have talked it all out.

Later, before leaving, she stripped off her shoes and waded into the lake, relishing the cool caress of the water around her ankles. Moonlight tracked down from a clear sky and twinkled on the surface like a million silver pixies. Recalling a rhyme she'd heard as a child—a tale of a sorrowful princess who drank down the moon and its magic restored her lover from the dead—Kelly dipped her cupped hands into the shimmering water...but when she brought them up to her lips, there was nothing in the bowl of her hands but cold black liquid. Thirst unquenched, she let it drizzle untasted through her fingers.

She dried her hands on her jeans, picked up her shoes and made her way back to the road.

* * *

Peter spent six full weeks in ICU—all of July and the first two weeks of August—before his transfer to the rehab unit on the seventh floor. During this interval, when he wasn't sedated, he and Kelly discussed little of any consequence—like their future together and how it had changed, or Peter's injuries, and in particular his chances for recovery—opting instead for mundane exchanges of small talk or simply silence. Sam was there almost constantly, darting in and out, as if pulled by other, unknowable duties. And Leona, whose meddlesome nature Kelly became fast unable to tolerate, sat there around the clock, stinking of booze, her very presence disallowing anything meaningful to pass between Kelly and her crippled son. She lied to him still, promising a full recovery, and sometimes Kelly had to bite her lip to stop herself from slapping the woman silly. It was a cruel and malicious lie. But as time wore on, Kelly thought she saw the truth twisting slowly into focus behind Peter's eyes.

"I'm going to get a job," she told her mother, hot on the heels of her confession about Kingston. "I'm going to get a job and find an apartment, and when Peter's feeling well enough I'm going to move him in with me."

Irene Wheeler, whose only sister had wasted her life on a man with no future, spun on Kelly like a jackal. "You most certainly are not," she snapped, making Kelly's father, Charles, avert his eyes. "No way. It's over for Peter, Kelly, and the sooner you face up to that fact the better it'll be for all concerned."

"It's terrible what happened to Peter," Kelly's father said, trying to soften his wife's well-meaning but rather harsh approach. "But your mother is right. It simply cannot work out, and with time you'll see that. He needs full-time nursing care—"

"Then I'll hire a nurse," Kelly said. "I'll…I'll…"

The tears were very close now.

"You'll call the registrar's office back right this minute, that's what you'll do," Irene said. She loved her daughter dearly, but there was no way she was going to sit by and watch her throw away a perfectly bright future over a dead man. And really, that's what Peter Gardner had become. Before the accident, she'd liked Peter very much, had even been secretly pleased with the idea that he might someday marry her baby girl. They were good together: smart, clean, honest kids. But now, all that had changed.

Irene's expression softened, and she snugged an arm around Kelly's waist. "Listen, honey. You'll get over him." Kelly buried her face in her mother's neck and cried. "You'll get over him and then you'll go on. Just wait and see."

Moved, Chuck Wheeler stood up to join in the embrace—

And Kelly bolted into the stairwell. "No," she cried like an angry child. "I'll *never* get over him, and I'll never leave him." Her stamping footfalls rattled the plates in the cupboards. "I love him…"

Kelly swept her bedroom door shut and flung herself onto the bed, sending an arrow of pain through her healing arm. In spite of her violent denial, a deep part of her knew her mother was right. Lying there sobbing, she felt the way she had as a third grader, when she climbed off the bus one day to find Snowball, her very first kitten, all bloodied and broken in the gutter, hit by a car and left to die. Sick with fear, she'd rushed him inside and begged her parents to drive him to the vet's. Her folks complied, but the vet only shook his head. "We'll have to put him to sleep. I'm sorry, sweetie, but there's no other way." Kelly objected vehemently, unable to comprehend why they didn't just patch him up. And when it was done, when Snowball was finally dead, she cried and cried and felt exactly like this, a vanquished warrior in a lost battle of truth who stubbornly refused to give up.

But that had only been a kitten, not her lover, and she was by God going to do it. She and Peter would get along fine on their own. Things were bad, horrible even, but their love would see them through.

With that resolve Kelly picked herself up and returned to the hospital. She told Peter of her intentions, and it took some coaxing before he agreed. He, too, was concerned for her future.

But, as so often happens, things did not work out the way Kelly had planned.

Peter still believed he was going to get better.

* * *

During the long months that followed, Peter allowed himself to acknowledge only the signs of his progress, scant as they were. The slightest encouragement from the staff took on the deceptive dimensions of promise, and he learned to endure the humiliations of his treatment with the stoicism of a man who is yet unable to see the true shape of the beast he must face. Time became a sluggish smear, highlighted by visits from Sam, his mother, and Kelly—and increasingly fewer visits from anyone else. In the first few weeks there had been cards and flowers and a lot of well-wishing, but this tapered off quickly, almost shamefully so. He began to feel forgotten, and this feeling sometimes made him question his very existence. The sedation heightened this sense of unreality—they told him he must rest through the healing process, which was ongoing in spite of his inability to perceive it—and he sometimes slept up to fifteen hours a day. When not sleeping or gawking at his visitors—for, with time, he came to realize that he had less and less of any consequence to say to them— Peter found himself floating in a chlorine-reeking pool or having his dead limbs cranked by some nameless physiotherapist. Without the continual encouragement of his mother, he might have despaired a lot sooner. But when they were alone in his room and the night outside was black and uncaring, she promised him a full and speedy recovery. And no one told him any different.

* * *

"We're going to have to tell him," Sam said. It was November 4. Outside, the first hard flakes of a brutal winter whirled on the gray pavement.

Remembering the clout she'd given him last time, Sam stood well back from his mother as he spoke. It was Friday night and she was really flying…but flying low. She had the tape player on and the photo albums out. The bottle in her lap was empty, and Sam was afraid that if she kept this up she was going to drink herself into oblivion.

"Tell who what?" Leona said, her rheumy eyes rolling his way.

"Tell Peter." He cleared his throat. "Tell him the truth."

"And what might that be, Mister Smarty Pants?"

Sam's Adam's apple bobbed apprehensively. "He's not going to get better, Mom," he said, flinching as he said it, expecting her to pitch an album at him or lunge up swinging her fists.

Instead, Leona's eyes moistened with tears. As if in shame, she hid her face from her son. A shuddering intake of breath seemed to overinflate her, and she appeared on the verge of finally facing the truth.

But just as quickly that look became a leer, and she returned to leafing through the albums, making Sam feel as if he'd never existed.

He turned and slouched back to his room.

And later, when the flap of the tape joined the bovine snores of his mother, he crept into his brother's room and lay down on his empty bed.

7

CHRISTMAS HAD COME AND gone and now January encased the world in its icy mantle. Sleet pecked at the thermal panes, and an incessant wind hammered the high tower of the hospital, whining through hairline cracks. Inside, the wards slept fitfully, dreaming uneasy dreams.

Peter lay on his side in his private room, not asleep, his back to the sleet-streaked window. He was listening to the wind and something else, something deep in his unfelt guts. Two things, really: one a grotesque and unwanted truth, the other a burbling, gaseous storm, brewing toward breaking point. He'd already tried calling the nurse with his chin-operated call button, but tonight it was that haughty bitch Louise Larue, who spent more time preening than she did looking out for her charges.

Earlier that day Dr. Lowe had changed Peter's medication, substituting a stronger laxative to relieve his chronic constipation. But whatever that medication was, it was working *too* well, and Peter knew that any minute now he was going to shit in his bed.

Uttering an angry oath, he chinned his call button again. He remembered only too well the last time he'd dirtied his bed. It had been in August, when the last of his "friends" showed their faces for the last time. Mike Gore, Rhett Kiley, and Jerry Jeter. They'd slunk into his room like convicts, full of guilty knowledge. Gore had brought along a box of pistachios, Peter's favorite, and had made the mistake of holding the box out for Peter to take. Following that blunder, a silence as impenetrable as a steel vault had enclosed them.

Peter had never felt so unmanned as he did on that day, the three of them poking into his room, guys he'd hung out with for years, guys into whose waiting paws he'd so easily lobbed hundred-yard passes, guys he'd gobbled Harvey burgers with or taken punches for in the after-game brawls that sometimes broke out, the three of them gawking at him like total strangers—or worse, reluctant acquaintances who'd come to a funeral to view the remains, only to find that the deceased had the uncommonly bad taste to still be alive.

It had happened then. Seeing his buddies ambling in like that, so damned easily, and understanding that life was like simple economics—even if you had been a millionaire, the game was over once you lost all your wealth—had soured something in his guts. Suddenly he was out of the race, no longer in possession of the essential currency of camaraderie... and this same sick thunder had growled in his belly then.

Suddenly, explosively, he had shit in his bed.

"Come on," Peter hissed in the stormy silence. "Come on."

But no one came.

He broke wet wind, the stink of it unbearable; nothing like it had ever come from inside him before. It was an old man's stink. The stink of an open grave.

Tears scalded his cheeks.

"Come on," he pleaded, shouting now. "Come on, you lazy bitch, come *on*."

That voice. That voice in his head.

This is it, man. This is what you are. All that physio and occupational therapy they've been putting you through isn't intended to help you get better. Its only purpose is to slow the decay.

"No." It was a roar, so huge it made his ears ring.

He broke wind again. Or was it…?

"Get *in* here." His head shot up like that of a cobra, his neck muscles flaring in a hood. "Get the fuck *in* here."

It was leaking out of him now. He couldn't feel it, but he knew that it was.

(*the stink*)

Peter's shouts fused together into a furious, unbroken bellow, like that of an air horn. He could hear footfalls now, quick and staccato.

Come ahead in, Larue, he thought bitterly. *Got a sweet-smelling surprise for you.*

(*this is what you are*)

"No," he cried again, as the night nurse poked her pretty face into the room.

"What—" she started to say.

Then the smell hit her and she knew. It was all over her face, the revulsion, and Peter wanted her out of his sight. He wanted to lie here in the stink of his own shit and die, because the voice in his head was right; it had always been right. His mother had lied.

This was what he was.

"Why didn't you tell me?" he said, spittle spraying from his mouth.

"Tell you what?" the nurse said. But she knew that, too.

"Why?"

Filled with pity and compassion, Louise approached Peter's bed, doing her best to ignore the smell of him. She'd seen this before with some of the other quads, this abrupt, savage awareness, coming so long after most people assumed they'd figured things out for themselves. The strength of denial was brute. Louise felt bad that she hadn't heard him calling before now. She'd been in the john, not preening but changing a tampon, and her partner was downstairs on break. Nights were usually so quiet up here, she hadn't thought she'd be missed for the few minutes her business would take. As it was, she'd barely avoided soiling her uniform…

Oh, Christ, why didn't they involve a psychiatrist in these cases earlier? Someone who could level with these poor bastards and know when it was best to do so?

She reached out to touch Peter's cheek, to comfort him—and Peter spat in her face.

"Get out, cunt. *Get out.*"

Biting back her own abrupt anger, Louise snatched a tissue from Peter's bedside dispenser and wiped the saliva away.

"Peter, I—"

"*Out.*"

Louise backed away, afraid now. Her fear was irrational—there was no way he could harm her—but she felt it nonetheless, deep, solid and cold.

"I'll be right back," she said as she left.

"Don't you dare," Peter shouted after her. "Don't you dare come back here."

Her footfalls faded in the dark.

* * *

"He's in a rage," Louise told Dr. Lowe over the phone. "He spat in my face…"

Lowe sighed. It was four in the morning. He lived twenty minutes from the hospital when the roads were bare, and they'd been issuing storm warnings all night. Still, he'd have to go in.

"Give me a half hour," he said, and hung up the phone.

* * *

Had it been possible to wish death to happen, to conjure it out of a hat, Peter would have done so willingly on this bleak winter's night. He was a quad, a human head grafted to a nerveless garbage heap that shit itself and pissed itself and would eventually wither and die. He would never move more than his head for as long as he lived. He would never walk again, play the piano again, make love again.

And he would never fly.

Peter's mind reeled like a toddler fresh off a carnival ride. Even parading before him as it was, the truth seemed incomprehensible. Maybe he had died and this was hell, punishment for sins unrecognized. Surely it couldn't be real?

Hell...that was it. He'd died beneath those huge rubber wheels, the same wheels that tramped over him anew each night in his dreams; he'd died and gone straight to hell. This was Lucifer's style, wasn't it? Let you stew for a few decades before popping up and bleating, "Guess what, motherfucker?"

The door creaked open.

"Who's there?"

The pale light of the corridor crept in, printing a stoop-shouldered shadow on the wall.

"It's me, Peter. Doctor Lowe."

"Don't come in here," Peter said. But a lot of the rage had drained out of him. Now he felt stunned, concussed by the immutable truth.

Lowe came ahead in. The reek of excrement was still there, but the doctor showed no sign that he noticed. He stood at the end of the bed, hands on the foot rail, eyes unreadable in the dark.

"Why didn't you tell me?" Peter said.

A sigh. "Because it wouldn't have registered."

Shame and fury battled for dominance in Peter's mind. Shame because he was lying here satcheled in his own shit, screaming at people who were only doing their jobs in the best way they knew how. And fury, not because the doctor was wrong, but because of the rehearsed smugness of his reply, as if he saved this line for all the new quads—"Because it wouldn't have registered"—waiting like a stage actor for that single elusive moment of purest dramatic effect.

Finally, shame won out. Peter apologized to Louise and the doctor and allowed the nurse to clean him up and then jab a sedative into his arm. Seeing the needle, he flinched in anticipation of the pain that never came.

But as the dope took effect and the door shut him in, the fury swirled up again, stewing like lava, waiting to erupt.

* * *

The next morning Kelly Wheeler left Peter's ninth-floor hospital room for the last time. She walked outside into the cruel January air with her coat half buttoned and her bare hands dangling at her sides. To the security guard stamping his feet by the parking booth, she looked like someone who'd just been clobbered with a nightstick.

The day was windy and brutally cold, the sun a high white blank in the sky. Powdery snow swirled in the gunfire gusts, and frost snapped at whatever exposed flesh it could find.

Kelly didn't notice. What had just transpired between her and Peter had erased the final chapters of her life. Now she was blank, like the sun. Empty and cold. She went to the bus stop, but let her bus drone past. After a while she began to walk.

* * *

She sat naked in the centre of her bed, lotus style, her face and hands stinging with chilblains. In the triangular enclosure between her legs lay a pastel assortment of pills: tranquilizers, analgesics, a dozen Demerol tablets her dad had left over from his back surgery, others. Ranged about her on the quilt lay the tangible remnants of her past, treasured keepsakes transformed into pockets of pain by a sadistic whim of fate.

She examined each of them in turn.

The torn halves of the tickets to last year's Sadie Hawkins dance. How surprised he'd been when she asked him, stammering like a kid, glancing over his shoulder to be sure it was him she was addressing. She'd known even then that if she hadn't made the first move they might never have gotten together. The desire was there, all over his face, like a rash that surfaced only when their eyes met... but a mover he wasn't.

A red rose, dried, pressed and sleeved in waxed paper. He'd waited on line at the Dairy Queen, where Kelly had been working for the summer, for almost twenty minutes on the hottest day of that August, one hand hidden behind his back, his sweat-dampened T-shirt plastered to his chest and that just-for-you smile on his face. And when he finally reached her window he poked the rose through the slot and pressed his lips to the glass. By the time she got it, the blossom was limp and droopy with the heat. But she kept every petal.

Pictures...

And The Book, as they came to know it. A dog-eared copy of the *Kama Sutra*. She'd picked it up in the Health section at the Coles bookstore on Elm Street and begun to leaf idly through it... and felt herself flush as she scanned random passages, not out of embarrassment (though the descriptions of positions and techniques left little to the imagination), but out of excitement at the prospect of bringing such forbidden ecstasies to her lover. She'd taken it up to the cashier, camouflaged amid a stack of $1.99 specials from the grab tables— such edifying titles as *Dogs, Lichens and Fungi of North America* and

Automotive Mechanics—and had almost slipped it through...but then the girl at the register, a plump redhead with mascara so thick it was peeling, said, "Oh, you're gonna love this one, sweetie," and flipped it open herself. "Here," she confided, winking and tapping a page near the middle. "Start right here. You'll give him a hernia."

They'd had a ball with that book, she and her man...and she'd given him everything but a hernia.

She went through it all, item by item, memory by sweet memory.

Then, almost dreamily, she scooped up a handful of pills.

8

ON A THURSDAY EVENING in the middle of January, Rhett Kiley and Jerry Jeter sat stageside at the Coulson Hotel and watched a stripper listlessly peel off her outfit. When she cut her tits loose—fat, pendulous things with nipples the size of bullets—Jerry thumped the table with his fist and grinned stupidly at Rhett.

Stunned fucker, Rhett thought, not unkindly. He'd always had a tolerant, big-brotherly affection for Jerry, and the sentiment seemed to have doubled since Jerry's football accident last fall.

"'Nother brew?" Rhett said, and Jerry nodded his bandaged head. Rhett hailed a waitress and ordered two cold ones. The quiff on the stage was down on her ass now, doing the old beaver shot for the pervs in the front row, and Rhett glanced at her disinterestedly.

What a drag, he thought, a sour belch burbling up from his guts. Barely twenty-one and already his life was on the skids. He'd been sure, so fucking *sure* the college scouts were going to pick him up, he hadn't even considered his alternatives. There was nothing else he wanted to do anyway. For Rhett, it had always been a pro-ball career or bust.

Well, it looked like a bust. Without a football scholarship, there had been little point in going to college. What was he going to be? A lawyer? A fucking pharmacist like brainy old Mike Gore? Right. If it hadn't been for his superstar status in high school, he never would have made it through. Even with the coach pulling strings for him, it had taken Rhett seven years to get his diploma.

The waitress came back with their beers. Rhett paid her, then drained half his bottle at a pull. He glanced at Jerry, who had his eyes glued to the stripper's snatch, and felt a twinge of envy for the guy. Jerry was no Einstein either, but he'd always had a cheerful, fun-loving nature, and he could run like the proverbial wind. Michigan State had picked him up on a nice juicy scholarship, but his first game out, Jerry had taken it in the head in a ten-man pileup and ended up under the knife. Epidural hematoma, they called it. He spent a month in the hospital after his transfer back from the States, and now, two months later...well, the poor little fucker was different. Maybe it'd wear off with time, Rhett thought halfheartedly, not really believing it. But since his surgery, Jerry seemed sort of...stunned. Yeah. That said it best. That bright, mischievous light was gone from his eyes, and instead of spouting wild ideas like he used to, he just sort of sat there, waiting for something to happen. He looked okay, maybe a little clumsy on his feet...but something was missing. Too bad. He could've been big. He could've made it to the pros.

"I've been thinking," Rhett said now, having trouble diverting Jerry's attention from the stripper. "My old man's been talking about retiring this winter, and he wants me to take over the business." Gord Kiley owned a Texaco station on Frood Road. Rhett was no mechanic, but Jerry could fix just about anything, and Rhett's dad already had a Class A mechanic on the payroll. "I've been thinking I might take him up on his offer," Rhett said. To this point he'd been doing little more than drawing unemployment insurance, cadging beers and smoking cigarillos. He lit one now. "Want a job?"

Jerry grinned. "Fuckin' A, Rhett, old buddy. I'm yer man."

Rhett puffed on his smoke and laughed. Fine pair they'd turned out to be. Football jocks turned mechanics. Who'd've thought?

"Fishing trip still on for this weekend?" Jerry said as the stripper strode bare-assed off the stage, her performance finished.

"Shit, that's right," Rhett said into the sudden lull. He'd almost forgotten—every year, third weekend in January. Gardner had dreamed up this gig back in the ninth grade, when the four of them first started chumming around together. Maybe that was why Rhett had forgotten; there'd been a lot of water under the bridge in the seven months since Gardner's accident. It hadn't even occurred to him to keep up the tradition. Gardner had made it into an annual event: "Something we should try not to miss no matter where our lives take us," he'd said, "as a means of keeping our friendship alive." Gardner was like that. Sappy. They'd even built themselves a hut back there in the woods, a condo on their own private lake. If they made the trip this year, it'd be the first time they did so without Peter.

"Think you can make it with that rag on your head?" Rhett said, thinking, What the hell. We don't need Gardner anyway.

"This shit?" Jerry said, fingering the soiled, turbanlike bandage beneath his Michigan State cap. "It's comin' off tomorrow."

"Then we're on. I'll phone Mikey tonight. I'm sure we can drag his nose out of the books long enough to drill a few holes in the ice. Whaddya think?"

Jerry thought that sounded just fine.

* * *

Rhett took over his father's business the following spring. The old man didn't retire; he died. Cancer of the prostate. They buried him three weeks after the diagnosis was made. The mechanic who worked for Rhett's dad decided in short order that he didn't approve of the new management and took a job at a competing station. Unruffled,

Rhett replaced him with an old lower-school chum, a big bearded Harley jockey who got off on boozing almost as much as his new boss. The station became a kind of late-night watering hole, and with each beer Rhett guzzled he watched his future grow dimmer and dimmer. Opportunity rarely knocked more than once, especially in a town like this, and Rhett cursed himself relentlessly for having missed his chance.

As Rhett had silently predicted, Jerry never truly recovered. Rhett had read somewhere that when they opened your lid like that and stirred your brains, you generally came up a few marbles short. Jerry was a case in point. He still liked his booze well enough, and he was a hard worker and a faithful companion... but he reminded Rhett of a spayed pup. That natural friskiness was gone, and although he was still only twenty, he seemed to prefer a snooze in the shade to a romp in a sunny field. Together they formed what Rhett's father would have called a motley crew, but between them they managed to keep Kiley's Texaco above ground. Barely.

They were sitting together one sunny Sunday that summer, drinking beer and feeling nostalgic, when Rhett decided they should pay Peter a visit. The idea came out of the blue, and he dragged Jerry into the company truck, gunned it over to the hospital and parked in a ten-minute tow-away zone.

But when they got to the big front doors, Rhett remembered how it had gone the last time they visited Peter, and said to hell with it.

They never saw Peter Gardner again.

9

ON JUNE 28, A YEAR to the day following her son's accident, Leona Gardner at last understood what had happened. It came in a staggering flash—and it was so tragically simple, it astonished her she hadn't grasped it before now. With this knowledge came an uneasy mingling of sorrow and relief…but for the first time in ages Leona Gardner knew exactly what she must do.

An odd serenity suffused her. She lit a fresh Tareyton, chugged some more Jack and flipped on the reel-to-reel. There was no hurry now. None at all.

Sammy's final report card lay face down on the coffee table in front of her, and now Leona flipped it open. He'd passed the tenth grade with flying colours, and despite herself Leona felt a faint glow of pride for the kid. He'd had to work hard at it, too, burning the midnight oil most nights. Poor Sammy, he was most definitely not a talented boy. He couldn't draw, couldn't use a hammer without blackening a thumbnail, couldn't even put out the garbage without busting the bag. The only thing he could do was play hockey, and Leona could see little of value in that. In spite of his gangly clumsiness, on skates the kid underwent a mysterious transformation, a change so striking that even Leona had to acknowledge it. The one time she'd gone out to watch him play—a Bantam game two years ago—his coach had proudly boasted that her son was going to be the next Wayne Gretzky.

Now there was a good one.

No, Sammy was not like his brother. For Peter the grades had always come easily, like the music and everything else. But what Sammy lacked in brains he made up for in determination; she had to give him that. He was out there right now, slinging cold cuts at the Sandwich King restaurant.

Gonna be a doctor...

Leona chuckled ruefully. For a while she let her son's music flow soothingly over her. When the tape was done, she got up and changed clothes, after digging the appropriate garments out of mothballs. Then she called a cab.

Dwindling finances, most of which Leona had guzzled in one form or another, had forced her and Sammy to give up their small house on Colby Street and move into a tenth-floor apartment in the rent-geared-to-income complex on Lorne Street. Thinking of it now—that hypocritical term, "rent-geared-to-income"—tugged another bitter chuckle from Leona. A slum by any other name. Overrun with snot-nosed kids, their pets and their fat single mothers, the place was a twenty-story embarrassment. But with the pittance she got from the government, it was all she could afford. She hadn't worked in over a year, and she had no intention of starting now. At least the money she'd gotten from the sale of the house had covered her debts, with a little left over for security.

The buzzer sounded. It was the cabbie.

Leona pulled on a sweater, locked the apartment door and took the elevator to the lobby.

"The Whipple Tree on Regent," she said as she climbed into the diesel Volvo. "And stop at the liquor store."

A misty rain was falling, dragging down with it the sulfurous reek of the smokestacks. Sneezing, Leona eyed the stacks with vague disdain. No matter what your vantage in the city, you could always see the stacks, bristling on the horizon like enormous blunt quills. They were steadily spewing eyesores…but each time she saw them, like a thousand other things, they put her in mind of her boy. The way he was. He'd worked his summers at Nickel Ridge, earning money for college.

Leona got out at the liquor store on Regent Street and came back with a forty-ouncer of Jack. At the Whipple Tree she bailed out again and disappeared into the shop. A few minutes later she was back, clutching her purchase to her chest. Seeing her coming, the driver climbed out to assist her. Whatever she'd bought, it was too bulky for the backseat, so he helped her stow it in the trunk.

"University Hospital," Leona said once they were mobile again. "And step on it."

The cabbie called in his destination, noticing a glassy flash in the rearview mirror as his fare raised a bottle to her lips.

* * *

The gruel they'd fed him for supper lay in a clotted lump in Peter's gut. A full year here and still he couldn't stomach the grub. Thank God for Sam. Three or four times a week the kid brought him a sackful of real food—barbecued ribs from Casey's, buckets of Chinese from the Peking Gazebo, spicy pasta from the Vesta Café, and more recently, heaped roast beef sandwiches from the Sandwich King, where Sam had a job for the summer.

Without Sam life would be twice the misery it already was. Relatives, friends—he never saw any of them anymore. Even his mother's visits had become sporadic…and when she did come in she was usually three sheets to the wind, still babbling about a cure. Sam was the only one who hardly ever missed a day, who made Peter feel as if he were still…okay.

But he wasn't okay. In the year since the accident he'd been back to the OR eight times. Twice to reset a poorly healed fracture, three times to release the deforming contractures that doglegged his lower limbs, once to remove a chunk of inhaled food from his trachea—that one had almost killed him—and twice to skin-graft the bedsores that had formed on his keester. He got bladder infections at the drop of a hat, gobbled more pills than a busload of blue-rinsers, and regularly upchucked his meals. He had to have someone brush his teeth, trim his nails and scrub his backside. And when he wasn't shitting his bed, a nurse had to slip on a glove and manually disimpact him.

Humiliation? He could write the book.

But somehow hope never abandoned him. That made him a fool as well as a gimp; he knew that well enough. Still, it was hard to give up. Maybe someday researchers really would come up with a cure—maybe even Sammy. The kid had made good on all his promises so far. To give up hope was to court the blackest of depressions, blacker by far than anything Peter had previously thought possible. On the few occasions he'd let his hope slip, he'd glimpsed that blackness and judged it worse than death.

There was always hope. No matter how slim.

His mother stamped into the room then, startling Peter from his grim reflections. She was dressed in black, with one of those overturned-ashtray hats on her head, the kind with the black lace netting and the long shiny pin. A church hat. Her gait seemed more unsteady than usual, but Peter attributed this to the large, paper-wrapped package she was lugging. He could barely see her eyes over its broadly curved rim.

As usual, the raw smell of booze preceded her... and something else. A green, piney odour that sparked formless, yet distinctly unsettling associations in Peter's mind.

It was coming from that package...

"Hi, Mom," Peter said, forcing a cheerful tone. "What'd you bring me?"

Apparently unaware that he'd spoken, Leona set her package on the floor below Peter's sight line, then kicked off the doorstop. When the door was closed she thumbed the latch, its soft snick shutting them in with the smell of cheap whiskey... and the cloying green reek of that package.

"Mom?" Peter said, unable to disguise the unease in his voice. "What are you doing?"

Leona made no reply, only glanced at him—but with such an expression of loss and bereavement that Peter almost cried out.

Now she was unwrapping that package, her back to him.

"Mom?" Peter said, his voice breaking like a frightened child's. "What are you doing? Is Sam okay?" This thought slammed into him like a gun butt. "Is he, Mom? Why don't you answer me?"

The crinkle of wrapping paper seemed impossibly loud. She tore it free, balled it up and stuffed it into the wastebasket.

Then, very deliberately, she swung Peter's call button aside.

That green smell was very big now, filling the room...

"Mom, look at me. *Look* at me."

And she did. She looked *at* him. Gray eyes swimming in boozy tears, she regarded her son as she might—

(an embalmed corpse)

Leona hoisted the funeral wreath onto Peter's thin chest, allowing its prickly weight to settle there. Peter had to wrench his chin back to prevent the stiff leaves from scratching his face. The smell of it made his head spin.

"Get it *off* me," he said, horror scuttling over his unfeeling body like sewer rats. "Get it *off*."

Unheeding, Leona reached out a mourner's hand and stroked her son's brow. Peter jerked his head aside, but she seemed not to notice. A grimace-like grin quivered on her lips.

"Why are you doing this?" Peter said.

While in his brain a battalion of remembered commands were instantly assembled. In a sweeping assault, they descended the neural pathways of his brain stem, their urgent purpose to recruit the wasted muscles of his body, draft them into service this one last time, endow them with the needed machinery to raise an arm and fling that wreath off his chest...but the futile directives toppled to their death in the chasm of Peter's shattered spine.

The wreath lay there under its immovable weight.

"Stop it, Mom, please. Get this thing off me. I'm not dead. *I am not dead.*"

Now she had a Bible open and she was reading from it, kneeling at his bedside, consigning him solemnly from this world to the next. Peter cried out to her, begging her to stop. The weight of the wreath was crushing him, stifling his breath—and now it seemed he really would die, right here at his own grotesque mock funeral. The mossy-sweet stench of the wreath swamped his nostrils like bilge water, and he was drowning in it.

"Please," he begged her, sobbing, swallowing his gorge, trying to stop the thick lump of his supper from geysering up his throat. "Please, Mom—"

"'And as they were afraid,'" Leona said, her eyes half shut, "'and bowed their faces to the earth, they said unto them, Why seek ye the living among the dead?'"

"Stop. Get it off me ...*please.*"

"'He is not here, but is risen.'"

"*Stop it.*"

Still unmindful of her son's shouted pleas, Leona got to her feet, leaned over the bed and placed a gentle kiss on his forehead. "Rest peacefully, my dear sweet boy," she said.

"Stop this," Peter bellowed, his anguish insane. "*Stop it, stop it, stop it.*"

In the hallway someone tried the knob, then hammered briskly on the bolted door. Distantly, Peter heard a shouted voice, "Open up in there. Open up now."

Leona backed away, sparing Peter a final glance filled with sweet memory and tearful sorrow before showing him her back. Then she reached for the door latch, twisted it, and vanished from the room.

Someone else was there with him now, the owner of that muffled voice, but Peter was far away, deep in the lime-pit blackness of his soul, a cry of perfect agony building within him. The supper the nurse had so patiently spooned into him boiled sickly in a stomach he could no longer feel.

And as that smothering wreath was finally borne away, it all gushed out of him—the tormented cry, his half-digested supper, the last remaining shred of his capacity for pain...

And his hope.

It all came up together, soiling the sheets of his bed.

10

IN SEPTEMBER OF THE following year, fifteen months after the accident, Kelly Wheeler became a full-time resident of Kingston, Ontario. Her reapplication into the phys ed program at Queen's University had been accepted, and by the middle of that month she'd immersed herself in the course load. Marti Stone, who'd already been there a year, had arranged shared lodgings for them in Chown Hall, a sedate limestone residence building located just a block from Lake Ontario. Their top-floor room overlooked the cobalt waters of the lake and Kelly fell in love with it immediately. In the twelve months Marti had been there she'd learned her way around both the campus and the city itself, and she did her level best to make Kelly feel at home. As always, Marti offset the melancholy Kelly carried with her like a yoke. There was just no moping when Marti was around. Her energy bordered on manic, and she maneuvered from party mode to sports to academia with a juggler's ease.

Kingston itself was a wonder to Kelly. Though essentially a working-class town, it housed a major university, a military college, a leading medical complex and, just for good measure, a maximum-security penitentiary. Kingston Pen, the most infamous of the prison sectors located in the area, was just a stone's throw from the campus itself.

In fact, from the roof of the teachers college—as Marti was quick to point out—you could see straight into the yard of the women's prison. An almost weekly occurrence were radio bulletins warning of escapees from the nearby Frontenac Institute, a minimum-security work farm on the eastern fringe of the city. At first this made Kelly antsy as hell. If they could break out of one place, they could break out of the other—and they had some real major leaguers over there, just a block away, wholesome guys like body-burier Cliff Olson and the ever congenial Shoeshine Boys—and Marti was forever catching her double-locking doors or nailing windows shut. But eventually, like most Kingstonians, Kelly relaxed into a quiet sort of wariness, no longer sleeping with one eye open... but still keeping her Louisville Slugger within easy reach of her bed.

The climb up from the pit of despondency had been a long and precarious one. On that bitter January evening eight months before, when Kelly roused as if from a nightmare to find herself naked on her bed with a fistful of deadly pharmaceuticals, she'd run gagging for the toilet, not because she'd stuffed all that crap down her throat but because she'd even contemplated doing so.

But perhaps "contemplated" was too strong a word. It suggested the persistence of will where for a few critical hours none had existed. She'd been driven to the medicine cabinet by the same sort of blind imperative that compels the salmon to batter itself implacably upstream. And like a dream, parts of that evening were lost to memory. She knew only that she'd left the hospital and, sometime later, gaped down in horror at her unclenching fist. The dye had run from the sweat-softened capsules, the stark pastels staining her palm, and some of the tablets had been crushed to a powder. Moments later, hunched over the toilet, she'd realized with a dull kind of shock that she'd sunk as low as she could without vanishing. And she decided then that it was time to fight her way back. Life was too precious.

But the way things had ended with Peter, as cruel and unexpected as a blizzard in August, had for those few lost hours made life seem unendurable...

* * *

It had been cold that day, the raw, glacial sort of cold that penetrated even the heaviest outerwear. Crystalline frost hung in the bracing air, and what little snow there was had been leached to a brittle powder. The bus let her off a hundred yards from the main entrance, and she hustled along the icy walkway, anxious for the well-lit warmth of the hospital. The arctic air jabbed at her eyes, and in the few moments it took to reach the automatic doors, tears formed frozen tracks on her cheeks. As she normally did, she stopped by the Ladies' Auxiliary boutique and scanned the magazine stand, hoping to find something that might spark Peter's interest. When he wasn't watching TV, he read voraciously, using a mouth-held page turner and a specialized book rest. She and Sam could barely keep up with his consumption. She picked up the latest issues of *Omni*, *Time*, and *People*, and a couple of Dairy Milk chocolate bars. Then she boarded the elevator and punched the button for the ninth floor.

The odour up here was distinctive, and it seldom failed to sicken her. It was the smell of human decay—bowels evacuated into lonely beds, urine leaked into baggy pajamas, flesh laid open in the weepy putrescence of bedsores. To Kelly it was the stench of slow defeat, of the toppling bastions of life against death, and it tortured her that Peter was a part of its source.

When she saw him that day, lying with his back to her, his hands arranged in a nerveless cross on his pillow, her immediate instinct was to flee. She came in at the same time every day, had done so for months, and until today Peter had always ensured that the nurses left him facing the door so he could watch her come in.

A dread premonition assailed her.

"Peter?" she whispered from the doorway.

But there was no response, and with a sigh of relief Kelly realized he was sleeping. She tiptoed into the room, deciding she'd sit by the window and read until—

"We have to talk," Peter said in a voice as wintry as the weather outside.

"Oh, you're awake," Kelly said, her mind filling with a hundred childlike evasions. For some time now a part of her had known this was coming, the same way a part of her understood that her eventual death was inevitable, but she rejected the knowledge with the same stubborn vehemence. To deal with it in any other way was to court a creeping insanity.

She plunked her package on the bed table and wriggled out of her coat, the words spilling out of her in a nonstop flood of hopelessness. "I brought you a couple of magazines. No porno, I'm afraid. Catholic hospital and all that. Did you go outside today? I wouldn't blame you if you didn't. Like my gramps used to say, it's colder'n a witch's tit out there. I nearly froze mine off getting here—"

"Kelly—"

"Did Sam—?"

"Kelly, please." His eyes were like glazed marbles. "Sit down."

"Okay."

She dragged up a chair, the sound of its legs against the tiles like the ratcheting gears of a guillotine, and positioned it next to the bed. Before sitting, she leaned forward to kiss him. It was like kissing a stone carving.

"I've had this conversation with myself a thousand times," Peter said, and Kelly's eyes filled with tears at the emptiness in his voice. "I sure never thought I'd have to say anything like it to you—"

"Then don't," Kelly said. "Don't say anything."

"It's too late for that, Kel." He looked up at her, and Kelly saw that same emptiness swirling in his eyes. "It's over. That's what we've both got to face. I'm not going to get better."

I know that, Peter. But that doesn't mean we can't—"

"Yes, that's exactly what it means. We can't. I can't." He looked away from her, his tone flat with resolve. "I want you to leave, Kelly. Right now. I want you to leave and never come back."

Kelly laughed, but it was a harsh sound with no humor in it. "I can't do that, Peter. I love you. I—"

"I'm serious, Kel. Dead serious." Now it was Peter's turn to laugh. "Dead. Yeah, that's it. I'm dead. Peter Gardner's dead. The guy you fell in love with. The guy who fell in love with you. I'm not him anymore. I'm a...thing now. A sill plant that needs constant watering, somebody to turn it to the sun every day."

"Please," Kelly said, the tears already spilling. "Stop this."

"I can't." He regarded her again, the planes of his face quivering in an effort to contain his misery. "Christ, Kelly, don't you understand? Every time I see you I'm reminded of the things I can't do, the things I'll never *be*, the things we'll never share. I can't take it anymore, and if you don't want to torture me you'll leave and never come back."

The fabric of a thousand heartbroken arguments shredded in the force of this unalterable truth, and Kelly could only sit there and look at him, tears streaming from her eyes. Months of buried yearning burst to the surface then and she wanted to throw herself on top of him, arouse him so intensely that her love would override the rent in his spine, give him life, make him see how empty the future would be without her. Giving in to it, she stood and leaned over him, her hands reaching for his face...

"Don't," Peter said, turning his head away.

Let's just give it some time, she wanted to beg him. *We can work it out.*

But she knew he was right.

She stood, pulled on her coat, and left.

* * *

"Penny for your thoughts."

Kelly gave a cry of surprise. She'd been sitting by the window, staring out over Lake Ontario, and hadn't heard Marti come in. Now, turning to face her friend, she scrubbed away the tears and did her best to put on a smile. "Something in my eye," she said.

"Sure," Marti said, whipping off her headband and unlacing her runners. "And I've got seven tits."

Kelly laughed—not a big one, but a laugh nonetheless. "I bet that makes you a hit on the dance floor."

"Cute," Marti said, shucking her sweat suit and tossing it on her bed. Her creamy complexion was flushed from her run and her green eyes sparkled with life. "But humor isn't going to get you out of this one." She put on a robe, then pulled up a chair and sat beside Kelly at the window. "I think it's high time you and I had a chat." She brushed Kelly's bangs from her face. "We're friends, Kelly. Best friends. I love you, you silly shit. And besides, we're roomies now, and the rule states there should be no dark secrets untold."

"What rule?" Kelly said, thinking that maybe she should get some of this off her chest. Lance out the poison. What harm could it do? Marti knew most of it. They'd talked for hours on the phone over the course of the previous winter, and Marti had been home to Sudbury for Christmas and the March break. But Kelly had never told anyone about that horrible January afternoon.

"My rule," Marti said, rolling up her sleeve and flashing an impressive bicep.

Kelly took a stuttering breath. "You asked for it," she said. And for the first time since its sorry inception, she told the story out loud.

* * *

"I spent the rest of the winter in a kind of walking coma," Kelly said, lacing her fingers around the steaming cup of tea Marti had fixed for her. "I just sat there, drowning in days, waiting for something to happen."

She'd been talking for almost an hour. Through it all, Marti had remained quietly attentive, her compassion evident in her eyes. Kelly had a true friend in Marti, and she was grateful.

"Why did you wait so long to tell me?"

"Shame," Kelly said, averting her eyes. "And fear. I thought I was losing my mind. I mean, how could life be so...bright and wondrous one minute, then black as a mine shaft the next? It was like standing on a high cliff and being unable to come up with a single reason why you shouldn't just fling yourself over the edge."

Marti stood, the mechanical swiftness of the movement indicating a sudden resolve. For Marti, life was reducible to a series of straight-forward choices. And she'd just made one of them.

"Get dressed," she said. "We're going out."

Arguments clanked in Kelly's mind like coins in a one-armed bandit. She knew what Marti wanted. She wanted to drag her out to a loud, smoky pub and get her bombed. In Marti's mind there was no better salve for a broken heart than a righteous, mind-curdling piss-up. Get so bent out of shape that you have to drag out your wallet just to introduce yourself...and then later, when you're sicking it all up, you sick up the hurt, too. Replace the heartache with simple physical pain—then set about the business of healing.

"What the hell," Kelly said, surprising them both. "Let's do it."

If there was any single moment at which Kelly Wheeler began her new life, it was then.

11

BUT FOR PETER THERE would be no new life. His mother's last visit had taught him that; the refusal of his body to respond reinforced it. And he tried, God knew he tried. In the withering reaches of the night, alone in his private room, he whipped his brain into a frenzy of concentration, focusing every buzzing synapse onto a single distant muscle, willing his finger or his knee or his baby toe to *move*. But of course it never did, and the frustration riddled him like a burst from an Uzi, bringing hot tears and hopeless, bellowed cries. For a while the nurses attempted to console him, creeping in with their flashlights like cat burglars and mouthing placatory phrases from the foot of his bed. But eventually even these reluctant ministrations were withdrawn, to be replaced by the pharmaceutical nightstick. Oh, yeah. His old buddy Lowe had an answer for everything.

"If he won't shut up, then we'll shut him up," Peter heard the good doctor say one sleepless night to a nurse outside his door. "He's not the only quad on the ward. Keep him quiet."

That had been his first lesson in getting along. There would be others.

At first, spending the hours in a warm narcotic haze didn't seem all that bad, measured against the razor-edged awareness his condition imposed on him—since his mind was the only thing still functioning, it remained almost painfully alert. The drugs brought dreams, and in his dreams he was whole again. Maybe even better than whole. In his dreams he could fly. But gradually he began to cherish his awareness, even if for little more than to follow the daily soaps. And the cost was merely compliance. Don't balk, don't shout, don't complain. Just do as you're told.

Just lie there.

And lie there he did. He lay there and read. Lay there and listened to music. Lay there and watched the tube. He did get around some, mostly at the insistence of his captors—and as the months droned past, that was precisely how he came to view them, as state-employed jailers who resented his dependence upon them. They bundled him into his motorized wheelchair—a technological marvel he controlled with his chin, allowing him a good deal more mobility than he would have thought possible—and parked him in the common room or the lobby or, weather permitting, on the rooftop patio overlooking Ramsey Lake.

For a while Peter lost what the other quads referred to as his patio privileges. In that black month following his mother's last visit, he'd racked his brains for a means to end his life. He even contemplated asking Sam for assistance, but he knew Sam could never do it; the mere mention of such a thing would haunt the kid for the rest of his days.

The solution came in a dark flash of inspiration, on a balmy, mid-September weekday, the last of a fleeting Indian summer. In spite of Peter's objections his keepers had wheeled him up to the patio that day; and what a day it was. Unmuddied by the late summer haze, the air was clear to the point of unreality, seeming more like crystalline tropical water than dry, breathable gas. On the rocky hills bordering the lake, bonfires blazed in the scattered maples, while the rest, a tenacious mix of poplar and birch, smoldered a warm and shimmering yellow. Stationed by the low frost fence that enclosed the patio, Peter felt at peace for the first time since his accident.

It was only later that he understood why.

Most of the other gimps had been out that day, too, their insectile limbs sheathed in flannel blankets—the Quad Squad, as Peter had come to think of them. The supervising nurse had been standing with her back to him, chatting with a workman—part of a three-man crew whose task it was to repair and repaint the rusted frost fence—when Peter unraveled the source of his calm.

He was going to end his life—if you could call it a life—on this perfect autumn day, and had in some way known it since they'd rolled him onto the deck. He'd noticed the missing section of fence, but its significance hadn't registered, at least not consciously. Located at the back of the building, the open section was just wide enough for a motorized wheelchair—and the drop was a sheer twelve stories to the paved parking lot below.

Devoid of emotion, Peter lined himself up with the gap. The nurse still had her back to him, as did the workmen, and the other geeks were submerged in their own grim musings. It was a good twenty-foot run to the edge, space aplenty to crank his chariot up to its top end, which Peter estimated at about six miles an hour.

He pressed his chin against the chin-control lever, eased the chair forward—then poured on the speed. Beneath his wheels bits of tarred gravel crunched and spat. The going was rough, the runty front wheels wanting to twist and pivot on the uneven surface, but Peter jockeyed his machine like a pro.

C'mon, baby, he thought grimly. *Let's do this right.* And there was nothing in his mind but that, the simple desire to get it right, to finish the job the beer truck had begun. *C'mon, babe.* No sweet memory-lane flashbacks, no unexpected regrets, just a simple desire to die.

Halfway to the low concrete edge a discarded milk carton deflected his right front wheel and almost toppled him. He lost the bulk of his speed and, once stable again, considered turning back for another run.

But a rearward glance changed his mind.

The nurse and two workmen were advancing on him at a run, the nurse waving her arms and shouting into the wind, the nearest workman sprinting like an Olympic athlete.

Doubling his resolve, Peter propelled the chair forward, marking the yards in a furious inverted countdown. "One! Two! Three! Fo—"

His front wheels struck the curb-high ledge dead on. The chair teetered forward, and Peter caught a dizzying glimpse of the parking lot before he slammed his eyes shut and released a banzai war cry, half triumphant and half filled with terror.

The workman's gloved hand brushed a handgrip…

And Peter went over.

He fell exactly four feet, landing on a narrow ledge he'd been unable to see from the deck. Only someone able to stand and lean forward could have seen it. He scraped his chin, raised a nasty goose-egg on his forehead, and crushed the bones in his baby finger. The finger didn't hurt. The chair took the brunt of the damage, and the hospital anted up for its repair. Dr. Lowe forbade him admittance to the rooftop sun patch for a month. By then the fence was intact, completing the circle of his despair.

* * *

Of it all, though, nights were the worst. The demons came out at night, shambling beasts with murderous intent… and what was doubly terrifying was the discovery that these brutes resided within him, in his mind, the place he now dwelt almost exclusively. They came out at night, when the gulf of his isolation was widest, churning up mud and chewing up light. The tissue that bred these aberrations was the stump of his amputated mind, the stuff that remained after the part that had housed his dreams—and the machinery to see them realized—had been cruelly lopped away. Bit by insidious bit, the demons took over, swarming over his psyche in hordes of malignant thought, laying waste to his peace of mind, spawning anger and hatred wherever they roamed. For a time he fought them heroically, clinging to the remnants of his dreams, philosophies and beliefs; but before long the door to his stewing subconscious blew open with an audible bang. And the offal began to ooze out.

The subconscious.

He'd read about it, thought it a pretty appellation for a cerebral pool in which all men must bathe, and then ignored it. It did its own thing anyway. You could feed it, true, but it was a shadowy precinct perhaps best left to its own devices. Prior to the accident, his had been a gentle corner of that pool, a tepid bath in which good dreams grew and raw talent resided.

But now, like his connections with the sentient world, the boundaries between his two minds had grown murky. In the profane jelly of that stump, evil things proliferated. The defensive checks the mind normally imposed—the selective memory of past events, trimming off the bad and embellishing the good, letting grudges die and nurturing love—these restrictions had been hacked away. Where initially he'd clung to his most cherished memories, playing them over and over like favorite movies, now he simply forgot them. In their stead, all the dirt of his past came spewing to the surface, becoming even more contaminated with its exposure to the light. The sunny days he'd spent on his grandparents' farm, the happiest days of his childhood, collapsed from memory into recurring flashes of his grandfather's face in his final agony, his limbs lashed to the bed rails in a chronic hospital while the cancer hollowed his bones. Revered images of his grandmother's mirthful face shattered into grisly replays of his daily visits to her bedside in that same last-stop hole of a hospital. Watching her flesh melt away and her cheeks cave in, seeing the clear light of recognition fade from her eyes into the cold luster of oblivion. God, but she was pale.

And the dream. Night after night, when at last sleep released him, there was the dream. The porcupine exploding in his face. His hands trying to guide that infernal bike. The beer truck rumbling over him, bearing a new and more hideous visage each time.

The dream was bad.

For a time, after the truth of his condition struck home, Peter refused to eat, refused all treatment, refused even to talk. When they suspended his sedatives, hoping to draw him out, he scored his own drugs from a wild-man paraplegic named Zero, who drifted in and out of the chronic ward like a bad smell. Zero was a hippie throwback who'd shattered his spine in a fall from a forty-foot scaffold ten years earlier. He'd been a roadie for a band called Powerhouse and had been on acid at the time. "You wanna talk about flyin'?" he'd chortled one night while he and Peter exchanged tales of battle. "*That* was flyin.'" Now he made a modest living designing heavy metal T-shirts for a local outlet. And he was pretty good. As a bonus for Peter's business—Zero supplied him with tranquilizers, analgesics, and the occasional joint, all of which Peter paid for with funds from his now defunct college savings—the artist designed a tattoo for him. The legend, CAPTAIN QUAD, formed an arc over a figure decked out in fighter-pilot gear, cutting through space in a wheelchair propelled by sweeping angel's wings. Zero had a friend of his sneak a portable unit onto the ward and did the tattoo himself, the quietly darting needles painlessly working their magic on Peter's left arm. Sam thought it was the coolest thing he'd ever seen.

Within the grinding monotony of the hospital, Dr. Lowe became the target of Peter's loathing. Whenever he saw Dr. Lowe he thought of a fat, sweaty child hunkered in the shadows of a shabby back porch, gleefully plucking the legs off spiders. In Peter's estimation, there was something in Harrison Lowe that thrived on human suffering, a skillfully disguised contempt for helplessness that in some way stoked an ageless fire in Lowe's secret heart. Nothing seemed to please the quack more than to parade into Peter's room with a bunch of students in tow and expound on the torments of quadriplegia, making Peter feel about as human as a fetus in a jar of formalin. His hatred for Dr. Lowe grew like a choking vine.

But it wasn't only the living Peter hauled across the keel of his loathing. There was his father. Angus Edward Gardner. Lord of the manor, king of the trembling household. Alone in the late night pall of the hospital Peter would lie there and relive every moment of his life in that joyless house. He could hear his father's voice even now, as clearly as if the heartless bastard were right there beside him: *"Peter. Get in here right now."*

Nothing he did was ever good enough for his dad—though he'd tried, with the same mulish persistence which, night after night, compelled him to try to move his limbs—and the taste that had come to his mouth when his father belittled him, a sour, rotten-fruit taste that made him want to gag, came hot on the heels of these memories. The old man was outdoorsy, liked to hunt ducks and moose, but Peter didn't share this enthusiasm. "Sissy," the old man would rag him. "Doesn't want to hurt the poo' little duckies." Peter had gone with him only once—and had ended up taking a beating. Hunched in the duck blind, half frozen in a late autumn drizzle, he'd sneezed as his dad drew a bead on a flock, the sudden racket causing the birds to scatter unharmed. Infuriated, the old man had brought the muzzle of his shotgun around in a smoking arc and thonked Peter on the forehead with it. The fists had come later. To his death, Angus had believed that sneeze deliberate.

No, nothing was ever good enough. Not even the music. His father had considered it a waste of time. Because of this—and he made no bones about letting his son know how he felt, usually in front of strangers—Peter took up sports with a vengeance, playing Little League baseball in grade school and then football in high school. But even this failed to impress his dad.

Peter remembered the defeated tears that had also come in the night, like these memories, while he lay on his back on the bottom bunk, listening to his kid brother's whistling breath and the drone of the TV in his father's den, wondering if the old man was going to burn them all to death with a forgotten cigarette. From an early age he'd learned to read the emotional climate in the house, fearing his father for his hair-trigger temper and fearsome, bellowing voice, pitying his mother for her dumb acquiescence to his will. By the age of four, he'd learned to shun his father's attentions, scant as they were, and to lie as a means of survival. "Who did it, then?" he could hear his father raging. "Who broke the fucking thing if it wasn't you? Answer me." His own name, when spoken by his father, became a kind of terrible accusation. He might be playing outside on a sunny Sunday morning, pushing his plastic cars along the paint-chipped surface of the porch, a small, healthy lad seeming lost in the racetracks of his imagination— but if his daddy was home, as he so often seemed to be when the day was fresh and somehow mocking, the boy kept one ear affrightedly cocked for the bellowed sound of his name: "*Peter*." It would rise from the airless basement of their rented triplex like a shouted oath, and the boy would spring to his feet—mouth dry, short legs threatening to drop out from under him—sprint along the narrow hall runner to the basement door, and fearfully drag it open. "Yes, Dad?" he would call in a voice too small to hear. But his father would hear it—oh, yes, his daddy would hear it plain as day. "Get down here," his voice would thunder. And the boy would start into the cobwebbed stairwell, small hands planted on the walls, fearing that at any minute his daddy's hand would dart out from between the risers and close around his ankle like a manacle. But he was never under the stairs, he was always back in his workshop, dressed in greasy coveralls over a checked flannel shirt, fishing around furiously on his cluttered workbench for some mislaid gadget or tool. And before his son had reached the bottom step he would stick out his head, an oily hank of hair dangling down to his chin, and he would roar, "Where is it?" his dark eyes shot through with red. "Where is what, Daddy?" the boy would squeak. "Where the fuck *is it?*" the old man would bawl. And Peter would fight to seal off his bladder.

How he'd hated his father then. How he had wished him dead.

That wish came true two weeks after Peter's fourteenth birthday, a bitter, sunless morning in March. Angus died in the middle of a screaming fit, his hateful heart finally giving up the ghost. He was pissed at Leona, who suffered his rage with a hangdog passiveness that always made Peter want to scream. Leona wanted to drive to her parents' farm in the valley, as she did every Sunday, and Angus was stalling, as *he* did every Sunday, hoping to spark a confrontation. In her quiet way, Leona nagged him until Angus rounded on her, screaming blue murder, slab-muscled arms bunched and ready to strike. But this time, instead of just cowering and taking his abuse, Leona ran for the kitchen, where she grabbed a knickknack off a shelf and pitched it at him, catching him on the bridge of the nose and bringing an alarming spout of blood. Surprised more than hurt by this defiance, Angus just stood there, cupping his nose and whining like a kicked dog, his beady eyes filling with tears—then his hands left his face and clutched his barrel chest, and he collapsed to his knees on the floor. A strangled curse escaped him (Peter was watching, crouched in the stairwell, peering down between the balusters, thanking God that Sam was still outside and wishing fiercely that his father would die die die), and then Angus vomited, a horrid yellow gout of half-digested breakfast and bile. In his night sweats Peter would see his father's face and remember thinking that his head seemed about to explode. It appeared to swell on his shoulders like the cartoon head of some infuriated Disney character, neck bagging out like an inner tube, cheeks bloating up until the skin shone a flat, cadaverous plum colour.

Stunned, Leona only stood there, a crazy blend of emotions in her eyes. A part of her thought she'd killed him, and that part was *glad*, oh, so very glad, he would never raise his voice or his hand to her again. But her eyes were full of fear, too. The fear that he was faking it in his cruel and cunning way, putting it all on so that she would rush to his aid, only to be met with the full force of his fury. And there was more. Dim flickerings of hope for a future without the constant yoke of her marriage. And fury—cold, untainted fury. Satisfaction. Pity. Sorrow. Joy unparalleled. It was all there and it paralyzed her and all she could do was watch.

Angus pitched forward—beefy palms spiking out to stop him, skidding in the repugnant splat of puke he'd spewed only seconds before—then he fell on his face and died.

Life after that was different. Freed from Angus's tyranny, they all breathed easier. But with their breadwinner's unlamented demise the few creature comforts they'd enjoyed were rudely snatched away. Unskilled and unimaginative, Leona found work where she could, discouraging Peter's naive insistence that he quit school and find a job. Even at fourteen he'd shown twice the courage of his dad. They would make do, she assured him. Her son's education was paramount.

But for all her apparent sacrifice, she'd trapped him in a web of guilt. He understood that now. She'd spun it slowly and skillfully, meaning to tie him to her forever. It was in the way she stood hunched over the stove at night, in her long-suffering glances as she plunked his supper down in front of him. The bitch had been trying to hold him, to own him. And why? Because she was nothing, a vacant shell, a soulless fucking humanoid who sucked at his soul like a leech. It became clear during these long nights of loathing why the old man had sometimes resorted to using his fists. She was a cheat, a low, infuriating cheat, and if there were some way he could even the score, feel his dead fingers close around her pale and scrawny neck, why...

But then there was Sam. Dear, loyal Sam, like a mutt who remains with a cruel master in spite of the whippings and the withheld feedings. Like the proverbial bad penny, Sam kept turning up. Some days he just sat there in the freighted silence of that room, waiting for Peter to say something...and Peter never did. Other days he served as a willing punching bag; still others he blotted his brother's tears. But he always came back.

He was the one. The only one.

Not even Kelly had bothered to return. Some great-fucking-love. In some dim way he remembered having told her to leave, having ordered her to...but if the shoe were on the other foot he would at least have tried to come back. Truth was, the bitch had been glad. Glad to be rid of him, just like all the rest. All his sweet memories of Kelly were spoiled in the endless blank of that room, like fallen fruit left exposed to a sweltering sun. She must have taken lessons from his mom. Parasites, that's what women were, bloodsucking parasites whose only intention was to gaff you by the heart and then slowly suck you dry.

But for all his ill-thinking of Kelly, the plain truth was that he couldn't shake her out of his heart. In the night's dark eye, after the worst of the pus had been lanced, Peter longed for Kelly Wheeler in a way that was perhaps more punishing than his desire for a return to wholeness. In turning her away, another, terrified voice reproached him, he'd acted rashly. Maybe they could have worked things out between them. There were specialized apartments in the city, with government-employed caretakers whose job it was to assist their handicapped tenants in every way possible. Kelly could have gotten her teaching degree, gone to her job in the daytime and looked after him at night.

Right, asshole. And how long before she got sick and tired of changing your diapers and picking up after you and having nothing to look forward to but more of the same? How long before she started making up thin-sounding excuses for coming home late while in reality she was getting the long lean hard one from one of her colleagues or some grinning dipshit she picked up in a singles bar? How long before she just pointed at the shrunken scrap of flesh between your legs and fell to the rug in hysterics?

The images that came on these nights were as brutal as they were cruelly vivid. He imagined her with another man—but was *another* a fair distinction? Didn't that presuppose that he, Peter, was also a man?—the two of them sipping wine and giggling, their harmless touching turning quickly into groping, hard-core foreplay. Despite his frantic efforts to obliterate these images, he saw Kelly open her mouth to receive the bastard's tongue, heard her moan with a passion the heat of which he had never come close to kindling. And he imagined her thinking of him as this heart-thief stripped off her clothes, laughing inside, freed at last of the childish notion that her love for him had been real. *Only puppy love,* he heard her taunt in a dreadful singsong voice. And then he saw the real man's tongue work its way down the curve of her belly and bury itself in that place she had promised was only for him. In tacky, blue-movie close-ups, he saw the man work her with a cock the size of his forearm, saw him ram her and jam her and heard her scream in raptures unimagined...

Of it all, this drove him closest to madness.

He still loved her. He would always love her. And trying to kill that love was like trying to kill something that had no life. It simply could not be done.

Months stretched into years.

Sam came.

Night came.

The dream came.

Peter's rage and resentment flourished inside him until it blazed like the coiled filament of some huge, unimaginable searchlight, burning brighter and brighter until one starlit night it simply winked out, taking the last of his sanity with it. For a period of time that was black and homogenous, he lay in a state of emotionless incubation, surfacing only long enough to acknowledge his brother's visits and to see that nothing had changed.

* * *

Until death came, and that changed everything.

TWO

—

AIRBORNE

12

September 23, 1989

IT WAS COMING OUT of the ditch, as it had each nightmare-ridden night for the past six years, slowly ascending the heat-baked slope to the road.

But tonight everything was different.

The sun was a bruise in the sky, its light a ghastly purple. The air was not air at all but a steaming, pine-scented soup through which the bike moved sluggishly. And the porcupine was no porcupine; it was a ... *thing*, with a humpbacked body of flesh turned inside out and the bristled limbs of an insect. It had a bat's parchment ears and a jackal's cunning glare—and when it rolled its eyes to face him, it grinned, grinned with a demon's yellow teeth, the spaces impacted with gore.

It grinned and he knew it was death.

The deep-throated bray of the air horn punched through the back of his helmet. He could feel Kelly's hands on his hips, knew she had screamed, but the sound was eaten by the air horn, that awful clarion, shrieking slaughter from the guts of a rolling chrome juggernaut. Brutal summer heat shimmered over everything, seeping inside, dulling nerves that should have been ready, slackening muscles that should have been primed.

The back wheel bucked hard—and Kelly was airborne, swimming in the lavender air. Now the world was filled with that hideous animal bray, over-spreading everything in an atmosphere of solid, bellowing noise.

And when he turned he faced the juggernaut, chrome teeth bared and glinting sunlight, hot breath reeking of grease. Its jaws fell open and a sticky tarmac tongue drew him in, past rolling rubber hinges into a dark and profane clockwork, where the rattle of an eight-chambered heart joined the mind-splitting howl of the clarion. Here he was fractured and chewed and his blood was tasted.

And when the thing shat him out, there was no pain at all.

Only nothing... nothing... *nothing*...

* * *

Peter opened his eyes, the horror of the dream exploding in the vise of suffocation. The wreath lay on his chest like a cinder block—but there was no wreath. The weight was death, that grotesque, raw-fleshed creature from the roadside. It straddled his chest, grinning as it sucked out his air.

He was dying.

* * *

In the drunkenness of asphyxia the room listed like a storm-lashed ship. His chin switch was there; he glimpsed its faint shine in the cold autumn moonlight. A touch and help would be there... but he couldn't lift his head. It was an immovable weight with a hole in the middle, his futilely gasping mouth.

He couldn't breathe.

Peter's mind fell into a flat spin as panic tore through him. An invisible hand had him by the windpipe, leaving barely a pinhole through which to drag air. He tried to give voice to his plight, scream through the sleeping corridors, but the effort only doubled the load on his chest.

The night-dark room grew darker still, death's shadow seeping in at its edges... and Peter thought of his mother. He wanted her here. The bitter contempt he'd nurtured for so long lifted like a sprung blind and now more than anything he wanted her with him. She would save him. She had once before, when the croup got him so bad he nearly died. It had been exactly like this, except that then he'd been able to move, to stagger clasping his shut-down throat to her room to waken her. She'd scooped him up and lugged him into the bathroom, where she cranked on the hot water taps and flooded the room with steam.

There, honey. Breathe easy. Breathe easy, now.

"Mom?" Peter husked. "Mom, please..."

The panic was massive, outstripping the capacity of his mind to contain it. It widened like a tornado's dark eye. And as his head thrashed to and fro and his neck swelled with air hunger, a crude stake of truth sledged its way down through his heart.

These were his last moments.

And he would spend them in horror.

Sam's face floated up in his mind, full of admiration and love. And Kelly's, rapt in the almost painful ecstasy of their union.

And his mother's...

A sound like a rusty hinge reached Peter's ears. My last gasp, he realized. And even as the darkness yawned and the panic soared, an intense feeling of peace suffused him. It began in the centre of his chest and spread like a gentle fireglow. Warm and renewing, he embraced it, welcomed it...

And finally he begged it to bear him away.

* * *

Merciful blackness entombed him.

No thought. No panic. No fear.

Consciousness faded—then abruptly returned, with all the rudeness of a dipperful of water slung squarely in his face.

Suddenly his mind was alert, his awareness crystalline…

Then a strange sensation (*I can feel I can* feel *it*) mantled his frame, a kind of…tug, as if his whole body had been mummy-wrapped in Scotch tape and the tape stripped away, all in a single brisk pull, producing a sensation more startling than painful.

It lightened him somehow, freed him…

There were footfalls in the hallway now, urgent, thudding footfalls, and a rolling clatter of equipment. They were coming to save him, Peter realized, and he delighted in the knowledge that they were too late. He wasn't breathing, wasn't even trying to breathe.

I'm dead you dumb bastards, you won't be turning my crushed-insect body five times a day or stuffing your fingers up my senseless ass anymore, 'cause I'm dead dead dead—

But if he was dead, why could he still see? And why was his mind more keenly alert than ever before, even when he'd enjoyed the peak of his health?

And why was the ceiling getting closer?

Floating? Am I floating?

The crash cart preceded a nurse and two interns into the room, all of them shouting commands. "Call a Code Blue. And find an anesthetist. Somebody ventilate this guy. Holy shit, I think we're too late."

Damn straight you're too late, Peter thought with morbid glee. No research, no miracle was ever going to make him feel again, walk again, live again.

This was it. His only way out.

He watched them assemble beneath him, scrambling about his bed like children who'd just shattered their mother's favorite vase and were now caught up in the foolish hope they could somehow glue it back together. He watched them down there, amused and a little annoyed, wishing they'd just leave him alone.

One of the interns knelt on the bed and began to administer closed-chest massage. The other thrust a curved green airway into Peter's mouth, then began to squeeze oxygen into his lungs with an ambu bag. Now another nurse appeared, red-faced from running up stairs, and started fishing around in the crash cart, pulling open drawers, scrabbling for the utensils of rescue.

Then someone jerked the covers off Peter's body and he saw himself, really *saw* himself, for the first time since he'd been able to just amble over to a mirror and check himself out at his leisure.

It was only then that the full impact of what was happening struck Peter Gardner. He was observing all of this from above, from the ceiling. He *was* floating, but not in his body, that misshapen mantis on the bed below. No. He was *outside* of his body now, just his mind, floating free...

And those bastards were trying to drag him back in.

No, he cried. But his mouth didn't open—couldn't open, with an airway jammed into it and an oxygen mask sealing it shut—and no sound issued forth. For a moment this muteness brought back the old and bitter impotence of paralysis, only worse, because now he couldn't even speak.

Then he understood.

They couldn't hear him in this... state of being. They weren't even aware of his presence. He was a spirit now, a ghost. All that Separate School catechismal mumbo jumbo had been true. He was dead and free of his body and his would-be rescuers didn't know it yet.

Peter watched, awed at the clarity of detail.

Now the anesthetist darted into the room, slit-eyed and scowling, and Dr. Lowe thumped in behind him.

"How aggressive do you want to be?" the anesthetist said as he took over ventilating Peter's lungs.

"Bring him back," Lowe said. "I want him back."

Some old quarrel passed between the two men like flint sparks in their eyes. Then the anesthetist removed the airway from Peter's mouth and slipped a laryngoscope blade into his throat. With the deftness of years he inserted an endotracheal tube, inflated its air-sealing cuff, then attached it to the ambu bag in lieu of the mask. With quick, even strokes he inflated Peter's lungs.

And for an instant, Peter heard the man's thoughts—

You're a fucker, Lowe.

Peter saw him glance at Lowe—who, while injecting drugs into Peter's IV, was busily studying the oscilloscope tracing of his almost flat-line heartbeat—and saw the physical expression of that sentiment on his face. But his lips hadn't moved, though the voice Peter heard had been as plain as if the words had been spoken aloud.

Now it came again.

Why don't you let the kid go?

"Adrenaline," Lowe said, his outthrust hand twitching impatiently. Then: *Come on,* Peter heard him say in another, more hollow voice. *Hurry up, bitch. Give me the shit.*

And something else? Had he heard something else? An echo of a distant, more urgent thought, weakly superimposed?

(Oh, Christ, I need a—)

But now the syringe of adrenaline was in Lowe's hand, the fine needle longer than any Peter had ever seen, and Lowe was aiming it at Peter's chest, puncturing the skin between his ribs, sucking back a crimson eruption of heart's blood before plungering the entire payload into his ventricle.

"We've got a rhythm," the anesthetist said, the flatness of his tone barely disguising his disappointment.

Way to go, Lowe. Another vegetable for your patch.

Peter felt another tug now, this one more abrupt than the first one had been, a hair-pulling, scalping kind of tug that jerked him forcefully downward.

Did that mean he was leaving this life?

Or coming back in to it...?

That long-ago dream of plummeting to earth from the stratosphere recurred as his essence was sucked abruptly downward. He resisted that pull with the entire force of his will... but the effort was useless. He met his body with the distorting force of a cannon blast. His last conscious perception was a voice.

Or perhaps a thought...

I hope you're proud, Lowe. I hope you're proud.

13

THE TEMPTATION TO ASK him inside was great. Almost over-powering. It was for that simple reason—the temptation, its unrea-soning sweetness—that she resisted. After all, she hardly knew him. They'd met only a month ago, at Chevies, a fifties disco in the east end of town. Marti had introduced them. "Kelly, this is Will Chatam. He works at Nickel Ridge." Good old Marti, still trying after all these years to matchmake Kelly into wedlock. This had been her third date with Will. Dinner and a movie. Nice.

Now she accepted his kiss, which was bashful and dry, shifted on the seat of his mint condition—as he seldom failed to pridefully point out to her—'53 Buick Super, and let herself out into the cool Septem-ber night.

Can I see you tomorrow?" Will said.

Kelly shook her head, suspending the motion when she saw the look of disappointment on his face. Quickly, she added, "Can we make it Friday?" and Will's expression brightened, the boyish grin Kelly had fallen for a month ago splitting it almost in two. "It's early in the term," she said, "and I've got a new dance class to prepare for. Gotta pick out the music, sort out routines…" She shrugged.

"Friday's great," Will said and keyed the ignition. "Dinner and a flick?"

Kelly formed a circle with her forefinger and thumb, then started up the walk...but as Will thunked the Buick into gear, she found herself on the verge of running back out to him and blurting, "Come on in, won't you? I don't want to spend another night alone in this house."

She let the words die in her throat. Plunging headlong into this thing would be a certain mistake. Since Peter, she'd done exactly that on two occasions, and both times she'd ended up regretful. Better to wait.

For what? that tempted voice objected. *Until your hair turns white? Until God swoops down in a flaming chariot and says, "Okay, Peter. Walk"?*

Will U-turned in the gravel turnabout in front of the house. Then, waving, he crept up the washboard hill. Wrapped in her own arms, Kelly watched him go, ignoring that final weak nudge which bade her give chase. She was a big girl now; she could sleep alone.

When there was nothing left but the receding purr of the Buick's eight cylinders, she turned her face skyward and gazed into the deepening night.

Stars like pinpoints wheeled high in the cosmic mystery, preparing to shift with the seasons. A restless breeze chattered in the trees, picking off leaves and stacking them into drifts against the house. A full moon twinkled like a distant headlight, and on the island far out on Ramsey Lake, gulls grumbled plaintively in their slumber.

Standing in the yard, letting the crisp autumn breeze frisk her body, Kelly recalled a proverb her grandfather had been fond of quoting—"Whatever goes around comes around"—and was struck by its aptness to the cycles of her life. The last place she'd expected to wind up after Kingston was back here in Sudbury. Somewhere during the middle of that four-year stint, which had been tough but mostly enjoyable, Kelly had vowed to return home only for the obligatory seasonal visits. It wasn't that she no longer cared for her folks or for the friends she had made and stayed in touch with over the years. It was just that a part of her had died here, a large part, and it seemed both pointless and somehow morbid to return to the site of its burial. An almost blind doctrine of forward motion had ruled her in the south— her blurb in the graduate yearbook dubbed her the faculty's all-time workaholic—and unlike Marti, who had more or less cruised through the academia, Kelly'd had her pick of at least a dozen prestigious high schools in the province, even a few choice spots outside the province. She hadn't even applied to the schools in Sudbury.

But on the very day that the first of the acceptances came rolling in, she got a phone call from her old alma mater, from the principal, no less. Old stony-face Laughren had retired the previous year and had been replaced by a young-sounding woman named Cole. Ms. Cole— "Call me Nickie"—had gotten wind of Kelly through the academic grapevine. And like Kelly, the progressive new principal had a special interest in gymnastics and modern dance, two areas of endeavor which, regretfully, had fallen into disfavor with the members of the Regional Board, dinosaurs all. It was Ms. Cole's intention to recruit a teacher who could revive these flagging specialties and let the brass say what they would. Miss Gambling, the crotchety old broad who'd held the job for the past hundred years (or so it seemed to Kelly, who could recall her own mother telling her horror stories about "that wicked old gym teacher at Laurentian High"), had suffered a mild stroke while proctoring a midterm exam, and until a full-time replacement could be found, the job had fallen into the floundering hands of the substitutes, most of whom couldn't do a push-up or a pirouette if their lives depended on it.

Was Kelly interested?

A huge and bellowed *No* had risen to her lips…but something had stifled it. Afterward she had tried to convince herself it was the

deal the principal was offering—the money was standard, but the
academic freedom she'd be allowed would take her years to achieve
under normal circumstances, and might never materialize at all.

But it had been more than the enticing deal, something she'd
been unable—or had simply refused—to acknowledge at the time.

Standing here now, cocooned in the night and suddenly cold to
the marrow, the reason she'd returned to Sudbury poked her in the
heart like an intrusive finger—and that reason was quite simply that
she'd had no choice in the matter. Free will had not been a factor.
Some force—call it fate, for want of a better word—had drawn her
back with the insistence of a giant's outreaching hand. It had been a
summons from a higher court... and she would die here.

Disturbed at the turn of her thoughts—and a little afraid—Kelly
started inside. As she mounted the path to the winterized cottage she
rented, something crunched stealthily across the gravel behind her.
Her heart was on its way up to her throat when a dog's cool muzzle
pressed itself into her palm.

"Chainsaw," Kelly said, her dark contemplations forgotten. "How
many times have I told you not to sneak up on me like that?" She
dropped to one knee and scratched the shepherd's thick ruff. The dog
lapped happily at her wrist, its big tail thrashing the hedge. "You want
to see a grown woman wet her pants?"

The dog belonged to Kelly's landlord, a mostly absent accountant
named Haas who owned the sprawling, Tudor-style home cresting the
hill leading down to the cottage. Chainsaw wasn't the dog's real name,
but that was what Kelly called him. It had to do with his bark, which had
frightened the daylights out of her until she'd been forced to confront
the big lunkhead one late night in July, coming home from a walk.

The big dog panting at her heels, Kelly recalled that night with
an unpleasant shiver. She'd come scuffing up the lane the two homes
shared, absorbed in the gloom of her thoughts, when the shepherd

released a volley of barks. Kelly froze, throat half shut, ears tuned to the tread of the dog's thick paws as it bounded toward her, the scrape and whip of its chain as it stretched to full length—

Hold, oh, Jesus hold...

But it hadn't held, and the big dog came charging across the yard, a twenty-foot length of chain snaking through the gravel behind it. Kelly braced herself for the killing leap—

Then this big goofy pup had its forepaws propped against her chest, not driving her down to rip out her throat but lapping her face until she began to giggle through her terrified tears. From that night on, she and Chainsaw had been the best of pals. Haas had even complained to her once that the dog no longer answered to its proper name, which was plainly, boringly, Herman.

"'Night, big fella," Kelly said as she let herself into the house.

Once inside, she glanced back and saw the poor mutt gawking lonesomely in through the sidelight. As she turned away, Peter's face flashed in her mind, like a single subliminal frame in a low-budget horror flick, and she remembered how alone he'd looked the last time she'd seen him—

Out of habit, Kelly trampled this line of thought. As she hung up her coat, she marveled at how time lost its meaning wherever Peter Gardner was concerned. Six *years* had gone by since the accident. She was twenty-four now. She had an honours degree in phys ed, taught grades eleven and twelve at her alma mater, and was finally banking some money. She enjoyed excellent physical health—

But the arm still acts up sometimes, doesn't it? The arm you broke in the accident—

"Enough," Kelly said aloud, derailing her thoughts and earning a green-eyed glance from her cat, an all-black tom named Fang.

In the living room she slipped a disc into the CD player and, after adjusting the volume to low, crossed to the big picture window overlooking the lake. Gazing out, she let Mozart soothe her aching heart. This same sort of sentimental crapola always got started whenever she met a new fella. Not that she'd dated that many since Peter. A half-dozen maybe, and she'd slept with only two of them.

Mistake. Mistake.

But this guy...

Will Chatam was different. Not different from the others so much —she liked clean-cut, easygoing, reasonably articulate men—as he was different from Peter. With her usual damnably keen insight, Marti had pointed this out with each of the others...

"You're doing it again, kid."

"Doing what?"

"Just look at this dude. Do those twinkly brown eyes remind you of anyone?"

Or "That thick shock of beach-blond hair?"

Well, this guy *was* different. In every way. Even Marti conceded that much. She had, after all, introduced them.

"He's nice, Kelly," Marti said after they'd left Chevies that night. "Not overly bright, not stunningly handsome. But nice. And he likes you. He'll be steady; wait and see."

Nice. Yeah, he was nice.

Kelly went back to the disc player, expelled Amadeus and slipped in Joe Cocker, tracking ahead to her favorite cut: "You Can Keep Your Hat On."

Damn. She should have invited him in.

And she shouldn't...

She'd used the others, she knew. For solace, for simple human companionship, and, during her two brief sexual flings, as surrogates, however inept, for the one she truly desired. Will was too...nice for her to do that to him.

She'd wait. And see.

"Abed," she said to Fang, who'd taken to twining in and out between her ankles, his customary feed-me ploy. "That's where I ought to be."

The big tom trailed her out to the kitchen, mewling around a yap full of spit, pawing at her shoes as she scooped out a wet glop of Tuna Surprise. Extinguishing the light on the cat's noisy dining, Kelly decided to forgo a bath and, after turning off the stereo, padded tiredly upstairs.

In her lake-facing bedroom she peeled off her clothes and let them puddle at her feet on the floor. Usually sloppiness disgusted her, but tonight she was too damned tired to care. As she crossed to the bed, her naked reflection in the bureau mirror caught her eye and she turned self-consciously to face it.

She had a teenager's body still—full breasts, a flat tummy, long, well-muscled legs—and the sight of it pleased her. It was a good body...

And a voice unmistakably like Marti's said, *But it won't be forever, kid. Nothing is forever.*

She had a sudden wild urge to phone Will Chatam, pretend she was calling from a neighbour's house and that she'd locked herself out, what a nit...

Then she flopped into bed. She kept seeing Will's boyish face, lighting up like a birthday cake when she told him she'd see him again on Friday. She fell asleep wondering how things would work out between them.

Later, as she slept, Fang came in and assumed his favorite snoozing position, in the V of Kelly's gently spread legs.

14

SAM WAS STUDYING WHEN the hospital called. Comparative anatomy. His application to medical school for the fall session had been politely rejected. On the fourth of September, undaunted, he'd begun his second year in the biology program at Cambrian University. He would apply to medicine again this year, and the year after that if need be. He'd come close this time—very close. The dean himself had told him as much, in a handwritten letter. His marks had been good, the impression he'd made during his interview excellent.

But close didn't count. He'd have to really buckle down this term. Sleep less, study more. Maybe even give up one of his jobs. The professor who'd interviewed him had expressed some surprise at Sam's reluctance to apply to med schools outside of the city. In response, Sam had only shrugged and said, "Guess I'm just a home town boy."

Because he hadn't relished trying to explain to this reed-thin, bespectacled microbiologist that his mother was a lush and his brother a quad. He hadn't wanted to admit to his fear that without him they would both probably wind up dead.

Sam had long since abandoned the idea of finding a cure for Peter's shattered spine. A little reading and even less common sense had brought that childish notion sharply into focus. The vow he had so somberly taken on the Paris Street bridge six years ago had been a sorry kid's promise, a small boy's desperate attempt to wish all the hurt away. But naive or not, that vow had been the catalyst which had started him on his way. By hook or by crook, he would become a doctor—about this there was no trace of doubt in his mind—and although discovering a cure was improbable, a life in medicine would bring him that much closer to his brother. As it was, he'd missed only about twenty days of visits since the accident, most of those due to out-of-town hockey games.

In the low light of his bedroom, Sam glanced at the digital alarm clock on his desk—1:04 A.M. Yawning hugely, he slapped his textbook closed. He had to be up at five-thirty, have the boxcar at Carrington's Lumber off-loaded by nine, then be back at the university by—

From his mother's bedroom across the hall came a sudden yelp; it sounded like a cry of pain…but then Leona's dry cackle followed, and Sam settled back in his seat, fright fermenting inside him. How many times had he been faked out by her middle-of-the-night shrieks? Too many to count. Apparently she had company, although Sam hadn't heard anyone come in. He should've known.

Sam had given up trying to keep the names of her boyfriends straight, mostly because none of them stayed around long enough for that little nicety to matter very much. They were all drunks anyway, beer-bellied losers she picked up at the Strand or the Prospect Hotel. And the hell of it was, she didn't *want* any of them hanging around for more than a night or two. She wore her promiscuity like a brand. She was punishing herself, Sam knew; herself and him, too.

He leaned back in his chair and pressed the heels of his hands to his eyes, trying to shut out the rutting, piggish noise of them over there. To see his mother this way both saddened and disgusted Sam. And what made it worse was that he had no one to talk to about it.

Peter flat out refused to acknowledge even the whispered mention of her name. And if the truth be known, Sam didn't blame him, not one iota. When Peter told him what she had done on that day, stumbling drunkenly into his room and laying a funeral wreath on his chest… Even now, the thought of it sickened Sam to the point of puking.

Across the hall a glass smashed. Leona shrieked again, but this time it was a shriek of fury, one Sam knew only too well.

"Awright," she shrilled, "that tears it. Get your fat ass outta here. *Now.*"

Sam lurched forward in his chair, the thick muscles in his shoulders bunching in almost painful readiness. He'd remained gangly until the middle of his fifteenth year, but then the hormones had walloped him hard and Sam had shot up like a bad weed. Now, at twenty, he was a solid one hundred eighty pounds.

"You don't shout at me," a slurred voice bellowed back at her. "No. You don't shout at me, you dipshit bitch."

Another glass smashed.

And Sam was out of his chair and across the hall, booting his mother's bedroom door open so violently the knob punched a hole in the drywall on the opposite side.

Sam came face to face with the biggest, meanest-looking redneck he'd ever seen… but the bozo had his shorts bunched around his ankles, his half-stiff dick cupped in one hand, and it was all he could do to fend off Leona's hailstorm of blows. Standing there ready to commit murder, Sam might have found the whole sick spectacle amusing had it involved anyone but his mom.

"Who the fuck is this?" the redneck squawked.

"That's my kid," Leona told him, her tone eerily calm now. She flashed her red eyes at Sam. "Don't you know enough to knock before you come barging into a room? Didn't I teach you any manners?"

As ridiculous as all of this was, Sam felt himself flush at his mother's reprimand. Meanwhile her suitor was busily jerking on his pants, darting nervous glances first at Leona and then at Sam, trying to avoid falling on his ass in the process. The room was a mess, stained sheets and rumpled clothing everywhere, all of it reeking of stale booze and rancid sweat. Against one wall the runny remnants of a tossed whiskey bottle oozed wetly to the floor.

Sam backed out of the room.

"You don't gotta go, Johnny," he heard his mother say as he pulled the door shut.

"Fuck that noise," Johnny said. "You're a fuckin' wingnut."

A few minutes later, after the man had stomped sullenly out, Sam heard his mother sobbing in the dark of her bedroom.

* * *

Unable to sleep, Sam went back to the books. When the telephone rang an hour later, it startled him more than the shouting had earlier on.

"Yes?" he said, his voice shaky. Late night calls were seldom very cheerful.

"Is this Mr. Gardner?"

"Yes, this is Sam Gardner. Who is this?"

"It's Shawna Blane. I'm a nur—"

"I know who you are," Sam said. "Is something wrong with my brother?"

"He's had another… spell, Sam. Trouble with his breathing. We had to put him on a ventilator this time. He's in ICU."

Sam sighed raggedly. This had happened once before, two years ago, but they hadn't had to ventilate him that time. Peter had recovered on his own. Dr. Lowe had taken Sam aside after that attack and explained the situation.

"It's only going to get worse," the doctor said. "This type of attack will recur again and again until either we do something about it or he dies."

"What can be done?" Sam said.

"There's a device that can be implanted under the skin. It gives off a series of electronic impulses which stimulate the diaphragm, kicking it into action automatically. Without it, I'm afraid, Peter will just go on having these attacks."

But Peter had balked vehemently at the very idea.

"Forget it," he told Sam. "One of the few things I can still do on my own is breathe, and there's no way I'm going to let them take that away from me, too."

On the other end of the line the nurse cleared her throat, breaking the brief but oppressive silence. Her words made Sam feel as if she'd been reading his mind. "Dr. Lowe had a surgeon implant the device he told you about last time, Sam. It's functioning well—"

"I thought you needed my brother's permission to do that."

"Not when it's considered a lifesaving procedure."

"I see."

Sam glanced up and saw his mother leaning in the doorway, the dim light of her gaze fluctuating between stupor and dull curiosity.

"Is he going to be all right?" Sam said into the phone.

The nurse hesitated, just slightly, but enough to swamp Sam with dread. "We think so," she said. "He's still unconscious. We came very close to losing him."

"I'll be right over," Sam said, and hung up.

Grabbing his jacket, he started past his mother—but she blocked his way with her body. Her nightie was filmy and Sam could see the tired sag of her breasts through the fabric.

"Where ya goin', Sammy?" Her voice was breathy and low…almost seductive.

Deflecting a knife thrust of revulsion, Sam took a quick step back from the boozy heat of her.

"It's Peter," he said. "He's sick."

"He's not sick," Leona said, her face clenching like a brawler's fist. She advanced on Sam menacingly, the gleam in her eyes insane. "He's *dead*."

But instead of backing down as he usually did, Sam took hold of his mother and shook her, shook her till her eyes cleared. Then he clutched her face roughly, forcing her to meet his gaze.

"My brother is not dead," he told her in a chilling monotone.

Leona pulled away, a growl rattling in her throat. Sam brushed past her into the hallway. "He's dead, damn you," she hollered at his back. "Why can't you get that through your thick skull? That... thing, that crippled fucking head is not my Peter. Do you hear me, Sammy? *That is not my Peter.*"

In the elevator on the way down, Sam hammered the graffiti-scrawled paneling, dulling the edge of his fury. In the grimy lobby he hitched up his collar, then thrust his fists into the pockets of his jeans.

The rail of his mother's voice dogged him into the cold autumn rain.

* * *

The sight of Peter, still as death, tubes snaking out of every orifice, caused time to fold back on itself for Sam. Suddenly it was six years ago and he was a skinny, pimple-faced teenager again, bumping into the nurse who'd led him along the too-bright ICU corridor to the hell his brother's life had become. Suddenly the tears were back, the guilt, the overwhelming sorrow.

He shifted closer to the bed, searching his brother's face for signs of awareness, finding none. The hiss of the ventilator and the beep of the monitors were the only sounds.

"Peter?" he said quietly, almost whispering.

And to Sam's surprise, Peter's eyes fluttered open. They strayed about unfocused at first, the eyes of a fighter tangled in the ropes.

Then they found Sam's eyes and cleared a little before filling with tears. A frail smile struggled for life around the tube in his mouth.

Sam touched Peter's forehead. "How ya doin', bro?" he said, unable to keep his voice from breaking.

His heart fell when Peter shook his head, the movement unutterably weary. A nightmare was born then, the first of many Sam would endure before the bond between them was broken. Peter was trying to say something around the tube, as he had so long ago—and again that eldritch feeling of time folding back on itself stole through Sam like a chill. Leaning over the bedside, he half expected Kelly to sidle in next to him or his mother to say in a drunken slur, "He's tryna say something, Sammy."

Peter's eyes shifted, sliding to their corners, indicating the ventilator that currently sustained his life.

"Uhnn," Sam said, reading Peter's lips. "Uhnn...fflug...idd."

Unplug it.

Horror clasped Sam's heart and gave it a squeeze. He looked into his brother's eyes, searching them for confusion, the dim fog of drugs; but he saw only the clear light of reason.

And with muscles functioning temporarily beyond his control, Sam found himself reaching for the plug. Suddenly the dismal vista that was the balance of his crippled brother's life flashed before Sam's interior eye like a convict's first glimpse of the chair, and he was doing it, he was reaching for that plug—because this cruel parody of life was worse than death, worse by far. It was a death unfinished, a careless oversight on the part of the Reaper. And how many more misery-heaped years would it be before that hooded goblin recalled its mistake? How much longer would his brother be forced to lie here in the tomb of his own festering corpse before his tortured mind finally followed? Suddenly Sam saw the fulfillment of his brother's request as his duty, the same humane deed he would grant an animal crushed but not killed in the road.

His fingers found the plug, tightened around it—

And abruptly recoiled, as if the full voltage of the outlet had jumped its restraints and coursed up his arm. When he looked back at Peter, shame burning in his eyes, Sam was relieved to find that he'd blacked out again.

Feeling like both a coward and a killer, Sam pulled up a chair and sat at the bedside, trying to shut out of his mind the atrocity he'd almost committed.

It was five days before his brother opened his eyes again.

15

AS WITH THE BEST of notions, the idea of a drive to the island was a spontaneous one. Friday afternoon, which was overcast, had given way to an evening too glorious by far to be squandered in a theater, and when Will suggested the island as an alternative, Kelly agreed without hesitation. It was an hour's drive through some of the most magnificent countryside the north had to offer. Rolling hills carpeted in dense pine forest, abrupt quartz cliff-faces jagging out of the earth, deep saucer-shaped valleys gorged with glacier-blue lake water. Then came the island itself, Manitoulin, a craggy, wedge-shaped hideaway whose sandy south bank faced the oceanic body of Lake Huron and whose every rugged inch lay steeped in native folklore. Once there, they would dine at the Inn on the Bay, an intimate lakeside chalet and Kelly's favorite eating spot in the province. Sumptuous Austrian cuisine served at candlelit tables overlooking a deep green gem of a lake…

The mere thought of it made Kelly's mouth water, and she could hardly wait to get underway. Responding to some nameless possibility, she threw a few extra items of clothing into a tote bag—just in case. And later, while waiting on the steps, she realized with something like shock that she was happy. Plainly, simply happy, for the first time in too many years.

Will, you bugger, she thought, I'm falling for you.

Absorbed in these thoughts, Kelly basked in the lazy evening, waiting for Will, relishing the sights around her. The westering sun threw out spears of rich golden firelight, setting the treetops ablaze and embroidering the scattered cloud cover with flax; Kelly could feel its heat on her face like a loving hand. The thin haze of August had burned away, leaving a clarity of colour that was almost painful to the beholding eye. The lake was a sequined tropical blue, the lawn a rich mossy green; even Chainsaw, scruffy as he was, looked clean and freshly minted as he scuffed his way down the hill. It was as if, overnight, the entire world had been lovingly refurbished, the old varnish scraped away and replaced with a shiny new coat.

Out of this mellow perfection Will's old Buick appeared, rattling good-naturedly down the hill. As it approached the house, a stray sunbeam turned the windshield into a mirror, creating the illusion that the humpbacked antique was unpiloted. Then Will's boyish features materialized behind the glass, his dimpled smile sparkling in the sunlight.

"Hornin' in on my gal?" he said to the shepherd as he got out of the car, his tan flight jacket and wash-faded Levi's fitting smoothly into this picture-perfect setting. Chainsaw trotted out to greet him, pressing a wet muzzle into Will's open palm. "Eh, boy? Tryna swipe my gal?" The dog only wagged its tail.

"All set?" Will said, his eyes resting speculatively on Kelly's tote bag before rising to meet hers.

"You bet," Kelly said. "Let's boogie."

And they were off, Chainsaw trailing them up the hill.

* * *

They had wine with their meal and, afterward, curled together in a love seat in the lake-facing lounge, brandy by a maplewood fire. The alcohol banished Will's sometimes stifling shyness, and before long he was regaling Kelly with tales of his childhood and yarns about his job as a slag-train engineer at the Nickel Ridge smelter. He was a fine, sensitive man, and Kelly found herself increasingly drawn to him. During the drive out from the city, she'd forsaken the picturesque sights and sat cradled in the crook of his arm, allowing herself an almost forgotten feeling of safety. It felt good to have his arm around her.

As the evening progressed and the alcohol lightened her mood, Kelly found herself reflecting on the items she'd stuffed into her tote bag. Along with a fresh change of clothes, she'd packed a gossamer nightie, a long, ghostly thing slit shamelessly high up the thigh and breasted with delicate lace. Apparently undirected, her fingers had snatched up the nightie and buried it deep in the bag...but what had her intentions been?

Now midnight had come and gone, and the proprietors were winding things down for the evening. Both she and Will were too far gone to make the drive home safely...and had she known this was going to happen? Willed it, perhaps? This place was famous for its intimate chalets.

Suddenly the question seemed to hang unanswered between them.

Breaking the momentary silence, Will giggled and indicated the bustling staff. "Looks like they're getting ready to turf us out."

"Think you can drive?"

Will giggled again. "No worries." He started to get up, then sat down again. "In a while."

Kelly laughed. Along with her glow, a cool sexual excitement had begun to flutter in her tummy. "Want to pool our pennies and rent a room?" she said, the words out before she could intercept them.

Will looked as if he'd swallowed an ice cube. "Uh...together?"

"Yes, together," Kelly said, feeling agreeably light-headed. "Come on. Let's go see if there's a vacancy."

They shuffled arm in arm to the desk. Kelly hadn't been this tipsy in years, and it felt fine. One of the proprietor's daughters, a blue-eyed girl of about sixteen, smiled knowingly, and Kelly thought, Are we being that obvious?

Agreeing to share the cost, they signed themselves in then retrieved their things from the Buick. After a brief inspection of the chalet, they sat in lawn chairs on the elevated deck, Kelly wrapped in a blanket against the creeping autumn chill, Will tucked in beside her. The night sky was sensational—moonless and vacant of cloud, stars packed so densely they cast their own silvery light—and they lay silent for a time in awe of it.

Then, surprising Kelly, Will slipped out to the car and came back with a Coleman cooler. From it he extracted an iced bottle of Mumm's, two plastic wineglasses and a scented candle. The candle he seated in a lathed brass holder, obviously new, and lit with a match from a complimentary pack.

As he poured the bubbly, Kelly said, "Did you plan this little sleep-over, Will Chatam?"

Will blushed furiously, his face a throbbing beet red in the candlelight. Still half looped, he accepted the implication in good humor, as Kelly had intended it.

"Moi?" he said, handing her a glass of spritzing amber fluid.

"Yes," Kelly said, "toi." She was content, ridiculously so—but something about the champagne chipped the edge off her devil-may-care mood. Suddenly the old voices were grumbling again, tossing up all the old warnings.

Wait, they cautioned her. *Don't be so eager to undress.* Her heart, though it had soared this evening, reminded her that it had been battered before. Its walls were weak. One more kick and it might give up for good. In the space of an instant her physical readiness, her healthy hunger for Will's embrace, had transformed into a wary, childlike watchfulness.

Kelly's smile slipped away. In that same instant Will seemed to sober. He set his wineglass on the trestle table and sat on the foot of Kelly's lawn chair. As he spoke, he stroked her bare foot.

"No, Kelly. I didn't plan it."

And she believed him.

"When we decided to come up here and I went home to get ready, I found myself just…grabbing things, without thinking." His blush had faded, but his words came haltingly. "Since meeting you, Kelly, I, well, I've been happy. That's the best way I can think of to describe it. And the thought of coming up here with you…I guess I got pretty excited." He looked down at her foot. His touch was warm and arousing. "To be alone with you, away…it made me crazy. So I just started grabbing things. I didn't mean anything by it."

Touched, Kelly took his hand. "I know that, Will." She chuckled. "Hey, I'm just as bad. You should see some of the things I stuffed into that bag…or maybe you shouldn't." Her smile came back then, genuine and only for him. "I like you, Will. I like you a lot."

"Really?" Will said, his expression like that of a lottery winner.

"Really," Kelly said, and kissed his hand.

They were quiet then, content in their closeness and growing affection. In the midst of that quiet a shooting star streaked across the top of the sky, seeming to go on forever before winking out at the rim of the globe. In its afterglow, Kelly made a silent wish. More fiercely, Will did, too.

When it was time to go in—and Kelly was still not sure what she wanted to do—Will spoke again.

"There's something else I want to tell you," he said. "I hope you won't think I'm weird or that I don't find you attractive, because believe me, I do. But…I just want to sleep with you tonight. Beside you." A lump formed in Kelly's throat. "When I was in high school, I played the field a bit. You know. Fooled around. But it didn't suit me. I can't just...do it. For fun." He was beginning to struggle and Kelly took his hand again, silently urging him on. "I cared for someone once, a long time ago, and it didn't work out. I think...being with her that way, too soon, made it harder when it was suddenly over. Do you understand?"

"Perfectly," Kelly said, relieved to have the decision taken out of her hands...and a little disappointed. "Let's go inside."

Smiling, Will slid the patio doors shut behind them.

16

THE WHEELS TRAMPED OVER his legs with punishing slowness, leaving him nerveless in the road, that horrific *snap* of bone—like teeth chunking into rock candy—reverberating in his skull. He could feel the sun baking his face, the sting of sweat in his eyes. He could feel Kelly's cool shadow pooling around him...

And then a tug, the same Scotch tape tug he'd experienced on the night he nearly died.

A tug...

Then he was afloat in the dense summer air, gazing down with cool detachment at the final moments of his normal life, watching his lover weep and the transport carve its ravening path through the bush. Floating nearer, he saw something else—his own lips moving as Kelly leaned over him on bloody knees.

He drifted closer, trying to hear what his last words had been; closer, and he could smell Kelly's sweat mingled with the sharper tang of her fear; closer, and now he could hear his own laboured breathing; and words, gurgling, half-whispered words...

"Uhmm ... pleassse ... help me ... Mommm ... "

With a force doubling that of the Michelins rolling over his legs, Peter's dream eye was jerked up and away from the scene, leaving the earth behind with the thrust of a moon-bound spacecraft.

And in his heart such a volatile mixture of anguish and fury roiled together that Peter had to scream to diffuse its potency. In his extremity he'd cried out to his mother like a frightened child. In his direst moment, he'd beckoned to the pathetic gin-swill she'd become, to the witch who'd left him for dead.

Love and hate clashed within him in bloody hand-to-hand combat. In the same stroke he wanted to tear out his mother's heart, dance on her twitching remains, howl like the warrior triumphant... and embrace her in loving forgiveness, bury his head in her breast and purge the pain through his tears.

The perception of skyward acceleration changed suddenly, leveling out and sharply increasing. In an instant the sensation of forward motion became a smeary, breathtaking blur. He was in a corridor now, narrow as a mail slot and infinitely tall, whistling along like a bullet with eyes. A U-shaped pocket of air formed in front of him, causing a resistance he could feel against the crown of his head like a restraining hand. Cranking some interior joystick, he compressed that pocket to a blister—

Then all resistance vanished and he was highballing through space—*Light speed*, he thought in the awesome clarity of this dream—the sheer exhilaration of it dousing the fires of his rage. Unable to help himself, he twisted his form through a series of deliberate spirals, kissing like a pinball off the flickering neon sheets the walls around him had become.

From someplace in the unseeable distance, faint but familiar music found his ears. Like a moth drawn to light, he bore down on its source—

And in an eyeblink his transit had ceased.

He was in a room he'd never been in before, strange... and yet not strange. Behind him stood his piano, its fallboard closed like a coffin lid, its surface flawlessly polished. On the lid near its centre stood a tacky sort of shrine, a gaudy memorial to himself, with the eight-by-ten grad photo he'd given to his mother ringed in candles and cheap plastic flowers. It infuriated him to see it there, and with muscles that magically responded, he flung out an arm to sweep it away—

But his arm passed through it, leaving it untouched.

That music...

It was the sonata, the last thing he'd played, the memory of it scratchy with years. But no... it was taped music, he could see the revolving spools of the recorder over the back of the couch in the next room. Moving closer, he realized it wasn't a separate room at all, but a section of one larger room that had been unfashionably partitioned off with a planter-divider and the bulk of the couch itself.

There were other familiar items around, bits of his past grafted into this drab room, and Peter examined each of them in turn. Above a mock fireplace hung the big, artless K-Mart oil painting he and Sam had pooled their resources to buy for their parents' anniversary twelve years ago. Seeing it now, Peter felt the same twinge of embarrassment he always felt when he remembered how excited the two of them had been, buying an original oil painting for their folks. Later he'd seen at least a dozen duplicates of that same "original" at one of those parking-lot art shows that come and go like a dream... and at half the price they'd paid. To his right, on a dusty knickknack shelf, stood the "World's Best Mom" figurine he'd bought and then hand-painted for one of her birthdays. And there were other things: the braided oval rug, now irretrievably soiled and uncoiling, that had lain at the foot of his bed; a row of athletic trophies, all of them his, neatly arranged on the mantel, the—

There was a moan, a plea from a tortured dream, and Peter whirled to scan the room. It had come from behind him, from the couch.

He noticed something then that had evaded him before—a pale hand dangling over the armrest, its limp fingers loosely clasping a tilted, almost empty bottle of whiskey whose base rested on the end table next to the couch. The hand twitched slightly, nearly losing the bottle; then it was still.

Not for the first time, the remarkable detail of this dream struck Peter in a concrete moment of thought. Curious, he drifted closer to the couch, intent on discovering who belonged to that hand...

But now the music swelled, rising in a sweet crescendo, and Peter remembered that day, the sweet power of *making* that music, the smooth feel of the keys as his fingertips whispered across them, each touch a fleeting embrace. And later, Kelly moving beneath him in a new kind of crescendo.

He found himself back at the Yamaha, brushing its lid with his palm, almost...feeling it. There was a tiny gouge in the wood, a fleck of embedded glass.

That hadn't been there before...

He sat on the bench, fingered the curve of the fallboard—and now he *could* feel it, its smoothness, its substance, its weight.

Ecstatic, he lifted the cover, baring the keys, stroking them tenderly...

And as the last chord of the sonata sounded on the tape, he arranged his fingers in the remembered positions and pressed. The chord, rich and clean, rose from the piano like a phantom, filling his heart with joy.

He was playing again, actually *play*—

"Peter?"

Peter flinched as if stung. That voice...

"*Peter?*"

There was a clatter from the direction of the couch—the bottle tipping over, liquid gurgling out, an ashtray wobbling to the rug. Then

Peter saw five pallid fingers crawl up the backrest, a vampire's fingers dislodging the lid of its daylight sleeping quarters... only these fingers belonged to a woman.

And that voice—

"Peter? Is that...?"

Then there was a face above the fingers, a familiar face—no, a cruel caricature of a familiar face. It was in the eyes.

It was—

(no not her please don't let it be her)

—his mother.

"Peter?" Her jaundiced eyes searched as if blind. "My baby?"

Peter hammered both fists into the keys.

And the drunken caricature came alive, clambering to its feet, lurching over the back of the couch with outspread arms.

On the tape, applause hissed eerily out—

And Peter awoke in his ICU bed, his mother's sobs and the spoiled-meat taste of loathing stalking him back. Hoaxed by the magical renewal of his body in the dream, he tried to sit up...

But of course he could not.

Despairingly, he wept.

* * *

Sam was there when his brother awoke from his coma. He'd been there almost constantly over the past five days. When Peter looked at him, Sam rose from his chair and lay beside his brother on the bed, being careful not to jostle the tube in his mouth. He stayed that way, ignoring the protests of the staff, until Peter slept soundly again. Then he made his way home.

In the living room he switched off the reel-to-reel, ending its monotonous flapping, and started down the hall to his room. The door to his mother's bedroom stood ajar, and although he didn't want to

Sam peeked inside, half expecting to see her snoring shape sprawled-over by some grizzled buffoon. But the bed was empty. No mother, no company, nothing.

Sam felt afraid.

Where was she? It was ten past four in the morning. Had she fallen down drunk in some dark corner and fractured her skull? Had some redneck taken her home and gutted her with a hunting knife? An image of his mother's body, naked and motionless in a dead-woman's sprawl, assaulted Sam's weary mind.

He was partway down the hall when he heard the sobbing.

Sam found his mother in the bathroom, huddled in the tub behind the stained shower curtain, a shapeless nightdress cowling her body. Like a toddler with a blanket, she clutched an empty whiskey bottle to her neck. Black eyeliner ran down her cheeks like the tears of a tragic clown. Her sobs were like laughter. Crazy laughter.

"He was here, Sammy," Leona said, her breath rustling in her throat. "Your dear sweet brother was here."

Sam's flesh crawled in cold handfuls.

His mother began to rock.

17

"I EXPRESSLY REFUSED YOU permission to do that," Peter said, his voice still husky from the tube in his throat.

Dr. Lowe fingered his collar. Behind him, arranged in a tight semicircle, a group of students looked on in horrified awe. Earlier that morning Dr. Lowe had come in to extubate Peter, but had neglected to mention the electronic device he'd instructed the surgeons to implant beneath Peter's skin. Peter had found out for himself when a nurse came in to calibrate it.

"It had to be done," Lowe said in his own defense. "Without this device, you'd be stuck on a ventilator indefinitely."

Peter's face reddened to the cast of old brick. "You had no right."

Lowe backed up a step. "Well, I can see there's little point in continuing this—"

"Don't you dare walk out on me," Peter roared. "Don't you *dare.*"

With an outstretched arm Lowe herded his students toward the door.

"Come back here," Peter shouted. *"Come back here."*

Lowe turned his back.

And Peter spat. Using a technique a school chum had taught him when he was a kid, he amassed a huge gob and propelled it along the curled chute of his tongue. The bulk of it caught Lowe behind the ear, where it dangled obscenely. Sticky satellites speckled his balding pate and the shoulder of his pinstripe suit. Unable to stop himself, one of the students burst out laughing, nervous laughter that was quickly stifled.

Lowe rounded on Peter in fury. "Don't you *ever* do that again." He dug a monogrammed handkerchief out of his breast pocket and wiped his ear with it.

"Stay out of my room," Peter hissed. "And stay out of my life."

Keeping one eye on Peter, Lowe hustled his entourage out the door. Peter heard him barking orders at a nurse—and knew that he was meant to hear every word.

"I want him sedated," Lowe said in that cool, imperious tone Peter had come to despise over the years. "And I want Psychiatry to see him today. He's agitated. Agitated and irrational." Underscoring the doctor's words, Peter heard the busy scribble of his pen on an order sheet.

"Nobody touches me with dope," he hollered. "If anyone tries, I'll bite off his fingers." Furious tears stung his eyes. "Do you hear me? I'll spit in the fucker's face. I'll—"

You'll what? a mocking voice interrupted.

You'll do shit, another voice answered. *That's what.*

Consumed with rage, Peter thumped his head repeatedly into his pillow, wishing it were a cinder-block wall.

* * *

Sam turned up around four that afternoon, freighted with books, his pocked cheeks rosy from the brisk autumn air. He'd gone first to ICU, and was gratified to find that Peter had been shipped back upstairs to his room. In the glow of his relief, Sam had forgotten about the implant. The palpable gloom reminded him.

He pulled up a chair and sat at the bedside. And although he secretly applauded Lowe for taking the initiative—what Sam didn't want was a dead brother—he decided to squat on neutral ground for the time being.

"Want to talk about it?"

Peter sighed. "What's there to say? The fucker went ahead and did it. I can't believe it, but there it is."

Handling it gingerly, Sam examined the compact device. Hooked by two fine wires to a disc-shaped plate beneath the skin of Peter's flank, the stimulator looked like nothing more than a scaled-down Walkman, with two small calibrated dials and a glassed-in indicator that resembled a voltmeter. Another wire ran to the wall above Peter's head, where it jacked into an outlet labeled ALARM.

"I feel like a bit of a jackass," Peter said.

"Why's that?"

"I really blew up at Lowe over this thing." He chuckled without humor. "Called him some nasty names. I even gobbed on him."

"You *gobbed* on him?"

Peter nodded, the corners of his mouth twitching in the closest thing to a smile Sam had seen on his brother's face in years.

"Not too bright, huh? Sort of like spitting in the judge's eye before the sentence is handed down."

"Maybe he had it coming."

"Fucking A he had it coming," Peter said, that impotent anger rising again.

As much of that anger as Sam had been witness to over the years, it still distressed him whenever it flared. Before the accident, it had taken a lot to set Peter off—a direct slur on their mother, perhaps, or on Sam himself—but now, anger was Peter's only defense, his only release. And as ugly as it was, that anger was therapeutic.

Sam drew it out.

"Maybe we should hire a lawyer," he said. "Sue the bald bastard's ass."

"Nice thought, but forget it. They're calling it a lifesaving maneuver." A defeated sigh escaped him. "And the hell of it is, they're right. I'm nothing but a fucking head, Sam, and still I'm afraid to let go. Some prize turnip, huh?"

Sam's stomach rolled threateningly. The one thing he could not stand from his brother was this kind of talk—but the sickness he felt now bubbled up from someplace much deeper.

(uhnn ... fflug ... idd)

He wondered if Peter remembered his mute, late night entreaty.

"Cut that shit," Sam said with forced levity. "Nobody wants to die. So you'd better not die, dickbrain, 'cause if you do, I'll come back here and kill you myself." It was intended as a joke, but the words hung heavy between them. "I meant—"

"I know what you meant."

A nurse came in then, carrying a small burgundy tray with a loaded syringe and an alcohol swab arranged side by side on its surface.

"Hey, welcome to the Cocaine Café," Peter said, doing a passable Cheech Marin. "What'll it be today, man? A hundred of Demerol to keep the feeb at bay? Or how's about ten of Valium? That oughta keep the kumquat quiet."

Afraid Peter would create another scene—there had been many over the years, each of them ending with these forced injections, like punishments—Sam got quickly to his feet.

"Stick around," Peter told him calmly, chuckling again, that same hollow, mirthless sound. "No pun intended." He grinned falsely at the nurse. "I'll go quietly."

Shooting a tense glance at Sam, the nurse swabbed Peter's thigh and injected the Valium.

"*Oww,*" Peter said, tipping a wink at Sam when the nurse flinched. Sam grinned, but he wasn't amused.

"Be sure to tell them I was a good little squash," Peter said to the nurse as she left.

Sam looked down at his shoes.

"Not so impressed with your big brother now," Peter said, more than a little shame in his voice. "Huh."

"That's bullshit and you know it," Sam said, feeling angry now himself. "The way they treat you, it makes me want to cave their fucking heads in." He sighed. "And yet, I know they're just doing their jobs. It's a trap, man. A god-awful trap." His eyes reddened with tears.

"Hey," Peter said. "Hey, man, I'm sorry. It's just that sometimes I get so damned angry I want to bust something, you know? Kick the living shit out of something...but I can't. So I crap on whoever's handy. God help me, I've even done it to you."

Sam started to object...but it was true.

"It's almost impossible to think of anyone else's problems when you're in this kind of shape, Sammy. But that doesn't excuse it. Christ, just look at you. Trekking in here every day, doesn't matter if it's shitty outside or you're sick as a dog with the flu, you're here. Studying, holding down three jobs just so you can keep me in toys and the old lady in booze." Sam flinched visibly; this was the first time since the incident with the wreath that Peter had mentioned their mother. "I don't know how you do it."

"Do you know why I do it?"

"Yeah, kid," Peter said, compassion lumping his words. "I do."

They were quiet for a time, the Valium having its way with Peter. Then: "You know, Sammy, I dreamed about her last night."

"Who?" Sam said, guessing he meant Kelly. Peter rarely mentioned her anymore—the bitch had run out on him, just like all the rest—but Sam suspected his feelings for her still ran deep.

"Mom," Peter said, making the word sound profane. "I hadn't even thought about her in years, let alone dream about her."

This was a lie and Sam knew it, but he decided to let it slide. He made no comment, expecting the discussion to end there.

But Peter pressed on.

"It was the strangest thing. It started with something similar to what happened on the night I nearly croaked." He told Sam about the floating, detached state he'd found himself in that night.

"Wow," Sam said. "I've heard of that happening. 'Sixty Minutes' did a thing on it a few years back, or maybe it was 'W-Five'. They called it an out-of-body experience."

"Yeah, I saw that program, too. And I've read about the phenomenon." With a nod Peter indicated his well-stocked library, which occupied a stack of shelves against the opposite wall. "Truth is, I thought it was all bullshit. Until now."

Sam regarded his brother with an expression of open wonder.

"Then last night I was having the dream." Sam knew all about Peter's recurring dream. "It was the same as always, except at the point where I usually wake up I was suddenly hovering in the air above the whole scene, just like the other night. I guess my subconscious just built the experience into the dream.

"But then I realized I was saying something, or my body was, down there on the road..."

He took the story right up to the point where he arrived in that strange, dingy room, following the pull of that eerie music. But as he described the room in the meticulous detail of the dream, he witnessed a peculiar transformation in Sam. Suddenly the kid was sheet-white, the hollows beneath his eyes a pale, unhealthy green, and he seemed to be having difficulty catching his breath.

"Sam," Peter said, concerned. "What—?"

"You saw the shrine?" Sam said. "And the couch? And that crappy room divider?"

"Sam—"

Sam raised a forestalling hand. He was trying to remember if he'd ever described the apartment to his brother. But no, Peter hadn't even allowed him to talk about the move. And without being able to stand there and study the room himself, even Sam couldn't describe it in such detail.

"Sam, what the hell…?"

"That was no dream," Sam said, recalling his mother's drunken claim of the night before.

(*He was here, Sammy.*)

"What do you mean?" Peter said, a hint of fear in his voice.

"You were there," Sam whispered. "You were actually there."

(*Your dear sweet brother was here.*)

* * *

The night following her son's ephemeral visit, Leona Gardner sat expectantly awake and painfully sober until just before dawn. With jittery fingers she rethreaded the tape again and again, barely noticing when at one point Sam stormed out of the apartment, slamming the door behind him.

The music had brought Peter back to her the last time.

It would do so again.

When by four-thirty nothing had happened, and the shivery, gut-sick shadow of withdrawal had consumed her, Leona cracked open a fresh bottle of Jack and guzzled her way deep into its fiery oblivion. Sleep stole over her sodden gray cells like death, and she dropped precipitously away. Anyone seeing her there on the couch—half sitting, her skin a diseased yellow, the shallow intake and boozy outflow of her breath barely perceptible—would surely have thought her dead.

On the table beside her, the tape flapped repeatedly…

But the music played on, distant at first, rising from the depths of some unseen chasm, then swelling as her awareness of it heightened.

Through slitted eyes she saw the dumb revolutions of the take-up reel, the loosely flapping tail of the tape, and now she sat up on the couch, her liver-eyes as round as saucers.

The music wasn't coming from the tape.

It was coming from the piano…

But the benchseat was bare, the fallboard closed over the keys.

Leona rose on slippered feet and wove her way toward the piano, shifting from handhold to handhold like a sailor on a yawing ship. She approached the instrument from its bent side, laying a trembling hand on its polished lid for support.

The wood vibrated beneath her fingertips.

With music.

Like a mother snatching a child from a burning bed, Leona grabbed the fallboard and slammed it open, revealing the gleaming keys, like the teeth of a friendly monster.

They were moving, up and down, like the keys of a player piano.

Leona dropped to her rump on the rug. Before her eyes the air above the benchseat began to ripple like a desert heat shimmer, and then to take shape, human shape…

Peter's shape.

Intent and miraculously whole, he sat hunched over the keyboard as he always had, still transparent but hardening, assuming the lovely substance of reality. His sandstone-coloured eyes were lidded in the rapture of creation, and his athlete's hands glided expertly over the keys. He glanced briefly her way, that funny, lopsided grin on his face, the one he always got when he played, then turned back to the keys.

Stunned, Leona could only watch… and then crab her way backward as her son's image underwent a hideous metamorphosis, his lithe body wasting, his strong limbs retracting as the tendons shortened with audible creaks. The clean refrains of the sonata deteriorated into the inexpert plunkings of a beginner, and finally into the furious poundings of a retardate. As if in revolt, the fallboard slammed shut like an alligator's jaw, severing Peter's fingers at the middle joints. Rotating on the bench, he held up his hands for his mother's inspection, grinning at her from a face that was otherwise inert.

I am not dead, the spidery ruin on the piano bench told her.

Not dead...

* * *

Leona awoke on the floor with her back jammed against the room divider, sweat oozing from her pores. On the coffee table behind her the tape flapped monotonously. She squinted at the piano in the dawn light—and saw blood drizzling from beneath the fallboard. She blinked and the blood was gone. The fallboard gleamed in the morning's new light.

Breathing hard, Leona rose stiffly to her feet. She stumbled toward the piano, meaning to lift the fallboard and examine the keys... but at the last minute she altered her course. If she raised that cover and found ten bleeding fingers underneath, she would run screaming off her tenth-story balcony.

From the uncapped bottle on the end table, Leona swallowed the first of the day. She sat on the couch, wiped a hand across her booze-slopped chin, and rethreaded the tape.

* * *

By midmorning Leona had passed out again. She came to just over eighteen hours later, sitting abruptly erect and uttering a startled cry. She gaped over the couch back at the piano, now a ghostly white shape in the unlit room, and felt a legion of invisible spiders skitter over her flesh. There was a terrible emptiness at the centre of her being, and a frightful clarity dawning in her mind. For a moment, almost fondly, she remembered another life...then she realized what was wrong.

She was sober.

When her eyes had adjusted to the dark, Leona reached for her bottle. It sat on the far side of the coffee table, precariously close to the edge, and instead of closing around its comforting smoothness, her trembling fingers sent it tumbling to the floor.

Leona cursed and jumped up, barking her shin on the corner of the table as she tried to save the precious intoxicant—this was her last bottle, and it was the middle of the night. She could hear the liquid gurgling out, seeping into the rug like spilled blood, and a degree of panic she had never known took hold of her like the hands of a frozen giant.

She groped in the dark for the bottle. When she found it, it was empty. She thought of sucking the puddled rug and then recoiled against the couch, clasping her abraded shin and sobbing like a frightened child. She was cold and alone and she wanted her booze...but she couldn't move. Her brain was working again, and it lobbed unwanted truths at her like live grenades.

That was no dream last night, sister, and it wasn't your son. It was the DTs, an alcoholic hallucination. Can't you see what you've done to yourself? You're a lush. A common drunk. You belong in a gutter... and what'll become of you when Sammy finally leaves? Have you thought about that? Ever slept in a Dumpster? Ever et garbage? Oh, you fool. You fool, you fool, you fool...

I'll call somebody, Leona thought frantically. That's what I'll do. 911. The hospital. I need help. Oh, God, I need—

Leona scrambled to her feet like a woman possessed. She stumbled out to the kitchen and groped for the light switch, found it, then stood blinking in the light, trying to get her bearings. When the glare became tolerable, she fell to her knees and opened the cupboard under the sink. Desperate, she fished around inside, knocking unused containers of Windex and Easy-Off and Borax every which way, until she found what she was after.

"My little ace in the hole," she crooned to the dusty bottle of Jack, thrusting it up to the light like a pagan idol. "I almost forgot about you." She unscrewed the top and drank deeply.

Sam found her there six hours later, unconscious on the kitchen floor, a fresh scab forming on her shin.

18

FOR THE NEXT TWO weeks Peter tried to duplicate the experience. These efforts had exactly nothing to do with wanting to visit his
mother again, if that was in fact what he had done. No. What Peter
was after was that gut-grabbing sensation of *flying*. For he knew that,
even in the fleetest of jets, never would the thrill, the sheer exhilaration of motion, match what he'd experienced in that shimmering
corridor of light. In contrast to all of the previous nights in which the
dream had haunted him, Peter actively sought the dream now, tried to
induce its occurrence.

The dream came, but that was the only constant. Each night, as
always, he awoke in a panicky fever, bare seconds before the truck bar-
reled over his legs. Nothing he could do or imagine would prolong the
dream beyond the thunder of the truck. Finally, in a funk of frustration, he gave up. And through some strange paradox, defeat was the
needed catalyst.

He felt low that night, lower than usual. For two weeks now he'd
allowed himself the hope that some new...what?...dimension? had
opened its gates to receive him. And this hope had inflamed the old
desire, the yen that had at one time consumed him. He wanted to fly
again, bullet through that vertical kaleidoscope of light until his senses

reeled and his heart galloped free in his chest. It was this desire—this *need*—that canceled any compulsion to verify the reality or unreality of recent events. That part of it didn't matter. So desperate was he to escape the featureless drone of his life that he would do anything, endure anything—and believe anything—to make it happen again.

Just once.

That afternoon the Canadian Forces air show had taken place outside his ninth-story window. The Sudbury Science Centre, which sponsored the show, had been its ground base, and thus the focal point of the breathtaking aerobatics. Strapped in his wheelchair, Peter had watched the show from the roof, which overlooked the science centre and its newly sodded grounds. At first he hadn't wanted to go out, but Sam had coaxed him until finally he'd given in. In the end he was glad…

Or so he'd thought at the time.

Now the memory of those sleek CT-114s, banking in a tight diamond formation or carving impossible loops, burned hot fire trails in his brain, and he ached to climb aboard one of them, feel his fingers close knowingly around the joystick. During the show, Sam had run down to the recruiting trailer the forces had set up and had scored a large full-colour poster of the nine red and white jets dwarfing the curve of the globe. At Peter's unthinking request, Sam had taped the thing to the wall at the foot of the bed. Now its presence seemed to mock him.

But, oh, the wonderful thunder they had made, rocketing past at Mach 1 and beyond, punching holes in the sound barrier and causing the air to resonate with an almost electric intensity. That resonance had centred in his heart as he craned his neck to glimpse those smooth metal underbellies, and it had rippled down through his bones, creating the closest thing to an actual physical sensation he'd experienced since the fateful day of his accident.

Lying here now, in the deep autumn quiet of his room, Peter discovered a tiny pocket of that sensation still intact, expanding outward as he drifted toward sleep, eeling its way through his body like a drug. He imagined himself humming like a tuning fork, his very molecules becoming so agitated they began to defy gravity... and float.

The thunder. The thunder was back.

Fearful of the dream, Peter opened his eyes... but the thunder was the real thing. Sleet tapped impatiently at the thermal panes, and flash-glares printed negatives of the room on his retinas.

A freak autumn thunderstorm.

Peter gazed through the bleary windows of his eyes at the bedside clock and discovered that he'd been in that vibratory semitrance for an hour, though it had seemed like only seconds.

Thunder cracked, rolled...

And Peter slept.

* * *

When he awoke he was sitting in the chair at the foot of his bed. But no... it wasn't *his* bed, couldn't be, because there was someone else asleep in it. The room was dark, the only light a pale yellow fan from the corridor beyond the nearly shut door.

It wasn't his bed, but it was his room. There was his TASH environmental control unit on the shelf by the bed. Technical Aids and Systems for the Handicapped. Great stuff. If you could blow out a candle, you could "control your environment." He had a twenty-inch colour TV, a Sony DVD player, a Hitachi CD player and a case full of CD's, all of which he could control with a slight puff of air—and all of it compliments of Sam.

Now his eyes scanned right, to the stuffed floor-to-ceiling bookshelves, and the nightstand in which he stored the few remaining artifacts of his old life, items too painful to list. And there was the poster of the CT-114s, its edges already curling. According to the digital clock, it was six minutes past five in the morning. The worst of the storm had passed, but sleet still ticked at the window glass.

He looked again at the sheet-covered hump.

Who's that sleeping in my bed?

With dreamlike ease *(that's what this is it's a dream)* Peter rose to his feet... and then off his feet. From a yard above his bed, he looked down at himself.

A sudden, panicky fear bludgeoned him. Was he dying again? Or worse, already dead?

So what if you are?

Yeah. So what?

But he didn't want to die. Not anymore.

He wanted to fly.

Dead?

No. The gimp Walkman was functioning perfectly, its red LED flashing with each electrical impulse it dispatched to his diaphragm. Beneath the sheets his chest rose and fell.

He drifted closer, noticing that beneath his eyelids the globes of his eyes flickered in the crazed, trapped-animal patterns of REM sleep.

He was dreaming.

Closer...

Then two things happened simultaneously. First, a breathless sensation of free-fall that was a lot like being sucked whole into a vacuum. And second, a repulsion so savage it seemed to tear his essence to shreds. Repulsion from the bony, misshapen mess in that bed, from the open-grave stench of the bedsores that cratered its butt, from the incomprehensible truth of its existence... and its identity.

The repulsion won out. In a heartbeat he was back at the foot of his bed, still standing but winded, punchy, reeling in the clutches of nausea.

A shadow crept by in the hallway, stretching itself out like ghostly toffee before vanishing in a squeak of crepe-soled shoes.

Shawna Blane, Peter thought, dull anger mingling in a brooding backwater of his mind with an old and bitter arousal. The animosity between them, which had begun about a year ago, had been born innocently enough. Peter had misread Shawna Blane, mistaking her pity for interest. And one late night as she was turning him, he had asked her to touch him. One of his unbidden erections—which he was somehow aware of, a sort of faraway ache perceived more by the brain than the groin—had bobbed up when she drew back the sheets, and it had made him wonder if, were she to stroke him, then maybe, just maybe, he might feel it, at least at a psychological level, and perhaps even ejaculate. Shawna had always seemed so cheerful around him, so friendly, touching his face, engaging him in an ongoing, faintly sexual banter—or so he'd judged at the time—that never failed to arouse him. Asking her to touch him that night, in the silent tomb of the vegetable ward, had seemed so... right. He'd sincerely believed that she wanted to.

What a chump.

Shawna had flipped out, called him a disgusting, horny little veg, and then slapped him in the face, where she knew he could feel it. Peter had retaliated in one of the few ways left open to him, by hurling insults at her in a voice that trembled with humiliation and rage.

Somewhere outside, a muffled voice called Shawna's name.

"Hold on," Peter heard Shawna answer. "I've got to tinkle."

Dream?

Peter didn't think so.

He crossed on unfelt feet to the door, reached for the knob... and watched gleefully as his hand passed unimpeded through its substance. With a smile, he glanced back at his bedridden body and thought he saw it vibrating, ever so slightly.

Then he waltzed through the thickness of the door into the muted light of the corridor.

* * *

Walking at first, then lofting like a gull on an updraft, Peter followed Shawna Blane to the ninth-floor loo. She closed the door as he got there... so he simply passed through it.

His timing was perfect. Shawna was just hiking up her skirt... and, sweet Jesus, she was wearing a garter belt. She wiggled out of a pair of bikini panties—revealing a set of powder-white buns which in their plump perfection surpassed even his wildest imaginings—then turned with what Peter chose to interpret as deliberate slowness... and before she perched on the porcelain hoop, allowed him a fleeting glimpse of heaven. He heard a faint, tinkling hiss as Shawna let go—and then, to his total shock and dismal disappointment, such a thunderous and sloppy passage of wind that he found himself instantaneously returned to his room, his formerly keen arousal burst like a balloon at a dart toss. In all his life, the few times he'd even considered it, he'd never imagined a beautiful woman capable of such a thing.

Floating above it, fighting a fresh wave of revulsion, Peter looked down at his body again. He could see an erection poking up under the sheets.

Then, out of the corner of his eye, he spotted a large commercial jet outside his window, landing lights twisting, the huge torpedo of its body declining with smooth majesty toward the Sudbury Airport, twenty miles north of the city.

All else was forgotten as he stood on the waist-high windowsill and watched the plane complete its descent. It was a 747, an uncommon visitor to this barren north country, and as always, its massive size astonished him. He had hopped up here—floated, really—the instant he'd spotted the airliner.

The yearning was deep now. Deep and compelling.

Peter leaned forward, to press his face to the cool glass... and met no resistance at all. With a gut-clutching lurch, he pitched forward through the window, leaving it intact. The frost-sugared lawn hurtled solidly up at him, and he felt as if his entire being had compressed itself into the dry well of his throat. Bare yards from the ground, he pulled up his nose...

And soared into the coming dawn.

* * *

He rose in a breathtaking vertical thrust, like a warhead, then angled east in a steady climb. Beneath him the twelve-story monolith of the hospital shrank into insignificance, then vanished in a purple haze. In seconds the entire sloping clockface of the city melted into that haze and he was high on the edge of dawn, the heavens above a cold, dark indigo, the horizon below a garish slash of orange. Higher he soared, and at the rim of the world the sun lifted its blazing head. Light the colour of apricots speared out in great fan-shaped rays, blinding him. Thrumming with a crazy mix of wonder, exhilaration and fear, he banked away from the furnace of the sun and sliced still higher through the air. When the globe beneath him revealed its curving hip, he paused, hung there at what felt like the outer margin of the atmosphere, and looked down.

It's a goddam dream it has to be...

There was a sound then, a faint, keening whistle underlaid by an almost subaural rumble, like a synthesized bass note. The whistling heightened until it reached a whining, ultrasonic peak that made him want to clap his hands over his ears—

The jet roared by a hundred yards beneath him at what Peter estimated was at least Mach 2. There and then gone, it materialized out of the sun, then vanished into the maw of the west, the only signs of its passing a clean white contrail and a crackling sonic boom.

Feeling like a god, Peter gave chase. He dropped to the level of the vapour trail and followed it, skimming along its dissipating surface like a glory-bound soul on a celestial speedway. Powered by his will, he cranked an interior throttle and felt that hand on the crown of his head again, that compressible blister of resistance he'd had to overcome the first time. Thrusting relentlessly against it, he felt it give with an audible *pop*.

He was back in the corridor now, barely aware of the jet as he arrowed past it. Throttling down, he slowed to a hover and waited, unable to imagine how far or how fast he'd traveled.

It was then that he spotted the string, slung over his shoulder and receding in the direction from which he had come. Slender as a thread, its slack length glowed with a faint blue light, reminding him of the fiberoptic filaments he'd read about in *Scientific American*, fine tendrils of glass along which light could be induced to travel.

Soulstring, he thought, recalling the title of a novel by a favourite author. *That's my soulstring.*

Jesus, this is real…

That whistling sound was back again.

Sick with excitement, Peter turned and prepared to meet it.

The jet came out of the explosive light of the sun like a dart hurled by a colossus. It bore down on him at breakneck speed, sunflares winking off its wing tips and tinted canopy. Matching its speed, Peter cut through the air above it, close enough to read the markings on its seamless frame. It was a Mirage 2000 in camouflage blues, packing twin Mantra 530s, sleek air-to-air missiles. It was a French fighter jet, part, Peter guessed, of the air show that had skipped to the cities south of Sudbury and would continue on a westward sweep for another few weeks until its completion in Vancouver.

As he shadowed the jet, Peter dug in his memory—a memory that lost almost nothing—and came up with the specs on this aircraft.

Capable of Mach 2.3, the forty-eight-foot fighter jet had a range of just under a thousand miles and a service ceiling of 59,000 feet. He had studied aircraft the way a bird-watcher studied birds and could name most of them at a glance.

Ho-leeee fuck, we're really flyin' now.

Like some ghostly hitchhiker, Peter lowered himself onto the tinted canopy. Clasping its raised lip, he glued his face to the Plexiglas, barely noticing that, like a ghost, he cast no reflection. Beneath him the pilot's helmet gleamed like an ivory cue ball. A gogglelike visor the same smoky tint as the canopy concealed the upper half of the pilot's face, and an oxygen mask muzzled the rest. Bulky chute straps looped his shoulders, and between his spread knees a gloved hand clasped the joystick.

The old thrill was back with a vengeance. *Wahooo,* Peter howled in childlike joy. *Ride 'em, cowboy.*

The jet banked sharply to starboard, dropping Peter's stomach, and in his mind he begged the pilot to cut the bird loose, belly-roll, loop-the-loop, do something delinquent.

And then he did.

The jet rolled through a sudden 360 and Peter tumbled off. When he tried to regain control he found that he couldn't and now he was falling, twisting toward the misty curve of the earth like a jettisoned sack of potatoes. An updraft caught him and spun him around, tangling him in that blue thread of light like a fish snagged in its line. In a fit of panic, Peter saw that in places his soulstring was ragged, nearly worn through.

Twirling like a drill bit, Peter fell.

And in the great vacuum of his descent, he blacked out.

When he came to he was back in his body, the sensation of free-fall still churning his guts. Dressed in a gaudy pink uniform, a cleaning lady stood hunched at the foot of his bed, the sound of the vacuum she was trailing a lot like the whine of a jet.

(dreamjustadreamjustastupidfuckingdream)

Starting as Peter's head came up off his pillow, the cleaning lady said good morning with a thick Italian accent, then resumed her labours.

"Gina," Peter said, for he knew all the staff by name, "open the curtains for me, will you?"

"Sure," Gina said, laying the hose aside and toeing the machine into silence. "It's a nice day outside, no?"

"Please," Peter said, the urgency of his tone making the cleaning lady stumble. "Hurry."

Gina swept the curtains open, flooding the room with morning light.

Peter craned his neck.

And there, high against a curving canopy of blue, was the spectral slash of a vapour trail, already dissipating.

Smiling, Peter thanked the woman, then dropped comfortably back to sleep.

* * *

When Sam sauntered in that evening with his book-loaded knapsack slung over his shoulder, he took one look at his brother and stopped dead in his tracks. There was something wrong, and although Sam could not immediately put a name to it, it struck him like a rush of poisoned air.

"What's up?" Peter said. "You look as if you just stepped barefoot in a cow pie."

Sam said, "I...uh," and then he had it: Peter was smiling. Not the forced congenial grin he sometimes managed but a huge, sparkling, face-splitting *smile* the likes of which Sam had last seen about eight years ago, on the day Peter's flight instructor handed him his pilot's license. Sam shrugged off his bad feeling—it was great to see his brother happy for a change—but a shred of it remained, like an itch just out of reach.

"You look great," he said as he drew up a chair.

"Feel great," Peter said, his smile widening.

For a clumsy moment Sam was at a loss, and he just sat there, staring. He'd been excited on his way over here from the library, where he'd spent the morning scanning the surprising volume of literature that was available on the out-of-body experience. The more he read, the more convinced he became that Peter had experienced just that. According to the literature, the OBE was generally accepted as the last stage of physical death, a sort of reluctant parting of essence and flesh. In the more legitimate works, large amounts of data had been amassed, individual case reports including statements made by patients who, through medical intervention, had been snatched back from death's very doorstep. What Sam found remarkable about these statements was their almost exact correlation with one another—and with what Peter had told him about his own near-death experience.

As with all things unusual, the OBE had its lunatic fringe, fire-eyed zealots who claimed they could leave their bodies at will, travel great distances at blurring speeds—attached the whole time to their bodies via an incredibly elastic thread—and return intact, refreshed and more intensely alive than the rest of us could even begin to comprehend.

But loony or not, how else could Sam explain it? His brother had been *in* the apartment...and their mother had sensed his presence. After reading about it, Sam had been eager to share with Peter some of the things he'd learned...but that smile. Somehow that smile had taken the edge off his excitement. Maybe he'd just leave the books in his knapsack and forget about the whole crazy thing.

Peter's head came off the pillow, the action as always making Sam think of a man buried to the neck in desert sand.

"Whatcha got in the sack, Jack?"

"I've been doing a little research," Sam said, thinking, not for the first time, that Peter seemed able to read his thoughts. He reached into the knapsack and withdrew the topmost book. "And I think I know what happened to you the other night."

"I do, too," Peter said, still smiling. "And it happened again."

"No shit?"

"No shit, bud." He made a shrill whistling sound through his teeth, jerking his head toward the window as he did. "Last night. And it was un-fucking-real, if you'll pardon my French."

He related in detail the happenings of the night before, beginning with his voyeuristic encounter with Nurse Blane—which made Sam blush and Peter roar with laughter—then moving on to his flight at the rim of dawn. By the time he was done Sam had all but forgotten his earlier inkling of dread.

"And you saw the string?"

"Sure did, Sambo. But it was more like a thread, a fine, glowing blue thread. I even gave it a name: soulstring."

"Yeah," Sam said. "That really says it."

"So what about these books?"

Sam held up the first of them for his brother's inspection. It was a plain black paperback entitled *The Projection of the Astral Body*.

"Well," Sam said, unaware of the terrible Pandora's box he was about to help open, "these guys claim you can learn to do this at will."

19

WILL SLAMMED THE DOOR of his Chevy pickup, hiked his jacket over his head and ran across the parking lot to the gym entrance door. A cold October rain was falling, promising an early winter, and Will was glad he'd put the Buick up on blocks the weekend before. Weather like this was hell on the chrome.

He jerked the door open and slipped inside. The corridor was empty, but he could hear tinny music in the distance, and the echoey shouts of kids. He grinned. He hadn't been in a high school gymnasium in years. He let himself in through a door marked GIRLS' ENTRANCE and took a seat in the stands. Kelly stood with her back to him on the opposite side of the gym, her fanny packed prettily into spandex tights, and Will felt a familiar tug of excitement. God, she looked good.

The music stopped and the ten members of the senior girls' Dance Club stood shaking their arms, breathing hard. They were practicing a jazz routine they were scheduled to perform at the Grand Theatre in early December. They were to be the opening act for the Osmond Family Christmas special, and even now the air of anticipation was palpable.

A new piece started on the deck, which rested on the sill of the gym office window, and the activity picked up again. Will recognized the tune; he'd heard it at least a dozen times over at Kelly's: Herbie Hancock's "Rockit."

"Okay, girls. Let's try the break-dancing sequence."

This was met with squeals of approval, and the students dropped into spinning contortions on the floor. Watching them, Will had to smile. Kelly was always so worried about how she was doing at work, whether the kids liked and respected her, and whether she was having any positive impact on their lives. It was obvious to him that they loved her. They were having fun, and their eyes were bright with admiration for Kelly.

Will didn't know that much about it, but he guessed this first year of teaching must be the toughest. It must be hard to appear confident in front of twenty-five or thirty teenagers, all of them strangers and a goodly proportion of them eager to see just how much they could get away with. "Don't smile until December," Kelly had said to him one night. "That's my motto for the term." Well, Will thought, if these kids were any indication, all her worries were for naught.

But there was more to Kelly's unease about her job than that; Will sensed this with an unerring instinct. This was her old high school, and although she claimed that she'd enjoyed her time as a student here, Will knew she was hiding something. Something big. Something that haunted her even now. Coming back here to teach had opened some old wound...but that was all he could piece together. On some subjects Kelly was pretty close-mouthed, and Will didn't like to push her. If she wanted him to know about her past, she'd tell him in her own good time.

Will glanced at his watch. It was a quarter to five. They had dinner reservations at Marconi's for six o'clock; then they were off to see a stage version of *One Flew Over the Cuckoo's Nest* at the Sudbury Theatre Centre.

It was October 14, Kelly's birthday.

"All right, girls," Kelly shouted, still unaware of Will's presence. "Let's concentrate. Candace, what are you grinning at?"

Kelly turned, following her student's gaze…and then she saw him. She waved and blew him a kiss, and Will felt his face bake with pride. Kelly held up two open hands, mouthed the words "ten minutes," then returned her attention to the girls.

"Okay, gang. One more time and we're out of here." She crossed to the gym office window, rewound the tape to the top of the Hancock tune, and put the kids through their paces again.

* * *

They went to Will's place after the play. He rented the top half of a duplex in the Flour Mill area. As she climbed the steps, it occurred to Kelly this would be the first time she'd ever seen his apartment. She hadn't been avoiding coming over; it just seemed they always ended up at her place. "It's cozier," Will often said. He liked the fireplace and the panoramic view of the lake.

The play had been a riot. Kelly hadn't read Ken Kesey's book, but she'd seen the movie at least a dozen times. Her favorite line was the one McMurphy drawled when they escorted him back to the ward from shock therapy: "The next woman that takes me on's gonna light up like a pinball machine and pay off in silver dollars." In the movie, Jack Nicholson had played R.P. McMurphy, and Peter had had that line down pat. Kelly had waited for it to come up in the play and was disappointed when the actor didn't use it.

She was surprised to find Will's living quarters sober and neat, almost austere, with old but well-kept furniture, gleaming hardwood floors and lots of uncurtained windows hung with plants. There were posters of classic automobiles in plain metal frames, a sturdy rack of bookshelves stocked mostly with adventure novels and westerns, and in the spare bedroom, a bench and a set of weights. The mirror in

Will's bedroom, like the one in Kelly's own room, was crammed along its edges with favorite photographs. Will was the fourth in a family of eight, five boys and three girls, and he kept cherished snapshots of each of them.

While Will fixed drinks, Kelly browsed through his collection of albums, all neatly sleeved in plastic and arranged in alphabetical order. Of all the differences between them, Will's taste in music brought the disparity in their ages—Will was thirty-four, Kelly twenty-four—most sharply into focus. Hendrix, Cream, Led Zeppelin, Springsteen, all of it reeking of the late sixties and early seventies.

"Are you an acid head, Will Chatam?" Kelly said as he handed her a gin fizz.

Will plunked onto the couch with a can of beer and loosened his tie. He'd dressed to the nines for the occasion, and although he looked dapper, Kelly thought he looked a little awkward, too. He was more at home in jeans and checked flannel work shirts.

"Yup," he said, taking a slug of brew. "Just dropped a hundred mics of the world's finest. Should be seein' colours any minute now."

He smiled and Kelly felt light-headed. When Will smiled at her like that, not the shy little grin he sometimes gave her but this wide beaming smile, Kelly felt her heart do a funky little flip-flop in her chest. Their eyes held for what seemed like a long time, passing a knowledge between them that Will understood, but which to Kelly was still an unsettling mystery. Then Will got up and selected an album.

They didn't sleep together that night either.

But it was close.

20

UNTIL DEEP IN NOVEMBER, a month marked by unseasonably cold weather, Peter spent his days reading the books Sam had brought him and his nights trying to leave his body. For the first long while his desire mixed destructively with his growing frustration, until it seemed he would never feel that freedom again.

Then, one late night, triggered again by the nightmare, it happened. It had been snowing that night, nasty dry pellets that fell almost horizontally, borne along by a snarling north wind. Through what he assumed was a process of association, Peter found himself back in his mother's apartment—but this time he didn't hang around. One glance at her snoring carcass stirred that old and deathless rage in him, and he got out of there before it could destroy his ride.

That night had been a rip, slicing like a swallow through the air, slaloming between power poles and stitching spirals around the smokestacks, buzzing the near-frozen surface of the lake like a startled pintail. Cranking up to hyperdrive in that psychedelic corridor of light, the landscape below reduced to a ravaged blur, slowing above cities with no names only to return at the same breakneck pace.

The books suggested that separation was most easily accomplished from a state of light trance, and for hours each day Peter strove to achieve this state, attempting to shut down the headlong race of his mind. This proved to be no mean feat. But gradually he developed a knack, and by the end of that six-week stretch he was batting over five hundred.

With his increasing ability to leave his body came an equally growing intolerance for the hospital and its tiresome routines—and in this arena, Dr. Lowe irked him most. Despite Peter's initially polite requests that he be left out of the doctor's teaching rounds, Lowe flat out ignored him, until finally Peter was forced into one of his towering rages, sedated—which effectively canceled his ability to leave his body—assessed again by a psychiatrist, and beaten once more into submission. In no other situation in Peter's life was this admixture of need—Lowe was the only physician in the area with so great a knowledge of the special needs of the quadriplegic—and resentment so potent. It made him wish there were something, *anything*, he could do to strike back.

Quite by accident, the opportunity—or perhaps more correctly, the ammunition—presented itself one snow-blown evening in November. He and Sam had been yakking about Peter's newfound ability, and Sam suggested that he try it with Sam in the room, to find out if Sam could sense or perhaps even see Peter's astral form, as their mother apparently had. Keen to experiment, Peter had psyched himself into a trance and escaped his broken body, that Scotch tape sensation of separation exciting him to a level that bordered on sexual. He'd woven tight loops around Sam, who sat by the bedside staring intently at Peter's face, waved his insubstantial arms and made a shimmering lasso of his soulstring. But Sam had sensed none of it.

Unwilling to waste the experience, Peter had slipped through the window and commenced an exhilarating glide down the face of the building, his intention being to skim away from the wall at a point just inches above the snow-crusted ground and then carve a tight loop back through his window.

But something he spotted through a sixth-story window stalled him in mid-trajectory. He eased in through that window, settled atop a file-cluttered cabinet and watched his nemesis, Dr. Lowe.

* * *

"Sonofabitch," Lowe muttered savagely. Hunched over his desk in the muted light of his office, the perspiring physician fumbled a key ring, trying to seat a stubby brass key into the slot of a locked desk drawer. The keys fell to the tiles with a cheerful little jangle, and Lowe rapped his forehead on the desk lunging forward to retrieve them.

In his brother's room, Sam cocked his head quizzically as Peter's mouth widened in a smirk.

Keys in hand, Lowe tried again, this time succeeding. After angling the desk lamp to illuminate the open belly of the drawer, he rummaged near the back for a moment and came up clutching a black leather pouch. He unzipped it and withdrew a small glass vial, half filled with liquid. His pupils were huge, his lips dry as he smacked them, and sweat stood out on his balding pate in coalescing gems. From a separate pocket in the pouch he took a sterile syringe, an alcohol swab, a rubber tourniquet—

Then Peter was back in his body, just like that, the transition too fast to be noticed.

"Peter," Sam was shouting. "Peter, wake up."

"Whoa," Peter said, surprised by a lancet of anger at his brother's intrusion. "What's up?"

"Sorry," Sam said, removing his hands from Peter's shoulders. "You just had this…freaky grin on your face and I guess I got scared."

"No problem," Peter said, his anger abating. "Did you see, feel, or smell me?"

"No," Sam said, slouching down in his chair. Peter was grinning again. "Nothing at all."

21

TO SOME OF THE staff who knew Peter Gardner and from time to time came in contact with him, his recent grinning cheerfulness seemed a sign that an important corner had finally been turned: he'd at long last come to terms with his lot in life, had realized how futile were his depressions and fits of anger, and had seen, perhaps with the force of revelation, how rewarding his life still could be. To others, Peter's emotional about-face was the tip of a much darker iceberg, a harbinger of impending mental collapse.

In the opinion of the nurse who sponge-bathed him now, on this frosty, late November evening, the latter seemed by far the more likely. His buoyant good cheer—and that *smile*—struck her as decidedly odd, considering the state he was in and would remain in for the balance of his vegetative life. When he asked her to reach into the cupboard of his nightstand and take out the bottle of cologne, this opinion was solidly confirmed.

"It's near the back, I think. Old Spice."

The nurse, whose name was Jannet Wade and whose ambition it was to transfer to the neonatal intensive care nursery just as soon as a spot became available, rooted through a hodgepodge of dusty mementos until her hand closed around a half-full bottle of cologne.

Seeing it there, held aloft in the prim nurse's hand, induced a dark undertow of memory in Peter that threatened to drag him under, and he came close to telling her to put it away again. Old Spice had been Kelly's favorite—in his mind he could feel her splashing it on him and then nuzzling that perky little nose of hers into his neck, could hear her cooing, "Mmm, that's nice. Wanna get lucky, sailor?"—and she had given him this bottle. "No reason," she'd said when he asked her why she'd bought him a gift with Christmas still months away and his birthday long past. "I just like the stink of it." It was the only thing he had left that Kelly had given him—

"What should I do with this?"

"What?" Peter said, jerked back to the present.

"I said, what should I do with this?"

He smiled. "Would you mind splashing some on me?"

The nurse's hazel eyes flickered to their corners and back again, checking the door, and Peter realized that even after all this time the "dangerous pervert" alert was still out on him, God damn that farting bitch Shawna Blane.

"I promise I won't bite," Peter said. "Or spit, or try to get you to stroke the old trouser snake." He grinned. "Okay?"

Jannet returned his grin, but it was forced. Flustered, she uncorked the bottle—

And suddenly that undertow of memory recurred, its intensity trebled by that sweet, unmistakable odour. Peter's grin flipped over in sadness, tears welling as the nurse splashed a tiny puddle of Old Spice into her palm.

"Where?" she said, her discomfort heightened by the turn in Peter's mood.

"My neck," Peter said, fighting tears with the full force of his will.

He closed his eyes as her warm hand brushed his skin, ashamed at the thrill her touch gave him, overwhelmed by the bright weight of memory. Choked with emotion, he asked her to leave. He did not open his eyes.

"Do you want the light left on?" Jannet said after replacing the cologne in the nightstand.

Peter shook his head.

She left him in darkness, her heels tapping out a receding tattoo in the twilight.

* * *

Tonight, Kelly thought as she clutched dress after dress to her body and judged her reflection in the mirror. If Will will, *I* will. The man was nice, as Marti had promised…but, brother, was he *slow*. It had been two months since their heart-to-heart talk on the island, two months of gradually upping their dating frequency from two nights a week to four, two months of necking and heavy petting and a growing, unfulfilled ache in her loins. Still, until recently, she couldn't have said with any real certainty that she was a hundred percent ready to do it. The part of her that hadn't felt a man's touch—several parts, really, and Kelly chuckled evilly at this thought—in over a year was way beyond ready, had been for months. But another part, a quiet, hurt, introspective part, was glad of Will Chatam's down-south slowness. She knew he wanted her—the tender urgency of his kisses told her that—but he made her feel as if *she* were the important thing, not what he could get from her. His sweetness was almost unreal.

Now, though, she felt that even the mousy, frightened part of her was ready.

Boy, am I ready.

She shooed Fang off the bed—the cat just loved to get crazy in all of those groovy dry-cleaning bags—flung a matronly looking tweed-thing onto the heap, and plucked up her last-chance-for-romance outfit, a years-old cotton one-piece, maroon, cut too low in the front and slashed tartily up the thigh. She held it to her naked torso, did a half-pirouette before the mirror...

And was swamped by her own backswell of memory.

Peter had bought her this dress for her birthday... seven years ago.

Clad only in panties, Kelly pulled the dress on, disturbed by how the brush of the fabric across her nipples excited her. She was big-bosomed, hardly an attribute for a gym teacher, and Peter had always been after her to "cut 'em loose." She'd modeled the dress for him like this, with no bra, and the lovemaking that night had been—

Kelly stomped the thought dead. She unzipped the dress and let it puddle at her feet, vowing that in the morning she'd stuff it into the Neighbourhood Services bag she kept on the back porch, stuff it down deep, where all these memories should be... Then she picked it up, smoothed it out—and decided to wear it. With no bra. And if *that* didn't put lead in Will Chatam's pencil, then she would by God enter a convent.

Kelly slipped out of her panties and hurried into the shower.

* * *

He was in a light trance, a state he achieved more easily each time he tried. All he had to do was shut out any background noise—both actual and the sometimes hectoring whine of his thoughts—picture a blank white screen... and drift.

He drifted.

But the reason he was trying to leave his body tonight kept stealing into his mind and giving it weight, killing its buoyancy. Earlier that afternoon one of the candy stripers had come into his room with the library cart, and although Peter had been in no mood for company, he'd allowed her to hold up some old copies of *Northern Life* for him to scan. In one of them, a yellowed issue from last June, he'd come across a squib in the local news section that had knocked him for a loop. It was a bulletin from his old high school, announcing the appointment of a new teacher, a hometown girl and a graduate of that very institution. There was an accompanying photograph, a grainy black-and-white culled from the Queen's University yearbook, and Peter had two thoughts almost simultaneously before asking the candy striper to leave.

Oh, Jesus, she's back.

And: *She hasn't changed a bit... not a bit...*

The last time Peter had heard any news of Kelly was maybe four years ago, when he bumped into her mom in the gift shop downstairs. Mrs. Wheeler was in a wheelchair then, too, with both feet in casts, recovering from bunion surgery. And she'd seemed only too willing to fill Peter in on Kelly's progress.

"Oh, she's doing famously down there in Kingston," Irene told him amicably enough...but Peter had sensed her unease. "We're so proud of her."

"What are her plans for after graduation?" Peter had asked, partly out of curiosity, but mostly just for something to say. In those days he'd still had a pretty big mad-on for Kelly.

"She intends to stay in the south," Irene said immediately, almost defensively, Peter thought. "She's very determined about that. She's going to find a good school and teach down there."

But Peter had never believed it.

Blank, he commanded himself now, repeating the word like a mantra.

Blank... blank... blank...

* * *

The hot water was heavenly, skilled fingers working the wire-drawn muscles of her body. First the back of her neck, where tension had tied crazy-knots, then the base of her skull, that creaky, ringlike joint that bore the weight of her worldly concerns. The smooth cliff face of her back came next, down that bony range of peaks to the twin round swells of her buttocks. Turning now, inching closer to the steamy spray, letting it riddle her face like a million Cupid's darts.

Eyes closed, Kelly plucked the soap from the dish and, turning, ran the bar over the dome of one shoulder. Her thoughts were a sleepy jumble, and she knew that if she were lying down right now she'd fall fast asleep. She focused on nothing, but was aware of a hundred dangling thoughts, like threads in a waiting loom. When the whiff of cologne struck her nostrils, she at first dismissed it, writing it off as a fragment of memory wafting up from a chamber in her mind where the lid had worked itself loose. It was Old Spice, her favorite, the brand she'd bought for—

Then a sound jerked her back to full alertness—a creak of floorboards? a footfall?—stealthy and close, and that scent of cologne was still in the air.

There's someone in the house.

Every fear Kelly had ever had about living alone fell on her now in an avalanche of grisly images—rape, murder, buggery, butcher knives, good old Normy Bates—and she parted the shower curtains and stepped out, flung a towel around her body and began searching in the fog for a weapon.

Soap-on-a-rope, club him with that. Spear him with the curling iron. Squirt hair spray in his eyes and run like hell.

Then Fang pushed his way into the bathroom, bushy tail up, green eyes lidded with contentment.

"You little shit," Kelly said, making the cat cringe. "You scared the crap out of me."

What about that cologne?

Nudging the cat out of the way, Kelly clasped the Wella Balsam hair spray in one hand, her heated curling iron in the other, and swung the door open with her knee.

* * *

Aloft above her on the steamy air, Peter looked on with a mixture of amusement and forgotten arousal. Seeing Kelly's naked body— trim and more lithe than he remembered it, slick and shiny-wet in the rattling pulse of her shower massage—made him realize what a pitiful boor he'd been reduced to. Fantasizing about self-involved scrags like Shawna Blane or any one of a hundred other bimbos that had come his way, passing themselves off as nurses; lusting after their slightest touch, sneaking into the toilet to catch a glimpse of naked flesh. The depth of the bond he and Kelly had shared, the coal-furnace heat of their union— that was what he needed. That was what he wanted back again.

She'd been easy enough to find—one call to directory assistance on his voice-operated phone had done it. The listing was a new one, and Peter's polite inquiry regarding her address had been courteously indulged. "Is that the Wheeler on Gloucester?" he'd asked. "No, sir," the operator said. "We're not supposed to give out that information… but this listing is for Lake Point Drive."

There were only about a dozen scattered dwellings along Lake Point Drive. Kelly's had been the third one he checked.

There was no one else in the house, no masked bandit or drooling rapist, and he wished he could tell her that. Truth was, she'd just have to find out for herself.

* * *

Cold and still dripping, Kelly returned to the bathroom. Fang had set up shop on the back of the toilet, and his look as Kelly strode shivering into the room like some freaked out graffiti artist, spray can in one hand and cattle prod in the other, seemed to Kelly a trifle sardonic. She'd been through the entire house, all three stories of it, right down to the unheated cement-floored basement, and had encountered nothing more sinister than a scuttling spider. In an uncharacteristic display of violence, she killed it. With the hair spray. Let it rain.

Shedding the towel, Kelly hurried back into the shower—the place was serviced by a quirky well and an even quirkier water heater—blaming her overwrought nerves and mulishly persistent memory for calling up that phantom whiff of Old Spice. As she shampooed her hair, heaping its shoulder-length thickness into whorls on the crown of her head, she decided that maybe she shouldn't wear that maroon dress after all. Enough memory-stirring for one night, thank you kindly. Altogether too much.

A sensation like a kiss touched Kelly Wheeler on the nape of the neck, high up, in the downy hair that grew there, and she screamed—a high, throat-slashing scream that sent the cat vaulting off the toilet lid and made her eyeballs throb as if molten. She thrust her back against the tiles and raked insanely at her neck, a child with a bat snagged in its hair. Blood from a period that was five days early coursed down her legs in thin crimson rivers, blood mixed with water that had suddenly gone cold.

When her screams died away, Kelly scrambled out of the tub, threw the door shut, and locked it.

She could still feel those lips on her neck.

* * *

Jerked out of his trance to the drab white walls of his hospital room, Peter Gardner discovered that the hollows of his eyes were flooded with tears. Sick with remorse, he turned his head to one side and let the salty pools leak out.

He hadn't meant to frighten her, God, no. He'd meant only to...

What?

The truth was he hadn't meant to do anything but look at her, just see her again. The urge to kiss her had simply come, and he'd acted on it without thinking.

But, Jesus, she felt me...

Yes. She had.

And what did that mean?

But the answer was obvious. It meant he wasn't merely a phantom, a flying consciousness that could in no way affect its surroundings. He was something more than that.

Perhaps much more.

Peter looked up at the ceiling with dry eyes, his remorse receding into a sense of awe that was bright, arresting... and faintly sinister.

* * *

"Hi, Will?"

"Kelly?"

"Yeah."

"Hi. I was just about to jump in the shower." He paused. "Are you all right? You sound kind of flaky."

"Yeah, you're right. I've got my period, and it's hitting me pretty hard." She sniffed. "Would you mind if we put things off for tonight?"

"Not at all," Will said, but his voice was flat with disappointment. "Is there anything I can do? Anything you need?"

"No, thanks. I just need to lie down. I'll be fine by tomorrow."

"Are you sure that's all it is? Your period, I mean?"

"Yes, Doctor." She hated to lie to him, but what was the truth here? That she was losing her mind? "That's all it is."

"Okay, babe. When will I see you?"

"How about tomorrow?"

"Sorry, I'll be doing my hair." He sounded relieved. "I'll be there with bells on."

Will, I'm scared. "'Bye for now."

"Take care."

She waited until he hung up, then softly cradled the receiver.

22

THE NEXT DAY, THURSDAY, was a light one for Kelly. Her morning roster was full, but her only obligation for the afternoon was a
grade eleven health-ed class at one o'clock. So far this term she'd spent
the free time marking papers or supervising members of the gymnastics team who had study periods. But today she slipped quietly out of
the building, leaving her BACK TOMORROW sign in the gym office
window. She wanted to get over to the university before classes let out
for the day.

She made the crosstown drive in ten minutes, thankful that a
speed cop hadn't been waiting at the end of the long, ice-patched
straightaway before the university turnoff. The day was brisk, the sun
a cold white spot bright enough to make her eyes water, and Kelly
nagged herself for having left her sunglasses at home. The backs of
her eyes had taken up a dull ache, and it was spreading to the rest of
her head.

In the parking lot outside the biology building, Kelly leaned
against her red Subaru, examining each face in turn as groups of win-
ter-clad students filed out. Although Sudbury was a relatively small
city, she hadn't seen Sam Gardner in at least four years. The last time
had been in the Regent Street Mr. Grocer. Sam had been strolling

down the frozen-foods aisle one way, Kelly the other. When he spotted her, he'd glowered angrily, pulled a rattling 180 with his cart, and stormed off in the opposite direction. Stung and bewildered, Kelly had only stood there, sobbing back tears. She'd always liked Sam, the admiring little brother, and in a girlish way had been flattered by his obvious crush. His reaction that day still baffled her—and it doubled her apprehension at approaching him now.

She almost missed him. She saw him all right—her view of the exit was unobstructed—but at first she failed to recognize him. Six feet tall, trim and swift-moving, his broad shoulders and long legs hinting through his winter fatigues at a well-toned body, the young man who breezed out alone through those big orange doors bore little resemblance to the scrawny, pimple-faced kid Kelly remembered. Gone were the bottle-thick glasses that had made his eyes look like single-celled sea creatures viewed through a microscope, replaced, Kelly assumed, by contacts. His once rampaging acne had retreated into a hale, ruddy complexion, and Kelly thought he looked more like a woodsman than an aspiring physician. He moved with the cool self-assurance of one whose life, though fast-paced, was focused and well ordered.

Kelly would soon learn differently.

"Sam?" she called. "Sam, over here."

Sam braked abruptly as he wound his way through the milling students, and when he turned his expression was blank. Kelly knew then that his life was not so full as it might at first have appeared, for that blank look was one of total surprise. A girl hadn't called after him like that in years—or perhaps ever.

Kelly's throat grew parched. She'd come out here to ask Sam a question, one born of her terror of the night before, and as he approached her across the ice-patched tarmac, that question reared up again.

Is Peter dead?

Some years ago Kelly's mother had told her of an incident, the truth of which Kelly had always secretly doubted. Not that she felt her mother had lied—Irene Wheeler, who pounced like a lioness on even the most innocent of fibs, truly believed the incident had occurred. It was the improbability of the event that made Kelly doubt her mother's perceptions, and in the end she'd chalked it up to a coincidental dream her mother must have had and then later confused with reality.

"Gramma's died," Irene had said as she hung up the phone that early spring morning, her eyes as dewy as the grass outside. "I knew it before I picked up the phone."

Kelly hugged her close, knowing how deeply Irene cared for her mother. "How did you know?" she said, her own eyes brimming now.

"She came to me last night," Irene said. "While I slept. Touched my foot and said good-bye." A fit of weeping had beset her then, and that was the last time the incident was mentioned. Kelly hadn't believed it then...but she thought she might now.

Sam stopped several feet shy of her and began shifting from foot to foot, as if preparing to bolt. A dozen emotions seemed at war in his eyes: mistrust and remorse, bashfulness and a terrible caged anger, delight at seeing an old friend and a callous self-reproach for feeling it.

Sensing her reading him, Sam looked away. Vapour jetted from his nostrils. He said, "What do you want?"

Kelly felt ridiculous. Surely if Peter had died Sam would have said so by now. She'd spooked herself in the shower, that was all. She'd been overtired, nervous, and, God help her, still a little uncertain about her decision to sleep with Will, and her imagination had run off on her. And on the basis of that she was standing out here in a cold November wind, mute as a Trappist monk, face to face with a living fragment of a past she'd vowed never to acknowledge again.

Still, to dismiss what had happened the night before—and the ensuing, almost blind compulsion to find out if her intuition was un-erring—meant ignoring every instinct she possessed.

"Can we talk?" she said, giving a nervous snort of laughter at the absurdity of the phrase.

The corners of Sam's mouth curled into a grudging half-smile, and for a second it looked so much like Peter's lazy, lopsided grin Kelly wanted to fling herself into his arms. The truth of what that urge meant seeped through her like a slow poison, withering six years' worth of carefully constructed lies, and for an instant she glimpsed that old and dread darkness again.

"Sure," Sam said, stepping closer but still not meeting her gaze. "What about?"

"Where were you headed?"

"The Sandwich King. On Paris Street."

"Come on," Kelly said, opening her car door and sliding in. "I'll give you a lift."

With a nod, Sam strode around to the passenger side and un-latched the door. He tramped the snow off his boots, tossed his knap-sack in ahead of him and climbed inside.

They drove mostly in silence, Kelly giving up early on the small talk, Sam suspending judgment until he'd heard what Kelly had to say. When they pulled up in front of the Sandwich King, a cheerful little restaurant bookended by a beauty salon and a Laundromat, Kelly had still not asked her question. She decided to soften it.

"How's Peter?" she said, doing her best to sound casual.

Sam retrieved his knapsack from the mat between his feet and, preparatory to getting out, cradled it in his lap.

"What do you care?"

"I care," Kelly said, feeling slapped, guilty, alien. "I just, I wanted to…" A fugitive tear appeared and she cuffed it away.

"If you cared," Sam said, his fingers scrabbling now at the door panel in search of the recessed latch, "you'd *visit* him. You dumped him, Kelly, just like all the rest. You—where's the damned handle?"

Then he found it and kneed the door open, ducking his head to storm out—but the door came sweeping back at him, cracking his knuckles and hammering his knee. Cursing, he shoved the door open again—and Kelly had him by the coat sleeve.

"Wait, Sam. I never dumped your brother. I loved him."

"Yeah," Sam said, his voice husky with emotion. "Some great way you've got of showing it."

Then Kelly understood. "Is he all right?"

"No, he's not all right," Sam said, turning with blazing eyes to face her. "He's paralyzed from the neck down. Or had you forgotten?"

Not dead, Kelly's mind sighed. *Thank God he's not dead.*

"What did he tell you?" Kelly said, her fear giving way to pity for this hurt, angry young man.

"The truth," Sam shouted in the closeness of the idling car. "His great true love. You walked out on him without so much as a fuck you or a fare-thee-well. 'Sorry, pal. If I need some vegetables, I'll get 'em at the supermarket.'"

"That's a lie, Sam. A dirty, malicious lie."

Sam groped again for the door latch. "I'm late for work."

"No," Kelly said, the quiet force of the word freezing Sam as effectively as a gun muzzle pressed to his temple.

Then she told him the truth, the real truth, each word a razor-slash in the meat of her heart.

* * *

"And I never went back," Kelly said, more of her seemingly endless reserve of tears tracking her cheeks. Beside her, Sam sat staring at the floor mat, his jaw rippling rhythmically. "I came close. Got as far as the door maybe a dozen different times. But there was no way I could face those empty eyes again." She dug in her pocket for a hankie.

"He told me you dropped him," Sam said, uttering his first words since Kelly had begun her story. "He said you came in that day and told him you'd found someone else. Someone...whole." Sam looked up at her, his own well of tears long since dried up. "I hated you for that, Kelly. Hated you and those three football fucking jerk-offs he called his friends. I hated you bad."

"I don't blame you, Sam. I hated myself for not trying harder. Maybe I should have gone back...but I could see it was killing him. I could feel him drying up inside."

She reached over and touched Sam's hand, wanting to comfort him, needing it herself.

Sam withdrew his hand. "Why did he lie to me?"

"Because he didn't want to lose you," was all Kelly could think of to say.

"I gotta go," Sam said, and opened the door again, more gently this time. He started to get out, then turned back to Kelly. "Why now?" he said. "Why after all this time did you come looking for me now?"

Kelly considered not telling him—he'd probably think she was nuts—but he deserved the truth. "I was alone last night at home," she said, "taking a shower, and I thought I could smell...Old Spice. It was the brand I used to buy for him." She tugged self-consciously at her hair. "It gave me a fright. I thought someone had broken in...but then I felt"—Kelly shuddered—"a kiss, right here, on the back of my neck. It's—"

Pretty nuts, she intended to say. *Just my imagination.*

But something flashed across Sam's face. Not doubt's shadow, not even surprise. Something else. Some internal circuit had snicked shut with her words, and as crazy as it seemed Kelly felt certain Sam knew something about what she was saying.

"Sam?"

"I gotta go," Sam said, and climbed out of the car.

* * *

It took a long time that busy day to sort it all through in his mind, but in the end Sam thought he understood. Kelly was right: Peter had lied to him because, once Kelly was gone, Sam was all he had left. Peter's fear of abandonment had blinded him to Sam's devotion, and the deceit was intended to kindle Sam's pity. It hurt him that Peter had believed such a deception necessary. But he thought he understood. He hadn't told Kelly about Peter's new... what? Power? Yes, that was what it was. What Peter had acquired was a kind of power, a triumph over impossible odds. To Sam it proved yet again what an extraordinary person his brother was. Fate had brought down its cleated fist and flattened him, and after six desolate years Peter had found a way out. What Kelly would undoubtedly attribute to an overactive imagination had in all probability been an actual visit from Peter, from his mind.

His soul.

In a moment of faceless dread, Sam considered confronting his brother on this, getting it out in the open before something really freaky happened... but Kelly was as taboo a topic as their mother.

And what had he felt when he turned to the sound of his name and saw Kelly Wheeler standing in the parking lot? How could he explain the rush of excitement that had coursed through him with an almost sexual intensity? Wasn't he just a little afraid that if he talked to his brother about this, Peter would look into his eyes and know what Sam had felt?

"One order of chicken fingers," a waitress hollered, shattering his dark contemplations. "One burger, no onions, two orders of fries."

"Got it," Sam mumbled, and slung the chicken strips into the fryer, wincing at the spit of old grease.

23

PARTWAY THROUGH DIALING WILL'S number, Kelly hung up the phone. It had been her intention to call him and cancel their date for tonight. That would make two times in a row, but after today, holding hands and munching popcorn at the Cineplex seemed like the last thing she wanted to do...

Still, it beat moping around the house. Her conversation with Sam had breached a hive of restless ghosts, and with the north wind bulldozing its way across the lake and sleet machine-gunning the windows, she didn't think she could stand another night alone in this house.

Opting for a bath instead of a shower, Kelly settled into the bubble-heaped water with a glass of wine, Kenny Loggins crooning soothingly in the background. The heat, teamed with her intolerance for alcohol, soon had her feeling heady and loose, and by the time she climbed out of the tub she was giddy. After gliding into a mink-coloured teddy, she tossed a match onto the kindling that was already stacked in the fireplace and added a few birch logs. She had an hour and a half before Will's scheduled arrival, and planned to spend it unwinding. She settled into a mound of throw pillows on the rug in front of the fireplace, gazed into the sprite dance of flames... and dozed.

The Big Ben chime of the doorbell brought her back. She stood, glanced down the hallway and saw Will peeking in through the sidelight. When he spotted her, still in her teddy, he looked away.

"Oh, shit." She grabbed her robe off the couch, threw it around her shoulders—and made a decision.

She tossed the robe back on the couch. Then she went to the door and invited Will in.

* * *

"Dressed kind of light for the movies," Will said, his embarrassed attempt at nonchalance endearing.

"I could go get dressed," Kelly said, ignoring the clangor of alarms in her heart: *This isn't your style, kiddo.* "But there's a nice fire burning," she said, helping him off with his coat, "and a freshly opened bottle of wine that'll just go to waste…"

Will just shuffled his feet and grinned.

Kelly led him down the hallway to the living room, aware that a generous chunk of her fanny was showing but no longer caring, and sat him on the floor by the fire. The lights were already low as she decanted the wine, and she prayed Will couldn't read the uncertainty in her eyes. She felt desperate and alone, and wished for nothing more than a sweet outcome to the evening, a rescue for her ravaged heart. Maybe Will would be her ideal lover.

There was only one way to find out.

"He's nice, Kelly," she could hear Marti saying. "He'll be steady, wait and see."

She sat beside him and snuggled. "Be good to me, Will," she murmured. "Please…"

Will set his wineglass aside. "I will," he said, and embraced her.

His kisses were gentle, probing, unhurried. He smelled clean, a faint scent of soap on his skin. His touch aroused her, but she was tense, clutching him, her yearning more intricate than mere physical desire. She wanted his touch to erase her memory, to confront that part of her which insisted on pretending it was Peter's touch she was feeling and not someone else's. Not Will Chatam's. She wanted him to make himself real.

"Be good to me," she urged in breathy whispers.

And soon Will was fumbling for his belt, his own arousal cranked to a fever pitch by the unexpected depth of Kelly's need. Teeth clenched, she helped him skin off his jeans, her breath singing loudly in her nostrils. She felt hot, but it was not a good heat. It was the heat of a dog day afternoon, of sudden illness, of flesh held cruelly over fire. He dragged his V-neck over his head, and for a heartbeat Kelly wanted to cry out. Who was it behind that sweater, she wondered in that brief, faceless moment, his penis thrusting angrily against his briefs, sweat standing out on his belly?

Then her hand was inside his briefs, stroking him, kneading him. "Oh, Kelly," she heard him breathe. "Oh, babe." His hands were under her teddy now, finding her breasts. She could feel his heart, pounding the cage of his chest like a small, fierce animal trapped in a hollow wall.

With gentle strength, Will pressed her back into the pillows. He unfastened the crotch of her teddy and touched her, gently, knowingly, then lay down beside her, pressing warm kisses to her lips and neck while his fingers described small, delicious circles down there, the pleasure of it gradually unhinging her mind, until she wanted this man inside her, Will, Will Chatam, *oh, please...*

It hurt when he entered her—it had been a long time—but the discomfort turned quickly to pleasure as Will moved smoothly and rhythmically above her.

"Will," she whispered in the crackling glow of the fire. "Look at me. Open your eyes."

And they made love that way, face to face, their eyes open and almost unblinking, bathing in each other's gaze.

* * *

"Do you want me to go home tonight?"

They were still by the fireplace, still naked. The blaze had flamed down to a scatter of blushing coals.

"No," Kelly said, a trace of her earlier desperation creeping into her voice. She took his hand and met his eyes. "Will, I'm sorry."

"For what?"

"For what happened here tonight."

"Really?" Offended.

"That's not what I meant. I meant for the way I was. I don't usually come on like that. I'm not that … aggressive."

"Who is he?" Will said.

"Who is who?" Kelly said, knowing what he meant but unprepared for his perceptiveness.

"You know who," Will said with compassion. "The guy who's got you by the heart."

Tell him. Get it out. Marti's voice. The voice of her own heart.

She did.

* * *

"I know it's been six years," Kelly said. "And until I got back to Sudbury, to my old school, I thought I had it all in perspective."

She'd told him the whole sad story, right from the outset, omitting nothing. The more she talked, the more she realized the importance of leveling with Will. He needed to know the truth.

"Does that mean you still love him?"

"That's what's got me puzzled. I mean, I guess I'll always love him, his memory. We were very close." She chuckled nostalgically. "We were virgins together. Do you understand?" Will nodded. "But I don't believe I love him in the sense that you mean. I understand that it's over between us, that my future doesn't include him. And yet... it's weird. Driving through town or walking through the halls at school, I get these flashbacks, these incredible emotional flashbacks, and time loses its meaning... I'm not twenty-four anymore, I'm not a member of the staff, I'm seventeen, and I expect to see Peter come waltzing around the corner to meet me."

Tears shone in her eyes, and Will wrapped an arm around her. Grateful, Kelly snuggled closer.

"I want it to be over, Will. I want him out of my heart. And most times he is. But, Jesus, sometimes the memories sneak up on me"— she shuddered, thinking of her experience in the shower the night before—"and I can't control them. That's why I'm so glad you've been patient with me." She caressed Will's face. "You're a wonderful friend, Will, and I care for you very much. I know you like me, and I know it must be hard to sit here and listen to me go on about another fella... but I'm glad you're letting me."

"Hey," Will said, returning her embrace. "I've got a pretty thick hide. I can tackle just about anything, as long as I know what it is. I appreciate your honesty, and I understand. When you care that deeply—and what's the point of caring if you don't go all the way?—it's a hundred times harder to go on when a disaster like this comes along and takes it all away." He kissed her. "I understand, babe, and if you let me, I'll help you. We can get through this together."

"Thanks, Will," Kelly said, feeling aroused again. "I care for you so much. And I'd really like you to stay with me tonight."

"I'll stay. And if it's any consolation, I think I'm in love with you."

Smiling, Kelly stood. She had no response for that right now, and none seemed expected. "Give it time," was all she could say.

"That's one thing I've got plenty of," Will said. He closed the fireplace doors and then stood.

Kelly led him upstairs to her bedroom.

Where they made love again.

* * *

The lovemaking was fine, so fine that at two o'clock Kelly was still wide awake. There was a smile plastered on her face, and her whole body thrummed with forgotten excitement. Beside her, lying on his side, Will slept soundly, his well-muscled shoulders rising and falling in the beat of his dreams. She reached out to touch him, to waken him and tell him that she loved him, too, to thank him for reminding her of how easy loving should be... but she withdrew her hand. It was two in the morning and she had a gymnastics practice at seven. There'd be time enough tomorrow—and the next day and the day after that—to tell him how she felt about him, to show him. She'd realized her feelings as they lay drowsing together after the second time. It had come to her all of a sudden, the way a forgotten name will sometimes leap to mind, as if an obstructing blanket had been whipped away. And there was nothing complex about it. It was a story as old as time. Will Chatam had stolen her heart... and she was glad. She was long overdue for a little happiness.

Lying beside him now, feeling his warmth and secure in his love, Kelly's past seemed more dreamlike than real. Will's gentle caring had obscured it, cast it in a welcome haze. For the first time in years she felt excited, alive...

But it was time to get some sleep.

Kelly climbed out of bed, freezing when Will stirred in reaction, then felt her way to the upstairs bathroom. On the top shelf of the medicine cabinet she found a dusty bottle of muscle relaxants a doctor had prescribed for her two years ago for a stitch she'd developed in her back. She'd taken only a few of them because they'd made her too dozy to function.

That was what she wanted now, something that would knock her flat, at least until the alarm went off; otherwise she'd be a wreck all day tomorrow, and Friday was her busiest day. She popped one of the tiny yellow pills, sent it highballing down with a gulp of cold water, then padded back into her room. Resisting the temptation to waken him, she snuggled in next to Will.

And drifted peacefully into slumber.

* * *

One of the really great things about leaving his body, Peter had discovered, was that he never seemed to need any sleep. While he was out of it, his body got all the rest it needed. The only time he suffered was when he ignored the signals his body sent him. If he strayed too far or for too long—as he had on his first real flight, when he'd played bucking bronco with the fighter jet—his soulstring would fray or a jabbing pain would develop in the front of his head. These, he'd come to realize, were warnings that it was time to turn back to his body. If he ignored these signals it would sometimes take days to achieve separation again. On one notable occasion—he'd decided to arrow straight up into the heavens and keep going until something radical happened—he ignored an ax-blow pain in his head and found himself suddenly dissipating, wafting apart like a thin puff of smoke. His return that time had been terrifying, a twisting, scattering free-fall for what seemed like hours, and the suffocating fear that he was lost, that he would never get back to his body. He'd realized then how badly he needed his physical self. No matter how decrepit, it was his way station, the place he went for refueling. Without it...well, he hated to think. When he finally found his way back that day, he opened his eyes to see Dr. Lowe and a nurse hovering over him. The nurse, he was told later, had called Lowe in to pronounce him dead.

It had taken him a while tonight to get free. He'd wanted to go back and see Kelly, watch her move, watch her sleep, but something in the wanting had thwarted him. He'd had to totally erase his thoughts before he could even begin to slip free. Before, his greatest fear had been of dying; now it was of never being able to escape his body again. Each time he tried, that fear lay on him like a stone.

He approached Kelly's place from the lake, riding the brisk north wind. November snow lay on the roof and surrounding fir trees in cheerful white heaps, which in the moonlight were luminescent. Her bedroom window faced east, and as he banked toward it, Peter saw a truck parked next to Kelly's red Subaru.

A cold suspicion stalled him in mid-flight, and for a moment Peter feared that jagged emotion might send him hurtling back to his body. But he steadied himself, deciding the truck was probably Marti's. It would be just like that cowgirl to own a four-by-four. It was coming on to Christmas, and Peter guessed they'd gotten drinking or something, perhaps while decorating the house—Kelly was a nut for Christmas baubles—and had lost track of time. Yeah, that was it. Marti was sleeping over.

He slipped through Kelly's bedroom window.

And when he saw the stranger in bed with her, one limp forearm draped over Kelly's naked hip, rage of such volcanic proportions slammed into him that for an instant he forgot his insubstantial form and flung himself at Will's sleeping shape, a jealous husband come home unexpectedly to discover the wife he trusted in bed with another man. Fury twisted his unseen hands into killer's claws. He was going to stomp this fucker to death...

Then a curious thing happened. Darkness enveloped him—and he was back in his body, eyes closed, head heavy on the pillow... but now he could *feel* the bed beneath him, the warmth of the sheets against his skin.

And he could feel something else, something...asleep beside him. No, inside him.

He opened his eyes—and then he understood.

He was *in* the stranger's body now, his own essence keenly alert, achieving through its presence some rudimentary degree of control. He could feel Will's sleeping psyche right next to him, a faintly pulsing warmth, and understood instinctively that if he trod lightly, did not jar his slumbering host...

His mind reeled.

Skin against skin, oh, it was like the sweetest intoxicant, the wine of the gods, and he could *feel* it, Kelly's warm hip beneath his pirated forearm, he could feel it all...

Joy and a fierce arousal doused Peter's rage like floodwaters rushing over a candle flame. Straining to recall the neural messages, he commanded the arm to pull back, to bring its fingers into range—and the stranger's left leg jerked an inch off the bed. After a moment, he tried again...

And now the arm moved, *glorious motion*, and he stroked Kelly's hip with his fingertips, the sensation reaching him through borrowed nerve endings. An almost painful engorgement made itself known to him, not as a faraway ache but as a throbbing scream of need, and with his free hand he reached down to feel, actually *feel*, the rigid spike of his arousal.

Inside him something stirred... It was *him*, whoever this heart-thieving bastard was, and Peter clubbed him with the full force of his initial fury, battered him beyond sleep into unconsciousness. The beating diminished the stranger somehow, shrinking his hold on his own body, and now Peter assumed total control.

He reached for Kelly again, snuggling closer. With a phantom touch he kissed the nape of her neck, but this time he felt it, too. Kelly moaned, stirred a little—and Peter lay still. He didn't want to waken

190   Sean Costello

her. Not yet. When she settled, his fingers found the waiting folds of her vulva; they were already moist, that single brush of his lips against her neck arousing her even in sleep. With a gentleness belying his desire, he stroked her centre until it became as engorged as his own...

* * *

In a half-lit recess of her drugged and sleeping mind, Kelly Wheeler began to dream. It was the day of the accident...but the accident itself was still far away, a nightmare as yet undreamed. They were in her bedroom and Peter was touching her, awakening feelings that were frightening in their raw intensity. In the dream she rolled onto her back, as she had all those lonesome years ago, and drew Peter down on top of her, murmuring his name, slipping off on a warm erotic tide...

* * *

Peter could feel her responding, but with her eyes still closed and her muscles slack with sleep. She reached out limply to embrace him, slurred his name, and Peter shifted his pilfered body over hers, sliding its penis home. Kelly moaned, but still she did not awaken. He buried his face in the crook of her neck, smelling her sweetness, and began moving in a dreamy rhythm.

"Peter," she breathed in a drugged whisper. "Oh, God, Peter..."

Peter felt a climax already building and he slowed, wanting to savour it, unwilling to lose it all in a fevered adolescent rush. Balanced on an elbow, he took one of Kelly's breasts in his hand, circled the nipple with his tongue...

* * *

The sun streamed across them in warm parallel bars, a dream sun beaming through dream venetians, and she clutched his muscular back, drew him in as deep as her parts would allow. Her head tossed from side to side, and an insane kind of laughter built inside her, the laughter of ecstasies unimagined, of a love so potent it threatened to fracture the mind.

(Peter...)

* * *

She was surfacing now, as restraint abandoned him, and he thrust with renewed vigor. Slick with sweat beneath him, Kelly thrust back. The heat between them flourished, geysered toward flashpoint...and as their juices mingled, Kelly opened her eyes.

And screamed, shrill and long, the force of her release converted to the lethal explosive of terror. She awoke crying Peter's name—and found a stranger on top of her, hips bruising hers, alien eyes rolled back in the perverse delight of rape. She screamed and flung him off and he landed in a heap on the floor, his head cracking hard against the windowsill, splitting the scalp and bringing blood.

* * *

In his hospital bed three miles away, Peter awoke in his twisted body, bewildered, exhilarated, afraid. He lifted his head and in the moonlight saw a spreading wet stain on his bedsheet. The thrill of release still rippled the muscles of his jaw.

The voice of reason immediately tried to insinuate itself—*You've been having some pretty hi-tech dreams lately, pal, but that's all they are, don't kid yourself, they're only dreams*—but the voice was weak, its conviction foundering.

You were alive, a new, firmer voice told him. *For a few incredible minutes that fucker's body was yours, and you were* alive.

Peter's smile glowed like the snow in the pines outside.

24

THEY WERE SILENT FOR a while, as if by unspoken assent. Will, still dazed from the crack his skull had taken on the sill, sat elbows on knees on the toilet seat, while Kelly, sick and ashamed at the way her erotic dream had transformed into nightmarish reality, drew the wound edges together with a bandage. The cut was long, but not deep enough to require stitches. She was glad of the silence, even at the cost of a shell-shocked boyfriend. It gave her time to think.

Her immediate reaction upon finding Will on top of her had been one of anger and revulsion. True, they had made love earlier that evening, and it was good, but in no way did that give him the right to take her in her sleep. Split scalp or not, she'd come within an ace of throwing him out of her house. Once she turned on the lights, however, and saw that Will was just as befuddled as she—and worse, blood was tracking down behind his left ear—she realized her anger was merely a front for her shame. Helping him into the bathroom, wobbly herself from the sedative she'd taken, she constructed in her mind a version of what had most likely taken place.

She'd awakened Will with the carnal thrashings of her dream— in all probability, she'd unknowingly reached for him as a substitute for Peter—and in a drug-induced stupor had failed to distinguish between dream and reality. Will hadn't jumped her in her sleep—a thought a tad too necrophilic for Kelly's tastes—she'd jumped *him*. Oh, God, and then she'd tossed him out of bed, split his scalp on the windowsill and quite possibly given him a concussion. His eyes were still glazed and unfocused. He looked like a boxer who'd just lost the title to a knockout.

"Are you all right?" she said now.

Will made a sound that might have been a word when it was conceived in his brain—"nnngth"—then cleared his throat. "I think so," he said. "What happened in there?"

"Don't you remember?"

"Not a thing," Will said, shrugging. "I was having this dream...I was in a scrap with some guy, only he wasn't a real guy, he was some kind of...spook, I guess." He chuckled without mirth. "Weird. He really smoked me, sort of snuck up behind me and hammered me senseless. Next thing I knew I was on the floor beside the bed, feeling like I did the time I O.D.'d on tequila." He chuckled again, and winced. "I was seventeen... What did happen in there?"

Kelly dabbed the last of the blood from Will's neck with a damp facecloth. "I don't know," she said.

But as the drug fog lifted and the shock tapered off, a devastating truth took shape in Kelly's mind. She was a young, attractive woman, intelligent, self-sufficient, sought after by men and almost certainly loved by the one she now ministered to—but she was a helpless slave of the past, as tied emotionally to Peter Gardner as Peter was to his bed. She could think of no other way to explain it. She supposed she'd known it all along, deep down. It was a truth that had bubbled to the surface before, like swamp gas in the sometimes wretched morass of her heart. But she'd always managed to deny that truth, to veil it behind some new and more brittle fiction: *I don't need Peter Gardner. I don't need anyone. I'm going to become a teacher, and a good one at that.*

Besides, who's got time for dates? I've got to work. I've got to study. And I can take care of the ache myself…

She looked at Will and knew she could never sleep with him again. It wouldn't be fair to either of them. God help her, she didn't even know her own feelings any more. A few hours ago she'd believed herself in love with this man, finally freed from her past… now look at her. The first time in six years that she decides to give of herself, really give, and Peter pops up like a ghost and ruins it.

It was a tough decision to make, but as long as she was tied to Peter she was better off alone. Better to make a clean break with Will… and do it right now.

"How do you feel?" she said, brushing a stray lock of hair from his forehead.

"Better," he said, stifling a yawn. "What time is it?" Kelly glanced at her wristwatch. Rose-coloured light dappled the frosted glass of the bathroom window. "Quarter to six."

Will moaned. "Should we bag it for another hour?"

"I don't think so, Will," Kelly said, taking his hand. "If you feel up to driving, I think you should leave."

There was a note of finality in Kelly's words that perplexed and frightened Will Chatam. He was totally gone on this girl, and the possibility that he'd said or done something to screw it up—especially now, after they'd just made love for the first time—filled him with dread and an abrupt, abiding self-loathing. Something had happened in that bedroom, something that was lost completely to Will. But it had finished them. He knew that with an almost preternatural certainty.

"What happened?" he said again, holding Kelly's gaze despite the tears he knew would soon come.

"I… can't tell you that, Will. I'm not even sure myself." She took a slow, ragged breath. "But I think it would be best if we didn't see each other again for a while."

She didn't say forever, Will thought, choosing to cling to this slim hope rather than face the hurtful truth that lurked between the lines. "If a woman needs space," his mother had once counseled him, "give it to her. Give her that space or you'll lose her." And despite an almost insuperable urge to challenge Kelly's words, to plead with her if that was what it took, Will decided to heed that advice.

"All right, Kelly," he said as he wobbled to his feet. Kelly reached out to steady him—and Will took her firmly by the shoulders, trying to break through the misty dullness in her eyes, wanting only to be heard and understood. "But I meant what I said last night. By the fireplace."

"I know," Kelly said, giving him a smile filled with warmth and affection. "Thank you."

He wanted to say more—Call me if you need me, I'll be there for you, Kelly, I love you—but he released her shoulders, kissed her lightly on the forehead, and turned away. "I can find my own way out," he said.

Then he was gone.

Hurt and bewildered, Kelly got into the shower. She stayed there until the water went cold, then set about getting ready for school.

* * *

The fiction proved almost impossible to sustain during that cruelly foreshortened day, and when the catastrophe occurred, Kelly came completely unstitched. The reins of her mind had slipped out of reach, down among the stampeding hooves of her thoughts, and there was simply no way she could concentrate on her job. In the aftermath of a single lustful dream, her life lay in ruins. Obeying her heart instead of her head, she'd broken things off with the sweetest guy she'd come across in years, a man who genuinely cared for her. She'd known all along that her feelings for Peter still existed, had even accepted the fact that in all probability they'd remain with her forever. But she'd always believed that time would scab the wounds over. She'd anticipated scars, the low-grade itch of slow healing…but she never would have believed that the ghosts of her past could scrape the wounds raw with only a dream.

But what a bizarre dream it had been. The tangible fusing with the imaginary so eerily, so convincingly. Every man who'd ever touched her intimately had left a sort of sensory memory on her skin, and Kelly felt confident that if she were to close her eyes now and each of them were to touch her in turn, she could name them with the slightest embrace. And though the man on top of her last night had been Will, the physical memories he'd awakened had been of Peter, right down to his lips on the nape of her neck, arousing her so intensely…

"Miss?"

Kelly turned to face her students, feeling her face redden but powerless to prevent it. How long had she been out of it?

The girls' gymnastic team stood in uneven ranks around her, exchanging puzzled glances and furtive remarks. She'd come into the abandoned gym to prepare for her morning practice and had spotted a loose bolt at the floor end of one of the guy wires supporting the low bar. She'd bent to fix it…then her thoughts had run off on her again, and she'd failed to notice that seventeen buzzing teenagers had come stomping into the gym.

"Miss Wheeler?"

It was Tracy Giroux, the team captain. Tracy liked Miss Wheeler, who'd taken a special interest in her early in the term, when Tracy was having a problem with drugs, and now she rounded on her teammates like an angry cat, surprising them into silence.

"Is something the matter?" the gymnast said, touching her teacher's arm. "Should we, like, cancel practice till Monday?"

"No, Trace," Kelly said, trying on a smile. "I was just thinking."

Before Tracy could say any more, Kelly raised her whistle to her lips and gave it a blast, a familiar action linking her to the here and now. The sound ricocheted off the polished surfaces of the gym like a bullet. In response, the girls formed lines, their lithe bodies preparing for a brief aerobic warm-up, then the more taxing maneuvers of the various gymnastic stations.

Lagging behind the others, Tracy gave Kelly a look that said "If I can help, Miss Wheeler, I will," and this time Kelly's smile was genuine.

Setting her teeth, she led the girls through their warm-up. Twice she forgot which move came next—Tracy picked up the slack in these spots, her evil eye stifling the snickers of her fellows—and during the running-in-place segment Kelly simply forgot to quit, continuing the repetitive motion until the girls began to complain. At this point common sense screamed at her to cancel the practice, maybe even the whole day, feign the flu and go home, take another pill and crash… but a more headstrong part of her rejected this approach, recognizing it for what it was, a yellow streak of weakness that disgusted her. Later she would wish she had succumbed to it.

"Okay," she said in her coach's voice. "Tracy, Shelley, Catrina— high bar. I'll spot. Ali. You, Petra…"

Her own voice became a distant drone as she split the girls into groups, assigning each to a different apparatus and appointing spotters, making sure everyone had something to do. Everything around her seemed subtly out of sync as she approached the high bar—the lights too bright, the clamor of the girls almost painfully high-pitched, the edges of physical objects impinging on her retinas so intensely they gleamed like surgical steel. Even the air in front of her seemed to twitch like a desert heat haze.

She boosted Tracy up to the high bar, aware of the girl's slim waist between her hands, the synthetic feel of her tights… but the more familiar her surroundings became, the more paradoxically alien they seemed. Tracy was a great kid, a talented kid, who'd merely started off on the wrong foot. Kelly had helped this kid, and it had felt good, fulfilling. Tracy was captain of the gymnastics team now, respected by her peers, fawned over by the boys; her marks were on the upswing—and wasn't that what this was all about? Wasn't that why she, Kelly, had gone into teaching in the first place?

Then why, suddenly, did it all seem so empty? Could a single confused dream destroy all she'd strived to achieve?

Tracy was coming to the end of her routine and the eyes of her fellows were upon her. Tracy was the team star, her skill and grace virtually assuring them a shot at the Provincials in the spring. She rotated through a giant hock circle, releasing the bar at the bottom of the arc and then spinning to reverse her grip.

She missed.

Tracy cried out as her Danskin-clad body whizzed past Kelly's unseeing eyes, flapping like a flag in a wind gust. Too late, Kelly threw out her arms and Tracy whoofed to the mat at her feet. There was a greenstick *crack* followed by a tortured cry, and Kelly clapped her hands to her ears and looked down. Writhing in pain, Tracy gaped back at her with shock and accusation in her eyes. Her left forearm was fractured, the bone gleaming ivory through the skin, blood snaking back to her elbow.

"Gross," one girl cried. Another bolted for the change room, hands clamped over her mouth. The rest only stood there, faces white with shock, dazed eyes barely comprehending what they were seeing.

Kelly, too, only stood there. Her right hand had gone to her own left arm, and now it massaged the puckered knot of scar tissue there.

Tracy's wretched eyes broke the spell.

"Karla," Kelly said to the girl standing nearest. "Run into the office and call 911. The rest of you clear out of here. Now."

As the girls scuttled out, glancing back over their shoulders, Kelly yanked the drawstring out of her sweatpants and knelt over the injured gymnast. Tracy shrank back from her and Kelly's heart broke all over again.

"Why didn't you spot me?" Tracy said, tears streaming from her eyes. "You were supposed to spot me…"

"I'm sorry," was all Kelly could say. "I'm sorry, Tracy."

After using the drawstring as a tourniquet, Kelly fetched Tracy a pillow and a blanket from her office, then waited with her for the ambulance to arrive.

"You were supposed to spot me," Tracy kept sobbing. "You were supposed to spot me…"

* * *

Will did something that day he'd done only once before, on the occasion of his brother's wedding: he called in sick. He'd been employed at the Nickel Ridge smelter since his middle teens, when his father, who at the time had been shift foreman, got him a summer job swamping out toilets. That rather unsavory task had taken him all over the sprawling industrial complex, from the starkly utilitarian administrative offices to the shafts of the mile-deep underground hive. But the sweltering, sooty, clanking environment of the smelter had immediately intrigued him. Something in its implacable toughness, its crude and tireless momentum, had made him feel right at home. Within its coarse walls, the world and all its concerns vanished in a sulfury haze. From his first glimpse of the place—and his first unearthly ride as an apprentice engineer on the slag train—he'd known what he wanted from life…the same way he'd known what was in his heart the first time he laid eyes on Kelly.

And until this morning, it had all been going so well…

Will shifted his work light to a more functional perch and squinted into the Buick's dark underbelly. He'd been sprawled beneath the old girl's chassis for about an hour now, tinkering distractedly with a bum shock absorber. In his present frame of mind, this was the last thing he should be doing—he was more apt to screw it up than fix it—but it beat going in to work, where his inattention might cost him a limb. Or his life.

Cursing softly, Will lowered his aching arms and puffed warm breath into the grease-smudged bowl of his hands. If he had any sense he'd go back inside and slip into a nice hot tub with a beer and a paperback novel. It was colder than a dead man's heart out here, he couldn't concentrate to save his soul, and the task was far from pressing. The Buick had been up on blocks since early October, and it would remain that way until the middle of June at the earliest.

He closed his eyes and heard Kelly tell him it was over.

No she didn't say that she didn't say it was over.

Not in so many words, perhaps, but as morning stretched into snow-blown afternoon, the truth worked its way home.

Will damned himself for not having been more assertive. Kelly was obviously a mess. Maybe he should have tried to reason with her and to hell with his mother's advice. The guy she was stuck on was a goner, no future there, and although Will felt no animosity toward him, he wished the bugger would die. By the sound of it he had no life anyway, and Will swore that if he ever wound up in a similar situation he'd take every measure in his power to end it. But the guy—what had she said his name was? Peter? Paul?—*had* no power, no physical power, at any rate. The power he did have, an apparently unbreakable grip on Kelly's heart, seemed a mighty one indeed. But couldn't she see it was hopeless? The guy didn't even want to see her anymore. And it had been years...Christ, why had he walked out with his tail between his legs? Why hadn't he spoken his mind?

Because there had been a lot more to it, hadn't there. More than just the girl he was sweet on making love to him while thinking of another guy. That he could handle. That sort of obstacle could be overcome with love, patience and time.

But how had he ended up on the floor with a bleeding goose egg and a boner still slick with her juices? Why couldn't he remember any of that? At first, he'd ascribed this lapse in memory to the crack he'd taken on the head. Memory loss was not uncommon with concussion. He'd suffered the condition once before, when he tumbled to the ice as a teenager, proving once and for all that he couldn't get the hang of ice-skating. The bump that time had been like this, split scalp and all, and to this day he couldn't recall the five minutes leading up to the fall, or the subsequent half hour. But the aftermath that time had been different. The long-term symptoms of concussion had plagued him for the balance of that long-ago winter's day and well into the following night—nausea, vomiting, headache, drowsiness, swirling black spots before his eyes…

But this time there had been none of that. Only the memory loss. And it struck Will as inconceivable, even had his head been caved in completely, that he should forget, without a trace, making love to such a beautiful woman. And yet the evidence had been there: his erection, still glistening even as its anger subsided in the rude shock of being tossed out of bed; the unmistakable rush of an orgasm just spent; Kelly's complexion, flushed and glowing as it had been the evening before, that wondrous evening spent entwined before a crackling fire. And the dream he'd had just prior. The furious beating he'd taken and the sense that, in the instant before the intruder fell upon him, he was awake and that it was all really happening…

What in hell had gone on there?

He wiggled the dolly to the right, grabbed a socket wrench and fitted it to a rusted-on bolt. Teeth flashing white with the effort, he cranked at the bolt until the wrench slipped and the skin of his knuckles took up residence on the shaft of the shock absorber.

Will cried out, a shout of pain pitching upward to a womanly shriek of heartfelt misery and loss. Tears puddled in his eyes as he lay on his back beneath the Buick, his throbbing hand clutched to his chest, and he damned himself for his lack of nerve, ignoring a stern voice—a voice that was so much like his mother's—which cautioned him that he was better off out of it, find a new girl, this one could bring only grief.

Sometime later Will rolled out from under the car, shuffled inside and flopped dispiritedly on the couch. He had no idea how long he'd lain out there under the Buick, the blood from his scored knuckles freezing to his skin, his mind thrumming like a runaway turbine. He knew only that by persistent degrees the run of his thoughts had tapered to a single compelling pinpoint.

He had to get Kelly Wheeler back.

He was in love with her.

25

THERE WERE A NUMBER of things Sam wanted to talk to his brother about—chief among them being his conversation with Kelly—but he decided to broach the subject of their mother first, then play it by ear from there.

"I know you hate talking about her," Sam said. "But I'm afraid Mom is really starting to lose it."

To Sam's surprise, Peter appeared unbothered by the subject, even a little interested. "What's the old girl up to now?" he said, as if anticipating an amusing reply.

"She's planning a séance," Sam said, the admission causing him obvious discomfort. "For tonight. She's hired some local psychic to come over and...summon your spirit. She still believes you're dead and your visit was...cripes, I don't know, some sort of sign? That you've forgiven her, maybe? That you want to communicate from beyond the grave?"

Peter was still glowing from his adventures of the night before, and not even the Froot Loop antics of his mother could spoil all of that. What had happened in Kelly's bedroom had been as glorious as it was inexplicable. The forgotten fire of functioning nerve endings, the matchless joy of motion...and the sure knowledge that, even after

Sean Costello

all this time, even after all that had befallen them, Kelly was still in love with him. That revelation had nullified his initial fury at the stranger's trespass. After all, there had been nothing left for Kelly after the accident but to carry on, go through the motions of living and hope that, when death came, she wouldn't have to face it alone. Though his embittered heart told him differently, Peter knew that it was he who had turned her away, and not the other way around, as he would have his brother believe. Who could blame her for taking comfort from another man?

But she wouldn't have to do that anymore.

"Séance, eh?" Peter said, grinning at Sam's troubled face. "Well, Sammy, you never know. That might just prove interesting."

* * *

As the hour approached—midnight, the medium had insisted— Leona was plagued by a steadily escalating panic. Furtive attempts at dousing that panic—frequent side trips to the toilet with complaints of a nervous bladder, sloshing back mouthfuls of Jack—served only to boost it to a higher gear.

The medium, Eliza Cook, sat in a trancelike hush at the dining room table while her assistant—a fat, dough-faced woman named Tabitha—gobbled Cheezies from a bowl Leona had set out prior to their arrival. Leona had found the woman's name in the *Northern Life* personals. "Eliza. Professional Medium. Tarot Reader. Fortunes told. Séances Held. By Appointment Only." Leona had held off as long as she could, waiting for Peter to return on his own. But he never had. Not outside of her nightmares.

Eliza guaranteed results.

Everything was in place. The windows were draped, those without curtains slung with blankets Leona had scavenged from her bed; all of the lights but one had been doused, the phone was unplugged, and Sam was out for the evening. Leona had insisted. She didn't want the brat busting in and spoiling the whole show, spouting lies about Peter still being alive.

It was ten before midnight, and this time Leona's bladder really was full. "I'll be right back," she slurred to the seer's assistant, who nodded and sucked an orange finger.

"She's gone," Tabitha whispered once Leona had rounded the corner. She stifled a burp, then reached for her Pepsi.

Eliza, whose real name was Myrt, shifted in her seat. A cramp in her lower back had been nagging her since before she sat down, but she hadn't allowed herself to let on. In this business, style was everything. In the half hour before midnight, she routinely made a show of "achieving the correct plane," which involved sitting as still as a statue and ignoring such minor annoyances as cramps, itches, and worst of all, boredom. Not that attention to detail was going to matter for much longer if this silly bitch kept hitting the bottle. Still, she was paying with queen's currency, two hundred dollars' worth, and she deserved the full show.

"How do I look?" Eliza asked her assistant, whose job it was to add, with properly timed oohs and aahs, to the drama of Eliza's illusions.

"Like a two-bit hooker," Tabitha said, giggling into a ham-sized fist.

"Kiss my—"

Tabitha toed the medium's ankle, transporting her instantly back into trance. A moment later Leona shambled into the room. At Tabitha's instruction she sat across from Eliza at the small oval table, hands clasped eagerly in front of her. Her eyes were round and swimming, but they never left Eliza's somber face.

With a porcine grunt, Tabitha stood. She lit the single stubby candle that was part of their gear, then waddled over and switched off the overhead light. Returning to her seat, she sucked the last sweet ounce of Pepsi from the can before setting the empty on the floor by her feet. Then she lowered her fleshy lids.

In a cathedral voice, Eliza began.

"We are assembled here this night to call up the unquiet spirit of"—for a terrible moment she couldn't recall her client's name; then it came to her—"Leona Gardner's beloved son, Peter." She raised her eyes to the ceiling, letting them rest on a huge and intricate water stain. It looked like a cartoon orgy up there. "Taken in the spring of his life, he wanders the labyrinths of the netherworld, lost and bewildered, seeking the light of his mother's love. Only she can deliver him from this trackless limbo. Only she can dispatch him to God." Eliza thrust her arms overhead. Cheap Asian bracelets chattered on her wrists. "Come to us now, O Sleepless Spirit. Give us a sign."

Leona's eyes flooded with tears. She did not want to send her son to God; she wanted him back, to play for her as he had been trying to do on that single wondrous night, to remain with her always. But she dared not open her mouth, dared not disturb the medium. She'd spoken at length with the assistant over the phone and had been forewarned against creating any disruption once the séance had begun. She'd answered a lot of questions then, too, personal stuff about Peter's life, and had assumed it important to the process.

As she lowered her arms and dropped her chin back to level, Eliza caught a glimpse of Leona's earnest expression and made a show of flashing her eyes, rolling them back in a splendid display of deepening trance. Her mother, a fraud in her own right, had always said Myrt would wind up in show biz.

The three women joined hands, closing the mystic circle. "Come to us now," Eliza repeated in her husky working voice. "Come to us, O Wandering Spirit. Speak through Mother Eliza."

Hovering above his piano, Peter smirked angrily. As before, the sight of his mother, the woman he had once loved more than any other, blinded him with blood-coloured rage. With the entire force of his being, he reached down and pounded the keys.

Then he flew at Eliza like a fireball.

* * *

Immediately on the heels of the piano's tuneless belch, the candle flame guttered with a tiny roar, as if exposed to a sudden draft. Startled, Tabitha looked sharply at Eliza. The medium sucked in a sharp gust of air, then her eyes popped open like blinds. Her fists clamped brutally shut, causing both Leona and Tabitha to wince. In the dancing light of the candle flame, Eliza's lips purpled to a sickly burgundy.

Leona gave a delighted squeal.

Tabitha, who had no idea what was going on, started to get up from the table. None of this shit was in their repertoire, and how in the *fuck* had Myrt got that piano to pitch a fit? In the past Myrt had always forewarned her about any of the cute little special effects she sometimes rigged. And she never got this downright peculiar. She looked like she was having a heart attack, and Tabitha decided it was time to put a stop to it.

But Eliza's grip tightened, and Tabitha thumped back down in her seat, stifling a cry, the small bones in the blubber of her hand grinding like faulty gears.

"Peter?" Leona cried. "Peter, are you here?"

Eliza's head lolled forward, her iron grip suddenly slackening. A fat bead of drool took a swan dive from her lower lip.

From the floor beside her Tabitha's empty pop can rose to the level of her nose. It imploded, then described a whistling arc through the air. It struck the K-Mart oil painting over the mock fireplace, punching a knuckle-size hole in the canvas before clattering to the floor.

Eliza, looking stunned, lifted her head and gawked hazy-eyed at Tabitha. "Wha—?" she managed to say.

Then a whining whirlwind surrounded them. Eliza's hair, hung in a tight Gypsy's braid, stood smartly at attention on the top of her head. A faint band of metallic blue light encircled them, crackling with malign energy. Transfixed, Tabitha turned to Eliza, fear and befuddlement in her eyes. Eliza, still shell-shocked, gazed back blearily.

"Peter?" Leona whispered.

And the whirlwind ceased. As if shot, Eliza recoiled against the back of her chair. She stiffened, eyes widening, lips curling back to reveal stained, uneven teeth. A run of meaningless syllables slopped out of her mouth, then she barked like a startled dog. Her face seemed at war with itself.

Then: "Hi, mom," she said in a husky masculine voice.

Tabitha clutched her heart.

"Why don't you throw these simple sluts out and clean up your act?"

"Peter?"

"Yes, Mommy dearest," Eliza said, turning to face Leona. "It's me. Remember this?"

Enraptured, Leona looked on as Eliza's face rearranged itself, muscles forced beneath wrinkled skin into configurations contrary to remembered patterns. Her eyebrows peaked into exaggerated arcs and her mouth shaped an impish grin, the effect one of a battered, effeminate Jack Nicholson.

"Heeeeeere's Johnny," Eliza sang out with maniacal glee: Peter's impersonation of Nicholson as the homicidal caretaker in *The Shining*, the one that had always gotten a roar out of Leona and Sam and Kelly and his football buddies. "Remember?"

"Oh, Peter," Leona moaned, tears glazing her bloodshot eyes.

"Fuck this," Tabitha squealed. She grunted and got to her feet, snatched her purse off the table and rumbled like a semi toward the exit. As she clasped the knob and hauled the door open, Eliza went momentarily slack. There was a blast of stale air and the door swung shut in its frame, salting plaster dust into Tabitha's hair. With a yelp she jerked the knob again, and this time made good her escape. Her footfalls sounded like receding thunderclaps in the hallway.

Eliza perked up again. Her eyes were like doll's eyes. "You want to see me, Mom?" she said in a voice that was not her own.

"Oh, yes, Peter, I do."

"I'm in room 908 at the University Hospital."

Leona flinched as if kicked.

"You can't miss me, Mom. I'm the head at the head of the bed." There was a dry, cackling laugh. "Oh, and one other thing…"

Eliza reached out, caught Leona by the front of her blouse and pulled her across the table until their noses touched.

"I am not dead."

* * *

Six years' worth of vaulted anger let go in a mushroom cloud of destruction. Its initial instrument, Eliza sprang to her feet and flung the heavy pine table on its side, snuffing out the candle and plunging the room into darkness. The table edge clipped Leona on the chin, a stiff wooden uppercut that sent her sprawling to the floor. Dazed, she got to her feet and lurched to the nearest wall, her nails scuttling over the uneven plaster like roaches. She found the light switch and threw it up.

"Peter?"

Eliza spun to face her. In the time it had taken Leona to turn on the light, the medium had pulled over a bookcase, stuffed a stockinged foot through the television screen and toppled a dozen dusty figurines to the floor. Now her face contorted horribly and she charged at Leona like a rhino, head down, shoulders hunched, heels thudding the tiles. Halfway across the room her toe caught the edge of a throw rug and she sailed head first into the back of the couch. Her head struck a steel strut, and when her body hit the floor, it was boneless.

Blind with fury, Peter quit his unconscious host and rose like a mist to the ceiling. At the sight of the destruction he'd wreaked, an arresting awe overcame him and he simply hung there, surveying it, a triumphant general in a hovering chopper. He had caused all of this. Peter Gardner, vegetable. This was fantastic. This—

"Peter?"

Leona stumbled into view beneath him, yellow eyes rolled toward him, withered hands upheld in the beseeching posture of the damned.

Pathetic.

Peter started toward her, so jammed full of hatred and fury and confused love that his thought processes were momentarily reduced to a maddening whine at the midpoint of his skull.

He started toward her—

And an eyeblink later he was back in his body, his rage condensing into a frustrated cry in the bullhorn hollow of his throat. As he opened his mouth to expel it, a nurse walked in with a sedative. She took one look at him, spun on her heel, and was gone. Peter caged the shout behind clenched teeth. His mouth felt full of ashes.

Looking down at his mother only seconds before, he had dearly wanted to kill her.

* * *

By 3:00 A.M. Peter had achieved a level of calm that was more or less compatible with rational thought. That wretched, murderous whine in his skull had subsided, and his rage had flamed down to cooling cinders. Now he lay in the pale winter moonlight, reflecting on what had taken place in his mother's apartment.

First, and most important, he'd influenced physical objects, actually made things move. When he pondered this fact—really thought about it—the sheer excitement it caused him was almost too much to bear. The piano keys had flattened under his touch (as they had the first time he visited his mother, he reminded himself; that single clean chord had not been part of a dream after all), and he'd crushed that pop can as effortlessly as a normal man might squash a paper cup. The possibilities this fact alone created simply boggled his mind. It was like being the Invisible Man. Jesus, if he wanted to, he could really put a spook on some people—his good buddy, Dr. Lowe, for instance. Wait until Harry does himself up, then make the syringe do a jig in the air. What a rip that would be. Or—God, *yes*—he could rob a bank. Just float in and cram a rucksack full of crisp new hundreds. He and Sammy could move to Tahiti…

But there was more, and Peter felt an odd blend of dread and astonishment as he contemplated the rest.

He'd entered that woman's body. True, he'd done the same thing the night before with the cocksucker in Kelly's bed, but that guy had been asleep. This woman had been fully conscious, and yet she'd been easy to take over. It seemed more a matter of intellect than anything else. He'd literally outsmarted her, tricked her narrow little mind into taking a powder.

And that made him wonder how long he could have stayed inside her. How long might he have pulled her strings?

Could I have taken her over permanently?

This thought, for all its incredible possibility, struck him as ludicrous. Even as he rode her he'd sensed his hold on her was tenuous. Some awakening force in the woman had gradually begun to repel him, and although he'd jerked her around like a mad marionette for a few minutes, he'd felt like a rodeo stuntman on the back of an irate bull. The effort had exhausted him.

And yet…

What if he got some practice?

What then?

Outside, the winter wind pounded the double thickness of the glass. The air in the room was cold enough to raise gooseflesh.

Peter closed his eyes and reached for the trance. It came easily, and he slipped out of his body like a blade whispering out of its sheath. Avoiding his body—he still couldn't bear the sight of it—he scanned the room for a likely-looking test subject.

There was a small cactus on the windowsill, looking oddly out of place against Jack Frost's handiwork, and Peter drifted over to it. After some hesitation he wrapped his hand around the green plastic pot—

And cursed. Nothing happened. He couldn't feel it and the plant didn't move.

He tried again, fury swirling up in him as his memory crosspatched to the first time he attempted to override the chasm in his spine and move his limbs.

Nothing.

Come on, you Christless fuck—MOVE.

Peter swung a substanceless arm through the crimson glare of his rage and the cactus toppled to the floor. It didn't smash against the wall as he'd hoped, but it did move. He looked down and saw it lying half out of its pot on the tiles, a dry scatter of earth and tiny Styrofoam pellets surrounding it. In the moonlight the pellets glowed like insectile eyes.

There, Peter thought in dark, solitary satisfaction.

There.

It was the anger. The rage. That was his battery; that was his power plant. All he had to do was sustain it.

Somehow he didn't think that would be difficult.

He settled into his body without thinking, content with his night of discovery. Then his eye caught the blizzard outside and he thought of Kelly.

Is she alone on this nasty night? he wondered. Thinking of me?

He closed his eyes and reached again for the trance…but now it eluded him.

Unperturbed, he closed his eyes and waited.

26

DECEMBER CAME ON WITH a battering cruelness that matched the climate in Kelly's heart. The advances winter had already made were dwarfed by a rapid-fire succession of some of the most violent wind and snowstorms the north had endured in a century. At midnight on the evening of Tracy Giroux's regrettable accident in the gym, Kelly sat alone before the big north-facing window of her home and watched the first of the blizzards come.

Tracy had needed surgery to set her arm. It had taken three hours, two metal plates and eleven stainless-steel screws. The tragic but predictable verdict was that she would be out of gymnastics for the season, and quite possibly forever. Kelly, weeping and wringing her hands, had waited with Tracy's parents in the emergency room at the General Hospital. Mr. and Mrs. Giroux, a pleasant couple from the valley, had done their best to console her, assuring her that it had been an accident and that she shouldn't blame herself. But it had done little good. Kelly wept for Tracy Giroux—for the hard fact that she would be out of gymnastics, the one thing in her life that had given her direction; for the loss of trust that would inevitably follow this incident; and for the suddenly doubled probability that Tracy would drift back to drugs. A lot had been lost in a moment's inattention. But she wept for herself, too—for the sweet dreams that had snapped with Peter's spine. An old voice rose up in her in the stark fluorescent glare of the waiting room: *Six years,* it yammered. *Six years and still he's got a stranglehold on your heart.*

Kelly bit her lip to quell its quivering and gazed into the worsening squall. From the rocky point on which her house stood, the lake narrowed back to the starless horizon like a runway into oblivion. It was out of this dark hiatus that the wind and snow came pelting. Normally Kelly enjoyed the time she spent at home alone, especially during storms. There was something about nature's tempests that always made her feel humble... and yet somehow eternal.

But tonight it only made her feel cold. She had banked a birchwood fire and bundled herself in a comforter, but it made little difference. The cold was lodged inside her.

Oh, Will, she thought unhappily.

And deeper, more sadly: *Peter...*

The wind harped through the latticework porch skirts, blew hellish baritone in the downspouts, rattled the limbs of the trees. In its force, the familiar creaks of the house became stealthy creepings... and for the first time in her adult life, Kelly felt afraid in that elemental way that is the exclusive province of the very young. Afraid of the storm and the night. Afraid of being alone. Afraid of the goblin-green eyes of the bogeyman. Something very peculiar had taken place in her bedroom the night before, in that maroon hinterland between sleep and wakefulness, something which had shattered the house of cards that had been her life since Peter. Maybe Will was right... maybe this was the cost of caring so deeply. Nothing was forever. When that kind of love got destroyed, where did you go from there?

A low black shape detached itself from the shadows of the porch and blurred toward her from the opposite side of the glass. Kelly flinched—and then Fang was sitting on the sill, peering mournfully in at her. Still wrapped in her comforter, Kelly shuffled to the door and let him in. He'd been off on one of his all-day romps, and what he wanted right now was food. Trailing him out to the kitchen, Kelly felt the familiar, almost seductive pull of routine.

Get busy, a familiar voice counseled her. It was a simple doctrine that had seen her through the last six years, forming a three-syllable backbeat to a life that had lost its engine yet somehow managed to keep running.

When the shit hits the fan, kiddo, when it seems that life has passed you by, just get busy and keep busy. It's the only way to heal.

Her mother's words, spoken with the flat conviction of a veteran. As a child Kelly had watched her mother live by this creed, hunched over the ironing board or the sink, furiously pressing or scrubbing, and had judged it a poor way to cope. But she had been young then, young and unspoiled, her world still a wellspring of alternatives. Now, with her head in a mess and her heart in a jar, there seemed no way out but to return to that droning existence. Just unplug her brain and keep busy.

No, she promised herself as she crossed the kitchen to the fridge, trying not to trip over Fang. Not this time. No more hiding. You can't deal with your feelings for Peter by burying them. Because no matter how deep you dig, the soil is too thin. It won't hold.

"What do I do?" Kelly said in a pleading whisper.

Face him, the answer came back. *Confront him.*

She fed the cat and returned to her post by the window, not much comforted by this resolve. Eventually she fell asleep there.

Outside, the storm raged on.

* * *

The trance was there, like a memory just out of reach, and for a time he groped for it futilely. Then he relaxed and let it come. In his mind's eye, he saw himself riding the black December wind, a questing Horseman of the Apocalypse lofting up and away. Within seconds, he felt himself vibrating like a struck bell…then he was free.

He thought again of Kelly.

And in the twinkling of an eye he was there.

She sat asleep in an easy chair by the picture window, her legs tucked under her and her body wrapped in a blanket. A big black tom-cat lay curled at the foot of the chair, snoozing soundly. There had been a fire going in the fireplace, but it had burned itself down to embers and the occasional sputtering flame. Rafting above her on the air, Peter watched the pale ember-light creep along the curves of her face, which was also pale, and beautiful. The stranger was not here tonight, and although Peter had lived through him the night before, he was glad of the interloper's absence. Some nameless instinct assured him that even greater ecstasies lay near at hand.

He commenced a slow orbit about the chair on which Kelly slept, allowing the vertigo these revolutions induced to calm him. With this motion came a clarity of thought, of *awareness*, which eclipsed the enhanced lucidity that had previously attended this state. He could feel himself…condensing, becoming a ring of pure thought. Describing ever-tightening loops, he enclosed Kelly's head in a scintillating band of blue light.

Jolted from its sleep, the cat sprang to its feet and backed away from the chair, its spine arched into scruffy spikes. It spat fearsomely and then bolted for the basement staircase.

Like a garrote sinking into vulnerable flesh, Peter slipped into Kelly's dreams.

And found himself there.

* * *

They were walking in Bell Park, their bare feet cold in the damp sand that fringed Ramsey Lake. The moon was out, high and nearly full, and the sky was plastered with stars. Hand in hand they strolled through the silvery moonlight, thinking secret thoughts of each other. It was the night he first told her that he loved her, that he meant to marry her and be with her forever. It had all come out in one shy, awkward lump, but Kelly had never doubted his sincerity. For a time she'd nurtured this night as a cherished memory; but as the years dragged past its coming in her dreams became a torment.

The images were vivid, as all of her dreams were vivid...and yet, as they reached the slatted bench where Peter had poured out his heart to her, the dreamscape took on a fresh clarity. Now she could actually *feel* his hand in hers, its film of nervous sweat in spite of the coolness of the night, the accelerating pulsebeat in his grip. There was sand between her toes, gritty and cool, and the grass they'd strolled onto was dew-drenched. Peter's dream-figure seemed to solidify, as if some essential sap had been magically siphoned back into it. He was suddenly gorgeously real, not just an image dredged up from muddy memory but whole and solid and real. His face beamed in the moonlight.

"Kelly," he began in his tentative way. "Kelly, I still love you." He smiled. "And I know how we can be together forever."

(no Peter that's wrong that's not what you said)

His grip tightened on her hand, hard enough to hurt.

"Forever, Kelly."

Kelly awoke with a start, cold in spite of the comforter, Peter's words a haunting echo in her ears. Her gaze darted around the room, disoriented, her mind stumbling back to the present with a grudging slowness. Tears leaked from her eyes.

It had seemed so real...

* * *

The similarities to the last time Kelly had come to visit him were almost too much to bear. It had been winter then, too, a day much like this one, filled with gusting winds and billowing snow and the despairing sense that she might never feel the sun's warmth again; it was there, a high, heatless blank in the sky, but it seemed dead and somehow traitorous. It was four o'clock in the afternoon, the first day of a bitter December.

Turn around, the voice of reason cautioned her as she made her way up the ice-scabbed walk to the entrance. *There's nothing for you here.*

Kelly hesitated, heedless of the slashing winter air. It was true. There was nothing for her here. She wasn't eighteen anymore. That part of her life was over, as irretrievable as the snowflakes that melted on her face. What did she mean to say to him, anyway? Hi, Peter, I dream about you? I dream that you still love me and that you want me back? I dream that you're whole again, better than whole... and sometimes *(like last night)* I can feel you inside me...?

An elderly couple brushed past her on the walkway, hatted heads bent forward, collars clutched snugly against the wind. The woman glanced back at her, the way a pedestrian will glance back at a doom-cryer stationed grimly with his placard on a street corner.

She thinks I'm nuts, Kelly thought. And maybe she was. After all this time, she was probably the last person Peter wanted to see.

But they had been in love once, and she allowed this truth to fortify her. They had shared that unique species of intimacy which seemed never to come along again after that trembling first time. She remembered that love and cherished it... and if she couldn't have it again, she should at least be able to approach the person she'd shared it with, talk to him openly and, if need be, beg him to release her heart.

She completed her trek up the walkway, feeling the cold and yet itchy with a nervous sweat. *What will he say?* her mind kept demanding. *What will he look like? Oh, God, I hope he's glad to see me...*

She strode into the lobby and its welcome breath of heat. Crossing the puddled tiles, she caught a departing elevator and punched the button for the ninth floor.

* * *

"Time for your bath."

Peter's neck muscles tightened, flexing beneath the skin like snakes in the act of swallowing; years of hefting his head off the pillow had left them thick and inordinately powerful. He had been paging through one of the books Sam had left him when the voice of the nurse startled him. Now his face darkened in irritation.

"I don't want a bath," he said. Parked halfway into his room was the crane-operated sling they used to haul him into the tub room. It reminded him of some robotic, baby-bearing stork. "I had one last month."

Unperturbed, the nurse tried a compromise. "A sponge bath, then."

Peter debated. If he kicked up a fuss they'd drag him in to the tub room anyway, and he was getting pretty rank. A sponge bath would take only half the time of a baggage run to the tub, and then he could get back to what he'd been doing.

"Deal," he said, flashing an ear-to-ear smile. The nurse responded in kind, but Peter saw her gaze twitch to his teeth and then away, repelled. He had let his teeth go. What the hell. They couldn't force him to eat if he decided he didn't want to, and they couldn't make him accept that fucking toothbrush. Having someone brush his teeth made him feel like a tarnished booby prize in a neglected collection of trophies.

The nurse went into the bathroom. Almost immediately Peter heard the sound of running water filling a stainless-steel basin.

His mind returned to the events of the past two nights. Discovering that Kelly still loved him had come as a gratifying shock. The feeling between them had never died. Stricken by circumstance, it had merely crawled into the shade to hide. And despite the best efforts of each of them to kill it, their love had endured there in the dark, beneath the damp dead leaves of a half-dozen autumns, like some secret mushroom that flowers only when exposed to the light.

And now he had seen that light. He could be with her again. Last night had shown him that. Not physically—never physically—but in a way that only the most smitten of poets could comprehend.

He could enter her mind.

The nurse was back in the room. She set the basin on the washstand, drew the covers off Peter's body, and flipped him expertly onto his side. Behind him he could hear her dipping her hands into the soapy basin, wringing out a washcloth, and some tattered recollection from childhood made him tense mentally against the water that might be too cold...but of course he felt nothing. Only the gentle rock and squeak of the bed told him that his keeper had begun to scrub him. He had no way of knowing, but he thought she might have started with his feet.

He closed his eyes and ground his teeth and waited for this humiliation to end.

* * *

Still in the same room, Kelly thought when the nurse at the desk told her where she could find Peter Gardner. That somehow made it worse. There had been no change, no advancement. If they'd moved him to another floor, even another room, it might have meant he'd regained some feeling in his legs, some vestigial function in his hands, maybe even progressed to a walker of some kind...

But he was still in the same room: 908.

She walked down the hall toward its end, but it was less like walking than gliding, a feeling of being conveyed along a track to which her feet were firmly glued. The closer she got to his door, the faster that track seemed to propel her, until by the time she was halfway there she was almost running. The lenses of her eyes had slipped into soft focus, and her stomach felt queasy and sick.

The door was open, partially blocked by the sling contraption they used to move him around.

Still the same.

Kelly maneuvered around it.

The room was silent, the window shades drawn. A gaudy orange curtain surrounded the bed. From within came a puddling sound of water, but Kelly didn't notice.

Marshaling the last of her courage, she clasped the curtain and drew it aside.

* * *

That first moment spun out interminably. When she saw the bent, unclad body on the bed, with its transparent skin and flaccid muscles, she felt a surge of relief. *Wrong room,* her mind insisted. *That's not Peter, no way.*

Then he opened his eyes, and for a heartbeat the warmth she had known in them kindled. She felt herself beginning to respond to that warmth, the stiffness leaking out of her muscles, a smile creeping onto her lips. Then it was as if an invisible wall had popped up and she'd rushed headlong into it. Peter's eyes continued to widen, the warmth Kelly imagined she'd seen in them erupting into an infernal, repellent heat. His mouth fell open and a horrible, inarticulate groan flopped out, the sound a victim of palsy might make in a pathetic attempt at speech. Kelly's hands flew up to her face and dragged at the corners of her mouth. The nurse glanced at her then backed up a step, her own eyes wide and questioning.

"Peter, I—"

"You," he cried, his lips peeled back in fury and shame. *"You."*

"Peter, please…"

"I told you *never* to come back here." Now his eyes were a dull, clotted red. "I told you. *Never.* Why did you have to spoil it?" He made a disgusted scan of his body, then looked back at Kelly. "Is this what you came to see? Huh? This senseless bone bag of a body? *Is it?* Well, take a good look, because this is what I am." There were tears in his eyes now.

"I'm sorry," Kelly said in a strangled whisper. Her hand fluttered out to touch him.

"Leave," Peter said, a sob twisting miserably through him. "Just leave."

Kelly did.

* * *

He wanted to hurt her. He wanted to punish her. He wanted to fuck her. *Hate*-fuck her. He hoped the stranger would be there tonight. Oh, yeah. There'd be some mean horizontal mambo tonight. *Damn her.* Why couldn't she have left it alone? What had made her come nosing around to see the incredible decaying man? Maybe she thought that would make her shut of him. Maybe she thought it would kill her love for him once and for all. And maybe it would.

But he wasn't going to allow that.

* * *

The next morning, fearful of another calamitous lapse on the job, Kelly called in sick. There had been no sleep last night—after leaving the hospital she'd driven about aimlessly until darkfall, then had wandered home and plunked herself in front of the TV, where she watched all-night movies on Pay—and there had been precious little sleep the night before. She filled that long day with familiar but mindless pursuits: vacuuming the immaculate rugs, mopping the spotless floors, making out her Christmas card list weeks ahead of her usual last-minute blitz. She thought of calling her mother (who would have zeroed in on her mood the way a ham radio operator zeros in on a fuzzy signal, and immediately begun prying) and left a message for Marti at work ... but these days Marti was pretty busy. She'd met a new fella—the boys' phys ed teacher at the high school in Chelmsford where Marti taught—and for the past few months they'd been going at it fast and furious. Suddenly Marti's schedule was full—and it had never had that many holes in it.

The urge to call Will was a potent one, but Kelly stifled it. She was hurting and vulnerable, and she didn't want him to see her that way. Besides, with this sudden resurgence in her feelings for Peter, muddled and perverse as they were, she could no longer be sure of what Will truly meant to her. She couldn't be sure of anything anymore. As lonely as she was, she was determined not to use Will as a substitute. If she was going to think of Peter while being intimate with another man, then she would forgo that intimacy. It wouldn't be fair any other way.

Somehow she made it to nightfall. She took another sedative and buried herself in the covers. After a while, in a semi-drowse, she climbed out of bed and brought down the shoe box she kept on a high shelf in her closet. In the light of the bedside lamp, she rummaged through the items in the box until she found what she was after.

Then she leaned against the headboard and smiled.

They'd had these pics taken in one of those four-for-a-dollar photo booths in the downtown Zeller's. Horsing around, Kelly had hiked her T-shirt over her head in one of them, exposing her unholstered boobs, and the expression on Peter's face was one of lecherous and delighted surprise. In another Peter was doing his infamous Jack Nicholson impersonation, complete with A-frame eyebrows and leering, toothy grin. Kelly was doing what she always did when Peter pulled that face, cracking up like a loony. She recalled the feverish embarrassment she'd felt when the store rent-a-cop jerked the curtain aside, an instant after her delighted squeal and a heartbeat before the next shot had flashed. Twin expressions of juvenile surprise adorned the next shot, the two of them goggling up at the cop, Kelly trying frantically to tuck in her T-shirt, Peter's eyes swallowing his face. In the last of the four they were locked in a tender embrace, as oblivious of the flash glare as they might have been of a sudden nuclear attack.

Kelly felt the tears coming.

Always the tears.

Leaving the light on, she sank under the covers and let the pill do its work. Sleep came grudgingly.

And brought dreams...

* * *

Peter was playing for her. She sat beside him on the piano bench, a girl of seventeen and still a virgin, so much in love it hurt (a deep, moist ache in that part of her which longed to know him), but their first episode of lovemaking was still weeks away, and she had to content herself with his nearness and the pledge that seemed inherent in his music. *I love you, Kelly,* the chords seemed to say. *I will always love you.*

What a splendid day that had been. Spring had triumphed over winter and now there were buds unfurling, crocuses blooming, children splashing gaily in the snowmelt. Sam and Leona were away for the weekend (Leona had tried to drag Peter along, as always twisting the screws of guilt, but Kelly had managed to talk him out of it), visiting Leona's brother in Toronto, and she and Peter were alone.

She dreamed of that day now.

Seated beside him on the piano bench, one hand perched on the firmness of his upper thigh, she watched the knowing pass of his fingers over the keys. Spring sunlight beamed through the big bay window in whose belly the piano stood, and smoldered in the blondness of his hair. She could even smell him.

Old Spice.

Now his hands left the keys and he faced her, his breathing laboured in the sudden, ominous silence. His nostrils flared and the pupils of his eyes grew wide, obliterating the irises with black. His hand covered hers and pressed it to his crotch, which bulged enormously under her touch. He grinned and his teeth were yellow.

"Peter," Kelly said, both fearful and aroused. "This isn't right."

And what she meant was that this wasn't the way that day had gone, but also that the way he was touching her was wrong; he'd never been forceful or rough. In the dream she tried to tell him that—but he jammed his mouth over hers, ramming his tongue down her throat. With his free hand he laid hold of her hair, while with the other he ground her open palm against his groin. A confounding blend of passion and revulsion gripped her now, and she half fought, half responded.

With an ease that was frightening, Peter lifted her onto the piano lid. Sliding her away, he hiked up her skirt and jerked her panties down to her ankles. Without hesitation, he drove three rigid fingers into her middle. She cried out in pain—

And awoke. Something deep inside of her tugged...

Then the tears came, hot and bitter, squeezed free on sobs that shook her to the core.

* * *

Two weeks later, on the sixteenth, Marti dragged Kelly out for some shopping. It was the first day of the Christmas break and Marti was almost delirious with the Yuletide spirit. Her relationship with her male counterpart at Chelmsford Secondary was progressing famously, and she thought he might pop the question on the Eve. It was for this reason that Marti was running on high octane on this snowy afternoon and failed to notice Kelly's sullen, distracted state. They were sitting at a table in the busy New Sudbury Shopping Centre food court, sipping pop and nibbling french fries, when Kelly burst into tears.

"My God, Kelly, what is it?"

But Kelly could only shake her head. Ignoring the inquisitive stares of passersby, Marti sat next to Kelly and hugged her until the worst of the deluge passed. Then she led her out to the car. Snow sifted down from a white sky in merry little flakes, and the air was pleasantly mild. While her aging Firebird warmed up, Marti turned to Kelly and tried again.

"What's up, Kel? You and Will have a run-in?"

Kelly released a short, acid chuckle. "You're way behind on the news," she said, sniffling like a child. "I haven't seen Will in weeks. And no, he didn't dump me, if that's what you're thinking." It was. "I dumped him."

"And now you're sorry."

Kelly sighed and faced the windshield, cold in spite of the already toasty heater. Though Marti was her dearest friend, it was Christmas-time and Marti was a Christmas freak; she loved every tinsel-flecked minute of it, from these mad shopping sprees to dressing the tree to loitering beneath the nearest sprig of mistletoe. Moreover, she was in love and contemplating wedlock, a circumstance that to Kelly had always seemed about as likely as global nuclear disarmament. Marti was vibrant, happy and alive. And in the face of all that, wouldn't it be dreadfully unfair of Kelly to unload all this crap onto her?

Kelly decided it would. Besides, over the past few months she and Marti had been...drifting apart. If there was any blame to be laid for this regrettable situation, it belonged as much to Kelly as it did to Marti.

But it was a blameless situation and Kelly knew it. People changed. Times changed.

Come on, Wheeler, tell the truth, to yourself if nobody else. Nothing has changed between you and Marti. She still loves you madly and you still love her. You just don't want to admit that your life is turning to mud. You don't want her to think you're losing your mind ... and aren't you?

The answer was an unqualified yes. How else could she explain the turmoil of the past two weeks? How would any half-competent psychiatrist explain it? At first glance, it all seemed remarkably straightforward, even in the apparent absence of a precipitating cause. All these years of suppressed emotion were finally leaking to the surface, eroding the structure of a life which, in reality, was more fabrication than real. You didn't have to be a student of Freud to figure that much out.

But wasn't "leaking" too mild a word? Because all that poison or suppressed emotion or whatever you wanted to call it was *exploding* to the surface, geysering out in a pillar of molten pain. And it was no catharsis. There was nothing healthy in any of this. With each passing night her mind dredged up some new and twisted mutation, some new distortion of the past. It had reached the point where she either spent her nights trying to stay awake or drugged herself so heavily that in the morning her dreams were banished from memory.

In her waking life she thought often of Will. There had been maybe a hundred times over the past two weeks when in the backwash of the previous night's dreams her resolve had gone to tatters and she'd picked up the phone and dialed his number. But she'd always cut the connection before the wire-hiss turned to ringing. The one time she did let it ring, there had been no answer. *At work,* she'd thought defeatedly, and deemed it a sign from the gods. She didn't think she could have spoken to him anyway. She'd only wanted to hear his voice.

Yes, she thought of Will often. But she never dreamt of him. Peter dominated her dreams now, as he had all those years ago. She'd dreamed of him when he was whole and their future still lay shiningly ahead of them. And she'd dreamed of him later, after the accident, when his image had turned a nightmarish yellow. But with time he'd withdrawn from her dreams, dropping back sporadically to leave tears on her pillow, but for the most part keeping away.

But now...

Since that night with Will—a night that still chilled her in its convoluted reality—Peter had ... come back.

Back to her dreams.

At first it had been good, within the context of dreaming at least, as fond wishes fulfilled. She'd felt so close to him in those dreams, bonded in every sense, at one with him in a way that only dreams could allow. He filled up her ache, like gold in a hollowed tooth.

But since the day she visited the hospital—an abortive mission that had induced its own breed of nightmare—the tone of her dreams had undergone a vulgar transformation. Not infrequently over the past several nights she'd awakened in a frenzy of masturbation, drenched with sweat and moaning Peter's name, her legs spiked back and her fingers buried deep in her works, Peter's presence so palpable inside her—and that was the operative word here, "inside," as if somehow he shared her skin—she wanted to scream with the sense of violation. Her orgasms came like cold dollops of ice cream dropped on her belly and then she turned on her side and wept, despising his intrusions, loathing herself, and yet stricken by his passing from her shell. And slowly, some hateful part of her began to look forward to this carnal delirium, to actively seek it out.

And the dreams weren't the sum of it. There were other things, events more subtle and difficult to define. Like the feeling she got sometimes when she was alone and the wind was snuffling at the fire-

place doors, the feeling—sudden and lacking any basis in reality—
that there was someone right behind her, the skin-prickling sense that
unseen hands reached out for her neck. When these phantom sensa-
tions came, she would whirl from whatever she was doing (on one
near-disastrous occasion she'd been stirring pasta into boiling water
and had knocked the pot to the floor, splashing her jeans and almost
scalding the cat) and affrightedly scan the room, certain beyond any
shadow of a doubt that someone had just darted out of the room. Then
she would prowl the entire house, the Louisville Slugger she'd kept at
her bedside in Kingston clasped murderously in her sweating hands.

But there was never anyone there.

There were subtle stirrings—pockets of electric air, hot, intimate
rushes—and throughout the house, objects seemed constantly... out
of place. Though neat by nature, Kelly had never been one of those
fussy housekeepers. When she vacuumed or dusted, she took no great
pains to return every plant or ornament precisely to its original loca-
tion. Yet even with that she'd begun to get the unsettling sense that
things had been shifted while she was out or asleep. A potted plant
displaced three or four inches from its usual spot. The glasses in the
cupboard rearranged. The boots in the rack slyly shifted. She would
look at these things and in her increasingly agitated state be hard
pressed to trust her own memory—and at the same time swoon with
the awful certainty that someone had access to her home and was
screwing with her mind, softening her up for the kill. God help her, it
had even occurred to her that it might be Will, crazy with jealousy or
rage. Jesus. Sweet, innocent Will.

Oh, yeah, she was losing her mind all right.

She turned in her seat and looked at Marti. In the silence, the
defroster had cooked two oblong eyeholes in the windscreen. "Forget
it," she said. "I just get a little nostalgic around Christmastime. You
know how it is."

Marti started to protest, but she knew Kelly well enough to read the signal. When Kelly dismissed an issue out of hand like this, no matter how obvious it was that she was hurting, there was no point in trying to push her any further. It would all come out in due time.

"Are you sure you're all right?" Marti said, deciding to test the water just a little.

"Right as rain," Kelly said, mustering a smile that felt like a muscle cramp. "Let's go find us some Christmas cheer."

"I'm here for you, babe," Marti said, touching Kelly's hand. "I don't want you to forget that."

"Thanks. But I just need some time to think."

"Ten-four," Marti said, and clunked the Firebird into gear.

THREE

—

ON WICKED WINGS

27

THE LOCKERBY CAB DROPPED Leona Gardner in front of the church. She paid her fare—part of it in quarters she'd pilfered from Sammy's piggy bank—and stepped out into the gentle snowfall. Fat flakes seesawed to the pavement like thistledown, and for a moment Leona was reminded of her girlhood, the first time she'd taken a close look at snowflakes and marveled at their intricate shapes. In the orangey glow of a street lamp, she squinted at a giant flake that had settled on her coat sleeve, trying to snag the receding tail of that sweet memory. But her vision was blurry, and before she could focus on it the flake collapsed into a droplet of water. Stalled on the steps, already five minutes late for mass, Leona realized that she'd forgotten having had a childhood. Her memory contained only misery.

She clopped up the long cement staircase, adding her boot prints to the hundreds of others in the light dusting of snow. Winded, she paused before the hand-carved doors and dug in her purse for her flask. One last pull to carry me through, she thought. Midnight mass was a long one, and the incense always made her feel ill.

Beyond the doors, organ music boomed in the cavernous nave, the voices of the choir rising in solemn harmony.

With a practiced twist, Leona uncapped the flask. A tip, a guzzle, another twist, and the flask disappeared again. Exhaling hot vapour, she composed her face, straightened her back, and entered Saint Joseph's Cathedral.

The caroling had barely begun, but some vestige of pride prevented Leona from entering the main body of the church. It was packed in there, and she could see herself being forced to march all the way up to the altar in search of a seat. After adjusting her hat—the same one she'd worn to her son's funeral, God rest his soul—she headed for the big wrought-iron candelabrum that stood inside the left aisle entryway. The entire church was adorned with these flickering fixtures, each of them presided over by a plaster-cast statue of an apostle or saint, which stood in a dusty alcove in the wall above. Through some secret irony, Leona had chosen Saint Peter's allocation of candles. Hands spread in blessing and welcome, the sober-faced saint huckstered coins in inanimate silence. Dutifully Leona rummaged in her purse for the last of Sammy's quarters. She deposited them, fifty cents' worth, in the strongbox, and lit a candle in her dead son's name. She knelt, muttered a Hail Mary, then shuffled to the north tower staircase. When the family was together, they had always sat in the balcony. The organist was up there, and Peter had insisted on sitting close to her, often paying more attention to her playing than to the incomprehensible phases of the mass.

Leona found a seat on the aisle about two-thirds of the way down. Catching a whiff of her, the woman she crowded in next to widened a disparaging eye, but Leona didn't notice. She unbuttoned her coat, let it droop off her shoulders, and reached for the hymnbook tucked into the rack in front of her. They were just starting "Away in a Manger," one of her favorites. She took up the chorus lustily, her voice gratingly off key.

* * *

"Skipping midnight mass?" Peter said as his brother wobbled into the room, his gray eyes barely visible over the stack of gifts he was lugging.

Sam snorted. "The last time I went to midnight mass was the last time you went, remember?"

"Yeah, I remember," Peter said as Sam set the gifts on the foot of the bed. "The incense made you sick and you had to leave. In a hurry."

"That's right." Sam grinned in remembered embarrassment. "Just made it out the door before I blew mom's turkey all over the stoop."

Sam held his breath, afraid Peter might clam up at his accidental mention of their mother and the evening would be spoiled before it had a chance to begin. But it seemed those days were over. Oddly, Sam felt little comfort in that. He took off his coat and pulled up a chair.

"Christ, yes," Peter said, taken up in the grisly reminiscence. "Amazing, isn't it, how ingrained us poor Catholic kids become with the fear of God. No way can a kid toss his cookies in God's holy condo and still expect a pass at the Pearly Gates. Shit, I can still see you running up that middle aisle with your hands over your mouth and your cheeks puffed full of puke."

"Fuckin' A," Sam said, recalling the terrible sensation of impending eruption, the horror of trying to hold it all in. "'Member the spray? I geysered hours-old stuffing all over the last three rows."

"Can it," Peter said, laughing. "You're making me sick."

"You ever seen what cranberry sauce looks like the second time around? The way it kind of curdles—"

"Fuck off or I'll spit in your eye."

Mom's going to midnight mass, Sam almost said. Whatever else she was, she was still their mother, and Sam felt they should at least be able to discuss her. She was a sick woman, an alcoholic, and sometimes Sam felt unable to cope with her on his own. In a way, Peter's "visits" had made her worse—for days after that séance she'd been practically certifiable—and Sam felt his brother should share in the responsibility, even if only with advice. Peter was nothing if not an intelligent, insightful human being.

But a dark look stole over Peter's face, as if he'd read his brother's thoughts, and Sam plowed ahead before the sudden tension could gain a foothold.

"Wanna see what Santa brought you?"

Peter brightened a little. Good old Sam. He plainly refused to let anything die. For the past six years Christmas had meant little more to Peter than June the first or February twenty-ninth. It was just another day spent prisoner in this nerveless bag of a body. But Sam always made it that tiny bit brighter.

"Not another toothbrush," Peter said in that cruel breed of humor Sam had still not gotten used to, and probably never would.

"Nope," Sam said. He patted the larger of three foil-wrapped boxes. "You'll never guess."

"So show me," Peter said, deciding to play along. If he knew Sam, the kid had gone to considerable expense to brighten his Christmas. The least he could do was pretend to be happy. "Could it be … a lifetime supply of Swedish Erotica DVD's? Olga Gobbles the Home Guard?"

Sam grinned. He loved his brother mightily. "Nope. Not even close."

Peter rolled his eyes in a parody of concentration. "Okay…could it be a new pair of shoes? No, wait…a spanking new flight helmet. Yeah, that's it."

"Wrong and wrong again." Sam glanced at his watch. "Too bad you'll have to wait another…eighteen minutes to find out."

"Cruel and unusual."

"Well...okay. Let's have a look-see."

Ignoring the parcels at the foot of the bed, Sam reached into a plastic IGA bag on the floor by his feet. He came up holding a foil-wrapped package about the size of a cigar box. He made a show of examining the name card.

"Oh. Here's one for me. 'To Sam from Pecker Pete.' Hey, man, thanks a bunch. Can I open it now?"

Grinning, Peter nodded. Every year Sam pulled the same crazy stunt. Since Peter had almost no way of shopping for Sam, short of browsing through the tedious fare in the gift shop downstairs, the kid always bought a present for himself and scribbled Peter's name on the card. Usually it was some sort of gag. Last year it had been a peaked cap—peaked caps were big in the north—but this one had a huge coil of fake dogshit glued to the bill, real enough looking that you sort of breathed through your mouth for a couple of beats until you were sure it was only plastic. The year before that it had been a huge rubber dildo in the shape of a rocket.

Sam tore off the paper with a flourish. He lifted the lid, peeked inside, and beamed like a delighted child. "Check—it—*out*." Daintily, with forefinger and thumb, he produced a flesh-coloured harmonica in the shape of a penis, complete with grotesque ropy veins. "A bone-a-phone." He blew a couple of discordant notes.

"Play dat funky music, white boy," Peter said, caught up in the fun in spite of himself. The kid always got through to him. "Man, lookit the helmet on that. Blow those skin-harp blues."

"Hairy sax," Sam said with a grin, waggling the thing in the air.

"Flesh flute."

"Cock clarinet."

"Pistol whistle."

"Okay," Sam said, showing his palms in surrender. "I give."

"C'mon," Peter said, curious now. "What's in dem boxes?"

"All right. We'll start with the big one."

* * *

The caroling went on for a good half hour, the raised voices of the congregation almost drowning out the high-pitched trill of the choir, all of it underpinned by the reverberating chords of the organ. By the time the singing was done, Leona could barely contain her tears. Both Peter and Sammy had done stints as altar boys, and when the procession filed out of the vestry—the priest resplendent in the red and white silks of the season, the sober-faced altar boys balancing tall golden candlesticks—she lost it completely, sobbing like a child, honking every few minutes into a crumpled hankie. The woman beside her elbowed her bespectacled husband, who'd been drowsing, and dragged him off to another pew. Leona didn't mind. The stuffy bitch's perfume had been cloying.

The opening prayers gave way to the first of the Old Testament liturgies, which the plump monsignor recited in a booming *basso profundo*. At first Leona did her best to follow. But her throat was parched, and an all-too-familiar drumming had begun against the delicate skins of her temples.

She needed a drink.

* * *

"You crazy son of a bitch," Peter said in unaffected surprise. This was miles more extravagant than anything he'd expected. "This must have cost a fortune."

"Nah," Sam said, blushing furiously. "I stole the sucker." It was an Apple computer, complete with keyboard, colour monitor, and all the handy-dandy attachments one needed to run the sweetheart with no hands. Peter could tell it was used, but it was in mint condition.

"You crazy son of a bitch."

Not wanting to cry—as he wound up doing every year—Sam set about gathering up the wrapping paper and stuffing it into the wastebasket, jabbering the whole time about all the neat things Peter could do with his new toy.

"They've got more games than Carter's got pills. I picked out a few of 'em for you. Pac-Man—I knew you liked that one—and a Chuck Yeager flight simulator that'll flip your wig. The guy gave me a demo, and within two minutes I was reaching for the airsick bags. It comes with a dozen of them—barf bags I mean."

"You crazy son of a bitch," Peter said a third time, still marveling. "What about word processing?"

"No sweat," Sam said, sitting again. He'd arranged the computer components on the table at the foot of the bed. Now he paused a beat. "You want to write?"

"Yeah. I've been thinking I'd like to record some of my experiences. You know, when I leave this piece-of-shit body."

Sam flushed again. "Sounds great." He still hadn't gotten used to the idea of his brother as a kind of living ghost. The story Kelly had told him that day outside the Sandwich King had made his skin crawl, and the look in his mother's eyes the night of her bogus séance had made him want to shake her until she finally snapped out of it. Her eyes had shone that night with the lunatic light of revelation, and Sam guessed she'd have been no more affected had God Himself materialized before her on a cloud of spun silver. It was creepy, and as much as Sam understood Peter's need for something meaningful in his sessile existence, he wished none of this had ever happened. Against his mother's instructions, he'd come home that night to find the apartment a shambles and Leona planted soddenly on the piano bench, stuporously stroking Peter's enshrined grad photo. When he tried to talk to Peter about it the next day, Peter had cut him off in a brutal stroke the likes of which Sam had never had leveled at him before. It had stung him deeply.

But what had stung him even more was the shine of cruel satisfaction in his brother's eyes. Peter had tormented their mother and enjoyed it. Enjoyed it immensely.

"Well," Sam said, getting to his feet. "It's a quarter past twelve and I've got to shag ass out of here." His eyes were fogging with inevitable tears. "Believe it or not, I've gotta work tomorrow, Christmas or no Christmas."

"C'mere," Peter said, his own eyes moistening.

Sam bent over the bed, cupped his brother's face in his hands and kissed him on the mouth. A tear fell, mingling with one of Peter's on his cheek.

"Fag," Peter said as his brother drew away.

"Fuck you," Sam said as he left the room.

"And your grandmother, too."

"See you tomorrow," Sam said from the corridor.

"Yeah," Peter said to the empty room. "You too, kid."

* * *

Gazing at the computer components through rainbows of grief, Peter lay alone in the Christmas morning silence and thought about who he had been. With the vividness of one preparing to die, he reviewed the highlights of his sentient life with pain and a terrible yearning. The images came in no discernible pattern. He remembered the ambulance attendants lugging his mother down the long flight of stairs in their duplex on Colby Street, her belly swollen to the size of a beachball, her pale face grizzled with pain; and his first glimpse hours later of his newborn brother, gray eyes scrinched shut, dark hair matted with a blood-tinged goo that had frightened him badly. He could still hear his father's voice, assuring him it was nothing to worry

about, his brother was okay, just a leftover smear of the juices he'd
stewed in for nine long months. With the same startling clarity he
remembered his first glimpse of Kelly Wheeler, long-legged teenage
goddess seeming so unattainable, swinging her locker shut in the last
mellow light of an autumn afternoon, ample breasts all but hidden in
one of those baggy sweaters she insisted on wearing. "They're gross,"
he could hear her saying of her breasts in that singsong voice. Ah,
they were anything but gross, and the first time he'd seen them—
the first time he'd *touched* them—he believed he'd died and gone to
heaven.

Other images marched through his mind in a solemn procession.
Inviting Kelly home and sitting beside her on the piano bench, dissolving the fib he'd told her about his beginner skill level in the most
moving private concert he'd ever given; the love they made later that
day, that first incredible love, its overmastering intensity; the four of
them—Peter, Sam, their mother and Kelly—going together to midnight mass…

For a moment he remembered what it was like to be whole, so
lucidly he almost tried to sit up in bed. With this memory came a
breath of the inner calm he'd once savored, the quiet confidence, the
easy belief in a shining future…

Then, like entrails scraped from a butcher's block, the whole thing
slid into a lime-filled pit. With deliberate strokes Peter filled the pit in,
putting paid to a past that was truly past, as irretrievable as an infant's
first breath. The accident had changed him. In one brutal stroke it had
reduced him to a heap of breathing rubble. A page had been turned,
a savage twist effected in the horror novel of his life. But now a new
page was turning; he sensed it with a certainty not even the healthiest
of nerve endings could so keenly relay.

It made him want to pray.

* * *

The trance came readily tonight, quelling the storm in his heart, setting him adrift on a warm narcotic sea. He left his body without a backward glance and slipped through the frosted window. Outside, snow fell in lazy, looping flakes, and an updraft carried him away. Behind him, slung about the hospital's concrete waist, a festive sash of Christmas lights flashed in random patterns. Across the lake, the Science Centre twinkled like an idling spacecraft. Few vehicles were afoot on this early Christmas morning, just a lone city bus sluicing back to the garage, and a cab without a fare. Ranged out below him, the strip-mined face of the land seemed to Peter like an old and tarted-up whore trying vainly to disguise its pockmarked features behind a mask of Yuletide cheer.

He veered toward the twin Gothic spires of Saint Joseph's Cathedral, thinking how much they reminded him of teeth. Rotted stubs of teeth.

* * *

"For a child is born unto us, a son, and dominion is laid on his shoulders."

A son, Leona thought wistfully, idly tuning in on the sermon. Even through her grief and the whiskey haze she could remember how it felt to have him growing inside her, nudging the walls of her womb with an innocent elbow or knee. Her labour had been so easy; Peter had come into the world kicking with a hale vitality... but the instant he'd slipped through her birth canal, a vast depression had consumed her. It had persisted for weeks, becoming at one point so black Leona had contemplated ending her life. The sense of loss, of amputation, had been total. It was as if her heart had been wrenched out along with her child. The feeling had passed, to be replaced by the wonders of the life she'd given. But it had returned with Peter's death. Now all that filled it was the booze. The fit was imperfect, more illusion than substance, but it got her by.

If only she could carry again...

A bitter cackle rose in Leona at the unbidden thought of conceiving again, of carrying a child the way she'd carried her Peter. Sam had been a horror, unplanned, unwanted, born after thirty hours of excruciating labour by Cesarean section.

No. Nothing could replace her boy.

Her tongue made a spitless pass across her lips. Far below, the priest knelt before the altar in a gesture of supplication, the flowing folds of his vestments pooling around him like a garish noonday shadow. The congregation had joined the choir in an upbeat rendition of "Today a Saviour Is Born," and Leona took advantage of the interlude to scrounge in her handbag.

And even before she got the cap off the flask, she could feel the emptiness withdrawing a little, filling, like cement slopped into a hole in the dirt.

* * *

He slipped into the church through the big mullioned window, its round shape reminding him of a docking port in some cosmic Spielbergian saga. Inside, the altar, the kneeling congregation, the resounding chords of the organ—all of it swamped him in a backswell of nostalgia, and he hung there in the smoky nave, remembering. As a boy he'd wanted so badly to try out that organ, with its uncountable buttons, pedals, and keys, that he'd actually looked forward to coming to church. And they always had to sit in the balcony, as close to the organist as possible. In those days the organist had been a scratchy, blue-haired dolly who'd frightened Peter with her cold black eyes, eyes that measured him harshly the one time he mustered the nerve to approach her during mass. She'd favored him with a witch's scowl that sent him cowering back to his seat, round eyes swimming with tears.

Could that wicked old fossil still be alive? he wondered now. Still lording it over her organ?

He rose on the perfumed air, gliding over the lip of the balcony the way a breeze kisses over a ridge. The organist had her back to him, but he could see from here that she was a much younger woman; her straight posture and hennaed hair told him that. She—

A bright dart of silver pierced Peter's eye.

A reflection...

He glanced down—and there she was, not ten feet below, the last person he'd expected to find here, tipping a flask to her lips under the reproachful eyes of all those around her. There she was, a wraithlike parody of the woman who'd once been his mother, who'd borne and suckled and loved him. There she was, the whore who in the hour of his greatest need had left him for dead.

Rage plowed into Peter like a steaming locomotive. His mouth yawned open in an unheard, killing scream, and he flew at his mother like a missile.

* * *

Leona's body jerked and then stiffened, the small joints in her back popping like corn. The flask flew from her hand and ricocheted off the pew in front of her, scarring the wood and blessing a small circle of worshipers in a mist of Jack Daniel's. A terrible inarticulate groan escaped her as she rose rigidly to her feet and her handbag thumped to the floor. Spittle roped down from her mouth, which had stretched itself back in a G-force rictus.

You bitch, Peter roared in a silence that was somehow infernal, maddeningly impotent. He had meant to pass through her like a cold

December wind, but a few feet from her his deliberate forward momentum had been converted to a passive, magnetic drawing, a resistless pull with twice the force of his initial attack. He had pierced her in a way that left him feeling unexpectedly warm...and paradoxically aroused.

He was inside his mother.

He struggled away from the baking heat of her, the spider-silk cling of her, trying to escape. He wanted *out*. But she would not let him go.

"Peter?" Her voice was husky, erotic. She stumbled into the aisle, the people around her shrinking back. "Peter?"

A forbidden excitement seized Peter then, an oedipal rapture that extinguished his rage as effortlessly as a wave crashing over a match flame. His mother's flesh enveloped him, awakening dark dreams and sinful passions, doubling, trebling, quadrupling the richest ecstasies he'd shared with Kelly Wheeler.

Staggering down the stairs, Leona flung her arms around her own heaving torso, as if to embrace the life that had suddenly infused her. The heel of one shoe snagged on a bald patch of carpet and sent her tumbling into the lap of an immensely fat woman, whose bloated cheeks reddened with anger. This crazy bitch was stone drunk in the house of God, the fat woman thought, and she heaved Leona to her feet with a thrust of her flabby arms. Leona regarded her with glazed eyes before staggering away, her own cheeks as red as a cockscomb.

"Oh, Peter," she babbled, "I love you. God knows I love you so much."

No, Peter shrieked. *Let go of me. Let go.*

Passion, anger and shame roiled within him in a witch's brew of emotion. He could see through his mother's jaundiced eyes the commotion her convulsions were causing. Even downstairs, twenty feet below, inquisitive heads were turning, curious faces angling up.

But she would not let him go. He was trapped...and worse. She was drawing him downward, away from the twisted warren of her mind to the barren heat of her womb.

And a part of him wanted to go. A part that was growing by the second.

No, he protested, bitterly vehement. *You left me for dead.*

"But you *were* dead," Leona crooned in that same husky voice. She took the last three steps to the railing in a lurch that almost toppled her over the edge. Hands reached out to stop her, and she batted them away. "Dead and buried in that shell of a body." Her hands clasped the guardrail and she smiled. "But now you're back. To be born again."

Far below, the priest interrupted the mass to look up.

A tattered hush blanketed the church.

No.

"Yes," Leona whispered. *"Yes."*

The opposing forces of disgust and desire were tearing Peter apart. With the entire force of his will, he resisted that dizzying downward pull through his mother's sick body. He had already passed the jackhammer thud of her heart, the coarse bulk of her diseased liver, and now the slippery coils of her guts enfolded him in a hissing serpentine tangle. Vivid memories of the womb seduced him still farther downward, the floating peacefulness, the constant nourishing warmth...

But it would not nourish him now. It was peeling and dry, and he would perish there.

NO.

Peter rocketed back toward his mother's brain.

Leona's eyes widened. Her arms left her chest and dropped stiffly to her sides. Her entire body began to tremble.

She climbed onto the railing.

Let go of me, Peter demanded.

"No," Leona said aloud. "Never."

A hand closed around her ankle. Leona glanced down and saw a heavy-set man in a gray suit, his free hand reaching for her arm.

"Never," she said again.

And pitched forward over the edge. She did a flapping half-gainer before landing on her back on the candelabrum, where earlier some three hundred worshipers, herself included, had lit a candle and knelt to murmur in prayer. The slim iron crucifix on the lower left corner poked through the meat of her thigh. The one on the right punctured her heart. Life's blood boiled out even as the years-old lace dress she was wearing caught fire. There was a faint pop of flame, then a sudden, all-consuming roar. Her hair, always unruly, came alight like a forkful of hay.

In the instant the cold iron pierced her heart, her hold on her son was relinquished. As he left her body, Leona suffered an agony far more intense than the impaling that would in the next few seconds end her life. She looked up and saw a shimmering blue shape, transparent, phosphorescent, vaguely man-shaped. It hovered above her a moment, its pulsing head inclined toward her as if in pity. Then it was gone.

An instant later, Peter awoke in his bed in a cold bath of sweat. He had felt the crucifix burst his mother's heart.

Pungent black smoke roiled up from the charred fabric of Leona's dress, becoming sweet as the flames found her flesh. Her eyes were still open, gazing heavenward with the frenzied blankness of sacrifice. They swelled, then exploded. Like reluctant Inquisitors the congregation looked on, many of them turning away to empty their stomachs of the festive dinners they had barely begun to digest. Several had seen that eerie blue shape, but few would remember it in the horror of the following minutes. Those who did were busy denying it to themselves.

Already charred, Leona's skin began to crack open, craters in a primordial crust, releasing black smoke and an awful, greasy stench.

An altar boy appeared with a small red fire extinguisher. Ten feet from the pyre, he collapsed to his knees and sicked up his supper. A grim-faced woman retrieved the extinguisher and doused Leona's charring corpse with foam.

It was an hour before her blackened remains had cooled enough that the coroner and his assistant could bag them.

Mass ended early that night.

* * *

The pain in his chest subsided only slowly. An hour later he could still feel the path the cold iron had taken through his mother's heart.

But even worse than this lingering bayonet of pain was the persistent sensation of her diseased flesh around him. Being inside her like that, being *held* by her, sweaty mental hands groping him in forbidden places—that had almost finished him.

He lay in the dark of his hospital room and felt the walls creep in on him. There seemed to be no air to breathe, and his heart felt on the verge of bursting.

You killed her, his mind indicted him. *Sweet Jesus, you* killed *her.*

His thoughts ran rampant. The same stubborn corner of his mind that had so resolutely denied his quadriplegia sought now to denounce the reality of the events in the church, to ascribe them instead to some hateful night sweat. He had dreamed his mother's death, something which, in his torment, he had for so long believed she deserved. None of it had actually happened. He'd slipped not into a trance after his brother's gift-bearing visit, but into a deep and nightmarish slumber. His mother was at home right now, in her seedy little apartment, sprawled drunk and mumbling on the couch. It had all been a dream, from the very outset. He'd left his body only in the yearning rhapsodies of his sleep.

But a greater part of his mind recognized this line of thought for the thin evasion it was.

It had happened. All of it.

His mother was dead, and he had killed her.

Guilt reared its ugly head then, and for a few fretful minutes Peter cowered before its unwavering gaze. Long-buried memories shone through like coins in dirty water, and he saw her again as she had been, through a child's unblaming eyes, remembered how his world had once revolved around her. How could he have harmed this blessed, gentle woman?

Ah, but then he remembered the wreath, its piney weight and her insane refusal to hear him, to *see* him, and his confused regret shriveled in a fierce sunburst of satiated loathing and fury. She had gotten her due. It was perhaps no coincidence that she'd met her end in the house of God. After all, wasn't his new power nothing if not godlike?

There was no reason for guilt. He had done a higher bidding.

Peter raised his head off the pillow and gazed out the window at the night. High winds had whisked away the cloud cover, and now the night sky was black, star-specked and boundless. Beneath its ancient canopy, Peter felt filled with wonder.

Excitement.

And an intoxicating sense of *power*.

He closed his eyes and slept, soundly and without dreams.

28

KELLY SAT CURLED IN the easy chair by the picture window, her long hair in a braid, a wineglass leaning empty against the curve of her hip. In the lamplight, her eyes were lost in the hollows of their sockets. The corner of her mouth had taken up an annoying tic, and now she pressed a finger against it, trying to still it. On the stereo, Elvis rocked his way through a medley of Christmas favorites. The frozen lake, barely visible past the boughs of the big blue spruce she and Marti had spent the evening rigging up, was a moonlit purple plain, flat and unblemished. The ice was still too thin for the inevitable snowmobiles. Humming along with the King, Marti slung the last of the tinsel onto the tree. The flashing lights played prettily on the plain white cotton of her jumpsuit.

In spite of Marti's thoughtful presence—it was Christmas Eve, almost Christmas morning, and Marti had a sweetheart waiting for her at home—Kelly felt thoroughly, dismally alone. She had always loved the Yuletide season. It was a time of magic, a time of love, hope, and renewal. The half dozen Christmases following the accident had been bad, but this one promised to be the worst of them. She had expected to spend it with Will.

Fondly, she tried to imagine what he was doing. Had he found another girl? Or was he as lonesome and miserable as she? It seemed that her entire mental repertoire these days consisted of making up her mind to phone him and then deciding against it...and of course dwelling obsessively on Peter. Peter filled her thoughts the way a tumor fills a body space, growing by insidious degrees until there is nothing left but a husk.

On the stereo Elvis cruised from "Here Comes Santa Claus" into "Blue Christmas." Attracted by the glitter of the tree, Fang pounced out from under the couch and attacked a low-hanging bauble.

"Shoo," Marti said, poking the cat with her toe. Fang bounded away, tail bristling...and Marti glanced at Kelly.

She was crying.

Marti laid down her skein of tinsel and sat on the arm of the chair. "Aw, babe," she said, patting Kelly's shoulder. "Tell me what's eating you."

"I can't get him out of my head," Kelly said, her words filled with frustration and despair. "I can't..."

Marti felt something wither inside her, a bright balloon of contentment with a tiny but unstoppable leak. She felt torn on this festive eve, torn between Kelly and her troubles and the compelling draw of her own blossoming life. Steve was at her place this very minute, waiting with a bottle of bubbly for her return, and she just knew that tonight he was going to pop the question—if she didn't blow it by showing up after he'd wined and pouted himself to sleep. It had taken all of her charm (and a couple of downright unseemly promises) to get away at all this evening, and when she'd called him a half hour ago to tell him she'd be along soon, he'd seemed a tad miffed, to say the least...but last night had been the Sudbury Board's Christmas party at Sorrento's, and Marti had been there. And she'd heard some things—overheard them, really—in the can that serviced the reception hall.

"Nickie Cole thinks she's on drugs," Marti heard a catty voice hiss, and in the gloom of her stall she cocked an ear. Nickie Cole was the principal at the school where Kelly taught. "Apparently they narrowly escaped a lawsuit—and it would've been a whopper, I can assure you—over that gymnast who broke her arm. Word is she just stood there staring into space while the kid went flopping to the mats. Now if that isn't cocaine, you tell me what is. And apparently it's starting to show on her. She fell asleep in assembly the other day, and a janitor had to wake her. A janitor. And she stumbles around in a stupor half the time."

There was a muffled snicker, then another voice said, "What's Nickie going to do?"

"I think she should blackball the quiff"—and Marti knew then who the owner of that catty voice was; it was that bitch Irma Finney, she of the Gorbachev birthmark and the lazy left eye, teacher of political science and gossip-monger extraordinaire—"bust her to hell. There's plenty of responsible teachers just waiting for a job like hers."

Infuriated, Marti had come close to doing some busting of her own; but over the course of the evening, she'd discovered the rumors were true. Kelly had fallen under the eyepiece of the probationary microscope, and unless she shaped up, come next September she might find herself with nothing to show for her efforts but three weeks' severance pay and a form-written farewell. Marti had come over today to warn her... but they'd gotten into trimming the tree, and, Jesus, the girl looked dragged out enough without all of this. Marti was afraid that one more piece of bad news might finish her.

"Do you mean Will?" Marti said now, deliberately skirting the truth.

"No," Kelly said. "Peter, dammit. Peter." She sniffed. "And Will. Will, too... but it's different."

"What's different?"

"Well, I think about Will. Miss him. Wonder what he's up to and whether he's missing me ... but Peter ..."

"What, babe? Tell me."

"It's like he's *here*," Kelly said, looking at her friend with frightened eyes. "In this house. Everywhere. Lately I dream about him all the time. Vivid ... such *vivid* dreams ... But when I'm awake, alone, it's like he's here, behind me, around every corner. Watching me. I can feel him ..." *Inside me.* But she didn't say it. Not yet. Not to Marti.

The balloon of contentment in Marti's chest lost the balance of its air in a single defeated whoosh. As Kelly's best friend, she'd tried over the years to help Kelly get her life back on the rails. And until tonight, she'd thought Will Chatam might provide that final curative nudge.

But to Marti's rising horror, it appeared as if Kelly had slipped to the very brink. She looked like hell, had given up the only guy since Peter she'd truly cared about, her job was on the line, and now she was talking like one of those weepy little crazies who can't let go of the past, but rather brood over it until finally it swallows them whole. She'd gotten through all that a few years ago, scarred but wiser ... but now she'd fallen back.

Kelly dug a wad of Kleenex out of the pocket of her jeans and blew her nose. "Oh, Christ," she said, suddenly falsely bright, her puffy eyes widening as she glanced at her watch. "Look at the time." She stood. "You'd better clear out of here, girl, if you want that hunk of ice on your finger." She began tugging at Marti's sleeve, leading her toward the hallway and the exit beyond. "I bet Steve's pulling his boots on right now, getting ready to go downtown and look for an open pawnshop."

"Hold it," Marti said. "Just hold it." She put an arm around Kelly's shoulders, ignoring her resistance, hugging her. "The ring can wait."

The pain came then, gushing out of Kelly Wheeler like water from a ruptured dam. It came in crashing, thundering waves that rolled over Marti with a force that staggered her... and frightened her. It frightened her badly.

"There," she soothed, stroking Kelly's hair. "There. Let it come. Let it all come."

And for a while she did.

As her sobs tapered off, the mantel clock chimed out the midnight hour.

"Merry Christmas," Kelly said, and laughed through her tears.

"Same to you," Marti said, releasing her. "Feel better?"

Kelly nodded. And it was true. She did feel better. "I'm gonna go powder my nose."

Marti smiled. "Better powder your whole damn face, babe. You look like whale shit."

"Thanks for noticing," Kelly said, and padded into the stairwell. She was partway up when the doorbell rang. "Nuts," she said, crouching, looking wanly at Marti through the railing. "Who could that be?"

Marti shrugged. "Carolers maybe? A student lynch mob?"

"Would you mind getting it for me? And sending whoever it is away?"

"Consider it done," Marti said, and hurried out to the door.

* * *

Marti peeked through the sidelight and grinned. Standing on the stoop, stamping his feet in the gentle snowfall, stood jolly ole Saint Nick, resplendent in his poppy-red suit and curly white beard. He had a burlap sack slung over one shoulder, looking sorrowfully empty, and a tiny foil-wrapped package in his mittened hand. Marti couldn't see his face—he was looking back at the dog, who stood with its forepaws on the bottom step regarding him quizzically—and she didn't have a clue who it was.

Then it dawned.

Steve, she thought in a rush of excitement. And I just wonder what he's got in that package...

She tried to see past him as she reached for the doorknob, but whatever he'd driven up in was hidden by a mounded snowdrift.

She swung the door open and smiled. "Ste—"

Santa turned to face her.

"Hi, Marti. It's me. Is Kelly here?"

"Will?"

"The same," Will said. He tried on a smile, but it came off looking like a twitch. Not only did he feel like an idiot, he was terrified. This was a harebrained idea, the zaniest he'd ever come up with, and if Marti had been ten seconds slower getting to the door, he'd've been long gone. Or so he told himself.

He stood on the stoop in the porch light, waiting.

Marti shot a glance behind her, then waved him in. Nudging him out of the way, she grabbed her coat off the rack and pulled it on.

"Now listen to me, Will Chatam. Whatever you've got planned— and I think I know what it is—do it. Understand? I can see in your eyes that you're losing your nerve, but think about this: she needs you. She needs you, and I think in her own mixed up way she loves you. So whatever scheme you've got going, go through with it." She grabbed his hand. "Help her, Will. She's hurting."

Nonplussed, Will could only nod. He'd been skulking about at the top of the hill for the past half hour, starting down and then turning away, itchy in this ratty old suit, waiting for Kelly's company to leave. When he'd first seen the car parked next to Kelly's Subaru, he'd come close to throwing in the sponge right then. What was he trying to pull, anyway? Dressed up like Santa and lurking in the trees. If she wanted him she'd have said so by now. It had been weeks and he hadn't heard a word from her.

But the plain truth was that he had to confront her. Today, next week, it didn't really matter. When he'd first thought of it, the Santa getup had seemed…well, like a cute idea. He'd thought she might respond to it and at least let him have his say. And what a say it was going, to be. When Will Chatam went for humiliation and rejection, he went all the way.

He glanced at the package in his hand, then back at Marti, who was stepping into her boots.

"Do it," she said. Then she kissed him on the cheek, whispered "Merry Christmas" in his ear, and stole out the door.

"Marti?" he heard Kelly call from upstairs. "Marti, who was it?"

Catching his breath, Will tiptoed into the living room and waited by the fireplace doors.

* * *

"Marti? Who—?"

Kelly stopped dead in her tracks, a breath darting into her like a small, startled animal. She'd changed into a nightie and quilted robe, a matted old thing her mother had given her ten years ago, and now she belted it around her.

Santa Claus was standing by the fireplace. He had Will's face, and a gift in his mittened hand.

"Merry Christmas," Will said, and shrugged. "Marti took off…"

"Will?"

"No less." His body was filmed in sweat. "Hope you don't mind."

The tears started up again, and Kelly ran to him. "Oh, Will," she sobbed, hugging his padded suit. "I'm so glad to see you."

A knot broke in Will Chatam's chest with an almost audible twang. They stood that way awhile, Will stroking Kelly's hair as Marti had done only minutes before. Then Kelly stood back from him.

"For me?" she said, tapping the glittery package with a fingernail.

"Uh-huh." He handed her the package, his face grimly set, the face of a man was has staked his life's savings on a single spin of the wheel.

"I didn't get anything for you."

"The hug was enough."

Kelly smiled. "Should I open it?"

Will nodded.

"You want to get out of that outfit first?"

"I'll wait." *In case you throw me out once you see what's inside.*

Still smiling, Kelly unwrapped the package.

There was a tiny ivory-inlaid jewelry box inside. When she opened it, it played a wistful little classical piece Kelly didn't recognize, but thought might have been composed by Vivaldi. Inside, snugged in blue velvet, sat a single delicate diamond.

Kelly's eyes filled with tears again. She kissed Will tenderly on the mouth. "It's beautiful, Will, and I want to put it on. But can we call it a friendship ring for now? Until I'm sure?"

Will plucked the fur-rimmed cap off his head. His face was alive with a mighty smile. "More than anything, Kelly, that's what I want to be. Your friend."

Kelly slipped the shiny gold hoop onto the ring finger of her right hand. It was a perfect fit. "C'mon," she said. "Let's get you out of that suit."

* * *

Peter awoke refreshed on Christmas morning, though he'd slept only a couple of hours. He refused the breakfast they brought him and told the attending nurse he wanted to be left alone. It was Christmas Day, he told her, and he wanted to enjoy it in peace. A dull ache in his chest reminded him of the night before, but the memory awakened only a delirious sense of anticipation.

The adventure was just beginning.

When the room was quiet, he closed his eyes and rose from his crippled body. It was like being lifted out of a vat of bland syrup in which you could somehow breathe, but only barely.

He slipped through the glass into the sunny glare of Christmas morning.

* * *

In his indecision of the night before, Will had parked his truck at the top of the hill. As a result, Peter saw only Kelly's snow-heaped Subaru in the turnaround. When he entered the house—this time through the bedroom window, hoping to catch her asleep—the furthest thing from his mind was that she might not be alone. His trespasses of the past few weeks had instilled in him a deep sense of ownership, and he'd all but dismissed the possibility of the stranger's return.

The discovery was like salt in an open wound.

He found them seated at the kitchen table, drinking coffee and giggling over the big floppy Santa hat her boyfriend had cocked on his head. The sight was even more infuriating than the first time he'd caught them together, and Peter simply hung there, paralyzed anew. As he watched them, the scene seemed to grow in brightness until it glared.

Kelly wore only a nightie, a ghost of a thing you could see through. Now she leaned across the table and kissed the guy, kissed him on the mouth, her eyes closing in utter contentment ...

That broke the spell.

The power was suddenly huge, uncontainable, and Peter aimed it like a sputtering flamethrower; he aimed it at the jackass in the Santa hat—and when he let it go, the exhilaration was tremendous.

But nothing happened.

They went on kissing and giggling, and Peter found himself stuck in the wall like a misflung spear. Unbelieving, he pulled himself free and tried again, this time targeting Kelly.

Again, nothing.

A swarming maroon filled Peter's vision—and when he blinked he was back in his bed. Back in the drowning pool of his body.

A nurse at the desk down the hall heard his agonized howl, but decided, wisely, to ignore it.

29

"GARDNER," COACH TESSARO SAID from the doorway of his cubbyhole office.

Sam, gearing up with his teammates, did not appear to have heard him. He was sitting hunched over his knees, lacing his skates, but close enough so that Tessaro's big voice should have reached him.

"Hey Gardner," the coach said again, and this time Rolly Sawchuck, the Sudbury goaltender, nudged Sam's shoulder with his glove. Sam looked around, stood, then started toward the office with a listless nod.

The kid was in a daze, Tessaro knew, what with his mother so recently dead (not to mention the way she died, Tessaro thought grimly), and the coach was having serious second thoughts about playing him. There wasn't much question that without him the team would suffer—at the tender age of twenty, Gardner was their key playmaker—but maybe the kid would suffer more. He wasn't at his best, not even close, and tonight they were in for a grudge match. The last time Sudbury had met the Ottawa U. Raiders, just before Christmas on Ottawa's home ice, the Ottawa team had been badly humiliated—mostly due to Gardner's scoring ability—and tonight tempers would be hot. Their goons would be laying for Gardner.

"Yeah, Coach?"

"Come in here a minute, would you?"

Sam angled past Tessaro's big belly, his skate blades thudding on the rubberized carpet, and stood before the littered aluminum table that served as the coach's desk. Tessaro closed the door and shot the bolt, then squeezed in behind his desk.

"Listen, kid," he said, looking squarely at Sam. "We all feel shitty about what happened to your mom."

Right, Sam thought. That's why so many of you showed up at the funeral.

"It was a hell of a thing." His gaze fell from Sam's. "I think it shows a lotta guts that you're out here tonight—and believe me, kid, we'd probably get our butts kicked without you." He shrugged. "But do you think you should be back in it so soon? I mean, it's only been a couple weeks, and we're in for a real barn-burner tonight, I can promise you that. That yard ape Kiley's gonna be gunnin' for you. You really smoked him last time out, and clean check or not, Kiley's gonna be on your ass like a rash." He met Sam's eyes again. "What I'm trying to say, kid, is that maybe you should sit this one out. You can stay geared up, watch from the bench, but—"

"No," Sam said, breaking a written-in-stone rule by interrupting the coach. "Kiley doesn't scare me." Bobby Kiley was Rhett Kiley's brother. And Rhett Kiley, full-time drunk and part-time mechanic, had once been a "friend" of Peter's. "I want to play."

A familiar flush rose from beneath Tessaro's collar, then gradually receded. "Okay, kid. You can go on. But I'll be straight with you. I see you fucking up out there, you're off the ice. Fair enough?"

"Fair enough," Sam said. "That it?"

At the coach's nod, Sam turned and clunked his way back to the locker room.

* * *

By 6:45 P.M. the arena was packed with fans, many of them already sipping spiked Cokes or swilling from forty-ouncers stuffed into brown paper bags. To their credit, the Ottawa team had managed a respectable turnout. Behind the Ottawa bench a mob of chanting fans hoisted a huge purple banner aloft while the team mascot, a guy in a brown bear costume, bounded up and down through the stands. On the Sudbury side similar festivities were in progress, all of it challenged for volume by the arena's organist, who keyed out something drab and repetitive.

In the Sudbury locker room, Sam lagged behind his teammates, who had filed out for the pre-game warm-up. Though heartsick at the death of his mother, ascendant over all of his emotions was guilt. The guilt was huge. It had begun Christmas morning, when he left the morgue to go tell his brother the tragic news, and it had plagued him unremittingly ever since. Peter had been up in his wheelchair that snowy morning, gazing trancelike through his ninth-story window. Sam had shuffled into the room swearing he'd be brave, that he would not allow the tears that were already falling—but before he'd gotten a word out, before his brother had even swiveled around to face him, Peter had said, "She's better off, Sam. We both know that."

"How did…?" But surely one of the nurses had told him or someone from Pastoral Care? Or maybe he'd heard it on the news.

Peter's wheelchair hummed through a hundred-eighty degrees. His expression was chiseled in ice. "She was a drunk, Sam. A whore. A liability."

For the first time in his life Sam felt as though he should be furious with his brother, utterly outraged. His inbred instincts of decency and respect cried out for that rage…but it wouldn't come. It just wasn't there. Peter was right. Their mother had been all of those things and more.

And in the cold light of Peter's words, Sam realized he was glad. Mother or not, the tormenting witch was gone, out of his life forever. And he was glad.

"Change your mind?"

Sam looked up into Tessaro's dark eyes. "No."

"Then get out there and skate."

Sam got to his feet. He plucked his stick from the rack, whacked its heel against the toe of one skate, and started down the damp cement corridor to the rink. In the pit of his stomach, all of his emotions were focusing into a single hot flashpoint, like sunlight funneled through a magnifying glass. Even the guilt. Especially the guilt. Like frenzied insects they orgied together...

And their single hybrid offspring was rage.

* * *

The players for both teams had been on the ice for five minutes, skating brisk warm-up patterns and flicking wrist shots at their goalies, deliberately bumping shoulders with their opponents. As in almost no other sport, hockey was a game of intimidation. On the ice, with two-hundred-pound slabs of muscle and padding hurtling at you at speeds of up to thirty miles an hour, fear was your ally. But only if you inspired it.

Sam stepped onto the ice and joined the carousel, slipping automatically into a practiced routine of limbering and stretching, flooding cold muscles with blood. After all was said and done, he was glad he'd accepted the spot on the Cambrian U. team. Though it used up a lot of prime study time—second year was even stiffer than first year had been—it also kept him sane. On the ice was perhaps the only place in the world Sam felt totally alive, totally in control. The frosty wind in his face, the good heat of all-out exertion, the grace the skate blade afforded the human body. He would have been incomplete without it.

But tonight Sam felt none of these things. He felt alone, angry, confused—

Pain roared up Sam's left leg from his ankle, spinning him around and almost dropping him to the ice. Out of the corner of his eye he saw a puck deflect away from him, and an instant later Bobby Kiley was barreling toward him from the opposite blue line. The burly centre scraped to a sidelong halt at the red line, inches from where Sam was standing.

"Ay, cocklips," Kiley said, grinning his greasy grin, his troll's face and shaved head gleaming with an unclean sweat. "It's you an' me tonight, rump ranger. Tooth and fuckin' nail."

Sam ground his teeth against the knot of pain in his ankle. Kiley was not only known for his brawling; he had one of the meanest slap shots in the league and the accuracy of a laser-scope rifle.

"Stay out of my way," Sam said flatly.

"Ooooh," Kiley baited, doing an effeminate little jig. "I'm shakin' all over."

In the sway of Sam's unflinching gaze, Kiley's grin faltered, and for a moment Sam thought the crazy mother was going to throw down his gloves right there. Then he was skating away, snorting laughter, snaring a puck and driving it at the open net.

* * *

The first period passed without altercation. A Sudbury defenseman drew a two-minute penalty for hooking. Gilles Peltier, the Sudbury right-winger, scored an unassisted goal at five minutes of play, and Bobby Kiley matched it less than a minute later. To the delight of the fans, Kiley snapped his stick in half over the ball-peen curve of his head as he skated back across the red line. It was Kiley's trademark, and even the Sudbury devotees roared their approval. Later in the period, Sam cross-checked Kiley in a clean play, knocking him sprawling, and everyone expected an immediate punch-up. But the big brawler only grinned and skated away. In a way, Sam was disappointed.

But the shit hit the fan during the first two minutes of the second period.

Closing full bore on the Ottawa net, Sam picked up the puck at the blue line, faked a slap shot, and lobbed it over the goalie's shoulder. The puck wobbled into the right top corner of the net, making the score two to one.

The crowd roared.

Bobby Kiley came out of nowhere, a snarling locomotive moving at top speed. Two feet from his target he spiked up an elbow and slammed it into Sam's right ear, sending Sam's helmet flying and dropping him to the ice like a flung sac of seeds. Twelve hundred perfect Os punctuated the astonished faces of the fans, creating a chorused boo that thundered through the cavernous arena. Sam landed hard on his left shoulder, numbness bolting down his arm like a shot of novocaine. A whistle blew and one of Sam's teammates gave Kiley a shove, but Kiley decked this new adversary with a single punishing jab. He swung his stick at another attacker, shattering the visor of his mask, then threw off his gloves. Ignoring the referee and the fast-approaching linesmen, Kiley skated a mocking circle around Sam, spraying him with chill mists of ice.

"Get up, numbnuts," he taunted. "C'mon, chickenshit, get up before I spear out your eyeballs." He chortled like a lunatic, stabbing at Sam with his stick.

"Back off, Kiley," the referee said, "or you're out of the game."

Kiley ignored the threat. The fans were on their feet now, thirsty for blood, shouting jeers and tossing debris onto the ice—and Kiley loved every minute of it.

Dazed, Sam started to climb to his feet. When he was halfway up, Kiley drove the blade of his stick into the back of Sam's knee, dropping him to the ice again. A linesman made a grab for Kiley, and Kiley shoved him away.

"That tears it," the referee said, giving another sharp blast on his whistle. "Kiley, you're out of the game."

"Nothing to lose, then," Kiley said.

A scrap broke out between an Ottawa defenseman and the Sudbury left-winger. One of the linesmen skated in to break it up and another skirmish developed. On the margins of the circle that had formed around Kiley and Sam, opposing players hugged and shoved, their fuses shortening by the second.

The fans were going wild.

"C'mon, fag," Kiley said. "Get up. Whatsa madda? Your momma not here to look out for you?" The light of cruel inspiration shone in Kiley's eyes then, and he leaned over Sam's heaving frame. "Hey, Gardner. Been to any barbecues lately?"

Sam's body jerked as if shot. He got to his hands and knees on the scarred surface of the ice and spat out a mouthful of blood.

Bobby's brother Rhett had clambered down to the boards with his perpetual companion Jerry, and now the red-faced mechanic egged Bobby on. "Good call, Bobby," he shouted, having caught his brother's last comment. "Serve him up a plate of fried Momma."

Still grinning, Bobby glanced proudly at Rhett as he glided past the net.

Then Sam was up and skating, head down, stick up, shoulders hunched like a rhino's. Rhett's eyes widened to astonished saucers, and he pointed a grease-blackened finger, trying to warn his unheeding brother.

He was too late.

Bobby windmilled around with his stick, meaning to slash his unseen attacker, but Sam came in low, catching Kiley in the midsection, driving him into the now vacant net. The iron crossbar connected with Kiley's thick neck, the force of the impact lifting the goalposts off their pins. Sam, Kiley, and the net collided with the boards in front of the goal-judge box. Regaining some leverage, the heavier Kiley scrambled free of the net and caught Sam's jersey by the right shoulder, twisting it down and over in an effort to disable Sam's punching arm.

But Sam was a southpaw.

Sam's fist arced over Kiley's right arm and smacked the brawler on the beak, cracking it. Blood exploded from Kiley's nose in a startling gout, spraying Sam's face and drenching the front of his jersey. Locked in the classic scrappers' embrace, the two players commenced a rapid-fire exchange of blows, hammering away with furious abandon, turning flesh into pulp. Sam felt no pain, only a grim satisfaction each time his knuckles ground into Kiley's ugly mug. A particularly well placed uppercut dazed the big brawler momentarily, and now Sam worked his right ear, mashing it into a bloody rag. Reaching around with his suddenly free right hand, Sam caught hold of Kiley's jersey and yanked it over his head, temporarily blinding him. Exploiting this advantage, Sam hooked a leg behind Kiley's and tripped him, the abrupt shift of balance slamming him down on top of his thrashing foe. Dangerously vulnerable, Kiley cried out for a linesman, but by now the entire rink was a bloody battlefield littered with sticks and gloves and writhing bodies. Skaters came off the benches and joined in the fray. Even a few junk-tossing fans had hopped over the boards.

There was no one to save Bobby Kiley.

Sam straddled Bobby's chest, clutched him by the throat, and rained blows into his face. Kiley struggled for a while, but under the steady piston of Sam's fist he soon lay senseless and still.

Sam continued to pound.

A half-full bottle of Jim Beam buzzed past Sam's ear and shattered on the ice behind him. Sam looked up at Rhett Kiley, still safely stationed behind the boards.

"Get off him, you fuckin' freak, "Rhett hollered, his face the colour of clay. "It's over. You're gonna *kill* him."

Sam drew back to hammer Bobby again.

"*Hey*. Let him up or I'm gonna turn you into a fuckin' zucchini, just like your fuckin' brother."

In that instant Sam came totally unhinged. Later he would have little recollection of the events that followed. He sprang off Kiley's moaning frame and rocketed toward the boards. Blanching, Rhett and his sidekick turned tail. Rhett was furious, but he'd seen what this fucker had done to his kid brother, who was three times as tough as Rhett could ever hope to be. He headed for the stands at a run, Jerry hot on his heels.

Sam barely touched the boards vaulting over them. Then he was up in the aisles, frenzied fans shrinking back, sparks flying from his skates where the blades gouged the greasy cement. He ran headlong into a soda boy, sending his tray of wares flying, and charged after the fleeing hecklers.

On the ice below, the chaos continued, both teams locked in blood-battle. The referee and linesmen had abandoned all attempts at keeping the peace and were now engaged in the delicate business of staying out of the way.

Through a rear exit, a dozen helmeted policemen tramped into the arena.

"Come back here," Sam screamed, a lifetime of repressed anger at last given vent. "I'll kill you. You hear me?" Tears tracked his sweat- and blood-streaked face. An incisor dangled from his gumline by a bare tag of tissue. "Come *back*."

Taking the corner at the top of the flight, Sam tripped over a discarded popcorn container and pitched to his face in the aisle. Ahead of him, Rhett and Jerry vanished through an exit, elbows still pumping.

Drained, hurt, humiliated, Sam climbed back to his feet.

"Hey, kid," an excited fan shouted. "Look out."

As he spun, Sam ducked his head, avoiding Bobby's slashing stick by bare inches. The blade struck the cement and splintered. Dazed and furious, Bobby threw down his stick and kicked at Sam with a skate. Releasing a warrior's cry, Sam came up inside the lethal kick, catching Kiley on the blunt knob of his chin with the last ounce of strength he had left.

Kiley's skates left the floor. His contorted face went blank, its only colour a grisly smear of blood he'd cuffed across one cheek from his still bleeding nose. This time when he landed, he did not get up.

Ignoring the congratulatory shouts of the fans, Sam headed for the nearest exit, needing all of his will to avoid collapsing to the littered cement.

On the rink below, the havoc continued.

* * *

After changing and stowing his gear, Sam slunk quietly out of the arena. He had no idea how the game had turned out, nor did he care. Tessaro had been right: he should have stayed out of it.

But in many ways tonight had been inevitable for Sam. The tension had been building inside him like steam in an unvented pressure cooker, and if he hadn't cracked tonight, it would have come some other time, some other place. He was glad it was out. He was hurting—his mouth was still slick with the taste of blood, and his tooth was so loose he could wiggle it with his tongue—but he felt good, purged somehow.

The air was balmy on this mid-January eve, and a cheerful snow was falling. After a few minutes' walk, Sam unzipped his parka. The air felt good against his neck and abraded face. He could not remember having been so tired, but even that felt agreeable. The fatigue lay inside him like a gentle narcotic, and he lost himself in the easy pace of his stride. A block up from the arena, he crossed the street to cut through the parking lot of the Ledo Hotel. Behind him, headlights flickered on and a car crunched out of the lot, the low grumble of its engine receding into the night.

As he reached the crest of the Paris Street bridge and the hospital came into view, it occurred to Sam to stop in and see Peter... but more and more often of late when he visited his brother after dark Sam found him sleeping—or rather, off in one of his "trances." It was weird. In the two weeks since their mother's death Peter had been almost manically cheerful—although Sam sensed something counterfeit and distracted in this cheerfulness—reporting to Sam each day of his increasing ability to leave his body. They'd set up the computer ten days ago—the morning after their mother's interment—and already Peter had mastered the word processing software. Yesterday Sam had walked in to find him busily tapping the keys with the mouth-held striker one of the occupational therapists had rigged for him... but when Sam tried to sneak a peek, Peter had scrolled the screen blank.

Sam picked up his pace. On his way past the hospital, he glanced up and noticed that Peter's window was dark.

Suddenly his weariness didn't feel so good anymore. Suddenly he wanted nothing more than to fall into bed, though he didn't relish the thought of that empty apartment. He still hadn't touched any of his mother's things, and he didn't know if he ever would. Maybe he'd have the Neighbourhood Service people come by and fish through the litter. The reel-to-reel was still on the coffee table where she'd left it. There were even a few of her empties left scattered about.

Christ, that godforsaken tape…

Sam turned down the last dark street before his building, thinking that maybe in the spring he'd give up the apartment and find a room in residence. Yeah, that'd be better. Maybe even meet a few girls. He chuckled at this thought, barely mindful of the big champagne-coloured Caddy that drifted past in the oncoming lane, high beams blazing. It rolled to the end of the street, the tarnished chrome of its bumpers gleaming as it glided beneath each mellow streetlight, then U-turned at the end of the block. Now it motored slowly back, its snow tires reeling up the tracks it had laid down during its first pass along the street. Sam turned to face it, squinting in the glare of the headlights.

Accelerating a little, the Caddy swerved into the curb ahead of Sam and braked abruptly, its rear deck fishtailing. The hood, a large circle of which had been cleansed of snow by the heat of the Caddy's big mill, seemed to go on forever, and Sam wondered why a sane person would expose such a cherry antique to a northern Ontario winter. This baby was at least thirty years old.

Assuming its owner needed directions, Sam started around the hood to the driver's side.

The Caddy lunged forward like a skittish horse, then nosedived as the driver stomped on the brakes. The front bumper buckled Sam's knees and he nearly fell. Angry and a little afraid, he whanged the hood with his fist and got out of the way. Cautiously he proceeded to the driver's side window, which was slowly humming down.

"Hey, man," Sam said. "You ought to be more careful—"

The words died in his throat. He was looking into the inebriated face of Rhett Kiley, underlit by the swampy green glow of the dash lights. And there were at least three other ape-size heads in there with him. The familiar reek of whiskey wafted out on a bank of cigarette smoke.

"Hey, boy," Kiley crooned. "You're the one ought to be careful."

Roaring with laughter, Kiley flicked on the dome light, killing that wicked green shine but revealing a frightening convention of psychos. Sam recognized all but one of them.

Next to Rhett sat Jerry Jeter (and wasn't that a tire iron in his grease monkey's paw?). In the back on the far side slouched a still-grinning but subdued Bobby Kiley. The other guy, a barrel-chested giant with the big-boned features of a pro-wrestler, Sam had never laid eyes on before. But of the lot of them, this guy looked the meanest.

Sam decided to shin it.

"Get him," Kiley said, shoving his door open.

Sam leaned into a sprinter's stride, swinging his gym bag at the wrestler who popped out of the back with an almost magical swiftness. He'd managed barely a step before he lost his footing in the light dusting of snow. As he scrabbled for purchase, the opening door clipped him in the Achilles tendon, spinning him around and flipping him to the pavement.

He looked up into a circle of sneering faces.

A boot shot out and caught him in the ribs, Rhett Kiley's boot, and Sam felt something splinter inside him.

"Hit a man when he's down," Kiley said. "How's it feel? Like it?" He lashed out again, grazing Sam's upper arm. "Huh? Gutless spider."

"Yeah," Bobby cheered from the backseat. "Cave his fuckin' head in, Rhett."

Sam tried to get up and the wrestler kneed him in the chest. "This the way you homos fight?" Sam rasped, clasping his damaged ribs. He was in a world of trouble here and he knew it. Tanked as they were, there was every good chance these crazies would kill him. "Three on one?"

"Fuckin' A," Jeter said, and popped Sam's knee with the tire iron.

Unable to help himself, Sam cried out.

"Listen to the piggy squeal," Rhett said. "Why don't you call your bowling-ball brother? He'll come save ya. Just like he al—"

Lightning quick, Sam sprang up onto one bent leg and drove a boot into Rhett Kiley's balls, doubling the big man over. Kiley's air rushed out and he puked up a bellyful of booze.

Sam was almost standing when the tire iron tagged him on the side of the head. Under the force of the blow, the commotion around him receded into a high-pitched pinging sound, like an approaching outboard heard from deep underwater. Drifting snowflakes turned into violent pinpricks of light, brilliantly coruscating, then faded to yawning black holes. Sam swung a fist that connected with nothing, registered a distant, hollow laugh, and collapsed in a boneless heap.

"Pick him up," he heard someone say. Far away.

(the wrestler)

Now he was rising effortlessly through space.

Floating…?

Billy Tyler, a bouncer not a wrestler, who owed Rhett a favor, drove a fist into Sam's exposed vitals, then kicked him in the face.

Sam free-fell into unconsciousness, the blows against his body perceived only as a patter of raindrops on a rooftop overhead.

* * *

Rhett tramped on the go-pedal, causing the Caddy to torpedo dangerously over the greasy snowfall. He grinned at the throb of aging pistons, imagining his dear departed daddy twisting in his grave. The Caddy had been the old man's pride and joy. This would be the first winter it had seen since Gord Kiley drove it new off the lot in 1961.

Ignoring the stop sign at the top of the street, Rhett careened through the poorly lit intersection, narrowly missing an elderly woman in a green Volkswagen Rabbit. Whooping in spite of the ache in his balls, he reached over the seatback and grabbed the bottle of Jim Beam, which had begun making the rounds again as soon as they'd piled back into the car. He guzzled a liberal dose, then handed it over to Jerry.

In the backseat, Bobby was enthusiastically recapping the trouncing they'd given Sam Gardner. When he got to the part where Jerry had popped him with the tire iron, Jerry grabbed the heavy twist of iron from the floor mat and cracked himself on the bean with it. This struck Bobby as hilarious, and he howled until he almost puked.

A few minutes later, swinging onto Paris Street, Rhett spotted a cop car in the lot fronting the Plaza 69 pharmacy.

"Stash the bottle," he said, and Jerry stowed it under the seat. Cruising at a respectable thirty, Rhett rolled past the lot and away. The cop didn't bat an eye.

Rhett sighed, sobriety trying hard to reclaim him. His brain was beginning to work again, and deep down, even though the jacked-up little cunt had really creamed his kid brother, Rhett felt a stab of guilt over the Gardner kid. They'd left him in the middle of the street, bloody and unmoving, and if that porch light hadn't come on when it did...well, Rhett guessed they might have killed him. Maybe he should've left Billy the bouncer out of it. After all, vegetable or not, Peter had once been his best friend...

Rhett leaned a little harder on the accelerator, an unwelcome cloak of remembrance settling over him.

Yeah, those had been the days. As far as Rhett was concerned high school could've gone on forever, especially the senior years. Those had been Rhett Kiley's glory days, though it had taken him a few extra semesters to get there. Quite a few, actually. Football, chicks galore, that special breed of companionship you just couldn't find outside of a team sport...and Gardner had been the best of them. Poetry to watch him play ball. Utter fucking poetry.

But they were dead days, Rhett reminded himself. And the intervening years—six of them, although it might just as well have been sixty—had worked on him hard. At twenty-seven, Rhett looked like a man twice that age. Uncountable gallons of beer had slung an apron of fat around his middle, three packs a day of unfiltered Players had played hell with his lungs, and a total lack of exercise, combined with an atrocious diet of sweets, french fries and burgers, had given him the bloated, puffy look of an aging Elvis. Bearing grease and engine oil had worked their way into his skin, and there was the permanent dank odour of sweat, smoke and internal combustion about him.

Dead days, all right.

Unmindful of Rhett's ruminations, Jerry jabbed him in the ribs with the bottle. "'Nother hit, Rhe—"

Rhett batted the bottle aside, sloshing some of its contents onto Jerry's grease-spotted jeans. "I told you stunned fuckers to stow that."

Jerry, who'd always admired Rhett—and feared him—stuffed the bottle out of sight. They were downtown now, rolling past the City Centre.

In the backseat Billy said, "Let me out here," and Rhett swerved into the taxi lane fronting the shopping concourse. He was glad to see the back of Billy Tyler. The guy was a psycho.

As they merged into traffic, a gloomy silence settled in the car. Rhett had remembered something else about Peter Gardner, and now his knitted brow darkened with an old, undying grudge.

Gardner had stolen Kelly Wheeler from him. Rhett had never dated the girl, but he'd seen her first, had even pointed her out to Gardner in the halls. The greedy prick could've had any other pussy he wanted, but no, he had to go for the Wheeler bitch.

High-pockets whore thinks her shit doesn't stink.

Rhett's grip tightened on the wheel and he tramped down spitefully on the gas, bulleting through the intersection at Elm and Lorne on the yellow, fishtailing dangerously. A city bus gave him the horn and Rhett leaned hard on his own, flipping the driver the bird. They were headed for Highway 144 now, and the lunar plains of the Copper Cliff mines.

There'd been some bullshit scuttlebutt about the bitch asking Gardner to the Sadie Hawkins dance, but Rhett never bought it. That wasn't how it played. His fucking *friend* got a sniff of that sweet little stinkhole and just had to have her for himself.

Well, Rhett thought, uttering a stunted chuckle. Not only can the sorry schmuck not get it up anymore, he doesn't even know where to find it. Serves him right. Too smart. Just too fucking smart.

But another, smoldering part of Rhett Kiley knew that Peter had quite simply been a better man, in every respect. No one had offered Rhett a football scholarship, but Gardner had turned down three of them. Kelly Wheeler would never even have given him the time of day if he hadn't been a friend of Peter's. Christ, the one time he'd gotten up the nerve to call her after the accident, hoping to catch her on the rebound, the snotty bitch had chewed him out over the phone, told him he had a lot of nerve and what kind of friend was he anyway?

Yeah, Kiley thought now. What kind of friend?

"Fuck it," he said aloud, bringing the Caddy to a sidelong halt on the roadside. They'd left the city behind, a faint parabolic glow in the congested night sky. Now, ice-scabbed Precambrian rock stretched out for miles on either side of them.

"Yeah," Jeter mimicked. "Fuck it."

Rhett smiled, showing a shiny gold tooth. "Let's get shitfaced," he said.

All and sundry agreed.

30

THE INTRUDER IS STILL around. And she's wearing his ring. Oh, fuck, that makes me furious. And what's worse, I can't seem to touch her anymore. Not since Xmas. Trying to only makes me crazy. As melodramatic as it sounds, I think her feelings for the guy are protecting her somehow, insulating her.

It isn't fair. Kelly's mine.

But I'll get her back. It's just a matter of time. I'll get back inside. Then we'll see who she really loves...

Peter stopped typing and listened, his heart triphammering in his chest. The sound he'd heard came again—a voice, drawing nearer—and Peter tapped the Save button and exited his secret file. He tasted bile as he let the key striker drop from his mouth.

It was Dr. Lowe, marching toward Peter's room with his usual entourage, and the sound of his voice—cool, dry, imperious—gave Peter an unexpected shock; it was the first time he'd heard it in three weeks. Lowe had been away on his annual vacation in Florida—in previous years Peter had looked forward to this break almost as much as Lowe did—and in the delirium of the past weeks Peter had almost forgotten his feelings for the man.

From the sound of it, the time off hadn't diminished Lowe's enthusiasm for torment. Stationed outside Peter's door, he launched into his usual pre-visit sermon, modulating his voice so that to his students he appeared a paragon of discretion, but to Peter his words were plainly audible. He rambled on about Peter's "increasingly frequent bouts of torpor, characterized by deathlike paleness, near total cessation of autonomic functions, and a decrease in blood pressure which, under normal circumstances, would barely be compatible with life."

Peter let the words rattle the chains of his rage.

Turns you on, doesn't it, Lowe.

"His body temperature drops precipitously," the doctor lectured, "and his respirations become undetectable. Were one to fail to examine him minutely—his pupils continue to react, albeit sluggishly, and he does maintain a recordable blood pressure—a diagnosis of death might result."

Peter tuned the man out. In another few minutes he'd come flouncing in with his followers, oglers on a medical midway, hungry for a glimpse of the talking head.

If the stupid little shits only knew what he was capable of—

Why don't you show them? a persuasive voice cut in. *Eh, bonebag? Why the hell don't you?*

"Maybe I will," Peter said with a whispered savageness that startled him. "Maybe I will."

Without knocking, Lowe strode into the room, students in tow. His smug smile slipped when his eyes met Peter's—the impotent anger he'd expected to find there had been replaced by something else, an amused secret light that danced gleefully—and the doctor looked away, giving the impression to his students of a child who has accidentally intruded on his copulating parents. The doctor tried to shift back into academic mode, but the transition was sloppy, and now the students looked ashamed, too.

"Come ahead in," Peter said, bugging his eyes. "I'll see if I can't go all catatonic for you."

Lowe stood silent, crimson creeping into his bronze Florida tan.

"I think we've picked a bad time," one of the students said, a young woman in a starched intern's jacket. Her gaze met Peter's with an open but compassionate frankness. "I'm sorry, Mr. Gardner," she said. Then she turned and walked out of the room. The others followed.

Still off balance, Lowe only stood there, his gaze flicking from his feet to the door and back again. Words perched on the runway of his tongue, but he seemed unable to get them airborne. In the silence, Peter realized this was the first time in years he'd been alone with his doctor.

"I know about you," Peter said with a taunting half smile.

Lowe's doughy face jittered up—and now he was the child again, only this time caught with his hand in the cookie jar. A thin shine of sweat broke out on his brow. His pupils telescoped madly.

"What do you mean?"

"I know about you, Harry. I know what you're into." His head angled up. "And I am going to kick your lardy white ass."

Lowe clutched the foot rail in a lame display of indignation. The doctor wanted very badly to dismiss Peter's words, to sling them back in the cripple's face...but he'd been caught so completely off guard that any meaningful response eluded him. Paranoia was like that.

He stood there a moment longer, then scuttled out of the room.

* * *

"And so, ladies and gentlemen," Lowe said to the members of the Medical Advisory Committee, his composure on the verge of landsliding away on him, "I trust you'll agree that, armed with this proposal, we can approach the board with confidence."

He smiled at the enthusiastic applause, but the smile was a brittle fabrication, on the brink of dissolving into a panicky grimace of need. He'd needed his fix before—the night his wife walked out on him, her last word as she climbed into his Mercedes—"Half!"—clanging in his ears like a fire bell; that had been bad—but the craving had never been this colossal, this totally overmastering. His hands, which had shaken so badly during his hour-long presentation he'd had to stuff them into his pockets, kept wanting to fly up and tear his hair out in big bleeding handfuls. Lunatic laughter hunkered on the curb of his teeth, waiting for a chance to go vaulting out of his mouth.

And through it all, one thought rattled in his brain: What did that gimp fucker mean?

(*I know about you, Harry.*)

What did he know? He couldn't know about the drugs. Could he? He was bolted to his bed like an anvil to a blacksmith's block. Sure, he tooted around in his wheelchair from time to time, but it was damned hard to remain inconspicuous—

"Fine presentation, Harrison."

Lowe cranked his eyes into focus and tried to disguise his startlement. It was Dr. Javna, chief of staff, grinning through his neatly cropped beard, one hand extended and waiting to be shaken. Lowe dragged his hand out of his pocket, doing his best to rid it of sweat. "Thanks, Chief," he said, pumping the man's hand. He noted the sudden shift of Javna's eyes and felt himself shrinking inside.

"You coming down with something?" Javna said, releasing Lowe's hand and rubbing his palm on his suit vest. "You're as clammy as a race horse."

"Could be," Lowe said, thinking, *Let me out of here.* "Feel fine, though." He raked his papers into his briefcase.

The chief leaned in, green eyes twinkling. "Well, you look like hell."

Lowe's gut cramped. *Christ, do they all know?*

"Maybe you should go easy for a couple of days. The project's in the hands of the MAC now. Kick back a bit."

Javna clapped him on the back. The sensation thundered through him. "Good advice," Lowe said. "Maybe I will." He smiled, barring back a scream, and dragged his briefcase off the table. "If you'll excuse me?"

Then he was bustling out of the room, trying not to run, forgoing the elevators for the echoey solitude of the stairs.

* * *

Shawna Blane scooped up a forkful of niblets and aimed it at Peter's mouth. Peter accepted the offering and chewed it dutifully. Three floors up, the MAC meeting was still an hour away from convening. It was six o'clock, a cold clear January evening.

Shawna had tried to palm this duty off onto one of the students, but they'd had a lecture to go to and Shawna ended up saddled with the job. She hated coming in here. Peter made her nervous, and he just went on getting weirder by the day. Little wonder when you thought about it, which Shawna tried to do as little of as possible. If you dwelt on this kind of god-awful luck for too long, you ended up imagining yourself in the same cruel shoes.

Shawna shifted back from the tray. She kept getting the unsettling impression that her charge was about to sit up in bed.

"If you move any farther back," Peter said, amused, "you're gonna have to pitch that shit at me."

Shawna blushed, the one thing she hated doing most in the world. Shifting a grudging inch closer, she rummaged in her mind for something to say—and while sawing off a hunk of veal it came to her. "How's your brother doing?"

"Sam? He's got the flu." The veal came up and Peter accepted it, his eyes narrowing with suspicion as he chewed. Shawna had been avoiding him for weeks, and besides, she hardly struck Peter as one observant enough to notice that Sam had been absent for a while. The kid had called early Sunday morning to explain that he was down with a bug and that it might be a few days before be felt up to coming in again. "Why do you ask?"

"I did a shift in Emerg on Saturday night," Shawna said. "Covering for a friend. I saw him there."

"In Emerg?" Peter said, almost choking on a mouthful of food. The alarm on his diaphragmatic stimulator glowed briefly, then winked out. "What was he doing in Emerg?"

Shawna gathered niblets off the tray. Peter's outburst had made her knife slip as she hacked anew at the veal, and cold yellow kernels had gone scooting every which way.

"I assumed you knew," she said. "He was pretty banged up. I figured it was a car accident, but the duty officer told me later that he'd been...beaten up. I'm sorry. I—"

"Did they admit him?"

"No. Dr. James wanted to—he was the duty officer that night—but your brother wouldn't have it. He went home."

"Get him on the phone for me, would you?"

"Sure."

Peter recited the number and Shawna dialed. It rang several times; then Sam's voice came on, phlegmy and thick, drugged sounding.

"Sammy?"

"Yeah." Slow, deliberate shuffling. "Hi, bro."

"How's the bug?"

Peter dismissed the nurse with his eyes. Relieved, Shawna gathered the utensils onto the tray and hurried out of the room.

"Better," Sam said. "Sleep a lot. How 'bout you?"

"Forget about me," Peter said, his concern doubling at the pain in his brother's voice. "Tell me more about this bug. I've yet to see one that can punch the crap out of a grown man."

"That's exactly how I feel—"

"Can the bull, kid. You always were a lousy liar. Shawna the she-bitch tells me she saw you in Emergency on Saturday night. She said you got the shit kicked out of you."

"Oh, that." He chuckled, but it sounded like rocks being rattled in a paper bag. "No big deal. Got into a tussle at the game, that's all. Broken tooth. The coach made me get it checked out at the hospital." The rocks rattled again. "You should see the other guy."

"Who was the other guy?" Peter said. In his capacity as older brother, he'd had to straighten out more than a few bullies in his time.

"I don't know. Some goon."

It was no use. Sam was a crummy liar, but over the phone he could hold out forever.

Peter decided to pay him a visit.

"When will I see you?"

"Maybe tomorrow," Sam said. His voice had faded, as though the mouthpiece had sunk below his chin. "I've been sleeping a lot."

"Yeah. You told me that."

"Take 'er easy," Sam said.

"You, too, kid. You, too."

* * *

Gliding into the unkempt apartment, Peter was struck at once by the memory of his first visit here. The shrine was still in its place on the piano lid. The furniture was all as it had been, and from his vantage by the room divider Peter half expected to see his mother's head pop up over the couch back, her bloodshot eyes scanning the room in search of him. There was a head visible there, just the crown, but it was Sam's. The TV was on, tuned to the evening news, and as Peter drifted closer he saw the kid's bare feet, propped on the edge of the coffee table.

Suspended on the stale apartment air, Peter floated over his brother's head—and then stopped, his heart filling with sadness even as his vision flashed white with shock.

Sam was asleep, but Peter could tell at a glance that only his left eye still opened, and even that to barely a slit. His right eye was buried in a shiny purple mass, and his nose, the size and shape of an Idaho spud, was taped and obviously broken. His parted lips revealed two ragged rows of gums interrupted by sparse white teeth. Peter estimated eight missing teeth, maybe more. A rank of at least ten stitches pleated the line of his jaw...

Peter looked away, dazed and glowing with fury. He could feel the sight of Sam's beaten face threatening to hurl him back to his body, and he steadied himself, needing to see the rest. When the vertigo settled, he looked down again.

Sam wore only his Jockeys. In this nearly nude state, the balance of the damage was painfully evident. A snug Velcro binder encircled his ribs, restricting his ability to breathe. Abrasions tattooed his chest like leopard spots, some of them already weepy with infection. There was almost no skin left on one knee, and the other was wrapped in a tensor bandage. A bruise the colour of a setting sun screamed out at Peter from the flesh of Sam's right thigh.

Jesus, kid, who did this to you?

Sam's body jerked, the discomfort the movement caused him reaching him even in sleep, and he moaned, a tortured sound, like wind in a twisting culvert. His eyes backrolled beneath their lids, live things straining to escape, and he cried out again, swiping at the air with a half-formed fist. The fist plunked down to the couch, and was still.

Dreaming, Peter thought, understanding the torment dreams could bring.

Peter touched his brother's forehead...

And with a faint twinge of guilt at his trespass, he entered his brother's dream.

* * *

There was no incestuous rush this time, as there had been with his mother, only a welcome surge of affection and warmth. He soared into the turbulent strata of his brother's psyche like a gull into stormy mists, feeling closer to the kid than ever before, at one with him in every sense.

But this euphoric sensation was promptly shattered as he reached the tornado's eye. There was a brilliant flash of light, *pain*, then a skewed glimpse of winter night sky. Jacked into Sam's dream, Peter felt himself falling—

Then a ring of angry faces surrounded him, steam jetting from flared nostrils, and pain exploded in his rib cage. One of the faces *(that's Kiley that's Rhett fucking Kiley)* hovered closer until it filled the sky, and now its mouth fell open, releasing a run of meaningless syllables. Peter tried to get up and something socked him in the chest. Pain flared afresh and then he saw another face *(Jerry)* and the dark, featureless oval of a third—

Then he was plunging back through space toward the hospital, slamming into his body, a black, killing fury unleashed inside him.

* * *

The screen winked out to a pulsing green bead, then it was blank. Peter could look at it no longer. His neck was killing him, his eyes had begun to ache… and his anger was making him crazy. After colliding with his body he had tried to relax, to achieve the trance again so that he could go back out there and find those three fucking bullies. But when he closed his eyes he saw his brother's face, beaten to a pulp, and he knew it was useless. He would have to calm himself first, channel the hate, make it work for him instead of against him. Needing a distraction, he'd switched on the computer and begun to write, but even that had turned into furious ravings.

The dirty bastards had knocked out the kids teeth.

That's it. Feel the hate. Feel it grow.

There was no sense going after them now. He wanted to relish this particular piece of revenge, and in his present frame of mind he would end it too quickly. Better to wait. Ponder the good old days for a while. Remember his three old compadres for the weasels they were. Kiley he could have expected this from, even Jerry. But Mike? What was he doing still jerking around with those losers? Hadn't he planned on becoming a pharmacist?

Maybe it wasn't Mike. You didn't see the third guy plainly. What if—

"Fuck that," Peter said to his empty room. "Who else would it be?"

All three of them had run out on a friend who was down on his luck. It only stood to reason that the same three jackoffs had trashed his brother's face.

Gonna put a hurt on you boys, Peter thought, and chuckled. It looked as if he'd inherited his father's temper after all. Now it was just a matter of dreaming up something special...

Peter's eyes settled randomly on the calendar on the opposite wall. It was a hospital-issue thing, with seasonal landscapes on thick glossy paper. It was open to January; today was the sixteenth...

And then he had it.

The third weekend in January, every year.

The ice fishing trip.

He had no way of knowing, but he was willing to bet that his three "good buddies" still honoured that tradition.

Peter grinned.

Payback time—

"Excuse me, Dr. Lowe?"

Peter heard the voice only faintly, but it intruded on his thoughts like a scream; it was coming from the nursing station down the hall.

Now he could hear Lowe's footfalls—he knew them as well as he knew his own voice—but the doctor didn't answer the hailing nurse.

Peter glanced at the bedside clock: 7:06 P.M.

The voice came again, closer now. "Dr. Lowe? You've got a new admission—"

"Not now," Lowe said, and Peter could almost feel the desperation in his voice. "I've got to get to my office."

Got you now, you rodent.

Lowe hurried by in the hallway. Peter caught a glimpse of him through the open door—a flash of suit coat and he was gone. A moment later the door to the stairwell hissed open and Peter heard his footfalls stamping hurriedly upward.

He closed his eyes, reached out for the trance...

And slipped away.

* * *

Finally he was alone.

Lowe locked his office door, darted to his desk and switched on the lamp. With mutinous fingers he dug in his pocket for his keys. They came out with a musical jangle. He found the appropriate key—

And froze.

"Who's there?" He squinted in the lamp glow, but could discern only the squarish humps of the furniture. "Is someone there?"

No answer.

Now his scalp felt tight; he was breathing like a long-distance runner. He hadn't exactly heard anything. It had been more of a... feeling.

Of being watched.

Paranoia, Harry old boy. High-grade paranoia.

And in that instant, for the first time in five years of mainlining drugs, it struck him.

I'm a junkie. Addicted. Hooked through the balls.

No way…

Oh, yeah, son. Straight through the silky fucking balls.

Lowe leaned back in his chair, waves of shock crashing over him—then he lurched forward, grabbed the wastebasket and spewed his supper into the plastic liner.

Jesus, I'm hooked, and that whining prick Gardner knows it. He hates me, and he's going to blab it all over the hospital—

But no. Of course not. How could he know?

And even if he did, he could be stopped. A simple malfunction in his diaphragmatic stimulator, late at night…

(tonight)

The thought solidified—then dissipated as a brilliant sphere of pain detonated at the midpoint of the doctor's brain. Lowe had a clear thought of ruptured blood vessels, then even that thought blew apart. His hands shot up and clasped the sides of his head, squeezing, folding the slack flesh of his face into a grotesquely puckered mask of agony and confusion.

He fought it.

What is happening to me?

It was a dying man's plea, mute and despairing—

But he would not die. He fought for control of his mind, for command of his rebellious body. If he could just get his hands on his dope…

Then it ceased. All of it. The expanding ball of pain, the bucking of his mind against its reins. Though badly shaken, he was lucid again, his body responsive to direction.

So this is what full-blown withdrawal is like.

The thought was little comfort.

He searched for his keys, found them on the floor between his feet, and unlocked the bottom drawer. He almost fumbled the leather pouch bringing it out.

Steady… almost there…

Barely able to control his fingers, Lowe unzipped the pouch. He dug out an ampoule, a swab, a syringe. He tore the swab free, wincing at the sting of alcohol in his nostrils, and removed the syringe from its wrapper. Running the needle through the ampoule's rubber seal, he injected two ccs of air and withdrew an equal volume of liquid. It was a potent synthetic narcotic, the colour of spun silver in the mellow light of the desk lamp, and he had to get it *in*.

After fishing a tourniquet out of the pouch, Lowe stood, brought one foot up onto the edge of the desk and hiked up his pant leg, baring his stockinged calf. With some difficulty he got the tourniquet snugged beneath his knee and, after rolling down his executive sock, began flicking at a vein with a fingernail. The vein, a small one near the ankle, became quickly engorged, as if sharing its owner's need. Though the gauge of the needle was fine, Lowe made it a point to avoid using the more accessible veins of his arms. A single bruised track could give him away.

He swabbed the vein vigorously, excited by its liquid shine. The needle, no thicker than a human hair, slipped painlessly into the vein. Lowe drew back a tiny cloud of blood, then shot the wad home.

He released the tourniquet and sat down. Warmth wormed its way up his leg like the tongue of a veteran hooker. It lingered teasingly in the cleft of his groin, then continued its ascent through his belly. Lowe closed his eyes, inhaled… and finally, gloriously, the drug reached his brain.

A smile of ecstasy creased his face.

The world drifted away, became a remote, colourless mist, without connection or consequence. The desk clock ticked; traffic droned by in the meaningless distance.

And the sweet dreams came.

* * *

If he was going to do it, it had to be now. Though Lowe had resisted him at first, there'd be no fight left in him now.

But, Jesus, he dreaded the thought of sinking back into that mind, or what in Lowe's case passed for one. It was a cesspool in there, a brimming slop pail more repugnant than anything Peter could have imagined. It reminded him of the time he and a friend had gone exploring in an open sewage culvert behind the Nickel Ridge smelter. It had been dark and wet and rancid in there, but to the two young boys they'd been, it had seemed a great adventure... until Peter's groping hand sank into the maggot-eaten face of a wino who'd crawled in there the previous winter to escape the cold and froze to death. But the spring heat had thawed him, oh yes, and then the flies had found him...

Entering Lowe's mind had been like that, like shoving your hand into a dead man's rotting face.

All the more reason, Peter thought in the dull light of Lowe's office. *All the more reason to fix him.*

He reached for Lowe's shiny pate before he could change his mind again.

* * *

Lowe's eyes snapped open. Colours bloomed in the darkness, blending, then resolving into the ill-lit contours of his office.

Why did I come up here?

He noticed his fix on the desk.

Oh, yeah. Time to do up.

He chuckled. What a numbnuts. Took the shit out and forgot to use it. He found the open swab—*dry?*—and a faint alarm sounded in his mind.

Dud swab, that's all. Dry run. Should send it back for a refund.

He chuckled again. Picked up the syringe. Cranked ten ccs of air into the ampoule and withdrew an equal measure of liquid. He reached for the tourniquet... but it seemed a long way off, coiled beneath the lamp like a snake cribbing in the sun, and he said to hell with it.

He flicked a vein in the crook of his elbow—

(wrong)

—and another alarm sounded, this one more insistent.

(not in the arm)

Nice vein. Do it.

The needle slipped in and the gold ran home. The rush was instantaneous, astounding, and a dimming part of Harrison Lowe wondered why he'd bothered with all those pissant little doses in the first place. This was the way to fly.

Fly...

He crossed unsteadily to his sixth-floor window. It was an incredible night out there, plump flakes sifting down, the sky a glowing white. Watching it, he felt himself lightening, losing mass, until soon it seemed he possessed no more substance than a snowflake.

He climbed onto the foot-wide windowsill.

Fly.

Lowe pressed his forehead to the glass, then the palms of his hands, letting the thermal panes take some of his weight. Senses heightened, he peered down the flank of the building, then up, intrigued by the eddying patterns of the snowflakes, the way the updrafts caught them and twirled them about like eager little dancers. Letting the glass take his full weight, he imagined himself aloft out there, floating gently on the updrafts…

There was a muted creak of strain followed by a gritty splintering sound as a crack etched its way up from the lower left corner of the inner pane.

The night air would support him, he knew it would, because he was *light*, barely there, a dream with wings—

!!Crraaaack!!

No.

Lowe shoved back and away from the window. In response to the sudden force, the glass blew out with a savage barking sound.

Winter air found him where he lay dazed between his desk and the windowsill, and it cuffed him harshly in the face.

Overdose, a panicked voice cried…but to Lowe it was merely a whisper. *Got to get up, got to get moving…*

Neglecting to conceal his stash, Lowe got to his feet and stumbled to the office door. Behind him, glittering snowflakes swept in through the shattered window, forming tiny white drifts on his desk. He twisted the latch, pulled the door open and stepped into the hallway.

A service elevator stood directly across from him. He punched the button and the doors slid open. He stepped aboard, thumbed the button marked B and leaned against the paneled wall. When the doors rattled open again, he stepped into a narrow basement corridor lined with pipes and ducts and floored with raw cement.

Aimless, he tried the first door he encountered.

The morgue was unlocked. It reeked of formalin. A few lights were on, picking up gleaming highlights, and in an unseen drain liquid chuckled obscenely, a sinister sound, low and somehow canny. Lowe locked the door behind him and scanned the big room.

There was a tarp-draped corpse on the nearest autopsy table. The slab beside it was vacant. Beyond the tables, stacked like oversize filing cabinets, a wall of refrigerated stainless-steel drawers mirrored his image in elongated funhouse reflections.

Lowe approached the corpse. Its covering drape was of a thick smoky plastic, and it made a sound like kicked autumn leaves when he drew it back. The woman lying stock-still beneath it was young. A teenager. *Beautiful*. Her naked body was perfect, full breasts sitting high, tummy flat, pubic mound bristling with flaxen hair. Her complexion was pale, perhaps a little dusky, but she might only have been sleeping, cold in this harsh, refrigerated air. There was no sign of injury at all.

Lowe began to weep.

And to remove his clothes.

When he was naked, he stroked the girl's waxen face. "I'm sorry," he said, tears beading on the rim of his jaw. "So sorry."

He turned to an instrument tray and selected a scalpel. In the artificial light the blade seemed an object of gleaming perfection.

Clasping the scalpel in one hand, Lowe dragged the blade across the extended surface of his opposite wrist. Blood spurted up in fine twin jets, spattering the undraped corpse.

After a moment, he opened his other wrist, too.

He climbed onto the vacant autopsy slab and lay on his back, still weeping, the backs of his hands resting in the table-side gutters. He turned his head and looked at the girl, her lifeless face staring blankly at the ceiling.

Then, slowly, he closed his eyes, wanting only to sleep...

But now there was a sharp, tearing pain in his forehead, a sense of something being forcibly extruded—and he realized with blunted shock that he was naked, that he was lying on a smooth metallic surface, cold as the grave, and that he could hardly breathe. It was as if something enormous had settled on his chest—*Too much I injected too much*—and his eyes were burning with light.

"Jesus..." It was a breathless whisper.

His gaze drifted to one side, away from the light, and now he saw the girl's cadaver, its torso drizzled with blood, his blood, dripping off its sides into shiny, candy-apple puddles.

Jesus.

He tried to sit up and couldn't. *Too weak.* He raised his hands a few inches, but they splatted back into the gutters.

"Help me," Lowe said in a breathless wheeze. "Oh, God, help me."

The light...

The light was so bright, blue light, coalescing above him, taking shape...

Awed and terribly afraid, Lowe closed his eyes for the last time.

He experienced a curious tugging sensation over the length of his body, not at all unpleasant.

And his last conscious thought before he died was that he was floating.

31

KELLY SAT ALONE AT her desk in the cluttered gym office and twisted Will's ring on her finger. When he'd given it to her three weeks ago, Kelly had slipped it onto the ring finger of her right hand...but sometimes, when she was alone, she shifted it to the corresponding finger on her left, as Will had intended. She did this now, thinking what a sweetheart he'd been since Christmas, patiently allowing her time to think things through.

She raised her hand to the light and admired the diamond. She'd finished off her day with a group of grade niners, tutoring them in the fine art of cross-country skiing. Many of them were already quite proficient—in these parts, cross-country skiing was a community pastime, right up there with snowmobiling, curling and ice fishing. But a few of them were nigh on hopeless...and Kelly enjoyed these students most. For her, the small triumphs were the most gratifying.

Kelly shuddered a little, recalling the interview she'd had with the principal at the beginning of the winter term and how easily she might have lost the job she cherished so much. When she'd returned after the holidays, there had been a single manila envelope in her gym office mailbox. On it had been her name, in Ms. Cole's neat back-slanting script, and an embossed heading: FROM THE OFFICE OF THE

PRINCIPAL. Kelly had slit the envelope open with real trepidation, afraid the verdict had already been entered.

But it had been only a request for a chat, as soon as Kelly could arrange it. She'd gone to the main office that very minute.

"There's been some talk," Nickie Cole had said, after inviting Kelly to sit. "And I'd like to clear it up right away." She stood at the window as she spoke, misting a series of spidery plants with a stylish brass spray can. Barely thirty, Cole looked more like a corporate executive than a high school principal—short hair, trim figure, snappy gray outfit—but Kelly didn't doubt for an instant that her own future as an educator depended on what was said in the next few minutes. "I assume you know what I'm talking about?"

"Yes," Kelly said. "I do."

The principal turned to face her. "Can you shed any light on it?"

"I believe I can," Kelly said.

And then she had told the truth, or as much of it as needed telling. She explained to Nickie about Peter, about the tragedy that had befallen them, and about the unexpected resurgence of her feelings for the man. Then she talked about Will. About the future she hoped they would share, and the sense of inner vitality his affection had restored in her. Later, when it was over, she supposed that something in her forthrightness had convinced the principal of her renewed stability. It had been a tense half hour, but it had been good to get things squared away.

It occurred to Kelly then that her ruinous obsession with Peter had all but vanished. She'd scarcely thought of him in weeks. For some obscure reason, it had all just…dropped away, like a reptile's restricting outer skin. And as destructive as the process had been, Kelly thought now that perhaps it had been necessary. A cleansing that should have come years ago, before she'd had a chance to wall it up. And that was exactly how she felt. Cleansed, and…happy. Yes, she was happy.

And like the last time this simple truth had made itself known to her, Kelly realized Will was at the centre of it.

Solid, loving Will.

Kelly stood, her complexion still rosy from the January air, and pulled on her coat. She'd intended to mark some papers, but suddenly she was too excited to concentrate. She was going to go home—Will had more or less moved in—and see how long it took him to notice where his ring had taken up residence.

* * *

No question about it now. I can kill. The proof is in a long cool drawer downstairs. Jesus, I wish I'd stuck around until they found him. What a trip that must have been.

And you know what, world? It felt Good.

Yeah, it did.

But there were problems, and I'll have to keep them in mind when it comes time to deal with the others. Control is not absolute, nor is it without restriction. Harry resisted me at first. He might've been a prick, but he was also very sharp. And tough. It was like trying to tackle a man in thick mud, until he injected his shit. Then it was easier. And hey, kids, that dope of his is pretty good stuff, even when it's only dirty seconds. Can't say I blame the bald fuck for getting hooked.

But even then he fought me.

It hinges on rage, of course. Pure, unadulterated rage.

No problem there—

* * *

"Hey, bro'. Whatcha typin'?"

Peter jabbed the keyboard with his mouth-held striker and scrolled the screen blank. Scowling at his brother, he dropped the striker and said, "Don't sneak up on me like that, man."

Sam blushed and apologized. "Sorry, Pete. I knocked, but—"

"Yeah, you're right," Peter said, his complexion draining back to its usual waxiness. "Scared me, is all. I guess I was pretty wrapped up."

"I'll say," Sam said, relaxing a little. "What're you up to? Plotting a spy novel?"

"Nah. It's nothing. Just practicing. It's embarrassing. I'm so fucking slow." The anger, always so close to the surface now. "One key at a time—plink, plink—like a frigging grade-schooler."

"Patience," Sam said, trying to sound light. Moving stiffly, he pulled up a chair and sat, keeping his left leg splinted in front of him. In the hallway outside, a porter rattled by with an empty dinner cart. It was seven o'clock. "Have you tried any of the games?"

"A few," Peter lied, his scowl falling away as he focused on Sam's face. Some of the swelling had gone down overnight, and his right eye had slitted open, but he still looked pretty rough. "Holy fuck," he said, appalled. "Your face. I'd forgotten how bad—"

Peter closed his mouth with a snap.

"How bad what?" Sam said. This was the first time he'd been in since the beating. "Were you ... ?"

Then a memory came to Sam, of a dream within a dream—or a dream *superimposed* on a dream—nightmare and reverie thrown together in an uneasy mix. He remembered awakening on the couch the previous evening and thinking that Peter had been right there with him—the feeling had been that immediate. Peter had been right there with him and had been about to save Sam from ... but that, too, had been a dream, a restless replay of the trouncing he'd taken from Kiley and his drunken crew.

A chill pawed its way up Sam's spine. He looked at his brother and felt naked. Worse than naked. He felt violated.

"Did you ... ?" Sam began.

But no, of course not. He'd learned to accept Peter's ability to leave his body, uncanny as it was, but surely that was the extent of it? Peter had come to the apartment while Sam slept; that much Sam had already surmised...

But had he *seen*? Seen into Sam's fitful dreams?

Sam dismissed the notion for the absurdity it was. Perhaps, in the receptive state of sleep, Sam had sensed his brother's presence. In their more recent discussions of Peter's ability, Peter had reported that he felt himself growing steadily stronger, more able to impinge on the tangible environment. Yeah. That was all it had been, just a feeling that Peter was there, close by.

(inside)

"Was I, did I, what?" Peter said, amused at what he perceived as his brother's leap of insight. "We're going to have to start speaking in complete sentences here, Sammy."

"You ... saw me?" Sam said, indicating the swollen ruin of his face. "Before now?"

"Yep."

"Last night?"

"Yep."

"Jesus, that's weird. That's really weird." A cleft divided Sam's brow. "Christ, man, what if I'd been ... I don't know, boffing a babe or something?"

Peter whooped. "A virgin like thou?"

"Who says I'm a virgin?" Sam said, his face the colour of a beet.

"You just did," Peter said, laughing again. "'Boffing a babe...'"

"Well, it's not impossible, you know."

Recognizing his brother's bruised ego, Peter backed off. "What about it, Sammy? Any prospects in your life?"

Unbidden, Kelly's face flashed in Sam's mind, as unexpected as his earlier thoughts of his brother invading his dreams, and he blushed again. He glanced at Peter and thought he saw something flicker across his face like the shadow of a predatory bird. Then Peter was smiling again, patiently awaiting a response.

"No," Sam said. "Nothing serious. Looks like it's going to be liver in a jam jar for a while yet."

"Liver in a *jam* jar? Where did you hear about that?"

"*Psychopathia Sexualis*," Sam said, getting into the rap. "Required reading for the Human Growth and Development course, Biology Two. Cram in the liver, stuff in your dick. Great for no-stick frying afterward."

"You are one sick puppy," Peter said, laughing.

And for a while they were just brothers again.

* * *

Later, on his way down in the elevator, Sam realized that he was hungry. He'd had nothing to eat since breakfast and now he craved something sweet. After exiting at the main floor, he crossed the lobby to the gift shop, where he grabbed a Mr. Big from the candy rack. As he dug in his pocket for some change, he noticed Shawna Blane and another nurse from Peter's floor buzzing over the daily newspaper. Shawna held it up for her companion's inspection, and Sam caught a glimpse of the headline: PHYSICIAN DIES IN BIZARRE HOSPITAL SUICIDE. Curious, he paid for his chocolate bar, then browsed through the curios and gifts. When the nurses left, he moved to the newsstand.

Attired in suit coat and smock, looking officious and smug, Dr. Lowe stared out at him from the front page of the *Sudbury Star*. The headline, as lurid as they got in this peaceful municipality, screamed out at him in bold black caps.

"Jesus," Sam said, trying to ignore the jab of dread in his gut. "Oh, Jesus…"

He picked up a copy and scanned the article. Then he paid for the paper, rolled it into a tube and limped back out to the elevators.

He could feel his heart drumming out quick, nervous rhythms in his chest.

He was breathless when he reached his brother's room—but some instinct made him pause just short of the open door. Dinner was over, the evening rounds completed, and the ward was winding down for the night. At the moment the hallway was deserted.

Moving silently—and feeling a bit ridiculous—Sam crept to the edge of the doorjamb and peeked inside.

There on the bed in the dimming twilight lay his brother. The computer was on, and in its dull green shine Peter looked chillingly like Rhett Kiley had looked in the glow of the Caddy's dash lights. The key striker was plugged into his mouth like some weird wand, and his face was pinched with concentration...and something else, Sam thought. There was an open delight in Peter's face, and it brought a memory to Sam the way a throttle brought juice to an engine.

One afternoon in grade school Sam had left his homework assignment on his desk and had been halfway home before he realized it. He'd made his way back at a run, and had been grateful to find his classroom unlocked. He went to his desk, grabbed his books and turned to leave. It was then that he heard the faint, strangled squeals coming from the science room across the hall. The door to the science room was ajar, and although the lights were off Sam noticed a shadow against one wall, rocking rhythmically to and fro. He'd crept to that door the way he was creeping now...and on the other side he'd found Ben Parrillo, a fat, dumpling-faced kid, hunched over an unlit workbench. Ben was hacking the head off a white mouse with a pair of scissors. Rodent blood had sprayed up his arm and speckled his double chin—and the look on Ben's face had been exactly like the one on Peter's face now: fixed, furious, transported, delighted. Eight years later, at the age of sixteen, Ben had stabbed his mother to death, then hanged himself from an attic crossbeam. He'd stabbed her sixty-eight times.

Sam flinched away, convinced Peter had seen him—and suddenly terrified that he had.

What's wrong with you? That's your brother in there. That's Peter.

Sam waited until he caught his breath. Then he went inside.

Again Peter scowled. Again he switched off his computer. "What did you forget?" he said, the words spiked with annoyance, reminding Sam of their father.

"Nothing," Sam said, trying to shake his disquiet. He held out the rolled-up newspaper. "Have you seen today's paper?"

Peter shook his head.

And Sam thought: *He's lying. Maybe not about the paper, but he knows what's in it.* He folded the paper out, holding it open for Peter's inspection.

What's that on his face right now? Sam thought as his brother scanned the article. *What is it now?*

But the answer to that one was easy. It was satisfaction.

"Well, ain't that a shame," Peter said. "Get it out of my sight."

* * *

Alone in the apartment that night, Sam sat staring at the reel-to-reel. After a while he reached out and switched it on. The tape was the last of numerous copies Sam had made over the years, and at this stage the sound reproduction was so bad that even at full volume large parts of it were obscured by tape hiss...but that didn't bother Sam. He sat on the couch, which still bore the greasy imprint of his mother's head on the armrest, and let his mind take him back to that day, the pride he'd felt, the unalloyed admiration. He remembered, too, the faint stab of jealousy he'd experienced when he saw Kelly dart down from the wing—just one more befuddling emotion in the hormonal soup of adolescence...but it had been there just the same, and now he remembered it. He remembered how his mind had tossed up a portrait of the two of them embracing back there in the dark—"trading spit," as Peter sometimes joked—and how something deep inside him had for an alarming instant been furious, green and blind and furious. The memory made him think of the thrill he'd felt when Kelly called out to him in the university parking lot, that fleeting first moment when his heart had soared and his mind tried to convince him that Kelly had shared his feelings all these years...

Sam looked down and saw that his nails had dug happy face creases in his palms.

Truth was, he'd been thinking a lot about Kelly lately...

With a child's furtiveness, Sam reached under the couch and withdrew his grade nine yearbook. It fell open to the correct page automatically: Kelly's graduating class, glossy colour photos of bright, ambitious faces. Kelly's was the last of them.

Kelly Wheeler.

Was that who Peter had been writing about? Was that why he seemed so determined that Sam never get a look at the screen?

He was still pondering these questions when the tape ended.

And began to flap.

* * *

Will was chopping vegetables when Kelly walked in. The heavy snowfall of the night before had dumped ten inches of the stuff on the driveway, and Kelly had been forced to leave her car at the top of the hill. The guy who did the plowing hadn't shown up yet, and as she shrugged off her coat she made a mental note to call him if he hadn't arrived before bedtime. Chainsaw had trailed her down the hill, yapping and gamboling like a pup. Now he stood gawking in through the sidelight.

Will greeted her from the chopping block. "Hey, good lookin'. Can I interest you in a stir-fry? It's from Yan's latest cookbook."

"Which one is that?" Kelly said as she hung up her coat.

"A Hundred New Ways to Wok Your Dog."

Chainsaw barked.

"Careful," Kelly said, laughing. "I think he can hear you." She kicked off her boots and strolled in to give Will a kiss, making a show of adjusting her ring. "Been home long?"

"Half hour," Will said, accepting her kiss but missing her cue. "You like frozen peas?"

"Love 'em," Kelly fibbed.

"Good. Listen. Why don't you slip into the tub and relax for a bit." He fluttered his eyebrows lecherously. "Then I'll bring in your dinner and join you."

"Dinner in the tub?"

"Why not?"

"Yeah," Kelly said, flashing the ring again. "Why not?" She glanced at the neatly diced vegetables, then began undoing her blouse. "Fast food?"

Will began chopping furiously.

Happy, Kelly thought as she turned away.

The tub was already filled, heaped with bubbles and breathing steam, just the way she liked it. The overhead light was on, but a candle stood ready by the sink.

Pleased, Kelly stripped off her things and sank into the waiting tub. The bubbles sighed along with her. A few minutes later Will brought in a goblet of white wine. Kelly accepted it with her left hand ... but nothing.

Come on, Will. Open your eyes.

Before leaving, Will lit the candle and switched off the light. Kelly was dozing when he came back with the grub—stir-fried shrimp with almonds and assorted vegetables. Will was a great cook and had practically taken over the job since his unofficial move-in. Kelly didn't mind. Julia Childs she wasn't. He was slow and methodical out there, blending things together with an almost religious solemnity. It was the way he went about everything, Kelly thought—including spotting this ring—and she guessed he'd never die from a heart attack.

She watched him strip off his clothes, as always aroused by the lean hardness of his body. Once naked, he arranged the plates on the makeshift trays he'd rigged for the occasion, then slipped into the tub facing Kelly.

"To us," he said, toasting her with his goblet of wine.

"To us," Kelly said, using her left hand again, slopping wine onto her chin.

"You gotta watch that booze, babe. It's wicked stuff." He scooped up a forkful of peas—

Then his eyes widened and his mouth dropped open and the peas plunked into the tub. His gaze went unfocused, striking Kelly in the vicinity of her chin, and he seemed on the verge of choking.

"Will?"

"You...you mean it?"

Then she understood. She linked her left hand with his. "I sure do."

Will tried to hug her across the supper trays, then settled back in the tub. "God, Kelly." There were tears in his eyes. "I love you so much."

"And I love you."

32

DROP YOUR COCKS AND grab your slush boots," Rhett said. "Just *look* at you fuckin' reprobates."

He'd let himself into Jerry's place through the unlocked front door, and now he stood in the living room archway, one fist wrapped around a frosty can of Coors. Startled from his boozy sleep, Jerry lurched off the couch and swung blindly at the air. Mike Gore, slumped in the chair across from him, just went on snoring. The night before, the two old friends had settled in for some serious drinking and had passed out watching Clint Eastwood kick ass in some nameless spaghetti western. Rhett, who was supposed to have joined them, had called around ten to beg off—something about a redhead with larbos the size of honeydews.

"You just about scared the shit outta me, Rhett," Jerry said, grinning stupidly. The animal rage that flared in his eyes when he sprang off the couch had been replaced by a look of mild bewilderment, Jerry's usual expression. He scratched his spiked thatch of hair, then kicked one of Gore's stockinged feet.

"Wha ... ?" the big man grunted, opening his puffy eyes.

"Wha?" Rhett parroted, and roared with laughter.

Gore shrugged up in the chair that had served as his bed and winced at the kink in his back. Then he squinted at his watch and winced again. His wife was going to murder him. He'd promised to call her last night if he decided to sleep over. Oh, boy.

"Let's get it the fuck in gear, gents," Rhett said. "It's four ay-em and the fishies are waitin.'"

As if on cue, Jerry and Mike gazed in tandem through the living room window. It was pitch out there, and a gusting wind rattled the panes. Angry flecks of sleet spattered the glass like flung sand. At a glance, Mike estimated that the mercury had plunged into the double negatives.

"I know what you're thinking," Rhett said, "but put it out of your minds. I didn't crawl out of the rack at three in the morning—and boys, I was not alone—to listen to you two butt bandits whine. We haven't reneged on this trip in ten years, and we're not about to start now." He grinned menacingly. "So let's get on with it."

Ignoring the muttered profanities, Rhett lobbed his empty into the general rubble and stamped back outside. He was relieved to find that Jerry had readied the snowmobiles. They sat angled on their trailer in the sideyard, snugged cozily away beneath form-fitting tarps. He found the Coleman stove under the cluttered workbench in the garage. The ice auger he found resting on the overhead crossbeams. The sucker was heavy, and he nicked a finger on the spiraling blade trying to muscle it out to the truck. Cursing, he corked the finger into his mouth and waited until the sting subsided. Then he went back to wrangling the auger. A few minutes later, comically bulked up in a snowmobile suit two sizes too big for him, Jerry stumbled out to help.

"Where's Gore?" Rhett said.

"Callin' his wife," Jerry said, and both men grinned.

* * *

They reached the halfway mark—the dead end of a dirt road about fifteen miles off Highway 17—at 5:32 A.M. From here on in, the going was strictly by snow machine. Mike rode with Jerry, whose machine was more powerful, and Rhett hauled the lightweight sled containing their gear. As always, Jerry took the lead. Their destination, a deep-woods lake not shown on any map, had been his father's best kept secret, and Jerry had fished it all his life.

The ride in took twenty minutes at a comfortable cruising speed of thirty. The hut was where they'd left it the previous year, nestled in the brush by the lake. Snow encased it to just below the roofline, and it took the three men almost an hour to dig it out. Once it was free, they dragged it on skids to a likely looking spot near the middle of the frozen lake.

"All right," Rhett said once the hut was positioned. "Let's get some holes cut."

"Fuckin' A," Jerry said, and stamped off to gas up the auger.

* * *

The snowfall had subsided, but the wind had come up again, whining and bitter. As it twisted across the lake, it picked up phantoms of snow and spun them in dervish circles. The sun, which had just sailed free of the trees, looked like a healing bullethole in the white belly of the sky. To Mike Gore, who numbly busied himself offloading gear, it seemed a vision of hell. Why he abandoned the fireside warmth of his home year after year to come out here and let these assholes try to kill him was beyond him. It hadn't really been fun since...well, since the last time Peter made the trip. With Peter along it had always been more of a legitimate fishing trip, just four good friends getting together to share in the rigors and rewards of a rugged winter sport. Sure, they'd downed a few cold ones in those days too, but it had never degenerated into these pie-eyed, falling-down puke fests.

As he did every year, Mike Gore swore this would be the last time he made the trip…but it was a lie. He'd keep on coming, and keep on wondering why. Pondering it now, he guessed it was probably just some juvenile attempt to keep the good old days alive. And yet, watching his two friends degenerate so drastically over the years, he began to wonder how good those old days had really been. For Mike, these were the best days of his life. He had a wife, two gorgeous kids and, all things being equal, he'd be the manager of his own pharmacy inside of a year.

There was a balky, ratcheting sound as Jerry yanked the ice auger's starter cord. The 8hp engine farted rudely, releasing a puff of oily smoke, then kicked over. When he triggered the throttle, the auger blade spun with an evil whir.

"Where you want the bait hole?" Jerry shouted, his grin triumphant. He just loved getting that auger going on the first pull.

"Up your arse," Rhett hollered back, laughing coarsely.

In response, Jerry swung the cumbersome auger overhead, displaying a wiry strength that seldom failed to amaze Rhett Kiley. With the whirring blade pointed skyward, he fingered the throttle repeatedly, waggling his head and shimmying his body, howling like a Ward C psycho. With his brown balaclava concealing all but his facial holes, he might have been lovable ole Leatherface himself.

"Cut the shit," Rhett said, a little unnerved by this display.

"Right," Jerry said, letting the auger down. "Sorry, Rhett, I—"

"Just drill the fuckin' holes."

Looking baffled and stung, Jerry seated the auger tip in the ice and squeezed the throttle. The randy engine belched, and the blade cored down about a foot into the ice. When Jerry drew out the blade Mike kicked the ice chips away, then emptied a clear plastic bait bag into the hole. An assortment of minnows—shiners, suckers, chubs—wriggled affrightedly in this new enclosure.

"Now," Rhett said, assuming his customary role as foreman. "Sink a hole here"—he pointed to a spot six feet from the shack—"and another in front of the condo. I'll rig the tip-ups while the drug dealer over here fires up the heater." He favored Gore with a grin. "Think you can handle that, Mikey?"

"Asshole," Mike muttered. But he slumped off to perform this task.

Once Jerry got the holes drilled, he leaned the auger against the shack and then just stood there, squinting into the snowy glare. A few minutes later he hiked back to the snowmobiles, a distance of about two hundred yards. Rhett spotted him there and hollered over the moan of the wind ... but then he realized Jerry was taking a whiz and left him to his business. When it came to his toilet habits Jerry was the original little girl. Grinning to himself, Rhett tramped over to the bait hole to select some bait.

By seven all was in order. The tip-ups were rooted by their holes, the lures baited, the men seated comfortably in the hut. Through the partially open door they could watch their tip-ups: clever rigs like arms rising out of the snow, with jointed elbows that fed line from a spool and jigged up and down in the breeze, luring the fish. The whiskey was cold, the heater hot, and Rhett could almost taste that first scrumptious pan-fried fillet. Even Mike had begun to show signs of enjoyment.

Only Jerry seemed quietly out of sorts. Rhett noticed this, but he was getting too blasted to give a shit. Maybe the dozy little wanker had a toothache. He wasn't drinking, which was weird, and he kept screwing his face into knots, as if trying to puzzle out some tricky mathematical problem. Rhett chuckled at this thought and took another gulp of whiskey. Poor old Jer. Since taking it in the head in that ball game, he could barely count out change for a dollar.

Seated across from Rhett, Mike grinned nostalgically. His postbinge ailments had diminished to a tolerable grumble, and although he was taking it easy on the rotgut, his head had taken up a comfortable buzz.

"Remember the trip we made out here back in…what was it? Grade twelve? The time Jerry wandered off to take a dump behind that old beaver dam and fell through the ice?"

Rhett snorted laughter. "Fuckin' A. Whadda dipshit. Froze just about cock-stiff before Gardner belly-crawled over and hauled him out."

"Look at him," Mike said. "Pretending he doesn't hear us." He nudged Jerry with an elbow. "Remember that, Jer?"

Lauhing, Rhett said, "I remember Gardner stripping down to his long johns and handing Jeter half his clothes…"

Rhett's voice trailed off, and a silence freighted with gloom filled the shack. Mike finally broke it, broaching a subject that had become oddly taboo over the years.

"Either of you guys ever go see him?"

"Nah," Rhett said, feigning indifference. "What's the point? The guy's crocked out, shittin' his bed, stinkin' to the high heaven. If it was me, I wouldn't want a bunch of dropouts hangin' around, reminding me of all the fun I was missing." This last was said with a trace of bitterness that was not lost on Mike.

"You're still pissed at him, aren't you?" Mike said. "Christ. It wasn't his fault you never got picked up by the scouts."

Rhett remained stubbornly silent.

"I've been thinking," Mike said, cutting to the chase. "What if we just…dropped in on him, all three of us. Monday, say. What the fuck? Surprise him."

"It's been a lotta years," Rhett said, his voice taking on a hard edge that made Mike uneasy. "How do we know he's even still alive?"

"We could check. I mean, don't you feel even the slightest bit guilty? Haven't you ever tried to put yourself in his shoes?"

Rhett snorted. "Turnips don't wear shoes."

"Fine," Mike said. "Forget I brought it up."

"Fuckin' A."

"I'll go by my—"

"Why don't you just *do* that, Mikey?" Rhett had risen to his feet, and now he loomed over Mike like a storm cloud. "I'm sure that'd make Gardner feel a whole helluva lot better." He screwed his face into a sneer. "'Hi, Pete. It's me, Mikey. Good to see ya, bro'. I'm a big-ass pharmacist now, gettin' my wick wet every night and drivin' a two-tone Eldorado. How's things in the patch?'"

Mike stood now, too, jabbing his finger in Rhett's face. Through it all, Jerry sat staring at his slush boots, his face still twitching and twisting.

"You're a crude, bitter, self-centred bastard, you know that, Kiley? What the hell's gotten into you, anyway? Holding a grudge against a guy who can't even scratch his own balls anymore, and why? Because he was better than you? Big fucking deal. He'd've done anything for you, man. For any one of us. Why he even bothered hanging out with us was always a mystery to me. The guy outclassed us by a city block. He was a good egg, Rhett, and we dumped him. Doesn't that mean shit to you?"

Rhett's hands curled into bloodless clubs inside his mittens. "You don't know the half of it, you ignorant ape. He stole my fuckin' *girl*."

"Girl?" Mike said, struck momentarily off balance. He knew he was risking a beating here—he was big, but five years behind a stack of pharmacology textbooks had left him soft and slow—but Rhett's comment, once Mike got the sense of it, made him want to fall to the ice in hysterics. "Kelly?" he said. "Are you kidding me?" This was all news to Mike. "Get real, man. That chick was way out of your league—"

"That's right, gentlemen. She was."

The furious red drained out of Rhett's face as he spun to the sound of that voice.

It was Jerry, looking up at them from his shadowy corner of the hut...but for just a moment there, his voice had been someone else's. He rose from the bench, poking his head into the flat white light that slanted in through the open door. His eyebrows were unnaturally arched, and the dimpled grin on his face was completely alien.

"Why don't you two assholes dry up?" he said. Then he went out the door, letting it slam behind him in a gust.

"What the fuck was that?" Rhett said, stunned out of his anger. He goggled at Mike in bewilderment.

But before Mike could answer, that balky, ratcheting noise ripped through the walls and the ice auger barked into life. A split second later the entire hut went airborne, levered up from behind as if clouted by a powerful gust, and now the two men were standing in the open air, facing Jerry Jeter...but it wasn't Jerry anymore; both men could see that right away. The man who stood waggling the auger blade at them looked nothing like Jerry Jeter. His face had rearranged itself in a manner that defied reason. He *looked* like Jack Nicholson, or as close as anyone could come to that look, as close as Gardner used to come; he looked like Jack Nicholson with his face crammed into the ax hole in *The Shining*; he looked totally fucking *crazy*, and when he came at them revving the auger, hip-thrusting the four-foot bit as if it weighed no more than a feather, both men took to their heels. Deadly intent writhed in Jerry's eyes, a coiled black fury that was somehow more terrifying than his awesome show of strength or the sputtering roar of the auger.

Rhett cut left toward the snow machines. Blinded by panic, Gore took three wild strides and plowed into the equipment sled, pitching forward across its width. In his struggle to get free, he tangled his legs in a loose length of rope. His rump stuck straight up in the air.

"Hold that pose, boy," Jerry cried with insane good humor. "I'm about to core you a new asshole."

Mike cried out to Rhett for help. He lay on his belly, balanced across the sled like an overturned tortoise on its shell, and the more he struggled, the worse he got snarled in the rope. There was no way he could regain his feet.

He looked over his shoulder and saw that Jerry was still coming, that killing light still in his eyes. This was no joke, and he could feel his bowels letting go.

"How's it feel, Mike, old buddy?" Jerry shouted over the bawl of the auger. "How's it feel to shit yourself?" He lowered the bit and cranked the throttle wide open. "Nice, huh?"

The bit poked through the padded seat of Mike's snow suit with a dull popping sound, its first revolution raking out a thick tuft of down. Mike screamed before the pain came, screamed at the vision that filled his head, a vision of his own body impaled on the bit of that auger.

The next twist, a bare second later, found flesh, and now the engine seemed to wail on the brink of explosion. Blood slurried out of the ten-inch hole in Mike's snow pants, ribbons of it snaking up the blades of the cold metal spiral.

Jerry watched with remote fascination.

Mike's shriek rose on the arctic air, a solid, unyielding skid of life against death. Rhett heard it, and it sparked his muscles into furious service. The snow machines were back on shore, just a few yards to go. He'd grab Jerry's, it was the fastest...

But something made him stop and look back, the grim hope that maybe this was all some sick fucking joke, some stupid prank dreamed up by those two crazy assholes to really piss him off. But as he whirled, already imagining how he was going to kick their silly arses, he saw Jerry plodding toward him across the ice.

He held the auger straight overhead, as he had when he cranked it alive the first time. It was still running, but only barely, because Mike Gore was skewered to its tip, limp as a rag doll and sluggishly spinning, the loose flaps of his pant legs making a torpid *whuff-whuff-whuff* sound, like the rotors of some hellish airship.

Screaming now himself, Rhett took the last lurching steps to the snowmobiles.

The keys were gone.

Oh fuck oh fuck oh fuck...

Hunched beside Jerry's machine, Rhett threw a glance over his shoulder. Jerry had dropped Mike's body and now he was running, teeth bared in a yellow snarl. Rhett's first inclination was to stand his ground. The crazy cunt had dropped the auger, and Rhett had always believed that man to man he could tear Jerry Jeter apart. But the mad fucker stomping across the ice toward him now was not Jerry Jeter; maybe the shot he'd taken in the head five years ago had started bleeding again, maybe that was it, but the fucker was wild; he'd flipped that shack like it was made of cardboard, and he'd hefted both the auger and Gore's two hundred pounds like a flag in a Santa Claus parade.

Rhett blinked his eyes. The picture didn't change. Jerry was still coming. He was thirty yards away now...and that snarl had widened into a grin.

At the end of his outstretched arm, keys dangled from his pincered fingers. Rhett could hear their teasing little jangle on the wind.

"Lookin' for these?" Jerry said in a carrying drawl, an unmistakable drawl; there was only one voice like it in the world. It was Jack Nicholson's voice—Jack slitting Brando's throat in *The Missouri Breaks*, Jack riding easy in the saddle of Peter Fonda's chopper—except Jerry couldn't *do* Jack Nicholson; he couldn't even bark like a dog. *Gardner* did Jack Nicholson; he did it so well that if you shut your eyes you'd swear the Hollywood wild man was standing right there beside you.

These thoughts streaked across Rhett's mind in the space of a heartbeat, but it was a precious heartbeat, maybe his last if he didn't light the fuck out of here. The possibility that Gardner had died after all and that his spirit had somehow possessed Jerry Jeter did not seem at all farfetched, not out here in the middle of this arctic no-man's-land, with the wind clawing at his eyes and Mike's mutilated body leaking blood into the crusty snow. But the *thought* of it; *that* made Rhett want to sit in a snowdrift and gibber. The thought of it turned his nerves into noodles and made his legs want to drop out from under him.

Run.

Then he remembered his extra key.

He threw off his mittens and ran his already numb fingers along the undersurface of his snowmobile's footboard.

Please... please...

It was in one of those little magnetic key boxes; he'd stuck it there last winter after installing a whole new ignition system because he'd lost his fucking keys, and where the fuck *was* it?

Lost the fucker, lost it—

He knew the auger was gone, stalled on the ice and slicked with Mike's blood, but he could feel it coming at his back; the skin tingled where the point would go in...

Jerry was close now. Very close. Rhett could hear the creak of the ice beneath his footfalls.

He shifted to the opposite footboard—and his fingers closed around the key box. He jerked it free and scrabbled at the tiny lid— the fucker was *frozen solid*—then it opened and he nearly fumbled the key getting it out.

A sliver of calm pierced Rhett Kiley then, and in his mind he reached out and grabbed it. He threw a leg over the padded seat, slotted the key in the ignition and turned the engine over.

The snow machine rattled into life. Engaging the clutch, Rhett cranked the throttle and the machine lunged forward, almost bucking him off as the front end reared off the snow. Throttling back, he swung toward the woods and aimed for a break in the trees. There was a half-tank of gas, enough to take him back through the woods and, if necessary, all the way out to the highway. In the short time they'd been here the wind had obscured their tracks, but he could still make out a few scattered tread marks in the snow. All he had to do now was stay cool, keep to the trail—

Behind him Jerry's snow machine whined into life. Jerry gunned it and the sound was like a roar, a bellowing, beastly roar. It rose and fell, rose and fell, as if the beast paused to scent the air. Then the clutch was engaged, and the insectile buzz of the accelerating machine angled toward him through the trees.

Something raked Rhett's cheek, and he realized he'd run off the track into the brush. He righted himself, wincing at the sting in his face, aware that the wetness drizzling over his lips was blood but beyond caring. Head down, he dodged around trees and half-buried stumps, already lost but still alive, alive and intent on remaining that way. He held the throttle wide open, calling on quicksilver reflexes he'd believed long dead.

But it wasn't enough. The bastard was catching up.

Blue smoke began to stream out from the seams of the engine's yellow cowling, and the hot reek of oil filled the air. He was running the sucker too hard, but what choice did he have? Jerry was right up his ass; he could almost feel that evil grin.

Jerry buzzed up beside him, coming in so fast Rhett was hardly aware it had happened; the sucker was just *there*, cruising along smoothly beside him—then his arm levered out and caught Rhett in the teeth and he almost lost it right then, his machine careening off into the trees. He managed to wrest back control, but Jerry tracked him like an angry hornet. The cunt was laughing, Rhett could actually *hear* him laughing—

And suddenly Rhett was furious.

He cut into a dense patch of brush, shielding his face behind the low windscreen, and broke into a clearing. It was a field, a farmer's field; he could see gray buildings in the distance. At a glance the place looked abandoned, the buildings drifted in snow—but if there was a farm, there must be a road.

Rhett tore across the flat in a racer's crouch. Jerry, swinging wide, came into view at the edge of Rhett's vision. The bastard was toying with him, not even bothering to look ahead. Panic rose in Rhett again, trying to douse his clear-headed fury, but he wrestled it back.

Rhett had seen the tumbledown fence. He didn't think Jerry had. Ducking low, he buzzed safely beneath it.

Barbed wire. A single rusty strand.

Jerry blew into the half-buried fence at seventy miles an hour. The sagging wire caught him beneath the chin, sinking into flesh the way a hot knife sinks into butter. Suddenly unpiloted, the snow machine crested off a drift and went braying into the air, doing a backflip before landing on its bumper in the snow. The barbed wire snapped free at one end, and while Jerry was still airborne it coiled around his neck with a sound like a horseman's lashing crop, finishing the job of severing his head. Jerry landed on his back. His head rolled down a smooth drift and came to rest on its stump, facing Rhett, giving the impression of a man buried to the chin in the snow. The grin was still frozen to its face.

Filled with a savage exultation, Rhett gunned his snow machine through a precarious half circle, slewing back toward Jerry's twitching corpse. For the space of an eyeblink it was lost from sight, obscured by a snow-heaped stack of cordwood; then it came into view again.

Its limbs were no longer twitching; now they were *flapping*. The fucking thing was trying to flap its way *up* again. Blood was jetting from the stump of its neck and still it was trying to get up...

Just nerves, a sane voice told Rhett Kiley.

Then the head in the snow opened its eyes.

Something slammed shut in Rhett's mind, the doorway to reason, and his exultant whoop pitched upward into the keening registers of terror. Describing a loop that nearly toppled his machine, he swung away from the convulsing monstrosity and arrowed blindly across what had once been the dooryard of this forgotten homestead. The swaybacked clapboard overlooked a freshwater lake; seeing it only as a clear path of escape, Rhett went howling toward it.

The sun blinked through the cloud cover then, as if endeavoring to soothe Rhett's cracking nerve, and its brilliance jabbed him in the eyes. In the great gleaming plain of white that ranged out before him, Rhett failed to notice the sharp eight-foot drop to the shoreline.

The snow machine whined into the air at its top end, sixty-two miles an hour. There was a sensation in the pit of Rhett's stomach like that felt in an elevator at the height of its ascent...then man and machine parted company, Rhett continuing his climb, the snow machine falling away. Reaching the top of his arc, Rhett experienced a giddy instant of weightlessness, and in that small space of time he thought he might just drift away on the wind.

Then gravity took over and hauled him down. He struck the twelve-inch thickness of the ice feet first, his weight carrying him through into a frigid bath of darkness. He sank like a granite slab, unable to move, his shocked eyes registering nothing but a shifting watery blackness. His boots struck bottom, a barely perceptible thud followed by an abrupt cessation of descent. The impact bent him at the knees, which creaked audibly, the sound transmitted through his stiffening tendons like voices along undersea cables, and now he mustered the last of his sanity, deliberately deepening that bend and pushing off with his feet.

Slowly, his lungs already screaming for air, Rhett bobbed toward the surface, rising through bubbling planes of darkness into a green, thickly filtered light.

The top of his head met something jagged and unyielding.

The ice.

He'd come up under the ice and now he scrabbled for a handhold on its crystalline undersurface. He found a brittle stalactite and clasped it with nerveless fingers. On the verge of inhaling chill water, he thrust his chin into the three-inch space between the water and the ice and gasped at the miserly air. He was rapidly losing sensation—his legs were already gone, his arms like two burning stakes in his trunk—and he knew that if he didn't either find his point of entry or smash through the ice *right now*, he was a goner.

He had a minute, maybe two.

Grunting with the effort, Rhett rammed a fist against the ice. The impact was puny, barely disrupting the fenestrated surface, and the contact drew blood.

There was no way he could break through from underneath. He had to find the hole and he had to do it now.

But he felt suddenly warmer, tingly, as if he'd lain too long in an overhot bath. It was not a bad feeling. Not bad at all. Sort of dreamy and light, as if during sleep he'd magically left his body. The water was shifting around him, swirling in mysterious currents—and now it lapped over his nose and mouth, causing him to cough in a racking spasm.

The shock slapped him into alertness.

Above him the ice groaned, as if beneath some ponderous weight. Rhett squinted up through the ice and thought he saw a shadow gliding stealthily above him. He had guessed the hole was to the right of him—and that was where the shadow appeared to be heading.

An idea of sheer insanity overwhelmed him.

Jerry.

The headless fucker was coming to get him, just as surely as Rhett's blood was turning to icy raspberry slush; he was up there right now, shambling toward the hole in the ice.

Rhett's anchoring stalactite broke away and the frigid water enveloped him. Fully submerged, he squinted in the slopping green light and saw something breasting through the water toward him. In a mind suddenly floodlit with terror, he watched as that indeterminate shape became Jerry Jeter. His still-grinning head was lashed to his belt by the hair, and it twisted with each stroke he took.

Losing half his air in an unheard scream, Rhett flailed away and tried to swim for it, a dying part of his mind promising the ice would be thinner near shore; he could reach it ahead of the demon behind him, smash his way through and the farmer would take him in...

Envisioning himself cutting through the water with Olympian strokes, Rhett Kiley sank to the muddy lake bed. Before he reached it his heart froze solid to his ribs, the blood inside it hard as rock.

FOUR

—

INTO THE FAR-OFF
FAIR FOREVER

33

IT WAS TIME. THE WET WORK was done, and in the four drag-ging weeks since Christmas, in the face of his maddening inability to reach Kelly, a plan had taken shape in his mind.

He had an objective now.

Still, a single element eluded him: How had she become immune to his invasions? What defense had she acquired that defeated him so easily, making it a torment for him to even look at her? It had been so easy before. She had almost come to welcome him.

A part of him knew the reason, but he rejected it with the whole of his being. There must be something else...

But soon, none of that would matter anymore. He was strong now. He was ready. He'd evicted her lover from his own thieving hide once before; he could do it again. He'd break through that protective shell or die trying.

And with any luck, this time the eviction would be permanent.

34

WILL'S LOVEMAKING WAS LIKE his cooking, unrushed, almost solemn, yet simmering with a passion that grew and grew until, in the instant of their release, it filled the world. Kelly sat astride him, her dark hair obscuring her face in the low winter light of her bedroom. It was a kind of consummation tonight, a celebration of shared feelings, and their movement continued through that instant without pause, seeking yet another peak.

Then a sensation like a chill November wind cut through them and they stopped, breathless, eyes wide and searching in this chancy light.

Will said, "Did you feel—?"

Then his eyes found a sputtering pocket of light, suspended on the air overhead. As he watched it, it seemed to swell, as their passion had only moments before, and now Kelly saw it, too. Frightened, she pressed herself against him.

"Will, what is it?"

But Will could only shake his head. It hung there a moment, an eerie blue witch-light that seemed to defy all earthly dimensions, a faltering smudge of luminous air that extended upward through the ceiling, as if bridging this world and some other.

Then it was gone.

"What was that?" Kelly said. Her good sweat had turned clammy.

"I don't know," Will said. "I really don't know."

* * *

The moon was a hard round porthole at the top of the sky and Peter took wing toward it, a mute cry of torment shredding him into smoke. He'd caught them in the act, rutting like animals—and still he hadn't been able to touch them. He'd been certain he could penetrate her partner (*Will*, that was his name, he'd heard her breathe it in passion), crush his loathsome spirit, grind it into so much dust and then expel it, claiming the untenanted carcass as his own. He was so *powerful* now. Look what he'd done to those ice-fishing back-stabbers...

But this had been like slamming into a plate-glass window. He couldn't even get close.

A single blaring thought thrust him skyward like some impossibly powerful jet fuel.

She loves him.

She really loves him.

But that couldn't be. Not after all they'd been through together. Not now that he could *be* with her again, able to share with her an intimacy hitherto only imagined. What *right* did that bastard have to interfere? Why had she let him come back?

She loves him...

Peter soared like a missile toward the moon. It seemed to be getting bigger now. Brighter. Closer. He wanted to smash into it, hurl himself into its deepest crater. He knew how to die. That was no great secret anymore. He didn't need a runaway wheelchair or a willing hand to unplug a ventilator or a syringe to piston air into his veins. All he had to do was keep going. Ignore the pain that spawned in his skull

even now and keep going until that pain roared like Niagara Falls…
then keep going some more.

There was nothing to live for now, and this realization came as a
kind of relief. Kelly had always been at the centre of his will to survive,
even during his darkest years, when he'd been unable—or unwilling—to admit it. His nightly intrusions into her dreams had caused
him no guilt, because in the depths of those dreams he'd witnessed
the truth. She'd still loved him then. It had been a confused love, a
hurt love, but it had been getting better.

And Will Chatam had killed it.

Peter's speed increased in exponential bounds, far outpacing that
of his previous runs in this shimmering slipstream of light. Where did
it lead? It was a question he'd contemplated before. The answer was
out there… and its cost was merely his life.

His shape began to sizzle.

Come on, you son of a bitch. Take me.

Take me.

He was coming apart. The pain in his head was splitting him in
two, his halves exploding into vapour. He considered turning back, a
fleeting thought without much heart in it, but he doubted now that he
could. He'd already come too far.

He focused on whatever lay ahead, trying to hold himself together
until he saw where this crazy carnival ride came out. There was a body
of light up there, just like those jacked-up TV evangelists always said
there would be, a blinding sunburst of immaculate white, and it drew
him into its radiance the way a porch lamp draws a fluttering moth.

It was an awesome light, but he was not afraid.

The corridor ended suddenly, a crisp edge of brilliance and then
nothing; it was like running off the edge of a roof…

And then he saw it.

* * *

An immense, slowly revolving disc, nebula-shaped, made up of countless millions of radiant pinpoints of light, like stars, only brighter, each of them the condensed essence of a life that once was—he knew this instinctively. A thrumming bass note, profound in its depth, emanated from that disc, which was enormous beyond comprehension, yet accessible to his expanded perceptions.

As he drifted closer, awestruck and at peace, knowledge in its purest form struck him like a thunderbolt, and in that staggering instant he knew the depth and breadth of every being that had ever lived and then died. He knew the passions of the world's greatest thinkers, the patience of the mightiest oak, the agonies of the most tormented soul. He knew the watery peace of the womb, the sorrow of a fallen leaf, the pointless fear of the dying. This was the archive of all knowledge and it gushed into him now like life's blood. He hung there unafraid, basking in its radiance, privy to nature's most coveted secrets. There was no time to label this the final hallucination of a dying man, nor was there any need.

It was real. All of it.

And it told him what he must do.

* * *

The trip back was instantaneous. One moment he was staring into eternity, the next into the blank green eye of his computer screen. His brain was alight like a city under siege, each of its billions of axons firing simultaneously, and for a wild moment he thought the contents of his skull might simply gusher out through his ears.

Then he began to grow calm, the rush of the preceding minutes drawing back like a scouring tidal wave. In the blandness of his room, every ounce of reason that was left in him rose up to denounce the reality of what he'd just experienced .... Then all reason deserted him, skittering away like rats from a sinking ship.

The digital clock clicked over in the silence. Peter glanced at its glowing face: 1:00 A.M., Sunday, January 24.

He smiled. He had the whole night ahead of him.

And there was a lot he needed to do.

With a practiced thrust of his chin, he plucked the key striker out of its slot. A technician from Biomed had rewired the power switch to the scroll lock key, and now Peter gave it a tap. When the screen came to life, he began to record his experience and all it had taught him.

* * *

The next day, Monday, Kelly was again distracted at work, unable to apply herself fully... but it was a healthy distraction this time, not irresponsible in the least. Her cheeks ached from grinning so much, and all she could think about was getting out of here. She and Marti were going out after work to shop for wedding gowns. Steve had indeed popped the question on Christmas Eve, and the four of them had decided over drinks to make it a double wedding in the spring.

After encountering that peculiar illusion in her bedroom the night before, she and Will ended up talking until three in the morning, speculating on the existence of ghosts. It surprised Kelly to learn that Will believed in them strongly, though he'd never actually seen one before. It was all tied into a strong Baptist upbringing (another surprise for Kelly), and an unswerving belief in the persistence of the soul. Neither could agree on exactly what they'd seen or felt in Kelly's room, only that it was strange and, for the time being at least, inexplicable.

Kelly recalled her mother's encounter with the "ghost" of Kelly's grandmother and tried to fit her own experience into the mystic framework of her mother's. But whatever this thing was, it had borne no distinguishable features, and Kelly had picked up no particular emanations from it. In all likelihood, it had been some fluky reflection from the lake. There was a large dome-shaped area of water out there that for some reason never froze—her father's theory was that there was a warm-water spring beneath the surface out there—and maybe the moon had bounced its light off that, the reflection striking the ceiling, creating that eerie pocket of illumination. Then a cloud had scrubbed it away...

But what about that cold-steel feeling in your heart? What about that?

Kelly didn't know. All she knew was that in the good light of day it all seemed rather hokey, some shared illusion best forgotten. Maybe they'd humped themselves into some sort of pre-epileptic state, and that blue light had been an aura, a warning to cool down or burn down. Kelly smiled at this evil thought.

Will, my man, you bring out the worst in me.

She was in study hall now, her last obligation for the day, and when the bell rang she pushed her way out with her students.

* * *

Sam came in that day around four. He'd just completed an organic chemistry midterm and he was feeling pretty glum. Since his mother's death, and the ensuing changes in his brother, study had become virtually impossible. He felt constantly uptight, driven to distraction. And to make matters worse, the easy channels of communication he and Peter had always shared had been suddenly and mysteriously closed off. The long discussions they'd had about Peter's adventures had ceased, and whenever Sam brought up the topic, Peter changed the subject abruptly. These days, when he wasn't out doing God knew what, leaving his body in that creepy, catatonic state that was so much like death, Peter had his nose stuck in that computer. It was making Sam regret having bought it in the first place. It had nearly broken him... and now it sat between him and Peter like a wedge. If he dropped in while Peter was typing—an activity that accounted for the bulk of Peter's waking hours nowadays—Sam was made to feel as if he'd interrupted a meeting of the U.N. General Assembly or something. It was beginning to piss him off.

He found Peter asleep on this frosty afternoon. He wasn't in a trance—Sam could see his breathing, and there was a hint of colour in his face—but he looked exhausted.

Sam paused in the doorway, trying to decide whether to leave or stay. Then he noticed that the computer was still on. Peter must have fallen asleep while using it. His striker was tucked beneath his chin, which rested on the slope of his chest.

An idea struck Sam then, one of such sinful proportions and yet so irresistibly appealing that he felt light-headed and had to lean against the door frame until the feeling passed.

Read it. Go ahead. Find out for yourself what the big secret is.

Was it stuff about him? he wondered for the hundredth time. Bad stuff? Was that why Peter was so secretive?

Common sense told him no. Peter loved him. They were brothers, and Sam should respect his privacy.

Do it, that other voice goaded, its insistence chilling Sam... and making him wonder what his dark heart suspected.

Do it.

Sam started into the room, moving on tiptoe, slipping his knapsack off his shoulders and setting it by the bedside. He leaned over his brother, checking to make sure his eyes were still closed, then looked at the flickering screen.

Only two lines of text were visible:

> *... all the fucking assholes, all the jackoffs I went to school with, all the selfish fucksticks in this hospital...*

The cursor blinked impatiently beside the last word, waiting for the next batch of hate.

Feeling ill, Sam reached out to scroll the screen back, praying Peter wouldn't stir. His finger touched the scroll key—

"He's been like that for an hour."

Sam straightened up with a snap, barely suppressing a cry of alarm. Pain flared in his healing ribs. There was a nurse standing at the foot of Peter's bed, a pitcher of water in her hand.

"You startled me," Sam said in a voice that trembled.

"That's an understatement," the nurse said. "You're white as a ghost." She smiled pleasantly, her gaze lingering on Sam's puffy eye, then set the pitcher on the side table. She was new. Sam had never seen her before. She said, "Are you a relative?"

"I'm his brother," Sam said, shame brewing sourly in the basin of his throat. "I was just going to shut off his computer…" He let his voice trail off, realizing that he didn't need to explain himself to this woman. But he was glad of her intrusion. It had prevented him from violating his brother's trust.

"Don't mind me," the nurse said. "I'll be gone in a jiffy." She glanced at Peter with compassion, something Sam didn't see too much of around here anymore, then up at Sam. "Poor guy, he must be beat. The night nurse said he's been at that computer since the wee hours. And he's hardly budged from it all day." The nurse blushed, realizing the blunder of her words. "I meant—"

"I know what you meant."

"Well, 'bye for now," the nurse said. Then she was gone.

The interruption hadn't disturbed Peter, who was usually a light sleeper. Relieved, Sam reached out to switch off the screen.

(all the selfish fucksticks in this hospital)

What about them?

Loathing himself, Sam scrolled back to the beginning of the file. The first entry was dated December 29.

> *Even now it aches where the crucifix punctured her heart. It aches like a battle scar, one that brings pride and trace memories of wars that resonate strangely through time. There is no regret, only a cold sense of justice, and I am glad. I am free of her now, and so is Sam. Too bad she was the first. I'd like a fresh chance at her. This time it would be no accident.*
>
> *And I would prolong her pain…*

Sam looked up from the screen, a tense, trapped-animal sweat needling his armpits. That was their mother he was reading about… and although he'd scanned only a single paragraph, he felt the same sick lump in his gut he'd felt when he leafed through a copy of *Mein Kampf* for a history project in the twelfth grade. He'd read about the same number of words—and had known immediately they'd been scrawled by a madman.

He looked again at Peter—so close, so loved, sleeping his peaceful sleep—then returned his gaze to the screen. The steady *tick-tick-tick* of the line-advance key was the only sound. It seemed huge and intrusive to Sam, but he read on.

Jan. 3

> *Locked out. Can't reach her. Can't get back inside. Tried to take him, it was easy before, tried to take him but I couldn't. They've locked me out. Locked me out of them both.*
>
> *But she's mine, and soon they are going to see that. I'll make them see. The accident took her away from me before, but I was mere flesh and blood then. Fragile, so fragile. But all that has changed now. Now I'm divine. Yes, that's the word. Divine.*

And our union is divine. She felt it in her sleep, our union,
felt it when I pushed the right buttons, felt it when I gushed inside
her mind, oh the union the glorious union.

Sam broke off. He was breathing hard. Uninvited, he'd peeked
inside his brother's secret heart—and found a can of worms there,
a rancid sewer of hatred and contempt, of dark lust and loathsome
trespass, of madness and megalomania.

Helpless, he read on.

Jan. 16

Lowe was scum. He whimpered like a dog when I cut him.
And I think he actually wanted to fuck that corpse. I'd have let
him, but it was too disgusting even for me. Jesus, I wish now that
I had. Think of what the tabloids could have done with that.

Sam spotted his own name partway down the screen, and he
scanned to it, thinking, He believes he killed Dr. Lowe, and he believes he killed our mother, but that's all it is, a fantasy, a twisted angry
fantasy.

... poor kid, he was busted up really bad. And that moment I
spent in his dream, just before I saw what those bastards did to
him, what a wondrous moment that was. I'd often wondered how
little Sammy felt, taking the brunt of the bitch's hate, bearing the
deepest scars from our dad. He's one tough sombitch, my brother,
and I love him. I owe him a lot.

In spite of his creeping dread, Sam felt his heart soar... but fear
quickly crowded that feeling aside.

He really did see. He really was inside of me.

Right inside—

Peter's head rolled on the pillow, his eyes fluttering open to slits, and Sam nearly screamed. A bubble of naked terror closed over him, and he felt as if his bones had turned to putty, his bowels to runny mud. He sat on the edge of his brother's bed and felt afraid in a way he had never known, a cold unmanning fear, the kind of fear a man must feel in the face of an angered god. If Peter awoke now, Sam would be caught in that most vile of all acts, breaking a loved one's trust.

And what might he do about it?

Sam held his breath and waited. Peter's eyes touched him briefly, glazed and half closed; they rolled ... then fell shut again.

Sam breathed. And although his heart bade him take his leave, he scrolled to the final entry. It bore yesterday's date, and it was the longest. Sam had a brief thought of how exhausting it must have been to tap all this out, letter by painstaking letter.

Then he read on, the fear mooring itself deeper inside him with each incredible phrase.

* * *

On the walk home, Sam's mind kept twitching back and forth between belief and disbelief. His brother's writings were so far out and yet so incredibly persuasive that Sam actually considered marching over to Kelly's place to warn her that his brother had turned into some weird kind of killing machine and that Kelly and her boyfriend were in danger.

But wasn't the rational explanation by far the more probable? Peter had despised their mother and Dr. Lowe for years, and when he learned of their death, he simply created these elaborate fantasies, giving credit to himself—to this weird, ghostly thing he became. It was pretty warped, but Sam thought he understood. And all that other stuff about Kiley and company—fantasy again. Those dorks were probably at Kiley's Texaco right now, sucking back beers and bullshitting one another about all the babes they'd banged.

But he said this guy Will was next... then Kelly. Kelly and himself, at the same time. Then, joined together as one, they would go to—

And here was the wildest fiction of all. All that funky stuff about The Light or the hereafter or whatever that long run of madness had been meant to represent. Total knowledge, a recycling plant for souls, a vast, slow-moving carousel ride into eternity...

Cripes, Peter has really lost it. He's insane.

And yet, Sam thought as he turned off Paris Street onto Regent, there was an undeniable texture of truth to the whole thing. What was Peter when he left his body if not a soul? And as such, could he not gain access to the afterlife, if one existed? And if he could do that, then maybe he really could do all the things he claimed he'd done... and intended to do.

Kelly's image materialized in Sam's mind, warm and lovely, her dark eyes filled with unspoken (and unspeakable) promise.

Drop it, man. You're turning as crazy as your brother. Just drop it.

Sam looked up. He was standing in front of his apartment building. Heart pounding, he hurried inside.

* * *

"What's up?" Kelly said, alarmed. She and Marti had been sitting on the couch, leafing through a wedding catalog, when Marti gasped and jumped to her feet.

Now she sat down again, shaking her head. "I thought I saw something at the window."

Kelly looked but saw nothing. "It must've been the dog. He's forever sticking his mug in the windows and scaring the life out of me."

"Maybe," Marti said. "And maybe it was some pervert with his joint in his hand."

Kelly laughed, secretly pitying any pervert who decided to take on Marti Stone. "He'd freeze it off tonight."

"Good for him."

"Come on," Kelly said. "Back to business." They'd picked out the dresses they wanted, white lace with veils and elegant trains, and were now involved in the happy task of selecting gowns for the bridesmaids. "The peach or the fuchsia."

"I think we should run with the Naugahyde."

"All right," Kelly said, closing the catalog. She'd seen the last of Marti's concentration for tonight. "Let's watch a movie."

"Yeah," Marti said. "*First Blood*." She chuckled. "Sounds like a health ed film for a bunch of prepubescent girls."

"You, Marti Stone, are a sicko."

Kelly got up and turned on the DVD player. They'd rented a couple of films at Bianco's Video: *The Man Who Would Be King* for Kelly and *First Blood* for Marti. She was really just killing time until Will got home. She hated it when he worked the night shift like this. She worried about him out there on that slag train.

Kelly glanced at her watch as she fed the disc into the machine. *Four more hours*, she thought impatiently. *Just four more hours and he'll be home.*

* * *

Sam couldn't think. When he entered the apartment, the first thing he did was turn on the reel-to-reel. He listened to a few scratchy bars, then switched the damned thing off.

God help me, he thought, madness nipping at his heels. *I'm turning into my mother. The next thing you know I'll be drowning in a whiskey bottle.*

He turned the TV on loud. A fat woman wearing Buddy Holly glasses and a baggy *Vuarnet* T-shirt spun the wheel of fortune with a dimpled fist. The clack of the wheel stalked Sam as he wandered through the apartment. He stopped at the piano—and plucked a memory out of the air before it could flit away on him.

He sat on the bench, lifted the fallboard and examined the precise rank of keys. "Middle C," he could hear Peter saying in his tutor's voice. "If you can remember that, the rest is a cinch."

Middle C...where is it? Sam wondered, recalling with fondness Peter's vain attempts at teaching him music. He'd been about ten at the time. He plunked a white key near the centre of the keyboard. It sounded right.

"'Chopsticks,' kid," Peter said through a cold mist of years, and Sam could almost feel his brother's arm around his skinny, ten-year-old shoulders. "It's the easiest tune in the world. Play this for that little redhead I've seen you eyeballing across the street and you'll have her knickers off in no time..."

Recalling the simple melody, Sam hunched over the keys. He aligned his index fingers like rigid soldiers and tried to play "Chopsticks."

Wrong.

He shifted his fingers one key to the right and tried again.

Wrong.

"Come on, stupid," Sam cursed himself, "can't you do anything right?"

He shifted two keys to the left and speared them savagely.

Wrong. Shit. Wrong.

On the TV behind him the local news came on. The lead story made Sam twist around on the bench, his breath snagging in his throat.

"Two Sudbury men were found dead today by a Kukagami area trapper," the newsman said. "A third, listed as missing, is also presumed dead. Provincial police are withholding the details, but sources indicate that foul play was likely a factor. From what could be pieced together at the scene, the three men were ice fishing when one of them went berserk…"

The scene cut to three faded photographs. Sam recognized Rhett's from his ninth-grade yearbook.

No…

Clammy with shock, Sam stumbled out to the kitchen, grabbed the phone book and began flipping through the pages, tearing some of them as he went. He found "Wheeler" and scanned the entries; there were six of them. Kelly's number was unlisted. He found her folks' number, started to punch it in, then got a better idea.

He hit 411.

In the other room the announcer continued his news break: "Police divers will resume their efforts to recover the third man's body at first light…"

"Information."

"Have you got a new listing for Kelly Wheeler?"

There was a pause; then a recorded voice recited the number. As he jotted it down, Sam thumbed the cutoff button. When he had a dial tone again, he punched in the number. It rang.

"Hello?" a cheerful voice said.

And Sam fell mute. It was insane. All of it. She'd think he'd lost his marbles. And hadn't he?

There had to be some sane explanation. Somehow Peter had gotten wind of what happened to Kiley and the others and had built it into his fantasies. That was all it was.

"Hello? Who is this?"

Sam glanced at the TV. There was a detergent commercial on now. He hung up the phone.

It was too crazy even to contemplate.

* * *

Over the next five weeks things settled down to a state Sam came to think of as normal. It meant ignoring his fears, but this seemed a small price to pay for the peace of mind. Peter seemed more like his old self—by turns moody and bright, reading novels again and speaking fondly of old times—and this calm period lulled Sam into a wary breed of contentment. His injuries were mending nicely; there would be a permanent scar below his right eye, and the appliance the orthodontist had fitted him with was driving him batty, but his ribs didn't catch him anymore, and his limp was almost gone. He'd even suited up for a game toward the middle of February, though the coach hadn't played him. There was a change for the better in the weather, too, and this lent credence to the illusion of peace. Kiley and his friends had indeed come to an untimely end, but the question of how Peter had known about it began to fade in importance with time. After all, he was Peter, and Peter had always been an exceptional person. Even Sam's secret, carnal longings for Kelly seemed to diminish a little.

For a time he felt almost content.

* * *

Peter used the time wisely, honing his powers and recording his thoughts, but also biding his time. Let her dwell in her girlish fantasies. Let the monkey she'd taken up with lead her into a cloud of stupid bliss. She'd be more vulnerable then. Her grief would cripple her, and then he could take her. Take her to the light.

Then she would understand.

35

"WHAT'RE YOU GRINNING AT?" Dave Sully said as Will climbed aboard the idling locomotive. Sully was the conductor and switch-man. He and Will had been workmates for the past eight years, and tonight was just another of the many night shifts they'd shared. "You get your doughnut dunked before coming to work?"

Will just beamed, and for Sully that was answer enough. He clapped Will on the back, seized his lunch pail—he always did that, from the very first shift they'd shared, snatching Will's lunch pail and rudely inspecting its contents—then took his seat by the rear controls.

"You gonna eat this Twinkie?" Sully said, already unwrapping the sweet brown cake.

"It's yours if you shove it up your ass," Will said, and then laughed as he always did as Sully puckered his lips into what passed for the most appalling-looking anal crater Will could imagine and crammed the Twinkie in through it. "You hog."

Once these nightly amenities were observed, the two men set about inspecting the slag train. Will, in his capacity as engineer, checked the controls for function, cranking levers and eyeballing gauges, testing the pressurized brakes. Sully, meanwhile, hopped down to inspect the railcars, making sure each of the eight helmet-shaped pots was securely locked in the upright position. A single pot had a twenty-five-ton capacity, which meant that, fully loaded, the train lugged about two hundred tons of molten rock. The temperature of freshly skimmed slag ran in the vicinity of 2,400°F. A single drop splashed onto an unprotected arm would fry a sizzling tunnel all the way through before its owner got a chance to scream. It was not a substance to be toyed with.

Satisfied all was in order, Sully climbed aboard. "Let's get this old whore rolling," he said.

"I hear that," Will said, and sounded the whistle. Cranking a lever, he eased the train toward the long brick smelter a quarter mile distant.

* * *

In the west, the sun sank slowly into peach-coloured mist.

Their first run went like clockwork. They picked up a load at number three furnace and propelled the eight sloshing pots along the two miles of track to the dump, stopping only once at the halfway point while Sully threw a switch. Ranged out in clattering succession ahead of them, the lime-whitened vats resembled a crude rank of cribs containing the infant offspring of the sun. The heat shimmer rose ten feet in the air, distorting the objects in its path.

At the top of the run, where the east face of the embankment flattened out, Will stopped the train and gave a short, sharp blast on the whistle. Thirty yards away, the door to the dumper's trailer swung open and Jack Miller lumbered out. Jack, a dull-minded chap with the most amazing beer gut Will had ever seen, spent the time between dumps napping like a baby in his chair. The whistle blast was meant to get him moving.

As he always did, Sully jumped down to watch the slag spills glow in the twilight.

Left alone, Will leaned back in his seat and closed his eyes. His thoughts were with Kelly, of course, and a contented smile played on his lips. Winning her back had been like the magical replacement of a missing limb, and he made a silent vow before the sinking sun never to let go of her again. When Sully climbed back aboard twenty minutes later, Will failed to notice the scowl on his face and the apparent blackening of his mood. He exchanged waves with the dumper, who'd made his way back to his trailer, and began reversing the train down the grade. Had his thoughts not been elsewhere, Will might have been alarmed at the change in his partner, at the way his typically smiling blue eyes had darkened, and at how they'd settled, cold and sullen, on Will's unprotected back.

He eased the train back toward the smelter, unbothered by the two-hundred-foot slope of the embankment, which plunged away on either side.

As sometimes happened, the next batch of pots had not yet been loaded, and the trainmen got a few minutes' break. As Will backed the locomotive into the loading bay, Sully hopped down and stalked grimly off toward the line shack. In serious need of a leak, Will strolled into the smelter to use the facilities.

Shortcutting across the roaring aisle—a narrow, twelve-hundred-foot corridor in which the raw ore was refined—Will was struck yet again by the dark magnificence of the place. To the uninitiated, it must seem a vision of Hell's own foundry, a subterranean chamber of horrors in which the damned sweated and toiled through eternity, the nature of their sins long forgotten in the blistering extravagance of their punishment. Enormous cylindrical converters, in whose bellies the molten ore boiled, spewed fiery vomit from mouths that were fanged with cooling rock. Amid the whir of turbines and the crackle of electrical panels, Satan's trustees strutted in bone-white helmets and goggly black gas masks, untormented on their high catwalks by the sulphury fumes that parched the throats of the damned. And above it all, like ghostly conning towers, the cranes hummed infinitely by, immense hot-metal ladles suspended from huge iron hooks, the whole sliding neatly between walls of crisscrossing beams painted danger yellow and the black of slow dissolution. All too easy to imagine that bubbling cargo consuming the naked bodies of the damned, only to spill them out whole again at the end of the line, magically restored, to be crisped in agony once more.

Aren't you a morbid son of a bitch, Will thought uneasily, feeling suddenly, unaccountably disturbed.

Forgetting his full bladder, he hurried back out to the train.

In the few minutes Will had been inside, night had fallen like a seamless curtain, and now the shadow-hung plant seemed to sigh, as if wearied by the prospect of yet another night of obligatory wakefulness. Approaching his locomotive, Will thought he could feel that sigh, and the heartbeat that sustained it, a dull, thudding tremor in the earth beneath his feet.

Will's earlier unease came oiling back, beading him in a rank, unpleasant sweat, which the night instantly chilled. For no apparent reason he found himself wanting to leave the plant. Just pack it in. Never mind punching out or changing back into his civvies or saying goodbye to Sully. Just go. So strong was this impulse, he was twenty yards past the train before he could arrest his own urgent stride.

He turned and looked back at the smelter, now a bulking silhouette against the purple night sky, and his formless apprehension fell away. There was no heartbeat here but the thrum of buried turbines, no sigh but the steady vent of steam. His dark vision was doubtless inspired by some unbidden trace memory of life without Kelly, for more and more in the void of her absence he had viewed it as no life at all. There was nothing sentient in this sleepless factory, save the men who peopled it.

Nothing...evil.

"Let's get this old whore rolling," Sully said, gliding out of the dark like a wraith.

"Jesus, man," Will said in alarm. "Don't do that."

But Sully had already boarded the train.

* * *

The trip to the dump was routine. At the base of the last long climb, as always, Will idled the locomotive while Sully hopped down to throw a switch, said switch being designed to prevent a runaway from barreling back into the smelter, diverting it instead into the shallow basin of the railyard, where its deadly momentum would be exhausted in a series of harmless back-and-forth runs. It was full dark now, and Sully's frame was quickly consumed by the night. His return was uncommonly prompt—Sully had never been one to rush on company time—and when he climbed back aboard, Will commented on it.

"That was quick."

But Sully just glowered at him, and Will decided to leave him be. Though customarily jovial, Sully was a private person. If he wanted Will to know what was eating him, he'd say so in his own good time. Maybe he'd called home from the line shack during their break and had gotten into a tiff with his wife. Will didn't know. All he knew was that it was good to be back out in the open. For some strange reason the smelter had given him the creeps, and he was glad to be out and away from it.

Two more runs, he thought. Two more runs and he'd be heading for Kelly's warm bed.

He threw the locomotive into gear, wincing at the wheeze of pistons as the engine battled inertia. After a few lagging moments the rig began to chug forward, bumping the cars ahead of it, slag slopping over the rims. Lulled by the steady *clack-a-clack-a* of the rails, Will settled back in his seat for the ten-minute ride to the top. The grade was gradual but constant.

At the dump site, Will gave his customary blast on the whistle. A gusty breeze had picked up, and when Jack Miller stepped down from the trailer his silver asbestos greatcoat belled out behind him. He yawned hugely, then slouched off toward the nearest railcar.

"Think I'll go join him," Sully said, jumping down before Will could reply.

Shrugging, Will stepped off the train and unzipped his fly. His bladder had inched its way up to his navel, and he stood there pissing forever. When he was done, he climbed back aboard and settled into his seat to wait.

* * *

"'Evenin', Jack," Sully said as he strolled past the dumper.

Jack grunted and twisted a flywheel. In response, a system of gears began to grind and the first of the pots tilted forward. This was followed by a huge splashing sound and an intense rush of heat as tons of molten slag slopped down the embankment on the opposite side. Tugged by the breeze, a bank of noxious blue smoke swirled up, breaking over Sully's body and sending sulfurous tendrils up his nose. Though long accustomed to the gas, Sully felt his windpipe cramp down to the bore of a drinking straw. He angled his face away until the worst of it had passed, then turned and watched the river of slag.

Lighting up the night in an orangey Halloween glow, it coursed down the slope in divergent streams before coalescing into a steaming, crackling pool a hundred yards out on the flat. Roosting gulls flapped up in alarm, and a bright, baking heat threw the night sky into shriveling waves.

There was a fresh whine of gears and the still-glowing empty straightened up, the rime of cooling slag that lined it tinkling like shattered glass. Heat belched out of the pot's fiery interior in a surge. From his vantage ten feet away, Sully could feel it roasting his skin.

Then he moved.

* * *

Without ceremony Jack shifted to the next pot in line and began working a new set of gears. The pot tilted forward, its payload gushing out—then a hand flicked across the coupling and laid hold of Jack's arm. With a fierce yank it dragged him across the coupling. On the way past, Jack's head clipped the side of the overturned pot, the impact numbing him to the pain and the stench of his own scorching hair. He caught a dream glimpse of Sully's baked face, brick red and utterly blank, then went airborne over the embankment. He landed on his back in the lava flow, suddenly hellishly alert and screaming.

In his seat on the idling locomotive, eyes gently closed in a catnap, Will heard nothing save the fitful whicker of the wind.

Jack rode the torrent down the slope, twirling like a kid on a water slide. For the first several seconds his asbestos greatcoat spared him, but the slag quickly scorched its way through. From the side of the train above, Sully watched him go. He seemed to melt, like a lump of butter on a tilted skillet. By the time he reached bottom, there was nothing left of Jack Miller but a puddle of grease and a pair of smoking workboots.

Sully stepped over the coupling, righted the empty pot, then moved to the next one in line. Skin from his scorched palms stuck to the flywheel like bark on a flaying birch. Slag spewed down the slope.

While Jack leveled the first pot, Sully had slipped past it on the embankment side of the train. Had his timing been off by a hair's breadth, he would have been cooked by the soup from the second pot. As it was, the soles of his boots had melted through to his socks when he tiptoed over the spill, and the skin of his face was blistered by the radiant heat.

Shedding more skin, he discharged the next pot of slag, then the next, all the way down the line, working his way closer to the locomotive. As he finished each dump, he reached behind the flywheel and tugged loose a short length of neoprene tubing, disabling the pressurized brakes.

When Sully got back to the locomotive, he found Will dozing. As capable an engineer as Will—they often traded jobs to ease the boredom—he slipped the train into gear.

Will's body jerked and he opened his eyes.

"Relax, man," Sully said in a hoarse whisper, his gaze directed out the window. "I'll take her down."

Will nodded gratefully, thinking idly that Sully must be coming down with a cold. Maybe that was why he seemed so cranky all of a sudden. He glanced back along the flank of the train, intending to give his habitual wave to the dumper, but Jack was nowhere in sight. He leaned back and closed his eyes again.

When they'd gained some speed, Sully twisted a valve and gradually bled off the air brakes. Inside of a minute the train was doing twice its normal descent velocity and rapidly picking up speed.

Will opened his eyes. He looked up at Sully, whose face was still turned away, then out at the blurring nightscape. "Hey, man," he said, alarm skidding like an ice cube down the back of his neck. "You'd better slow her down."

Sully didn't respond. They'd already topped thirty miles an hour, and at this rate they would easily double that speed before the track leveled out again.

Will started to get up, but Sully rounded on him and shoved him back in his seat.

Will was totally flabbergasted. "Have you gone fucking crazy?" he shouted over the deafening rumble of the train. "Slow us down."

"She's mine, asshole," Sully said through puffy lips, and Will noticed then that his face was covered with blisters and his boots were steaming with smoke. And that was not Sully's voice...

But there was no time to argue or to ponder this bizarre transformation in his friend. Sully had lost his mind—that much was certain—and he was going to get them both killed if Will couldn't slow the train down. A quick glance outside told him that to jump would mean certain death. The rocky embankment sloped away at a treacherous angle on either side. His only chance was to stay with the train and pray the brakes had enough juice to slow them down. There was a tricky spot back near the switch point, a tight curve where the train might derail at this speed. If he could make it past that, they'd be out of danger. Beyond the switch point the train would behave like a marble in a shallow bowl, rolling back and forth until friction ground it to a halt in the natural basin of the railyard.

Then Sully would have some serious explaining to do. If he was suicidal, he could fucking well do it on his own.

Working against the acceleration of the train, Will charged at Sully, driving him backward into the controls. Apparently unaffected by the attack, Sully slammed a fist into Will's face, mashing the ball of his chin. Stunned, Will collapsed to the floor. Beneath his back the floorboards bucked and strained. He tried to sit up.

Then Sully was kneeling astride him, raising his fist like a bludgeon. The fist came down—and Sully's eyes cleared. He gaped at Will like a man kicked awake from a nightmare.

"What...?"

"Get off me." Will howled. *"Get off."*

Sully rolled into a corner and huddled there, taking blinking glimpses of the deadly situation he'd created.

He doesn't remember, Will thought as he lunged for the forward controls, and somehow that made this crazy situation all the more terrifying. He was totally out of it. It made him think of the first time he'd slept with Kelly, that period of temporal dislocation and the unexplained traces of their union.

Will tried the brakes. They were dead.

He shot a glance through the windshield. There was no speedometer on the train—its top end was only twenty-two miles an hour—but he estimated their current speed at about fifty.

And they were coming into the curve.

"Brace yourself," Will shouted, his voice all but swallowed in the clattering pandemonium of the train. *"Brace yourself."*

Like a huge and remorseless hand, centrifugal force leaned against the inner flank of the train. Positioned over the inward wheels, Will felt their rumble cease as they parted company with the track.

We're going over.

There followed a sickening moment of what felt like free-fall; for a split second the rattling din of the train simply ceased, and all that was left was the eerie whine of the wind. In his mind's eye Will saw them going over the edge, like a runaway freight train in a Saturday afternoon western.

Kelly's face floated up in his mind, clean and beautiful, and in his extremity he cried her name.

He tensed for the impact...

Then the world was filled once again with the screech of friction, the tortured strain of the couplings, the bone-deep shudder of the train.

Gradually that tilting hand was withdrawn.

Will let out a triumphant whoop and scaled his way back to his feet. They were past the curve now, closing fast on the switch point. They were still gaining speed, but the angle of the rightward track was not all that sharp. Once they blew past that they'd be fine—

The train veered left, toward the smelter.

Will swung on Sully in disbelief. "You didn't make the switch?"

Sully climbed to his feet, bracing himself like a man in a falling elevator. At the sound of Will's voice, the white and confused horror in his face fell away, and he smiled.

"That's right, Bubba."

Then he leapt through the open door.

"*Sull-leeeeee.*"

In the starlight Will caught a glimpse of his partner's body breaking apart on the rocks. Then it was gone.

Slack with horror, he stumbled to the control panel and began desperately working the levers...but it was pointless. The brakes were dead.

And now the smelter loomed into view.

Alternatives streaked through Will's mind like tracer bullets, all of them ending in catastrophe. Incredibly, the train was still gaining speed, and he'd already seen what would happen if he jumped.

There was only one hope, and it was a slim one.

Will threw himself into Sully's seat at the back of the cab. It was low and padded, bolted to the floor on a metal disk. There was a seat belt, old and frayed, and Will looped it around himself, his fingers fumbling before driving the tongue clasp home.

Seizing the armrests, he planted his boots on the floorboards and, through eyes as big as silver dollars, watched the smelter race toward him.

He prayed the next set of pots had not yet been loaded.

* * *

The first man to spot the runaway was the transportation supervisor, Chet Spinrad. He glanced up the line and saw the yellow locomotive thundering out of the night toward him like a phantom. He couldn't believe his eyes.

"Ho-leee shitfire."

He hauled out his walkie-talkie, thumbed the talk button and jerked the mouthpiece to his chin. "Hey, Bernie," he shouted, aware that his voice was scaling up the ladder into unintelligibility but unable to stop it. "Hey, Bernie, you readin'?"

Bernie was the slag skimmer; it was his job to load the pots. "Yeah, Chet. I'm here. Whatcha squawkin' about—"

Bernie's voice was eaten by the roar of the train. It screeched past Chet not ten feet from where he was standing, tossing up cinders, rocking like an all-night disco. Chet caught a glimpse of the cab's interior, but he could see no one aboard.

"Get your ass out of the loading bay," Chet bellowed when the train had passed. "There's a runaway comin', and it's movin' like a bat out of hell." He began to sprint toward the smelter, his scuffed white hard hat jouncing on his head.

"Y'don't need to tell me twice," Bernie sent back. Then his voice got chewed up in static.

On board the train Will braced himself. He'd thought he might lose some of his speed on the flat, but it hadn't worked out that way. He was highballing now, sailing on air, suffused with a terrible exhilaration. As he rounded the last bend before the loading bay he opened his mouth and screamed, a low curdling hoot that pitched upward into the shriek of a startled chimpanzee.

He closed his eyes—

And when he opened them again the smelter was gone and Kelly was there on the windshield, like a film projected on a movie screen. She had her back to him and she was naked, long hair loose, head rolling erotically on the glistening shelf of her shoulders. This bizarre mind-camera panned down her back, and Will saw that she was not alone. There was a man beneath her, and she was riding him. He had time to think that the mind was a remarkable thing, throwing up such twisted images in this moment that was probably his last. Then the camera zoomed in on her partner's face. It was emaciated and pale—and it was looking straight at him, its yellow smile openly triumphant.

"She's mine now, asshole," the image said in an echo of Sully's words, and Will heard them not in the cab but in his head.

"Forever."

And in that instant Will knew it was him. It was the quad, and somehow he'd made this happen. As if to confirm this awareness, the mind-camera pulled back and Will saw his decrepit body, saw Kelly's lovely rump riding up and down on the ropy stump of his penis.

Forever, Will heard him say again.

Then the image vanished and the smelter was there. The train stormed into the narrow loading bay at eighty-three miles an hour. Braked and bolstered, the next eight slag pots stood directly in its path.

And they were full.

The locomotive's blunt metal snout struck the coupling bar of the first railcar, the impact ramming the line of pots twenty feet farther down the track. Slag sloshed out in fiery combers, splattering the tracks and the steel-beamed ceiling, causing flashfires all up and down the platform. Still screaming, Will shot forward to the limits of his seat belt. In the instant of collision he believed it would hold, and he enjoyed a fleeting moment of hope—

Then the worn fabric gave with a dry farting sound, and he was bursting through the windshield. He struck it head first, and the shower of glass turned to stars in the tunnel of his vision. Semiconscious, he flipped once in the air and landed on his back by the tracks. There was pain and steely thunder, and he felt like a bug in a rolling barrel—but he was alive. The ground was beneath him and he was raw with pain and he thought, *Ha. You didn't get me you crazy bastard. You didn't get me.*

The world stopped reeling and Will sat up. He'd been thrown about twenty feet. Something knifed him in the side—*busted ribs*—and his neck creaked unstably as he swiveled it around to look.

The train was still moving, the empty pots piling up one on top of the next, the entire row twisting from back to front.

If he didn't get up and get moving, he'd be crushed.

He scrambled to his feet, aware that his left leg was broken but no longer feeling the pain. In hobbled strides he started away. Men were appearing on the opposite side of the tracks now, rushing toward him, and he threw out his arms to them.

But now they were shrinking back, white eyes darting from Will to a point above and behind him.

A pocket of scalding air struck Will Chatam from behind—and he knew why the men had backed away.

The whine of sprung gears filled the narrow aisle, muting the thunder of the train. Will lurched forward, his mind white with panic, managing barely a step before the first meteorites of slag sizzled through the back of his work coat. The pain, exquisite beyond the capacity of his mind to comprehend it, cranked the white of his panic to a blinding, sun-blasted chromium.

There was no thought.

No time.

The lip of a curling wave of slag struck Will Chatam in the back of the neck and seemed to freeze him there. He opened his mouth to scream and a column of liquid fire boiled out. His eyes fixed for a blank instant on the unbelieving eyes of Hector Witty, a crane operator who'd rushed out to witness the commotion. At the Ledo later that night Hector would tell a spellbound circle of listeners that those eyes had glowed hellfire red before running like half-congealed egg white down the doomed trainman's cheeks. It was as if, before erupting in a grisly lava burst, his skull had filled up with slag.

A split second later Will Chatam was gone, a toppling pillar of fire.

36

THE CANDLES HAD BURNED themselves down to stubs, and now Kelly snuffed them out, the act somehow doubling her worry. Will was an hour late. Not a long time in ordinary terms, and there were at least a dozen harmless explanations for his tardiness. Maybe his relief had been late or there'd been some trouble with the train. Will often complained about the antique equipment they were forced to work with. Or maybe he'd had a problem with his truck.

But it was unlike him not to call or to have someone at the smelter do it for him. And tonight was to have been a special night. It was the first day of the March break, and Kelly had promised him a late candlelit dinner. She'd even drawn them a hot bath, as Will had done on the night she accepted his proposal. He'd said he'd be home on time even if it meant skipping his last run.

Kelly went to the kitchen window and looked out. Nothing. The hill was dark, no sign of Will's truck in the turnaround. She could see Chainsaw out there, snoozing on the stoop, but that was all.

As she turned away, a flicker of light caught her eye and she swung back…but it was only a distant streetlight, the illusion of movement created by the wind in the trees.

Kelly's worry turned to fear. The simple explanations fell away like dressings from a terrible wound, and now she felt certain he was hurt.

Or worse.

Gooseflesh pebbled her skin as she hurried to the kitchen phone. She was wearing the mink-coloured teddy Will liked so much, and now she felt naked, stupidly vulnerable and exposed. She paged through her personal directory to S, followed her finger to "smelter," then placed a hand on the phone.

It rang and Kelly's hand flinched away. A cold sweat stood out on her arms, and her heart broke into a lurching stride that thundered in her ears. She giggled at her own raw nerves. Then she snared the receiver.

"Will?"

"No, ma'am. This is Chet Spinrad. I work with Will out here at Nickel Ridge. I got your number from his mom—"

"Is he all right?"

For a moment there was no response, and Kelly thought she might scream. Then: "There's been an accident, Miss. A terrible accident. I thought you might've heard about it already on the news. I—"

"Is he all right?"

"I'm sorry, Miss Wheeler," Spinrad said, "but Will Chatam is dead. It was a runaway train. He got caught in the slag."

Kelly looked up from the phone, her entire being screaming out a furious denial. Her gaze settled on the window—and now there were headlights at the top of the hill, starting down, and a triumphant laugh escaped her, an abrupt barking sound that hurt her throat. *Sick fucking joke,* she wanted to holler into the phone, but relief left her mute and she slammed down the handset instead.

Kelly ran to the window. It was a Blue Line cab, and now she had her explanation. Will's truck had refused to start—he'd commented only recently that he was going to have to drop a new starter into it—and he'd grabbed a cab home. He was climbing out now, paying his fare; she could see his hunched silhouette in the porch light. She didn't know who the crackpot on the phone was, but she hoped someone kicked his lying ass.

Kelly waited until Will had started up the walk, then darted to the door. When she swung it open, swooning with relief, she found Sam Gardner standing there, blushing at her state of attire and yet solemn, so dreadfully solemn.

"I heard about it on the news," Sam said. Chainsaw was nuzzling his gloved hand. "I'm sorry, Kelly. More than you can know." He touched Kelly's arm. "Can I come in? I've got some things I need to tell you."

Kelly fainted.

* * *

The first clear message to reach Kelly's brain was that she'd had a terrible dream. She'd dozed off in Will's lap and dreamed he'd been killed in an accident at work. Crazy. She could feel the firmness of his leg beneath her head, the gentle stroke of his fingers in her hair.

The next thing that registered was pain. She had a walloping headache that radiated outward from a single throbbing focus at the back of her head.

She opened her eyes and looked up at Sam, and for a mad instant her brain tried to rearrange his features into Will's.

Then she remembered.

"Oh," Kelly said and sat up too fast, adding a new percussion instrument to the furious ensemble in her head. She lifted a hand to the back of her skull. There was a tender, spongy knot back there. It felt as if it stuck out a mile.

"You bumped your head on the floor," Sam said. "I carried you in here." They were on the living room couch.

"Is it true?" Kelly whispered, the pieces of the evening's puzzle lumping cruelly together in her mind.

Sam nodded.

Then Kelly was in his arms, clutching him, the depth of her grief filling him with a ghastly emptiness. More than anything he wanted this girl in his arms. He could admit that now, after all these years. There was nothing more to lose. He wanted this girl in his arms...but not like this. Never like this.

Kelly buried her face in his neck and bawled, there was no other word for it. She bawled and shuddered and soaked his collar. Sam held her, soothing her as best he could. After a while, once the worst of it had passed, she lay like a rag doll in his arms. It was like holding a beautiful child.

And the whole time he held her, a shattering truth bored deeper inside him: his brother was a murderer, an assassin, the perfect criminal.

And now he had to convince Kelly Wheeler.

* * *

He would do it tonight. There was no reason to wait. The sooner he released Kelly from the prison of her body, the sooner they could enter eternity as one.

An hour earlier, still glowing from the rush of the kill, Peter had debated trying to explain his intentions to Kelly, to describe to her the glorious future that awaited them both in that awesome nebula in the heavens. Once he was inside her, it would be a simple matter of thinking, his thoughts thus becoming her own. But as the trance came on, he decided against it. She might not understand. She might be afraid, and that fear might make her balky. She was a strong-willed girl, and he needed her pliable. If she fought him he might not succeed. He would have to take advantage of her puny grief, turn it against her. He would try to make her death painless and quick. But if she had to suffer, little matter. What price immortality? What price a marriage of the gods?

As he quit his body, Peter remembered the sensation of the slag striking his back, the agony that was both hellish and blackly exquisite. He'd been forced to reenter Will's mind in the instant of that agony, for in that last split second it had appeared as if the bastard might throw himself clear of the spill. Peter had bound him there the way a rope bound a hanged man to his fate. And he'd felt it.

So hot, so final…

He took his time traveling to Kelly's place. The night was sweet, his last on this impermanent plane, and he savored it. His only regret was that he would be unable to say goodbye to Sam.

He entered the house through the big picture window, its molecules tickling his form.

And when he saw them there on the couch, the two people he cherished most in the world, locked together in a cheating embrace, rage ripped into his heart like the hack of a dull blade and he roared, roared and reeled back the way he'd come, the molecules in the glass not tickling him this time but mincing him like meat in a grinder.

He awoke in his bed and that roar found a voice.

He screamed in fury, the sound insane.

* * *

Sam twisted on the couch and scanned the room. He'd felt something just now, a frigid draft… but it had been more than that. The air had twitched, and for an instant Sam caught a whiff of an animal's den, a thick smell of pelt and a rampant, beastly rage.

Peter.

The clammy hand of terror squeezed Sam's balls. All the muscles in his body turned to taut cables and he groaned, sickened that he should feel such withering fear of the person he loved most in the world.

His gaze ricocheted wildly around the room...

But there was nothing. The feeling or illusion or whatever it had been was gone, vanished as quickly as Sam had sensed it, and he was left to wonder if it wasn't only his nerves. When he'd heard about Will Chatam's death on the news, every nerve in his body had begun to twist and spit like a live wire.

He returned his attention to Kelly. *You've got to get on with this*, he urged himself. *It's for real and you've got to tell her.*

But a yearning part of him didn't want to move, choosing instead to linger in a fantasy of its own. Kelly's weeping had subsided, the only indication that she wasn't just resting the occasional hitch in her breathing, or a sob. Sam was painfully aware of her scent, her skin, her scanty attire.

Then her face stirred against his neck, moist lips brushing his skin, and Sam felt a thrill snake through his body. Under the circumstances he felt ashamed.

"Oh, Sam," she moaned in a voice without life, without hope. "What am I going to do?"

"It's Peter," Sam said, not knowing how else to begin, throwing himself into it before he could change his mind.

He felt Kelly stiffen against him.

"What do you mean?" She lifted her head and fixed him with puffy eyes; they looked bruised in the low light of the living room.

"My brother," Sam said. "He did this. He killed our mother and Dr. Lowe and Kiley and those other bastards...and he killed your friend."

Kelly pushed herself away. Aware now of her near nudity, she grabbed a pillow and clutched it to her chest. "I think you should leave, Sam," she said, her voice shrill. "I can't take this. This madness. Why are you here, anyway? You'd better go." She buried her chin in the pillow and started to rock.

Kelly was in shock—that much was plain—but he couldn't leave her now. His brother might strike at any time.

"Listen, Kelly. You've got to believe me. Peter can leave his body; he's some kind of freaking ghost and he can hurt you. He can make you hurt yourself. He killed your friend. I don't know how, but I know he did. He said he would. I read it in—"

"Stop this, Sam." Her eyes were shiny and fierce.

"I read it in a journal he keeps on his computer. If only I'd believed it sooner, your friend might still be ali—"

Kelly stormed to her feet. "I want you out of here, Sam Gardner." Her face twisted itself into a parody of amusement. "What is going on here? Has the whole world gone stark raving mad?"

"He was in your dreams. Think about it, carefully. Your life may depend on it. He was in your dreams and he made you ... do things."

For a moment Kelly's face cleared. It was as if all expression had been slapped away from it. My God, she thought, he's right. Hadn't she sensed Peter? Not once or twice but night after night after night?

Until Will came back. Then the dreams had ceased.

"No, Sam. That's crazy. That's—"

"And he was *inside* Will. He took you from inside Will. You must remember that."

She did, she remembered—but it was mad, insupportable, insane, and she wanted Sam out of her house. She wanted him out and then she wanted to crawl into a corner and dream this all away, wake up to a fresh new day, a fresh new life.

Kelly pointed at the door. "Get out, Sam. I mean it." She stumbled to the hall closet, reached inside and took out her Louisville Slugger. She brandished it. "Get out now."

Sam stood, hands upheld in placation. She meant to use that bat; there was no doubt in his mind about that. Still, he had to keep trying. "Kelly, please, I—"

Kelly swung the bat. Sam stumbled back, almost tripping over the coffee table but avoiding the brunt of the blow. The bat's business end clipped him on the shoulder, missing his ear by an inch. He had a momentary thought of rushing her, but dismissed it when she advanced on him again.

"I'm serious, Sam. Take your bullshit and get out of here."

Sam hurried down the hallway to the door. It was no use. She was in a frenzy. And why shouldn't she be? She'd just lost her lover to a grisly death and here he was trying to feed her this lunacy.

He opened the door and placed its bulk protectively in front of him.

"My number's in the book, Kelly. Think about what I said and then call me. Please. Before it's too late."

He caught one last glimpse of her there at the end of the hallway, a sleek Amazonian goddess, backlit by the moon and pumped full of battle—then she was stomping toward him, roaring like an engine of destruction.

Sam pulled the door shut and ran up the hill in the starlight. Curled up by the hood of Kelly's car, Chainsaw watched him go.

* * *

Sam ran the eight blocks to the hospital. In the last quarter mile he developed a stitch in his side and now it seethed like a brand iron. He limped up the hill to the entrance, breathless and clutching his side. The only course of action he could think of was to talk to Peter, try to reason things through with him.

But he was afraid. He'd betrayed his brother both in thought and in deed, and now he would have to face the consequences.

It was 1:35 A.M. Under normal circumstances, anyone trying to visit at this hour would be turned away. But Sam knew the woman at the desk.

"Hi, Vicky."

The receptionist looked up from her Harlequin romance. The switchboard in front of her was peacefully blank. "Sam, what's up? Is your brother okay?"

Sam smiled. "Yeah, he's all right. I just got back from a hockey game and I thought I'd peek in on him, see if he's up. You mind?"

"'Course not. You go ahead."

Sam thanked her and slipped into a waiting elevator, his smile feeling like a healing scar on his face. He punched the button for the ninth floor. His fear was very big now, lying bloated in his gut like some ghastly pregnancy.

The doors slid shut and the elevator began its ascent. One wall was mirrored, and Sam was startled by his own reflection. In that first split second, it had been like looking into the face of his mother: the same socketed eyes, haunted things cowering in shallow caves; the same crooked mouth, joyless and thin...

The doors hissed open and Sam stepped out. The ward was dark, the only sound a distant radio tuned to a soothing FM murmur. As he crept past the nurses' station he heard the girls in the tiny back office, chatting quietly. They were unaware of his presence.

He turned down the last corridor and tiptoed toward his brother's room, the blood thrumming turbulently in his veins.

* * *

Kelly shuffled into the dining room and relit the candles. She was trembling violently in spite of the housecoat she'd wrapped herself in after putting the run on Sam.

An image kept recurring in her mind. An image of Will on fire. He was burning alive and screaming her name, stumbling out at her from every dark corner, a lifelike prop in a carnival house of horrors.

"Oh, Will," she sobbed, slumping into the chair he would have occupied. "Please come home. Let it all be a mistake."

She gazed into the capering candle flame. It threw a surprising amount of light, a warm, romantic glow that played on the objects in its reach: the empty plates, polished and waiting; the gleaming silverware her paternal grandmother had bequeathed to her; the single red carnation she'd picked up at the florist's on the way home from the supermarket; Will's diamond engagement ring.

"Please, Will. Come home…"

* * *

The computer was on, its stagnant green glare the only illumination in the room. Peter lay facing it, the screen itself only inches from his chin, but from the doorway Sam couldn't tell whether he was awake and reading the text or asleep again. He prayed for the latter.

He took a halting step into the room.

"Peter?"

No reaction.

"Peter?" Sam said, louder this time. He took another few steps into the room. He was at the foot of the bed now, his brother's face obscured by the bulk of the computer screen. It was a bad moment and Sam hurried past it, nearly stumbling.

"Pete—?"

Peter's head rolled up and around, the cables in his neck splaying grotesquely, and for a bewildering moment Sam thought his vision had shifted out of true. His brother's image had doubled in that green, horror-show light, reminding Sam of poorly matched transparent overlays, and now he opened his double mouth, his four eyes narrowed into baleful slits, and released a sound that was less a shout than a lion's warning cough, fierce, blunt, primitive.

Of what happened next Sam would never be certain. Without actually moving, Peter's body convulsed. Then a shimmering sphere of what could only have been pure thought struck Sam in the solar plexus and sent him reeling backward like a well-hit tenpin. Just shy of falling, Sam stamped and pinwheeled into his brother's bookcase, knocking a shelf of paperbacks to the floor.

"Did you fuck her?" Peter bellowed, his eyes like overripe grapes. "Eh, Sammy? Did you give her the old line drive?" He sneered. "You sneaky bastard. You're not my brother anymore, do you hear me, Sam? *You are not my brother.*"

Punched and gasping, Sam only stood there, his shock total. He felt boneless, fragile as a porcelain figurine, his brother's words striking him like pegged rocks. It took him a moment to get the sense of what Peter was saying... then it came.

That cold feeling on Kelly's couch, that whiff of an animal's den.

It had been Peter after all.

Sam tried to defend himself. "I was only—"

"Stuff your shitty excuses. You *fucked* her, didn't you." Peter's head stood straight up, his neck muscles so prominent Sam thought they might hoist him right off the bed. "Well, I'm warning you, *bro'*. Stay out of my way. She's mine." His face composed itself now, drew its frenzied features back in. Sam got an image of rats slinking into a hole. "Kelly is mine, Sam. Remember that. I'll hurt you if I have to. I can do it."

Peter's head fell back, striking the pillow with a thump of dead-weight, and Sam saw that his body had begun to vibrate; it shook the whole bed. And that illusion of doubling had recurred, only more explicitly this time.

Now there was something rising out of Peter's body, a faint blue glow, like a shadow on sun-dappled snow. The blue shape was rising, condensing...

(*I'll hurt you if I have to.*)

Sam ran.

(I can do it.)

There was a stairwell across from Peter's room and Sam burst into it, slamming the heavy door into the wall. He took the risers in precarious threes, leaping onto each cement landing. He'd never known such naked terror, such crippling confusion. That was his *brother* back there—but what had he become? At each turn Sam expected to see that cold blue fireball swooping down on him, and was there really any point in running? Where could he hide from such a force?

Peter, what have you become?

Sam ran. He ran down the stairs, ran through a restricted exit into the parking lot Peter had tried to launch himself into five years ago; he ran through the sleeping streets. And when he got home, his heart close to bursting in its secret chamber, he called Kelly's number.

There was no answer.

37

KELLY GAZED INTO THE dancing candle flame. It soothed her somehow, drawing a warm hypnotic curtain over this tragic turn of events. A part of her understood the truth was still there, it would have to be faced. But for now she allowed this counterfeit peace to permeate her. She was deep in shock.

Images began to unreel in her mind, but now they were pleasant ones. She saw Will climbing out of his Buick on that mellow autumn afternoon before their drive to the island, looking like one of those impossibly handsome actors in a light-beer commercial in his denim jacket and jeans. She saw the rigid set of his jaw as he made love to her and heard her own voice urging him to let it go, let that private hurt out. She saw his delighted smile in the candlelight, the diamond ring he'd given her reflected in the pools of his eyes. "Do you mean it, Kelly? Really?"

"Oh, yes, Will, I do, I really do." It was a desperate whisper. "I do—"

Kelly gasped.

The candle flame. She could see Will's shape in the candle flame. He was burning, reaching out to her, begging for help. Responding to his pleas, Kelly plunged her fingers into the flame. Will had died by fire, had been consumed by fire, as Peter's mother had. How horrible that must have been, flames licking and charring, the pain shrieking to a chorused pitch until it glutted the mind and destroyed it, the pork-like stench of one's own burning flesh ...

What was he saying? Was he begging for help?

Or beckoning?

Kelly's fingers began to blacken and blister. The smell of cooked meat brought the cat padding around a corner. It stopped at Kelly's feet and looked up at her, head quizzically cocked.

Come with me, Kelly, Will beseeched her from the heart of the flame. *I love you. Be with me forever ...*

"Yes," Kelly murmured. "Yes ..."

She withdrew her fingers from the flame and let her injured hand dangle at her side. There was no pain. Fang sniffed her burned fingers, then darted for the basement stairwell.

With her good hand Kelly removed the candle from its base. It was only a stub now, the wick close to drowning in a pool of hot wax. Grasping the candle by its butt, she dipped the sleeve of her house-coat into the flame. The quilted material caught with a tiny *flump* of combustion. Black smoke wisped up, thin and pungent.

You and I, Will promised. *Forever.*

The flame curled up Kelly's arm, reaching for her elbow, spread-ing like an autumn grass fire. It sent a tongue into her hair, and the ends ignited. There was another, stronger *whumpff* as the side of her housecoat caught.

And still his face was in the fire, beckoning—

The pain finally opened her eyes. *No. That's not Will.*

Kelly turned and caught her own reflection in the window.

I'm on fire.

She screamed, blundered sideways in panic—then there was a tug, a brisk shearing sensation that prickled her skin. It was as if every last hair on her body had been plucked free in a single simultaneous pull. An eldritch glow enveloped her, a shimmering halo of blue that seemed to emanate from her very pores—

Peter?

Then she was scrambling for the bathroom, pain streaking up her arm to her brain. The flames had spread to her back; she could feel them baking through her housecoat.

She was on fire.

Kelly tore off her housecoat and flung it into the tub she'd run a few hours earlier. There was a baleful hiss of flame, then an acrid belch of black smoke. Chunks of smoldering material clung to her arm, and now a thatch of her hair was blazing.

Kelly jumped rump first into the tub and dunked her head. Water scummed with old bubble bath sloshed onto the tiles. She was aware of the smell now, as she sat there shivering: the charred and soggy mass of her housecoat, the sweet, crisped smell of her skin, the nauseating stink of her hair.

The phone had started ringing, but she couldn't hear it.

* * *

Sam stood at the kitchenette window, staring out at the night. From this vantage he could just make out the hospital's east flank. Flat and featureless, it rose against the night sky like a doorway studded with lights; most of them were off now, but a few still twinkled with life. It made Sam wonder what sort of late-night dramas were being played out behind those curtained windows, how many lives were quietly giving up the ghost.

And it made him realize, with sudden, inarguable clarity, what he must do.

He turned and strode out to the foyer, grabbed his coat from the rack … and slumped tearfully against the doorjamb.

It was no use. Peter was his brother. Sam would sooner kill himself.

He let his coat fall in a heap on the hallway runner. In defeated shuffles he made his way into his room. He had a dim urge to try Kelly's number again, but he'd already let it ring off the wall. There had been no answer. Maybe he was already too late.

The feel of her limp and sobbing body tried to insinuate itself on Sam's surrender, but he blocked it from his mind. He opened his closet, reached behind a tote bag stuffed with hockey gear, and brought out a latched balsawood box. Originally it had contained assorted Italian wines. Now it housed Sam's most cherished mementos—the hockey crests he'd accumulated over the years, press clippings from out-of-town games, team photos, a folding pocket knife his father had given him—but mostly, it contained souvenirs of his life with Peter. He fingered through these items now, unmindful of the late hour, the sweetness of nostalgia somehow nullifying the awful truth of the present.

Here was a Polaroid of Peter climbing out of the two-seater Cessna he'd used for his first solo flight. Their uncle Jim had joked later that Peter's smile had been harder to look at on that sunny spring day than the polished steel blades of the prop. And here he was in a grainy clipping from the *Star*, hoisting the city trophy overhead. Sam could just make out Rhett Kiley's grinning mug on the sidelines. Another shot, this one a thumb-printed Kodachrome, showed Peter and Kelly on Peter's motorcycle. They'd been doing a test run that day with all the gear they meant to take with them on their trip.

How perfect they looked together. How much in love they'd been...

No, Sam thought, Peter could never hurt Kelly Wheeler. And that was true. The Peter Sam had known would no more have harmed another human being than he would have snatched an old woman's purse. But Peter had changed. He'd perhaps said it best himself when he raged at Sam from his bed: "You're not my brother anymore." It had taken six years of torture and humiliation, but that beer truck had finally snuffed out the last remaining shred of Peter Gardner. What was left in that ninth-floor hospital bed was…something else.

Peter was dead.

And unlike their mother, Sam knew it wouldn't be enough to just sit by and ignore the remains.

He went back to the front door, picked up his coat—

And the phone rang.

"Sam?" The word was a sob.

"Kelly. I tried calling you. Are you all right?"

"He was here, Sam." And in his mind Sam heard his mother's voice, creaking back from the grave: *Your dear sweet brother was here.* "He tried to kill me…burn me…"

"Are you hurt?"

"Not bad…can you come? I'm so afraid."

"I'll be right over. I'll get a cab."

* * *

She was still wearing the teddy. It was soaked, plastered to her skin, but the last vestiges of Sam's adolescent longing for this girl had died. The feeling ran much deeper now. It was love. A strange, forbidden, impossible love. The sight of her only fortified it.

He helped her dress her wounds. Two of her fingers were bad— black, blistered, already weeping—but Kelly refused to have them formally ministered to. "Just wrap them," she told Sam, and he did. He found a burn medication called Flamazine in the bathroom cabinet and spread soothing dollops of it on her fingers, then on the lesser injuries on her arm.

That done, Kelly trundled upstairs to get dressed. When she came back, wearing jeans and a bulky turtleneck sweater, she joined

Sam on the couch. In the unflattering light, her face looked swollen and bruised. Her hair clung to her skull in a singed, matted mess; Sam could smell it from where he was sitting.

Unable to meet Kelly's gaze, he began to speak in a slow, unbroken monotone. It was half past three in the morning.

"He's gone crazy, Kelly. It kills me to have to say this, but my brother's insane. When I read that stuff on his computer, I thought it was just…delusional. You know, all that bitterness and hatred, and suddenly people start dying off, people he's resented for years. I just figured that, since he could leave his body—and I knew that part was true, Kelly, I knew that for sure—I figured he just sort of…fantasized the whole thing. Took credit in his mind.

"But then I came to the stuff about your friend." Sam hung his head, feeling an absurd pang of rejection at Peter's decision to keep all this from him. "He said he was going to get Will, Kelly. Get him out of the way." He regarded her with woeful eyes. "But how could I have known it was true?"

"You couldn't have," Kelly said.

"So I went back home, sick inside, wondering what I could do for my brother. How I could help him be well again."

Tears tracked Sam's ruddy cheeks and Kelly brushed them away. She knew what it was like to love Peter Gardner so fiercely.

"That computer, it's full of the craziest stuff. Stuff about past lives. He thinks that you and he are soulmates, that you've been lovers since the beginning of time, tragic lovers who've been repeatedly thwarted on the brink of consummation. That's exactly how he put it: repeatedly thwarted.

"And he thinks he's seen heaven, or something like it. A vault of souls, a plane of perfect peace, total knowledge, eternal life." Sam looked directly at Kelly. "He wants to take you there. To this place. He wants to kill you—make you kill yourself—and then take you there.

Be with you forever in this imaginary afterlife." Sam buried his face in his hands. "It's crazy… so fucking crazy."

Kelly blinked, saw Will's face in the candle flame, and shuddered. She was too confounded to speak.

"He's dangerous, Kelly. I don't need to tell you that. He's a killer, and he's going to try for you again. And again, until he gets you."

Kelly took Sam's hand and squeezed it. Her eyes were shiny with fear. "What are we going to do?"

"Stop him," Sam said. "There's no other choice."

"When? And how?"

"Tonight."

Then he told her how.

38

THE TELELPHONE BURRED, THE sound inconsequential in the whine of Peter's rage. He became aware of it by the fifth ring and chinned his answering device. There was an electronic clunk as the line was engaged, then a low, tidal hiss.

"Yes?" Peter said, directing his voice toward the amplified receiver. His unexpected expulsion from Kelly's mind had left him feeling sluggish and sick.

"It's me." There was a pause, swollen with tension. "I'm with Kelly."

Peter's head came up off the pillow. "I told you—"

"No. I'm telling you," Sam said, his words coming all in a rush. "She doesn't want you, man. She wants me. I'm with her now, at her place. I know what you've been up to, I read—"

Sam's words were cut off by a low, malevolent chuckle. "You're thinking with your dick now, bro'. If you know what I've been up to, then you know I can break your back like a twig. Don't fuck with me. I mean it. Stay out of this."

"I'm already in it. I'm in it to stay."

"Have it your way—"

But he was talking to the dial tone.

Peter closed his eyes, threw his head back on the pillow and fell into a trance. It was as if a switch had been thrown.

* * *

Nine floors below Sam stood by the lobby pay phone and tried to wrest back control of his body. All the nerves seemed to have run out of it at once—that evil chuckle, so cold and maliciously confident—and the air seemed too thin. For Sam this was the final stroke, the last stage in the slow metamorphosis of his life into bloody nightmare. It had begun six years ago with Peter's accident, and the transformation would soon be complete.

He was about to murder his brother.

No, that's not true. That thing upstairs is not your brother. You've got to remember that. It killed your mother, it wants to kill Kelly... and it'll kill you, too, if you let it. For once in your life show some balls. Do the right thing.

Skirting the reception area, Sam slipped into a back stairwell. He took the risers in awkward strides, clutching the railing, that sensation of breathlessness heightening with each reluctant step. He felt sick and terrified, uncertain of his will.

Just do it, a steadying voice said. *Do it and get it over with.*

When he reached the ninth-floor landing Sam paused, gasping for breath, trying to bar all thought from his mind. Then he opened the door. After glancing both ways, he took the ten quick steps to his brother's room.

It was dark in there now, not even the green glow of the computer screen to aid Sam's probing eye. The only light, scant as it was, came from the red LED mounted in the wall above Peter's bed. The size of a dime, it flashed with each mute cycle of Peter's diaphragmatic stimulator, printing spectral red highlights on the chrome. The bed was a vague black hump in the gloom.

Sam hesitated in the doorway, listening for his brother's breathing. He heard only silence.

"Peter?" he whispered, braced for a sudden attack. He stepped into the room and toed off the doorstop. The door sighed shut behind him. He twisted the bolt.

"Peter?"

Sam approached the bed in darkness, groping like a blind man for the reading light. The worst moment came then, as he reached across his brother's shriveled body for the pull chain. His vitals were exposed in that terrible instant, and in his mind Sam saw that blue fireball punching through his belly and frying his guts.

He found the pull chain and tugged it. A soft yellow light flickered on. In its glow, Sam searched Peter's face for signs of awareness. There were none.

Peter wasn't here.

Moving cautiously, Sam stripped the covers off the bed. Then he slipped the pillow from beneath his brother's head.

* * *

Kelly stood in front of the picture window, gazing out numbly at the night. A dense overcast had gorged the sky, and now it was lowering. It would probably snow before morning, if morning ever came. This night seemed endless. Endless and dark.

She wrapped herself in her arms and closed her eyes. Oddly, she felt little fear at the prospect of facing Peter, only dull resignation. Sam's idea had been to tie her to something immovable, Kelly's big poster bed or one of the vertical beams in the basement, so that when Peter came he'd be unable to make her harm herself. But Kelly had refused. If she was to survive this night, she would have to do so on her own terms. To be free of Peter at last, she needed to face him alone. He had mentally raped her, brutally murdered the man she loved—and now she had to show him that her love for him was dead. From what Sam had told her, that seemed to be the key. The good love they'd shared as kids had festered in Peter's bitter heart for six years that must have crept past like centuries. And now he was insane, some kind of impossible killing machine with only one weakness.

His feelings for her.

She must show him her hate; she knew this instinctively. It might be the only way to stop him.

He wasn't Peter Gardner anymore.

Kelly shrieked and jumped back, her thoughts cut short. Something had shifted in the purple shadows of the porch. She'd caught the movement in the corner of her eye—a hunched, swift-moving shape. Now there was a crunch of dry snow, muted by the thickness of the glass...then Chainsaw poked his snout around the edge of the window frame. Head cocked, he regarded Kelly with soft brown eyes, eyes that seemed to say, "Come on, Kelly, come out to play."

"Chainsaw," Kelly said, a little hysterically. "You silly mutt. How many times have I told you not to sneak up on me like that?"

A smile twitched on her lips and the dog perked its ears. In a way, she was glad to see him out there. It was foolish, but his presence made her feel safer. She knew that if he could, Chainsaw would protect her, even at the cost of his life.

But what could he do against a ghost?

After a last winsome glance, Chainsaw turned away. She could hear him crunching back to the steps and then down. Not for the first time, Kelly thought of the irony of her relationship with the mutt. A little love—and the occasional can of Dr. Ballard's—and she had herself a pretty fearsome watchdog. Chainsaw patrolled the grounds around her place every night, while the house up the hill went unguarded. She wondered if the landlord could sue her for dognapping, and weren't these crazy thoughts to be having with Will only hours dead and some ungodly force about to try to kill her?

A huge shadow vaulted into Kelly's line of sight from beyond the porch railing. It touched the railing briefly, then blurred toward the window.

Chainsaw came through the glass in a shattering explosion. His forepaws struck Kelly's breasts and drove her to the floor. Her head struck the rug like a rock, then the dog was at her throat, boring in, his carrion breath hot beneath her chin. His hind paws clawed at the rug between her legs, jerking him forward in short, killing jabs. Kelly opened her mouth to scream, but the musty reek of the shepherd's pelt reached down her throat and stifled it. She could feel his teeth against her skin, blunt knobs of hard enamel, probing for blood. Only the thick woolen neck of her sweater prevented him from goring out her windpipe in a dripping snarl of tendon, blood vessel and cartilage.

Kelly got her hands up between the dog's forelegs and tried to shove him off. The dog's keel-shaped chest heaved against her fingers, but he didn't yield.

On the right side of her neck, where the dog's upper teeth dug and ground, Kelly felt the skin give way with an audible pop. Blood coursed over her shoulder in hot streamlets. With her bandaged hand she groped around her for a weapon, a pointed shard of glass, the bat she'd used on Sam, anything... but her fingers found only rug.

There was another pop now, and more blood.

"Peter," Kelly screamed, and the dog faltered for a beat. "Peter, stop this." Chainsaw lifted his head—

Then he was boring in again, roaring, maddened by the sweet taste of blood. Kelly clutched the ruff beneath his jaw and tried to choke him, but it was like trying to choke a tree trunk.

The dog was going to kill her.

Kelly's clawed fingers plunged into something wet, a warm, lip-less mouth in the dog's hairy neck. *A cut*, Kelly realized with a glee that bordered on insane. She could feel something pulsing against the backs of her fingers in there.

There was a third pop of skin, and now she could feel the hard grit of teeth against bone. Her bone.

With a primitive howl Kelly tore at the wound in Chainsaw's neck. The dog yelped in pain, but it did not back off. Kelly dragged down on the lip of the cut, trying to dig her nails into the pulsing cables inside. One of the dog's hind paws rammed her in the crotch, the nails poking through her jeans.

But she continued to tear at the wound.

The dog was shaking its head now, the way a puppy will shake an evening paper to shreds, trying to get a deeper purchase on her throat. She could see his eyes. They were scarlet.

Her index finger hooked a hot, throbbing rope.

She yanked.

Blood surged out of Chainsaw's neck in dark, divergent streams, the pressure forceful enough to spatter the TV screen six feet behind them. His growls turned into grotesque wet gurglings and his hind-quarters thudded to the floor—but still he tried to rip out her throat.

With a tremendous heave Kelly rolled the dog off her chest. Chainsaw tumbled away, clambered to his feet, then collapsed in a twitching heap. That scarlet rage flashed in his eyes again, as Kelly backed away. Then he was looking up at her beseechingly, confused and mortally wounded.

Overcome by a great rush of sorrow for the dog, Kelly fell to her knees at its side, unmindful of her own bleeding injuries.

"Peter," she screamed, throwing her head back, the blood like war paint on her face. "You dirty bastard, I hate you. Do you hear me? I fucking *hate* you."

Chainsaw was whining now, licking Kelly's wrist, and a cold March wind blew in on them both. Sobbing, Kelly held the animal's head—

Then scrambled back as the dog's bloodied pelt began to spit and crackle with profane electricity. Blue light streamed out of the shepherd's dying eyes in jagged, coalescing bolts that swirled and sizzled overhead.

No, Peter said, and Kelly heard the word—inside, like a secret thought. *You don't hate me, Kelly.*

You love me.

And now you're going to prove it.

* * *

He looked so peaceful. Peaceful and alive. His mouth was set in a ghost of a smile, and every few seconds the globes of his eyes flickered beneath their lids. It was as if he were only sleeping.

Sam had been standing at Peter's bedside for about twenty minutes. The pillow felt impossibly heavy now, an anvil instead of a sac stuffed with feathers, and Sam couldn't lift it any higher than his belt.

He felt paralyzed, like his brother.

Standing there watching him sleep (*no, not asleep, he's not asleep*) Sam was reminded of when they were kids and Sam would sometimes have trouble nodding off in his saggy top bunk. When these times came, he would poke his head over the edge and look down at his sleeping brother. He'd seemed like a god to Sam then, the five-year difference in their ages somehow vast and incomprehensible, and Sam remembered feeling safe with Peter so near. No one could harm him as long as Peter Gardner was his brother. He had wondered what Peter dreamed of on these nights, hoping he was included but doubting it, imagining instead that Peter's dreams took him to wondrous places, all the places he told Sam about when they sat together beneath the droopy old willow by the creek, just the two of them, Peter spinning dreams, Sam sitting rapt and attentive. "Gonna fly right up to the moon someday, Sammy. Maybe even Mars, who knows? Yeah. Be the first man on Mars, what do you think about that?" To Peter all things were possible, and it made Sam wonder how he'd put up with such a wimp of a kid brother.

But Peter had always stood by him, advised him, protected him...

Sam thought of that demented Nicholson smirk, and that made him think of the big Indian in *One Flew Over the Cuckoo's Nest*, Peter's favorite movie. He remembered how the Indian had pressed the pillow over Randall's vapid face after his lobotomy, not to punish him but to release him.

And as he remembered it, Sam felt his arms stretch out to rigid poles as he mimicked the act involuntarily, felt the pillow molding itself gently to the contours of his brother's face...

Sam dropped the pillow like a hot coal and stumbled into the bathroom, where the contents of his stomach came up in the sink. He turned on the light, wiped his mouth with a paper towel and threw up again.

Then he returned to the room.

He couldn't do it. He just couldn't do it.

* * *

Kelly opened her mouth to scream—then that horrid blue light was gone and something touched her on the nape of the neck.

It was like a kiss...

She stood, edging away from the ruined window, her sneakered feet crunching broken glass. Her fanny met the back door and she huddled there, closing her eyes.

Chainsaw whimpered once and was still.

Kelly.

(Stay calm don't let him freak you out.)

Kelly, can you feel me?

A soothing warmth oozed its way down through her body, like golden butter melting under a hot sun. It felt good, so good...

"Yes."

Feels good, doesn't it?

"Yes..."

All set for the trip?

Yes. Of course. The trip. My, how her girlfriends envied her. Spending the summer motorcycling across the country, seeing all the places they'd only read about. What freedom.

The whole summer...

Kelly's hand closed around the doorknob and turned it. She saw herself performing this simple act, but her arm seemed ten feet long, her hand distant and remote, not her own.

Her mind was filling up with smoke...

She was eighteen again. It was the last day of school and they'd just made love—and she'd finally felt it, that delicious rushing release. The intervening years had been only a dream, a cruel nightmare suffered in the summer cool of her bedroom, asleep beside the one she loved.

And I love you, Kelly.

With these words the warmth inside her intensified, becoming a compelling, euphoric heat—

But now there was a cold blast of air, nasty shavings of ice in her eyes, and Kelly paused, shaking her head in an effort to clear it. She was on the back steps, oblivious of having come out, the door behind her left open to the elements.

She could feel him inside her now, in this single lucid moment, not as a lulling warmth anymore but as a sly invading presence, a slow poison, a killing drug.

The hard fist of dread struck her then. He'd taken her so easily, unmasking that part of her which still cherished him, that part which had been frozen in time and then methodically buried, disinterring it with a single whispered phrase: *I love you, Kelly...* Upon hearing these words, she'd felt the fight run out of her like sap from a felled tree, and suddenly she'd *wanted* him inside her. It had felt like some mystic liquor decanted into the dusty vessel of her soul. It had made her feel whole again. More than whole.

It made her feel divine.

(No. It's a mind game. He's going to kill you.)

Heeding that voice, Kelly grasped her burned fingers and squeezed. The pain made her cry out—but it brought with it a savage clarity and she flung herself into the snow, kicking and flailing in an effort to dislodge him. For an instant that unpleasant tugging sensation began in her scalp—

Then she heard a single soft word... felt it, in her heart.

Kaitlin.

Kelly sat stock-still in the snowbank, eyes wide, heart racing—and felt the sleet turn to cool summer rain against her face. There was a wobbly sense of time falling away, like plates of ice from a towering iceberg...

Then she blinked and saw the land slope away into darkness, the road's muddy shoulder a blur in the jittering coach light. Lightning fractured the sky and Kelly saw the coach driver crack his whip at the galloping horses. From behind them came an answering pistol crack, then a hot crease of pain as a slug grazed her arm. "Oh, Liam," she cried, "I'm hit." And the man beside her roared, returning fire through a rent in the canvas canopy. "Bastards." he screamed—and Kelly thought: *Peter?* "You've hit my wife." Now the road took a hard right, nothing but a rutted track in the flank of a hill, and lightning flashed again. In its glare Kelly saw her own soaked attire—*my wedding dress*—and now the man beside her was turning, his brown eyes filled with concern in the wild pyrotechnics of the storm. "Ay, Kaitlin, are ya hurt?" But before she could answer the front wheels plunged into a washout and the coach lurched toward the gully. Now the rear wheels hit— and Kaitlin saw the right one go spinning off over the edge. Liam's side of the coach dropped like a stone, sending a roostertail of muck into the air. Another slug punched through the canopy, and now Liam was clutching his throat, blood gurgling out between his fingers to stain his silk ruff. There was a *snap* as the horses broke free—then the coach was going over the edge. In that endless moment Liam regarded her with fondness and a terrible regret. Then he flung her out and was gone, over the brink and down, and Kaitlin was plastered with mud in the roadway, the rain sheeting down, the wind snapping at her robe, the horsemen drawing up around her, high, faceless horsemen...

Ireland, Peter said in that even, soothing tone. *Eighteen—*

"Seventy-three," Kelly said without hesitation. She was on her feet again, starting down the slope to the lake.

You remember.

"Yes," Kelly said, tears freezing to her cheeks. "I remember."

They had been lovers then, she and Liam—Liam DeBlacam, merchant seaman, landowner, son of a Newgrange shepherd.

And now a fresh flood of memory came, vivid and wondrous. Her girlhood on a farm in the Celtic highlands, her love of horses and her talent for weaving, her mother's hale face and her father's fearsome but loving strictness...

(Stop this. It's a mind trick and he's going to kill you.)

But no. This was no trick. She'd been there. She'd lived it. The memory came from a secret vault where, even now, other memories stirred from their hibernal slumber. She'd loved him before, in another place and another time, but with the same all-consuming passion.

Yes, Peter said. *Many times. So many times...*

Sasha...

It was the whispered voice of the ages, secret, serene, compelling. And now a new memory came.

* * *

"Sasha."

The word was a knowing sigh, and Sam felt his hackles rise at the sound of it. He leaned forward, searching his brother's face in the mellow glow of the night-light. Warm shadows played over Peter's face as his mouth widened in a canny smirk...

Then he said it again. Breathed it.

"*Sasha...*"

* * *

Stripped naked and cold in the sea air, leering men with coarse hands looping crude lengths of hemp around her chest, cinching them cruelly behind her.

(*Oh, dear Jesus, I'm tied to a stake*)

Cold, so cold, and all of them staring, a terrible bloodlust in their eyes. "Burn," they chanted. "Burn." And her only sin had been to fall in love with the deacon's son, so young and uncertain of his faith and yet pledged by his father to spread the word of God, not the legs of a peasant's daughter. So they'd come in the night and dragged her away, raped her in that stinking jail, and then brought her to trial on some trumped-up charge of witchcraft. "Oh, David, where are you? Can you not stop them?" But he didn't even know. The ropes were chafing her skin, and now a grinning troll of a man tossed an armload of tinder at her feet, then another. And the deacon glowered, his eyes like bloodless bayonet holes in the dusk. "And the Bible saith, 'Thou shalt not suffer a witch to live. Behold the mistress of witchcrafts that selleth nations through her whoredoms, and families through her witchcrafts.' Now a boy waving a lit torch scrambled out of the mist. At a nod from the deacon he lobbed the torch at her feet, a boy of no more than ten, and as the torch struck the tinder and the tinder caught fire, the boy darted forward and pinched her breasts, spat on her legs, then turned and scampered back into the crowd. There were whoops and cheers of approval. And the chant beat on: "Burn, witch. *Burn.*" Flames licked up in a yellow hoop, crackling tongues merging with deadly swiftness into solid pillars. The heat was terrible, stealing her air, the smoke making her head spin. The crowd drew back from the pyre, their eager faces thrown into hideous corrugations by the heat. A burning branch tumbled into the narrow circle at her feet, and its tip branded her ankle. Crying out, she kicked it aside, but others fell in to replace it. She screamed—and then a man galloped up on horseback, plowing through the crowd, trampling those in his way. "David," Sasha cried. "Oh, David, thank God—" But now they were dragging him down from his mount, obeying the deacon's bellowed commands. David battled them fiercely, slaying three with his sword and another with his musket before they pinned him screaming to the ground. And the deacon's black raiment fluttered in the firewind.

No, Sasha. Nooooooo...

"Oh, God," Kelly sobbed. "Oh, God."

She was standing on the lakeshore now, that shattered voice from the past echoing through the ravaged galleries of her mind. The moon had found a worn spot in the cloud cover, and as if in a dream Kelly saw the hazy white disc reflected in the patch of open water at her feet. She studied it. It seemed to call her.

She stepped into the water. It closed over her shoes, cold as liquid ice.

It was always like this, Kelly. And it always will be, if we let it. Lovers through time. Tragic lovers... but we can change that now.

Change it forever...

That strange hair-pulling tug came again, a sense of something vital being snatched away...

And then she saw him.

He rafted above her, a shimmering phantasm in the shape of a man, lacking any discernible features and yet unmistakably Peter. Kelly experienced a brief razor stroke of awareness—*I'm up to my knees in freezing lake water*—but it passed when the wraith above her extended a shimmering hand.

Without hesitation Kelly reached out to accept it.

come

That same discomfiting tug began in her fingertips and rippled through her body. Simultaneously Peter's shape began to shed its glow and solidify, taking on the hues of life and the features that were distinctly his own. He was naked and perfect, unchanged since Kelly had last seen him whole. Only his smile glowed now.

Their fingers met and Kelly felt lighter than air, free as a distant star. She glanced down and saw her body advancing into the lake, approaching the thick lip of ice that ringed the circle of open water. She was already in past her waist. She had one urgent thought—*Sam, please hurry*—but it was torn apart like ground fog in a high wind.

Am I going to die, Peter?

He drew her to him, embraced her.

No. You're going to live forever, as one with me.

The notion brought a flood of tranquillity, reducing the freight of her mortal concerns to ash. Kelly looked down again and saw the water lap over her breasts, cold and black, that livid lip of ice only inches away...and she saw something else—a fine, glowing blue thread, stretching back to her body like an enchanted leash.

Awed, she turned back to Peter, aware only now of her nakedness. Touching him, feeling his touch, was like the most intense physical rush multiplied a thousandfold, and she tumbled helplessly into the depths of her arousal. He'd shown her so much in just a few stunning moments, and she trusted him wholly.

He would not harm her.

(that's you down there, and you're going to drown)

But there was only Peter.

When Kelly looked down again, this time from much higher up, she saw the water lap over her chin.

They rose hand in hand, gathering speed, Peter's smiling eyes holding her in thrall—

And Kelly stopped. She looked down and saw the crown of her head bob beneath the surface. There was a panicky feeling of suffocation, but it quickly passed. She started off again, then hesitated once more, a cleft forming in her spectral brow.

Thirty feet below, her untenanted body ceased to move.

She had heard or perhaps felt something...vital, and now she groped for it; it was like trying to hear a whispered voice in a roomful of chattering people, and she clutched at it, the way a drowning man might clutch at a floating reed.

Then she had it. It was a single syllable, a whisper of breath.

A name.

Will.

Now the thought was joined by an image, Will's loving face, and Kelly thrust it in front of her like a shield. Peter saw it, and his expression of calm reassurance fell away.

You killed Will.

Peter looked down and saw Kelly's thick hair floating on the lake like a discarded wig. He tugged at her impatiently.

That doesn't matter, Kelly. Nothing matters now. Only us. Only our love. Come with me now, before it's too late.

Understanding dawned like a dead sun in Kelly's eyes. She held on to Will's image. It was burning now. Burning up.

You killed him. You destroyed the only person I've loved since you. Why?

Peter glanced down again, the movement furtive. To Kelly he looked like a sneak thief who had just heard distant sirens.

Why?

Because he touched you, Kelly. He put his filthy hands on you. You're mine.

Kelly felt fury twisting inside her like something runny and half alive.

No, Peter. I am not yours.

She released his hand and withdrew. She looked down for her body and saw only a closing black eddy of water. The circle of ice gaped like a fiendish mouth.

Panic seized her.

I don't want to die, she cried. *Leave me alone.*

Kelly, please…

No, Kelly screamed, watching Will burn on the silver screen of her mind, letting the flames kindle her rage, oh, blessed sweet killing rage.

She spun away.

You're coming with me.

It was a petulant bellow, the final barked threat of a paper tiger, and Kelly glared at him spitefully. His form buzzed like cheap neon, and now his face was changing in the cold March sky. It was like watching a demon dissolve its false shape, and Kelly felt fear at this awesome display. The warmth in his eyes exploded into cold blue flame and he roared at her, showing her finally, what he'd truly become.

Bitch.

Then he was rocketing toward her, all human shape gone, transformed in an eyeblink into that malign blue light, yawning open like a vortex into hell. It swirled around her, stalling her, dragging her back—

And Kelly screamed, *NO*.

Kelly, please… That petulant whine.

No.

Forsaking him, Kelly whirled toward the patch of open water below. She tried to advance toward it, but she felt thick, heavy, drugged. It was like trying to swim through a vat of cold syrup. She could feel herself… fading, blacking out.

Dying…

God, please help me. I don't want to die.

There was a blur of motion—then she was under the lake, deep in its seamless domain, searching for her drowning body. She found it easily, floundering at the end of that strange blue cord—but when she reached it, it repelled her.

It faced her, opened its eyes, and grinned. *Good-bye, whore,* it said, precious air bubbling out.

Get out, Kelly shrieked. Then she struck her body like a hot bolt of lightning. She penetrated her own flesh—*oh, it's so cold*—and expelled him like an evil thought.

She turned and peered into the shifting darkness, the water numbing her to the marrow. The moon was still there, reflected on the surface overhead, and she slogged toward it through the killing depths. Her body had advanced only a few yards past that smooth lip of ice and now she thrust her face into the air, sucked at it, drank it in. Choking, she staggered toward shore, her soaked woolen sweater drooping from her torso in heavy folds, and collapsed in the frigid shallows. Regaining her feet, she blundered shoreward again, this time falling on dry land. Lying there shivering, gasping, she turned and glared up at him.

He was flickering, fading.

"You can't have me," she said, sputtering up lake water. "Even if you kill me, I'll never be yours. I hate you. You're not Peter anymore. You're a monster. Peter's dead."

I am not dead.

And as it had so often before, Peter's rage sought to work against him. He could feel it trying to drag him back to his body, but he would not go back, he—

"Fuck off," Kelly said, and laughed. She sat up on shore, struggling to conceal the fact that she was freezing, on the verge of blacking out. She waved a dismissive hand. "Bring on the dogs, you bastard. Bring on anything you like. I'll buy a gun and be ready. But you can't touch me now. Not anymore. You'll never touch me again."

There followed a moment when she feared she'd gone too far, that he would harden into that fearsome warhead Sam had told her about and punch a hole in her chest.

Then he grunted and reeled away. It was as if unseen cables had been jerked from behind by powerful hands. A look of impotent rage boiled in his face, and Kelly understood that his unending fury had finally defeated him. His body was tugging him back the way an aggravated parent might tug a naughty child.

It's not finished, Kelly, he cried.

Then he was gone, a faint streak of light, the tail of a dying comet.

Kelly sagged backward on the snow-crusted rocks. She could see the house at the top of the hill, visually inverted, uninhabited, nothing there but Chainsaw's body—and the phone.

The house looked a mile away.

She flopped onto her belly like a giant tadpole and began to crawl, her limbs feeling numb and vestigial. As she looked at it, the house seemed to withdraw along a dark tunnel, its well-lit windows fading to yellow smudges...and then nothing.

Kelly fainted dead away on the hill, her heart stumbling off in a precarious rhythm, her core temperature plummeting toward that of a corpse.

* * *

Impotent rage seethed within him as he dipped and tumbled toward the hospital, toward the ramshackle base camp that was his body. He was out of control—and he'd been so close. Another few seconds and she'd have been his—

Peter's involuntary retreat ceased. It was like running headlong into a cinder-block wall. A whining buzzsaw of pain slit through the top of his skull—and now a chunk of light blew out of him and was extinguished; it felt like flesh being torn out, *clawed* out, and he screamed; he screamed and the gulls rose up from the island far below, a screeching, wheeling white cloud.

Understanding followed the pain.

Sam. It was a roar.

Sammeeeeeeeee...

Another chunk blew out of him, and another, crippling gouts of the thing he'd become, and now he was moving again, flipping and cartwheeling like a dead autumn leaf. He tried to hold himself in, the way a gut-shot soldier will clutch his uncoiling innards, tried to smooth out his flight... but it was pointless. He was a rag in a twister's sucking funnel.

Sam wasn't just shaking him awake.

Sam was killing him.

The hospital came into view, a smooth black promontory in dawn's brooding light, and Peter tumbled toward it. He felt no regret, only a blind, delirious fury, and the consummate bitterness of betrayal. He'd ignored Sam's threats, judged them angry but empty words.

He'd been wrong.

He twirled toward his ninth-story window like a plummeting aircraft, the March wind wailing in his ears. When he struck it, the window exploded, the double pane pulverizing into sequins. They showered Sam where he stood at the bedside with a pillow seated tightly over Peter's face.

Sammy, no...

It was a feeble whisper, an unheeded plea.

Too late.

As Sam straightened up, removing the pillow, Peter caught a glimpse of his own dead face, fish mouth gaping, eyes mashed shut, airless chest jeweled with broken glass. In an agony of dissolution, he merged with the corpse on the bed. It was like sinking into raw, refrigerated meat.

Sam looked down at his brother's corpse.

It grinned.

Then it sat up, and Sam screamed.

39

DR. HANRAHAN WAS THE intern on call for the chronic ward. So far it had been a pretty laid-back rotation, nothing like the rat race she'd stumbled into during her stint in obstetrics the month before. Most nights she slept right through, curled up on a cot in the sleep room down the hall.

But tonight the call had been an urgent one—a possible respiratory arrest in 908—and now she thumped down the hall with the nurse, the utensils of her trade jouncing in her jacket pockets. She knew the patient in question, a quad in his middle twenties. The remote alarm on his diaphragmatic stimulator had sounded, and the nurse had paged her right away. She'd said something about hearing glass breaking down there, too, but Hanrahan had still been half asleep and the information barely registered. They rounded the last corner before Peter's room—

And stopped dead in their tracks.

"What the hell…?"

Now it came again, a deep-throated lowing sound more animal than human. Barely aware they were doing it, the two women clutched each other in the hall, exchanging fearful glances; then they separated, embarrassed, the renewed silence refuting the existence of that sound. If it had been there at all, it had been one of the old chronics, moaning in his senile sleep.

They started along the hallway again, more cautiously now—and froze a second later when a terrific crash came from Peter's room, and a brilliant blue light began to flicker beneath the closed door.

* * *

A crackling blue bolt struck Sam in the throat and sent him reeling into the wall unit. The TV slid off its perch and exploded. As Sam collapsed, the entire wall unit let go and came crashing to the tiles, narrowly missing him. He clambered to his feet, still clutching the pillow.

Peter's corpse was sitting up in bed, its eyes pearly-blank, its scrawny arms flapping like the limbs of some haywire mechanical toy. Its mouth worked soundlessly...then that deathly moan rolled out and Sam felt his bladder let go. The air was saturated with a dense electrical charge, and when Sam clutched the bed rail for support the shock nearly snapped his wrist.

He took a step toward the bed—and Peter's DVD player sailed past his head, missing him by inches. It shattered against the wall, jags of plastic and fractured circuit board buzzing through the air like shrapnel.

She's dead, Sammy. The words were blunt and hollow, as if spoken through an oil-filled tunnel. *I drowned her. Drowned her like a rat.*

Sam threw himself onto the bed, arms extended like pile drivers, eyes bulging in disbelief. His fingers closed around his brother's dead neck, the force of the attack driving Peter's body onto its back.

"*You're* dead," Sam cried, jamming the pillow over Peter's face again. "You're fucking *dead.*"

Peter's body began to rise off the bed, supporting Sam's weight with ease. Barely sane, Sam released the pillow and it tumbled away;

and now Peter was staring up at him, hard cobalt light twisting in his eyes. His corpse quivered between Sam's straddling legs, coursing with some awful energy, and now his flesh began to bloat and distort, throwing itself into hideous folds and excrescences. That killing light poured out of his eyes and surrounded them, blinding Sam to the horrid transformations that were still taking place beneath him.

This is your eviction notice, Sambo, Peter crooned. *I'm moving in.*

Suddenly flaccid, Peter's body dropped to the bed, dumping Sam to the floor. As Sam lay there, something jolted up through his balls and centred in his skull, and Sam felt like a sheet of wet paper, two giant hands tearing him in half. His mouth fell open, but his voice was gone.

You're going to die, Sammy.

He felt the cold breath of these words in his heart.

And it's going to be horrible.

* * *

"Hey. Open up in there. *Open up.*"

The commotion in the room had reached a frenzied peak—then it ceased. That unearthly radiance flickered and flared like a living thing; then it, too, was extinguished, as if someone had pulled the plug on a freaky acid-dream light show. A few of the ambulatory patients had poked their heads out of their rooms, but the nurse hustled them back inside. Finding the door locked, Dr. Hanrahan had used the nearest phone to call Security. The guard was thumping down the hallway right now, key rings jangling.

"Unlock this door," Hanrahan said urgently.

"What's the prob—"

"Just do it."

After finding the right key, the security guard unlocked the door. He started to pull it open, but Hanrahan placed a restraining hand on his arm.

"Let me," she said with quiet authority. She opened the door just wide enough to admit her head.

It took the intern a few moments to credit what she was seeing—Sam Gardner, whom she'd spoken to only once, standing in the dark by his brother's obviously dead body with a pillow clenched in his fist, the wall-size window that overlooked the science centre glassless and blowing cold air, the room a shambles—then she withdrew her head. It took another few seconds to piece together what had most likely taken place in that room. Then she dismissed the guard and signaled the nurse to join her.

The two women stepped into Peter's room, bits of shattered glass crunching under their feet. The intern knew the history in this case, knew of the steadfast devotion of the young man who stood with his back to her now, and felt a great weight of pity in her heart. Pity and admiration. What courage it must have taken to free through death his brother's tortured soul. What selfless valor. She met eyes with the nurse, and in one of those extraordinary moments that could only be described as telepathic, a conspiracy of silence was born. Obviously a pact had been made between the brothers, a contract against the horrors of quadriplegia. Peter had held out for as long as he could—*Six years*, Hanrahan thought, shuddering in the wintry air—but now it was over, and there was no sane reason for what had happened here tonight ever to leave this room.

Hanrahan glanced at the wreckage around her and guessed that in his grief Sam had stampeded through the room in a guilt-ridden rage. He'd pitched something heavy through the window, a chair, maybe, and that queer blue light had been nothing more than an electrical discharge from the shattered TV.

In her mind the intern filled out the certificate of death—cause: respiratory arrest, resuscitation unsuccessful.

Hanrahan came into the room and placed a hand on Sam's shoulder. Sam didn't react, only stared at his brother's body.

"It's all right," the doctor said. "Your secret is safe with us. Why don't you come away from here now? We'll take care of all this."

Sam didn't reply. He stood there a moment longer, staring. Then he turned and ran out of the room, the pillow still clenched in his fist.

* * *

The duty officer in Emerg looked up tiredly from the chart he was working on. A tall, red-faced young man bolted through the department with a pillow in his hand, then burst through the ambulance entrance and disappeared. Curious, the doctor followed at a fast walk, reaching the dispatch ramp in time to see the man grab a uniformed driver and lead him toward an idling ambulance. He spoke urgently to the attendant, but his words were lost to the inquisitive physician. A few moments later, the white and orange van was ripping up Paris Street, dome lights flashing.

Shrugging, the doctor went back inside. He'd find out soon enough what the trouble was.

* * *

"Down the hill," Sam said, running ahead. *"Hurry."*

The paramedics followed, picking their way through the patchy snow cover, a stretcher casting a thin dawn-shadow between them.

Sam sped surefootedly down the hill. He could see her in the gathering light, an unmoving hump by the edge of the lake. When he reached her, he hunkered beside her, expecting the worst. He shook her briskly, got no response, then probed her neck for a pulse. It was there, thin and erratic. His fingers came away bloody.

"Hang in there," he said, then shouted "Down here," to the paramedics.

When they reached Sam and Kelly the paramedics set down the stretcher and promptly began assessing the damage.

"Oh, boy," the first man said, two fingers pressed to Kelly's wrist, "She's hypothermic. Feels like atrial fib."

"Let's get a move on," his partner said.

And they bundled Kelly onto the stretcher.

* * *

Cold. So cold...

She could hear her teeth chattering, feel the cramps in her frozen muscles...but there was a comforting hand on her head, stroking her, and she knew she'd be okay. There were urgent voices, too, and a terrible wailing noise, but these things seemed unimportant.

She concentrated on the hand.

Now there was a quick stab of pain in her arm and her eyes flew open. Blue light strobed across the low, white ceiling and in a panic Kelly tried to sit up.

"Easy," Sam said, continuing to stroke her hair, which was clotted with tiny icicles. "You're okay. They're starting an IV"

"But the light..." Kelly rasped. It trailed across the ceiling again; then she understood. She was in an ambulance. The light was the dome light, nothing more. She looked up at Sam.

"Is it over?" she said in a small, frightened voice.

"Yes," Sam said. "It's over."

Kelly took his hand and blacked out again.

And the ambulance peeled into the dawn.

* * *

"They're not going to keep me," Kelly said. They were at the University Hospital, in the emergency room holding area. Three hours had passed. Kelly's lips were still blue and she was shivering, but she'd kept down some tea and she felt a lot better. She sat up on the stretcher and looked at Sam. "What time is it?"

"Almost ten," Sam said.

"God, I hate the thought of going back to that house," Kelly said, needing to say something, anything. She felt numb, shell-shocked. "It's a mess…" *And Chainsaw's still there.* She shuddered, a brief, jolting spasm. "I guess I could go to my mom's, but I'm not sure I'm up to her just yet."

"You could spend a few days at my place," Sam said in that same inflectionless tone. "There's plenty of room."

Kelly touched his hand. "I'd hate to impose, especially now…"

"Nonsense," Sam said, flinching at her touch. "You'll be good company."

"Well, thanks, Sam. I believe I will."

"Then it's settled. Come over as soon as they let you go."

He drew her a map on the back of a public health pamphlet, and left the hospital for the last time.

* * *

The morning's cool light inched its way through the apartment like an alien anthropologist, patiently unearthing the debris of an extinct society. It crept under the coffee table and revealed a dusty bottle of Jack, drained to the last sour drop and lying dead on its side. It stripped the obscuring murk from the couch where Leona had lain, reshaping it from a formless gray hump into the swaybacked ruin that it was. It extracted from its mask of shadow the dormant reel-to-reel… and Sam switched it on.

There was a moment of static-laced silence…then those first haunting chords, evoking a different age, a different set of possibilities.

He lifted his chin and remembered.

The shrine was still there, framed in a crisp oval of sunlight on the piano's white lid, and as he listened, he walked over to inspect it. After a few lingering moments, he removed the photo from its circle of adornments and turned it facedown on the lid.

And the music played on, scratchy with age but still sweet, so bittersweet.

He sat on the edge of the piano bench, a tall, strongly built lad with a pockmarked face and a tendency to slouch. He sat and listened to the music, his dry gaze settling on the orderly rank of keys…and now a strange, lopsided grin tugged at his lips and he plunked a single key.

Middle C.

The note was clean and perfect, like the day outside.

He hunched over the keys and began to play along with the tape—flawlessly, as he always had. His grin never faltered.

And when the piece was done and the tape commenced its infernal flapping, there came a hesitant knocking at the door.

Aren't you going to let her in?

He didn't move.

The voice was like a cancer in his heart.

Come on, Sammy. We're going to have to learn to share.

When the knock came again, Sam got up to answer the door.

END

LET IT RIDE

Chapter 1

(Anticipated publication date: fall 2012)

Friday, January 18, 1:35A.M.

RONNIE SAID, "THAT FUCKING brother of yours," the coke revving her up, making her aggressive, "treats you like an errand boy."

Dale drove the big Dodge Ram without looking at her, knowing the eye contact would only make her worse. He flicked the wipers on, fat snowflakes melting as they struck the windshield. Outside, Asian district neon reflected off the accumulated snow, drifts of it smothering the city.

Ronnie said, "You should be partners by now, fuck sake. Look at him, king shit in that big house in Parkdale—where are we? Cabbagetown. Half a duplex with a plugged toilet, those fucking rappers upstairs playing that street shit half the night."

She paused to do another hit off her coke mirror and Dale said, "It'll come, Ronnie. Ed's just showing me the ropes. He came up this way himself, doing runs for Copeland. It's the way it works."

"The ropes," Ronnie said. "Listen to yourself." She hefted the gym bag off the floor between her feet, 250K worth of Randall Copeland's heroin. Copeland controlled the drug trade in the Greater Toronto

Area and all parts south as far as the border. "I was you? I'd take this bag of shit and start up on my own. Someplace fresh. Miami, maybe."

Dale took the bag from her and tossed it on the back seat. "You're talking shit now, Ronnie. This is *Copeland's* dope. Not even Ed fucks with him. Why don't you just mellow out."

Ronnie just stared at him, that hard shine in her eyes that made Dale nervous, giving him no idea what was going on inside her head. It made him realize how little he really knew about the woman. He'd met her through his brother—one of Ed's discards, a hand-me-down, like a sweater—and six months later they're engaged. True, she was fine: that black leather coat flared open to show a little cleavage above a tight red top, legs that went all the way up, all that thick black hair. But she never talked about her past, only hinted at its flavor, almost like a threat when she got pissed at him and wanted him to know it: *"There's a lot you don't know about me, Dale, so I suggest you just back off."*

He said, "Listen, we're almost there. I'm gonna go inside and do the deal, you're gonna wait in the truck. Ten minutes tops. We're late, so I'm probably gonna have to put up with some shit about that." Late because Ronnie's 'quick' stop for blow wound up costing them an hour. "When I come out we're gonna take the money to Ed, collect our two grand and that's the end of it. Okay? Fuckin' coke, makes you hyper."

Ronnie said, "At least I'm awake," but the edge was gone from her tone, something else on her mind now. She slipped the smeared coke mirror into her bag, her trim body moving to the *Santana* tune on the radio.

Dale slowed the Ram and turned left, then left again into an alley behind a closed Vietnamese take-out joint. He parked behind a black Mercedes and killed the engine, pocketing the keys. He reached over the seatback for the bag and Ronnie leaned into him, her manicured fingers squeezing his thigh.

"I'm sorry I bitched you out," she said, close, minty breath warm in his ear. "I just wanna see us get ahead. We deserve more."

"It'll come," Dale said, suspicious as he always was when she turned on the lovey-dovey shit. But man, she knew how to play him. He said, "Couple more years, maybe we'll move into the top half of the duplex."

"Don't push me, Dale."

Grinning, he grabbed the gym bag. "Ten minutes, okay?"

"Let me come in with you, baby."

"The mood you're in? I don't think so."

"I'm fine now, honest. Come on, they won't mind."

Dale got out of the truck, sinking to his ankles in wet snow. "Forget it, Ronnie. These guys are wrapped way too tight. They think they're in a Jet Li movie or something. I go in alone."

"But—"

"Lock the doors. This is a bad neighborhood."

He closed the door on her protest. *Stick with the plan.* He'd fucked up more than once already, Ed bringing him into his office to ream him out, like Ed was his father instead of his brother. But Dale never took it personally. He *was* a fuck-up a lot of the time, the dope getting him into shit he sometimes couldn't even remember. He'd been clean a few months now though, even caught a few twelve-step meetings when the itch got strong enough. Truth was, Ed's last talk had shaken him. *"Keep it up, Dale, you're going to find yourself in a bind I can't pry you out of. In this world, blood only runs so thick."* Ed could be spooky sometimes.

Dale banged on the restaurant's steel service door, then glanced back at the Ram—shit, Ronnie smoking in his brother's truck, like he needed more trouble with Ed. He turned to say something to her about it and the service door opened on its chain. An Asian guy the size of an outhouse stuck his face into the gap, shark eyes sizing Dale up, then got the chain off and let him inside. Dale followed him into a storage area where the head gook, Trang, and another guy—all three of these dudes decked out in the same sky blue leisure suits with pink button-down shirts—were shooting darts and drinking beer.

Dale stumbled over something and Trang missed his shot, looking none-too-pleased about it as he turned to face Dale. "You're late," he said and let his jacket fall open, giving Dale a clear view of the big semi-auto tucked into the front of his trousers.

"Yeah, Mister Trang, I'm sorry. I was…unavoidably detained. But I got your product right here."

"It makes your brother look bad," Trang said, not letting it go, "showing up late for a quarter million deal." He touched the black leather briefcase that lay on its side on a service table next to him. A caress. "I should tell him."

"Sorry, Mister Trang. It won't happen again."

Trang's gaze ticked over Dale's shoulder now, registering mild surprise. He turned to look at his pals and when he faced Dale again he was smiling, showing small yellow teeth. "But I see you brought us a gift," he said, the smile widening. "Blowjobs all around, eh boys?"

The other two joined Trang in a good laugh and Dale turned to see Ronnie right behind him, strolling past him now, cool as ice, going straight to Trang as the other two flanked him to wait their turn.

Dale said, "Ronnie?" but the girl wasn't listening.

She sidled up to Trang with lidded eyes, giving him her smokiest smile, one hand going to his thin chest, the fingers of the other loosening his belt.

Ronnie said, "I'll blow you…"

And Dale saw her hand close around the pistol grip, saw her shoot Trang in the balls and draw the gun from his pants as he fell, tugging once as it snagged, then dropping to one knee to gut-shoot the big one, capping the third guy in the throat as he reached for his piece.

The reports slammed Dale's ears, flat claps of thunder in the cement-walled room.

Then Ronnie was moving, sweeping the briefcase off the table, turning to Dale to hand him the gun.

"See?" she said. "That's how easy it is. Now come on."

She started for the exit but Dale stood frozen, gaping at the scene: Trang screaming, both hands on his bloody crotch, and the big guy, holding his guts in, the pink shirt blooming red…

Ronnie's voice: "Dale."

"Jesus, Ron…"

"Look at me, Dale."

He turned to look at her.

"It's like I told you," she said, her green eyes wildly alive, "there's a lot you don't know about me. Now *come on.*"

Head spinning, Dale broke for the exit, running full out, gun in one hand, gym bag in other.

* * *

In the truck Ronnie got right back into the coke, turning the radio up loud, laughing when Dale came out of the alley too hard, fishtailed in the wet snow and sideswiped a parked van.

"Fuck," Dale said and Ronnie whooped. He couldn't look at her, not now, afraid that if he did he'd grab Trang's gun off the console and shoot her with it.

Slowing as he turned north onto Yonge Street, Dale said, "You know what you just did?"

"Made us five hundred K in under a minute?"

"Killed us, that's what you did." Picturing Ed when he heard about this, Dale wanted to cry. "Copeland's guys are gonna waste us and there's not a thing my brother's gonna be able to do about it."

"Like we're going to sit around and let that happen. The airport's a thirty minute drive from here. If you can't handle it, pull over and I'll take the wheel."

"The airport. Right. In this weather."

Ronnie considered this a moment, then picked up Ed's satellite phone, dialed 411 for the flight information number and waited while it connected, shushing Dale when a recorded voice came on and told her all flights had either been canceled or delayed until further notice. She hung up and said, "Fuck it then, we'll wait it out. How's the Harbor Hilton sound? Room service. Jacuzzi. It's not like we can't afford it."

"Copeland knows everybody in this town," Dale said, his voice rising to a petulant whine. "There's no place we can hide. Shit, maybe we should call Ed, tell him Trang went crazy or something, tried to rip us off. Gave us no choice."

"Forget it, Dale. You lie about as well as you fuck."

"Nice, Ronnie. Real nice."

"You know what I mean. He'd see right through you."

"Look," Dale said, struggling to catch his breath. His heart was triphammering, the image of Trang clutching his ruined crotch making his stomach sick. "I know a place. It's about five hours north of here. My uncle's hunt camp on Kukagami Lake. It's the last place Ed'd think to look."

Ronnie said, "A hunt camp," like it was a toilet. "If we're gonna drive, drive *south*, fuck sake. We take turns at the wheel, we're in Miami in two days."

Dale sped the wipers up a notch, the wet flakes heavier now, angling straight in at the windshield. He said, "They got dogs at Customs, Ronnie, can smell dope on your breath. Forget about it. There's no way we're gonna try that. No, if we're gonna run, and I don't see as we've got any choice now, we're gonna have to ditch the dope or sell the fucker before we leave the country. We lay low at the camp—

it's a cottage, Ronnie, a real nice place on the lake. Heat, electricity, everything. We stay there a day, maybe two, then drive to Montreal. I know a guy there'll take the shit off our hands. Then we head for Europe or maybe New Zealand. Someplace Ed never heard of."

"What if your Uncle's there?"

"He's in Daytona till the end of March, same drill every year. Trust me, the place is abandoned."

Ronnie was quiet after that, the fading adrenaline rush making her sullen. Dale had seen her like this before, brooding silences that went on sometimes for hours and made him edgy, afraid he'd done something to offend her and he'd wake up in the morning to find her gone.

But right now he liked her this way just fine. He needed time to think.

He got on the 401 and followed it west to the 400, pointing them north now, into the bellowing throat of the storm.

* * *

The weather broke all of a sudden, four in the morning, just south of Parry Sound. An hour earlier they'd been sitting at a dead stop behind a tractor-trailer jackknifed across the highway, flares everywhere, an O.P.P. officer coming right up to Dale's window and asking him where they were headed. Dale just stared at the guy and Ronnie said, "Kukagami eventually, but we'd be happy to make Parry Sound tonight, find a hotel and get out of this weather." The cop said that was a good idea, gave Ronnie a little smile and went on to the next vehicle. Dale saw Ronnie tuck her gun back into her bag, a nickel-plated Colt .380 she carried with her everywhere, and thought, *This is a nightmare, somebody wake me up.*

The drive in the snow, slow and hypnotic, had settled Dale's nerves a little. But seeing that cop stroll right up to the window like that, and then Ronnie, ready to shoot the man in the face, brought it all back, hard. He was a fugitive now, running from his own brother. The law, too, if the cops got involved. Christ, three dead Asians. They must be dead, the way they left them.

He kept thinking maybe it wasn't too late. He could call Ed, tell him the truth. This wasn't his mess, it was Ronnie's. Maybe—

"I know what you're thinking."

Trying to get some ice in his voice, Dale said, "You're a mind reader now, too?"

"You're thinking of calling your brother, right? Telling him it was me? You had nothing to do with it?"

"Would I be lying?"

"*Fuck* those guys, man. This is petty cash to them. Your brother'll get his wrist slapped and life'll go on. Meanwhile we're sipping gin fizzes in the Florida sunshine."

Dale glanced at the phone and Ronnie said, "Okay, you want to call him?" She picked up the receiver and held it out to him. "Go ahead. See what he says. Better yet, call Copeland. It's his dope, anyway. And you know how forgiving *he* can be." When Dale didn't move Ronnie set the phone back in its cradle on the console. "You're in this, Dale. Don't kid yourself. You *are* it. Fuckin' slant, thinks I'm gonna suck his dick. *What* dick? I hate those slippery creeps, think they can have whatever they want." She said, "Did you see the look on his face?" and brayed wild laughter.

Dale tuned her out. Let her rant.

Traffic got moving again after that, the drive to Parry Sound slow but smooth. Then, almost without his noticing it, Dale was driving on centre-bare blacktop under a white sky, a dull moon shining through like a beacon, guiding them north.

* * *

They stopped for breakfast at an all-night joint along the highway, Ronnie bringing the cash and the drugs inside. She ordered black coffee, bacon and eggs over hard with white toast and home fries and ate it all without saying a word. All Dale could stomach was dry toast and a few sips of apple juice. He'd lost his appetite for food. What he needed right now was inside that gym bag. He kept thinking about that first sweet rush when the tourniquet comes off, the warm calm that washes over you like tropical surf. The only effective antidote for fear he'd ever found. And he was shit-scared right now, more afraid than he'd ever been. Every minute that passed without dealing with this was a minute closer to the grave. Until now he'd always been able to turn to his brother when he got in a jam, Ed always coming through for him. But this…this fucking mess didn't *have* a solution. At least not one Dale believed he could survive.

They reached the hunt camp at 6:30 A.M., dawn breaking clear and cold as Dale parked the Ram in the yard and got out to find the key. The road in from the highway had been plowed and sanded, only the winding cottage road, a distance of about a mile and a half, requiring 4-wheel drive and a little care.

Dale found the key where Uncle Frank had hidden it since Dale was a kid, in the flared nostril of a figure on a thirty-foot totem pole Frank had picked up at a yard sale someplace.

Dale got the cottage door open and Ronnie pushed past him, saying, "I'm going to bed." She snatched the truck keys out of his hand, dropped the gym bag on the couch facing the big picture window and took the briefcase upstairs with her. Dale said, "Make yourself at home," and listened to her—boot heels stabbing the wood floors up there, the squeak of bed springs and then silence—before getting his coat and boots off, turning up the heat and taking a stroll through the place.

Being here, amidst Uncle Frank's weird antler furniture and hunting trophies, made him feel like a kid again. After his mother died and his father buckled down for the serious drinking, Dale had come up here as often as he could. Uncle Frank had always treated him like a prince, teaching him to fish, letting him take the power boat out by himself, and telling him stories about how crime didn't pay and he didn't have to turn out like his brother if he didn't want to. What Uncle Frank never understood was that Dale wanted nothing more. Nobody messed with Ed, that was the thing. Ed always got what he wanted, one way or another, and Ed never felt fear, something Dale had lived with since his mother died, a withered stick figure in a hospital bed, eaten alive by cancer while still in her thirties. Fucking fear.

In the kitchen Dale checked the fridge: a half-used jar of jam in there, six cans of beer and not much else. He helped himself to one of the beers and sat on the couch facing the frozen lake, one hand resting on the gym bag. The beer was flat and Dale set it aside, no comfort there. He pulled the gym bag onto his lap and unzipped it, removing one of the kilo bags of heroin. It occurred to him as he hefted it that a few good snorts would get him there, but not like blasting it would— and remembered Uncle Frank was diabetic.

He found the syringes in a kitchen drawer, thirteen of them left in a box of fifty, as seductive a sight as anything he'd seen in their crisp, sterile wrappers. He scooped them out of the box, got a teaspoon from the cutlery drawer—four of those corncob-shaped spikes in there, taking him back to his childhood again—found a wad of cotton in an aspirin bottle and a book of matches by the fireplace. There was a moment when he reconsidered, a part of him not wanting to blow his clean time, then he punched a hole in the kilo bag with his pocket knife and measured out a hit with the teaspoon.

* * *

Dale came awake with a kink in his neck, sitting on the couch with his head slung back, a strand of drool connecting his chin to a wet spot the size of a saucer on his Joe Cocker T-shirt. The sky beyond the picture window was dense with cloud cover now, and a light snow was falling. There was no sign of Ronnie.

Dale glanced at his watch, mildly surprised to see that it was past four in the afternoon. He gave his head a shake and leaned over his works, spread out on the raw-pine coffee table in front of him. A quick inventory told him he'd already used three of the syringes, though he only remembered the first. The reason he was here tried to come back at him and Dale decided it was time for a little pick-me-up. He got it done quickly, nodded off briefly, then got up to go to the john. That done, he felt around in his coat pockets for his cigarettes before remembering he'd left them in the truck. He got his boots and coat on and went outside.

He was halfway across the yard when he heard Ed's satellite phone ringing in the truck. He thought, *Fuck,* and tramped quickly through the snow to answer it, Ed's voice coming at him before he got the handset to his ear.

"Dale? Answer me, you little fuck-up. Is that you?"

"Yeah, Ed, it's me."

"It was the coke whore, right? Your fian*cée*? Tell me I'm right, Dale."

He thought of lying—for all the good it would do him—then thought, *Screw her. I told her to wait in the truck.*

He said, "Yeah, Ed. It was Ronnie."

"I fucking *knew* it. Dale? You know what I've got to do now? I've got to go see Copeland and explain this to him. Tell him how my dipshit brother and his coke whore slaughtered three of his best customers. How you then stole his product *and* his money and made a run for it. Jesus Christ, Dale, how many times have I told you? When you do a job for me, you repre*sent* me. How many times?"

There was a pause, Ed waiting for an answer, but Dale couldn't think of what to say, the dope making him want to giggle.

Ed said, "Are you high?"

"Maybe a little."

Ed gave a dry chuckle. "You're a piece of work, bro, I'll give you that. A real piece of work. All right, listen. This still might be fixable. Here's what we're gonna do. Where are you now?"

Dale said, "We're—" and felt the phone snatched out of his hand. He turned to see Ronnie in her jeans and red tank top pitching the phone as far as she could into the woods. When she turned to face him she had the .380 in her hand, the stubby muzzle aimed at his heart.

She said, "I ought to shoot you myself, save Copeland the trouble."

The sight of that muzzle, the tension in Ronnie's trigger finger, Ronnie barely dressed out here in the snow, cut through Dale's buzz like a scalpel blade. He said, "Ronnie, wait, Ed was pissed, sure, but he sounded okay about it, like he could smooth things over with Copeland."

"Did you tell him where we are?"

"No."

"Dale?"

"*No.* You took the phone before I could."

Ronnie lowered the gun, turning into the wind to go back inside. "I can't sit around here much longer," she said, not looking at him. "We leave together—tonight—or I leave alone and to hell with you."

Breathing hard, Dale followed her inside.

* * *

Ed looked across his desk at the two men Copeland had given him as enforcers, Frank Marshall and Gord Wood, Mutt and Jeff in expensive suits, loyal members of Copeland's organization for twenty years. He said, "I know where he is."

Frank said, "So where is the prick?"

"Watch your mouth," Ed said. "He's still my brother."

Frank shrugged his big shoulders. "Sorry, Ed. Where's he at?"

Ed got up and stood behind them, knowing it made them nervous. Trang's kid brother had called him in a panic about an hour ago, describing in broken, rapid-fire English the bloody mess at the restaurant. Fortunately for the kid, he'd been out picking up Harvey burgers during the exchange and had come back to find two men dead and his brother with his dick blown off, unconscious and bleeding to death on the floor.

Ed said, "When we were kids Dale got drunk one night and decided to take our old man's car for a joyride. But the dummy ran over the dog backing out of the garage. Dad loved that little mutt. Anyway, Dale panicked and decided to run away. Drove all the way to our uncle's hunt camp on Kukagami Lake. That's where the little fuck-up is."

Turning in his chair, Frank said, "So what now?"

"Now I gotta go see Copeland."

Gord stood. "I'll get the car."

Ed said, "No, I'll do it. You two take Frank's truck, it's got four-wheel drive." He went to the desk and started drawing a map; Frank got up to look over Ed's shoulder. "It's a long drive," Ed said, "but easy to find." He handed the map to Frank. Frank tucked it into his pocket, knowing what was coming. Ed looked him in the eye. "He's an asshole, no escaping that, so far over the line right now Jesus Christ himself couldn't save the kid. But like I said: he's my brother." He opened a desk drawer and brought out a snub-nose .44. From a small pocket on his vest he took out a single round, kissed the tip, then chambered it in the revolver. He handed the gun to Frank. "Quick and painless, understood?"

Frank said, "Yeah, Ed. It's my specialty."

"Good. Call me when it's done."

About the Author

SEAN COSTELLO is a practicing physician who lives and works in Sudbury, Ontario, his home since 1981.

For information on previous and upcoming titles, visit the author's website at www.seancostello.net